HARD HITTER

by

Kaylee Losey

xoxo Kaylee Losey

DORRANCE
PUBLISHING CO
EST. 1920
PITTSBURGH, PENNSYLVANIA 15238

122

Dorrance Publishing Co
585 Alpha Drive
Pittsburgh, PA 15238
Visit our website at *www.dorrancebookstore.com*

ISBN: 978-1-6393-7300-0
eISBN: 978-1-6393-7697-1

CHAPTER 1

In a rare and likely brief moment of calm at Rosewood Medical Group's physical therapy office, Raelyn DeRose plopped herself into the chair behind her desk and put her feet up. Unable to fully finish her dramatic sigh of relief, the three-bell chime of her phone went off, letting her know that Amala Jones was sending her yet another wedding-related email. Amala was the little sister of Raelyn's best friend, Amira Jones, who was getting married at the end of July. While it had originally been her plan to assign Raelyn the maid of honor position, Indian tradition dictated that Amira put family first, so Amala got the job instead. Not that Raelyn was complaining really; she was just as involved in the wedding planning process, but without the pressure, and she didn't have to worry about giving a toast in front of five hundred guests- a small wedding by Diya Jones's standards, but it would have to do.

Amira was determined to put together a wedding that was the perfect blend of American and Indian tradition. She would wear ivory rather than red, but her dress was a two-piece, adorned with embroidered patterns that were traditionally found on an Indian *lehenga*. She had even tried to fit the groom for an Indian *sherwani*, but somehow the tall, freckled, and red-haired Brody Kalahan just didn't look quite right in something so obviously...not Irish. He wasn't opposed to the elaborate and expensive sword that typically went with the outfit, though. Raelyn believed the most recent argument was how ridiculous Brody would look in a tux holding a sword, but somehow she thought Amira was going to lose that battle. Men and weapons, what could you do?

Raelyn put her feet back down and logged into her computer to check Amala's email titled "Bachelorette Party Itinerary." Raelyn clicked the email open and began to read quietly to herself. "Wedding is Coming- He bent the knee to his queen and now we prepare ourselves for The Long Night," Raelyn grinned as she continued. Of course Amira would have a *Game of Thrones* themed party; she had always made a big event of watching the show while it was still running. She would drag all of her girlfriends, sisters, and cousins to her house on Sunday nights to indulge in too much food as they all sat back and watched scenes of dragons, heads getting chopped off, and high-born lords having serious, conspiratorial conversations in rooms filled with naked women.

Raelyn scanned the itinerary, wondering how similar her own bachelorette party would have been if her engagement last year hadn't taken a flying leap off the Mackinac Bridge and into the shallow bank of Lake Michigan. It was for the best, she reminded herself as the thought popped into her head. She now had much more time to focus on her career, and to spend with her girlfriends.

"Oh, you've got to be kidding me," Raelyn groaned as she read the final piece of the itinerary.

> *Invite your kings, princes, or your wildlings. Brody and his King's Guard will be joining us for a bonfire to cap the night off.*

Raelyn's Bernese Mountain Dog, Harry, rested his large head in her lap, sensing her distress as she let out another groan, re-reading the line to make sure she had read it right. She placed her hand on Harry's head and gave him a few scratches behind his ears. Surely Brody's "King's Guard" meant his groomsmen, and his groomsmen would of course include the best man.

Raelyn typically wasn't opposed to the men joining in their events. She didn't have a problem socializing with men in general; as a matter of fact, her closest friends growing up were all boys and she often enjoyed the opportunity to get lost in conversations about MLB or NFL draft picks, March Madness, fantasy leagues, or any other athletic event under the sun. Her girlfriends always seemed to glaze over in disinterest when she tried to bring up the sports world with them.

No, the problem here was that the best man would now show up with his perfect sandy blonde hair, his perfect beard trimmed just the right amount, his *perfectly* bulging biceps in a shirt that would show off his beautifully sculpted form, and absolutely ruin her night. The best man, AKA Emerson Yates, was a dangerously sexy, seductive, combative, manipulative son of a bitch. He was also Raelyn's ex-fiancé.

This was the night she had been looking forward to since Brody had proposed, knowing her best friend was going to go all out for her girls to celebrate the end of an era, and the dawn of a new stage in her life. Of course she was also looking forward to the wedding, but as the best man was going to *have* to be there, she would inevitably spend the night dodging his attempts to get back in her good graces. Or just back in her bed.

As if hearing her anguish from across the parking lot that separated Rosewood's physical therapy offices from the women's center, Raelyn's phone rang and Amira's picture lit up the screen.

"Oh my God, Rae, I am so sorry!" Amira said by way of greeting. "I didn't realize Amala was going to send that before we got off work. I told her I would talk to you at lunch and break the news that the men-folk would be joining us later on. Do you hate me?"

"No, of course not," Raelyn said, rubbing Harry's ears again. "We're going to have to see each other eventually. It's fine, Amira, really."

"I told Brody he needed to pick someone else to be his best man, but he told me I was being *ridiculous*," Amira scoffed at the last word.

Raelyn grimaced. "How did that go over? Seems a little risky so close to the big day."

Amira laughed dryly. "Oh, he'll pay for it somehow. I haven't decided how to punish him yet, but it'll come."

"Seriously, Amira, don't go punishing him on my behalf. Besides, we kind of expected him to pick Emerson. They've been best friends since law school and they work together now. Really, we should be grateful your mom insisted on Amala being your maid of honor, or else I'd be walking down the aisle with my ex-fiancé." Raelyn cringed inwardly at the image in her head.

"*That* would have been a disaster," Amira agreed.

In an attempt to move the topic away from her and Emerson and onto literally anything else, Raelyn said, "By the way, I'm loving the *Game of Thrones* theme for your party. Do we get to carry swords? Because that might make the whole evening more entertaining."

Amira laughed, amused. "Sure, I'll find you a *Longclaw* replica stat."

"Replica?" said Raelyn. "If I'm going to be facing my ex again after what he did, I want the real deal."

"Ah, yes, let's give you endless tequila shots and a sword. That jackass won't stand a chance," Amira said dreamily.

Harry's tail wagged at the sound of Raelyn's laughter. He had always been such an intuitive dog, even as a puppy. He always seemed to sense anyone's change in mood and was able to address it accordingly, making him the perfect office dog. Every now and then the other attached offices would borrow Harry to help ease high anxiety patients, kids, or patients who had just been delivered bad news.

There was a light knock on the door and Alexis, the petite office secretary came sweeping in with an armful of mail. Alexis had fair skin and a sheet of long, straight, flaming red hair. Wearing a high-waisted emerald green pencil skirt with a classic black shirt, Alexis always looked styled to perfection, all the way down to her matching emerald heels.

The secretary placed the stack of mail on Raelyn's desk. "Alexis, you don't have to get my mail for me."

"Be grateful," Amira said on the other end of the phone. "Our office secretary just takes Snapchat selfies all day."

"Thank you," Raelyn said to Alexis, and she began sorting through the stack of papers, magazines, and catalogues.

Alexis shrugged. "Oh, it's no problem. I needed to stretch." The corners of her mouth pulled up in an attempt to conceal a grin. "And that hot nurse doing his clinicals with Dr. Huang was walking by."

"Get that girl hooked up!" Amira shouted, clearly listening in.

Raelyn laughed. "I'll see what I can do, though I doubt she needs *my* help attracting attention."

Alexis grinned with confidence. "Thanks, Dr. DeRose." And with that, she left the office, closing the door behind her.

Raelyn was still sifting through the mail on her desk when the cover of her newest *Sports Illustrated* magazine caught her attention. She gasped, "Oh my God." Flattening the magazine on top of the rest of the mail she said, "Amira, have you seen this?"

Sounding confused Amira replied, "Um, seen what?"

Raelyn read the headline in red over the close-up picture of the famous ball player, "'Hard Hitter Quinn Casey Exiting Early? What does this mean for the Kings of LA?'"

"Wait, 'hard hitter' is referring to baseball, right? Not some weird sex euphemism?"

"Yes, it's baseball," Raelyn laughed under her breath. "His team has been in the past four World Series Championships and they've won three out of four of them, so they've been referring to them as the kings of L.A."

Raelyn studied the cover, looking at the handsome features of Quinn Casey's face in deep concentration. His sharp jawline and light brown eyes, almost golden, staring back into hers. There was more than a five o'clock shadow peppering his strong, square jaw, but it suited him, along with his dark brown hair just visible beneath a royal blue baseball cap. Raelyn felt a tug in her chest, and warmth spread through her, down between her legs as she studied his intense face.

A flash of memories played through Raelyn's mind: The first time she saw him throw a baseball, Quinn teaching her how to swing a bat, spending hours in the fort they'd built in the basement at her parents' house, watching the same movies over and over, the two of them jumping and coming together in an awkward pre-teen embrace after winning a neighborhood game at the park. They had been so young and could barely go a day without seeing each other- at least until the night of their high school graduation.

Staring back into his intense gaze, she wondered when he had gotten this hot. Sure, he'd always been attractive, but *now?* He was practically a sex symbol waiting for a line of bad puns to be spewed about his bat and his ballpark.

Amira's voice snapped her back to her office, and Raelyn swallowed, telling herself the warmth she felt between her legs was simply because she was going through a bit of a dry spell where men were concerned.

"Quinn Casey? Why does that name sound so familiar?" Amira asked.

"I told you about him a while ago, back in college, remember? Our local, hometown sports hero...we were friends when we were kids," Raelyn said, a furrow creasing her brow as she continued to study the magazine cover. "I wonder why he'd be leaving early. I mean, he's on a roll, and I can't see them selling someone who's such an asset to their team...I read something about him ditching his baseball career for a modeling gig." Raelyn laughed to herself at the thought of the Quinn Casey she knew leaving the sport he loved to pose half-naked for designer magazines. "I thought it was just a ridiculous rumor, but he's certainly changed since we were friends."

"Oh, that's right!" Amira said, recognition dawning. "He's that super hot one who's always in *People* magazine with *Victoria's Secret* models. I actually bought a copy of *Men's Health* because his picture was just...breathtaking. I couldn't pass it up."

"Yeah, that's the one," said Raelyn, feeling a little annoyed at the mention of all the different models he'd been seen with.

"Didn't he blow you off when you met up in college?" Amira asked, now in full-fledged gossip mode. "You guys were supposed to catch up but then he ended up having sex in the booth instead?"

"They did not have sex in the bar booth," Raelyn said flatly.

"Maybe not, but I guarantee they didn't go far before tearing each other's clothes off."

"Right," Raelyn sighed, trying to ignore the memories from that night and the new images forming in her head.

"I can't say I blame her, whoever she was," Amira said. "Now that I remember who you're talking about, the *Men's Health* issue was phenomenal, but he was in the *Sports Illustrated Body Issue* last year, and I have to say I would definitely give his bat a swing."

"Amira!"

"I wouldn't mind taking him to third base," she continued.

"Oh sweet mother, please stop the puns!"

"I'd handle his foul balls."

"Ew!" Raelyn couldn't help laughing now.

"If he's the pitcher, I'll gladly be the catcher."

"First off, you're getting married," Raelyn interjected. "And second, you're a gynecologist. If you've seen all those magazine photos of him with countless women who have probably been with countless men, you might want to think again about that fantasy."

"Ah, well, a girl can dream," Amira sighed. "But I really do have to get going, I have a patient in the waiting room."

"I should get ready for my next patient, too," said Raelyn.

Just before she could hang up, Amira said, "You're really okay about Emerson being at the bonfire? I can totally kick him out- it is my party."

"It really is fine," Raelyn said. "Besides, making a big deal about it would only make it seem like I'm not over it, which I am. I'm still mad at him and probably always will be, but I'm glad we're not getting married."

With that, Raelyn wrapped up her call and hung up. She set her phone on her desk, now holding the magazine with both hands. She studied the once-familiar face again before flipping to the page with the cover story.

CHAPTER 2

"No, it's totally fine, I promise. Yeah, they're just blowing it out of proportion," Quinn Casey said into the phone for what felt like the 174th time today. "It's just a sprain, I'll have surgery and some PT and then I'll be back in the game."

Ever since *Sports Illustrated* published their latest issue with a seriously misleading headline, Quinn had been receiving non-stop phone calls from friends, people working for news centers, various reporters, and even a few previous hook-ups wanting to get together for pity sex. Quinn didn't do pity sex. And he certainly wasn't interested in answering reporters' questions of what he was going to do with his life now that his promising career had crashed and burned at only twenty-nine years old.

Quinn stared down at the article on his kitchen island that he'd been reading over and over since it was delivered. The only thing really misleading was the headline; the article itself was pretty accurate. That was the problem these days though; people couldn't be bothered to actually read a whole news article, they just liked the shock of the headline and created their own story. Quinn re-read where he'd been quoted saying that he was being set up with the best sports medicine team in California, and that even though he knew what he brought to the team, he was confident they'd remain the *kings of Los Angeles* in the upcoming season.

He had just set his phone down when it began to ring again. Quinn let out a groan of frustration and threw his head back, exasperated. How did all these people have his personal phone number anyway?

Just then Quinn heard his front door swing open and footsteps making their way into the kitchen. Mitch Hemlock, a tall, clean-shaven man with brown hair, green eyes, and the beginnings of a pretty solid dad-bod walked through the archway and into the large, immaculate space and pointed at Quinn's phone, still ringing on the island. "Do not answer that!"

Quinn breathed a sigh of relief, his hands coming together in prayer. "Oh, thank fucking goodness, Mitch." He swore he had never been more excited and grateful to see his agent walk into his house unannounced. Quinn jogged past Mitch and into the entryway where the inside door had been left open. He didn't want any reporters or paparazzi trying to get into his house or get a peek inside, but was instead met by Zoey Nunez, his publicist, walking through the door and closing it behind her.

With another great sigh of relief, Quinn wrapped Zoey in a tight hug and whispered, "Thank you, Mamacita, you're a life-saver."

Zoey's body tensed up briefly, surprised at this sudden and rare show of affection from her client. She gave him an awkward pat on the back, as he was significantly taller than her. Unlike most women in her position, she didn't let out a dreamy sigh or try to feel up his thickly corded forearms or biceps. Nonetheless, he gave her his signature devilish grin and a quick wink before heading back into the kitchen where Mitch was handling his phone.

"We're getting you a new number," Mitch declared.

Quinn leaned back against the counter, stretching his long legs out in front of himself and crossing them at the ankles, far more relaxed now that he had been saved from this nightmare. He quirked an eyebrow up. "Again?"

"Yes, again," said Mitch. "You need to stop giving out your real number to all these women. You sleep with them, they go home, they don't get a call, and I'm willing to bet they sell your number out of spite."

Quinn let out a low whistle. "That's cold."

"So is sleeping with a woman, telling her that she's 'not like all the other girls, ya know?' and never calling her," Zoey said in a challenging tone. Her dark, chestnut brown hair fell in a wave over her shoulder as she dug in her purse for her tablet.

Quinn gave her another grin. "Ah, Miss Nunez, you know my secrets. I'm just trying to be authentic."

"You're trying to *come across* as authentic," Zoey corrected him, "while lying through your teeth. There's nothing authentic about it, which is why you would be completely lost without me here to make you look good."

"Maybe you should be there next time I bring a girl home from an after party," Quinn said mischievously. "It could be fun and you'd be able to make me look good in the morning."

Zoey rolled her eyes, clearly not taking the bait. "Oh sweetie, who broke you?"

"What do you mean?" Quinn said with the slightest trace of a laugh in his voice. Zoey was the one person in Los Angeles who knew Quinn on a personal level. She was with him nearly every day, made all his appointments, and managed his mishaps, but she still didn't know everything about him. With a slightly guilty pang, he realized the only thing he really knew about her was that her golden-olive skin tone was a result of her unique Greek-Mexican heritage, and that she was about the only gorgeous single woman in the area that he'd labeled as off-limits.

"Every guy who drowns himself in some vice- drugs, sex, alcohol- has been heartbroken at some point. Are you sure you're not taking your anger or heartache out on the rest of the female population?"

Shaking his head, he grinned. "Zoey, we've been over this a hundred times. There's no girl. No one who broke my heart, no...just no one. I am who I am, Zo. Don't try to change me."

Unconvinced and, as usual, not ready to drop the subject, Zoey pressed, "Oh come on, Quinn. Did she cheat on you? Beat you at your own game playing the field? Pick your best friend over you?"

There was a moment's pause before he responded flatly, "I've never been in love."

An image of golden blonde hair blowing in the wind underneath a baseball cap- *his* baseball cap- came to him, along with a pair of bright blue eyes. He remembered teaching her how to swing a bat, though she probably didn't need him to. He remembered her friendly smile inviting him to join her overdone birthday party when he had come to the beach by himself, and taking her hand when he finally agreed to join at the prospect of being able to throw a baseball at something. Then the image of her across the high school gymnasium kissing a guy who was most certainly *not* him, and the sudden pain in his chest and sick feeling in his stomach when he realized that they really were *just friends*.

"Maybe I'm wrong then. Maybe you were just born to be the center of everyone's attention." Zoey shrugged. She didn't believe this, of course, but she was at least dropping it for now.

It took Quinn a moment to come back to himself, realizing he had been staring hard at the edge of his long, hand-carved dining room table where no one ever really ate meals. The pain in his chest and the rolling feeling in his stomach suddenly felt new again, not having visited that memory in quite some time.

He shoved the memory back down and looked up with a grin he hoped looked normal. "I think you're right. Plus, it's kind of hard to settle down when I'm on the road all the time."

Mitch clapped his hands together like he was about to relay a football play. "Okay, we're going to get you a new phone with a new number, then we've got a press conference, and ESPN wants an interview."

Zoey nodded. "I'll get his responses ready."

"Good. Quinn, go get dressed and let's get going," said Mitch. "Twenty minutes?"

Quinn pushed himself up off the counter, nodding and heading out of the kitchen to the stairs. At the top of the stairway, he spotted a slightly disheveled looking brunette making her way out of his bedroom. She smiled when she saw him.

Aw shit, he cursed inwardly. He forgot this one had slept over. *Nice job, Case, I thought we learned how to avoid that ages ago.*

He sighed and then put on his best smile. "Hey baby." He traced one hand lightly down her bare arm. "My agent and publicist just barged in. I'm sorry, I thought we'd have the morning to spend together, I'd even bought stuff to make breakfast."

That was a lie.

The brunette, Julia? Julianne? Jenelle?, gave him a sympathetic smile. "Aw, that's okay. I'll give you a call and we can do this again sometime."

"I would love that."

Another lie.

Quinn wrapped his arms around her and gave her a slow kiss—enough to make her feel special, but not enough to make her want to drag him back to bed. They pulled apart and she slowly headed down the stairs with a dreamy look over her shoulder, biting her bottom lip. Jesus, he should get an Oscar.

He rolled his eyes on his way to his bedroom. What didn't women get? If he's not a gentleman enough to walk her to the door, why would they think he's enough of one to give them a phone call?

He dressed quickly and brushed his teeth. He didn't have enough time to shave, so he was leaving the house a little more scruffy than usual. Running a hand through his dark brown hair, flecked with natural auburn highlights, he tried smoothing it down, then messing it up, then combing it, before giving up and grabbing his baseball cap and pulling it over his unruly hair. He had yet to eat breakfast and that was far more important than styling himself to perfection. If he had interviews and press conferences, there would no doubt be someone there to worry about his look for him.

Rushing around the kitchen he threw ingredients into a blender for a power protein smoothie, poured it into a cup and walked out the door, followed by Mitch and Zoey, who were both on their phones. As usual, an all black Chevy Suburban was waiting for them out front and they all slid into the back.

"She was cute," Zoey commented, hanging up and getting ready to dial a new number. "Did you tell her you'd call her?"

For a moment, Quinn wasn't sure what she was talking about but then remembered the woman whose name just wouldn't come to him. "I didn't have to, she said she'd call me."

"We're on the way to get you a new number," Zoey scoffed.

"Worked out perfectly, didn't it?" Quinn cocked an eyebrow and then stared down at his soon-to-be old phone.

Zoey shook her head and rolled her eyes. "You're impossible."

Quinn simply shrugged.

"You probably don't even remember her name. Why don't you try finding a woman who's worth remembering?"

Another flash of blue eyes and long blonde hair, seeing her in the stands cheering him on at his high school baseball games, his jersey number painted on one dimpled cheek. A feeling like a brick dropping in his stomach brought up the memory he most regretted- *graduation night*. Quinn shook his head. "I don't do love."

Zoey gave him a challenging stare before sighing, resigning herself to continue her phone calls.

Staring at his phone, he thought about the fact that out of all the people who had called him that morning none had been his friends before his life changed, before all the glamor and the money, before being labeled a sports hero, a hard-hitting legend, or even earning the title "rookie of the year" six years ago. Not a single family member had contacted him, not that he had expected them to. He didn't really have much for family, and he had no idea if his mom even knew what he'd made of himself. Honestly, if his family had contacted him he would assume it was just for money, so he couldn't say he was upset they hadn't been in touch. The best friendships of his life hadn't been completely left behind, but he'd lost touch enough to feel guilty when he thought about them. What would he give to hear from those friends again? To hear from *her* again?

Quinn sighed, looking out the tinted windows at the bright California sun. He had given all of himself to earn this life, to build himself up from nothing. He loved this life, really, he did. And even though he knew his injury was being blown into something bigger than what it really was, the idea of an injury having the potential to destroy his career made him sweaty and anxious. He was not ready to put this life behind him. Sometimes it just felt like something was missing. He pulled on his mirrored aviators, leaned back in the seat, and closed his eyes.

Back in his living room later that night, Quinn broke out his new phone and began the process of transferring the important contacts into it so that he could let them know his new number. They hadn't had time to do the transfer at the store, and he didn't really need his own phone when his publicist and agent were with him all day making phone calls and arrangements for him.

Mitch and Zoey were still with him, going over upcoming appearances, interviews, and doctor's appointments, and logging them into their schedules. Mitch came into the living room to debrief Quinn on whatever arrangements he had made.

"Good news," Mitch began. "We got your surgery scheduled- the morning after next! We got you put right at the top of Dr. Nichols's list and he will perform the surgery at 8:30 Sunday morning. The faster you get in, the faster you can recover and get back on the field."

Quinn's eyes widened. "That's great! So, I'll be able to play next season?"

Mitch grimaced. "Physical therapy is extensive for this procedure, but you will be able to get back out there," he added quickly, seeing Quinn's expression fall.

"How extensive?"

"Well, it goes in phases. The first phase is about six weeks, and then they say you can start strengthening and conditioning again," Mitch said. "Since you are at a professional level and will need to fully recondition after being out, the doc says you should expect to be out for at least a year."

"A whole year?" Quinn exclaimed, then let out a sigh. "Shit, so I won't be playing again until the middle of next season." What the hell was he supposed to do with a whole year and a bum arm?

"That seems to be what they're thinking." Mitch nodded.

Quinn unconsciously rubbed up and down his bad arm, feeling that little twinge at his elbow. It didn't feel that intense, but it had been made pretty clear how bad it could get if he kept playing without surgery. "Right, okay. So, you've got the details?"

Zoey pulled out her phone and leaned over to show Quinn all her notes she had taken regarding what to expect before and after surgery when a familiar ringtone went off from the phone next to Quinn on the couch. His old phone.

"You haven't switched them yet?" Mitch said, peering at the phone screen to see if a friend or foe was calling.

"The new phone wasn't charged yet," Quinn said, looking at the number. It was a 231 area code, but the rest of the number was unfamiliar. Quinn's brow furrowed, wondering who would be calling from his hometown, or at least close to it. "That's weird, it's from Northern Michigan."

"Family calling to check in?" Zoey suggested as Quinn swiped to answer. His team and the people in his life knew very little about his life in Michigan, just that he'd grown up just outside of Traverse City and had been fought over pretty aggressively by college recruiters.

"Hello?" Quinn was acutely aware of how uncertain his voice sounded.

"Hi, Mr. Casey, this is Sandra Burke, the home nurse you hired to look after your mother," the friendly voice came over the phone. Quinn's mouth went dry, his voice catching in his throat, and he found himself unable to speak. He had received email updates from Sandra on a monthly basis, just to know that his mother was still alive, but hadn't talked to her over the phone since he had hired her.

When Quinn failed to respond Sandra continued, "Of course I'm calling about your mother's health. I didn't think this was appropriate for an email. Her liver and kidneys are failing, Mr. Casey. I know we haven't had the best communication, but your mother has progressed to stage five of chronic kidney disease. She has started her dialysis treatments, though it is unlikely that she would be considered for a transplant due to…" the woman hesitated, "the factors that led her to this stage."

Heroin use. They won't offer a kidney transplant to a patient who essentially chose to destroy her body. And why should they?

"I thought you should know in case you wanted to come see her…Even if it's just to say your goodbyes."

Quinn closed his eyes, unsure of how to respond. He knew this day would come eventually, and he never knew how he would feel to get the news. He did not have a good relationship with his mother. He really didn't have any kind of relationship with her. She had spent his entire childhood and adolescence either passed out from drinking too much or in a dazed trance from heroin use. Repressed images of needles littering the bathroom counter filled his mind, his mother sitting in her ratty green chair staring out the dirty front window, completely unresponsive for hours. Quinn had spent his childhood taking care of her as best as he could, making sure she ate enough to stay alive and making sure the house stayed clean enough to ward off social services.

He had been silent for quite some time and became suddenly aware that both Mitch and Zoey were looking at him with deep looks of concern on their faces. "Sorry," he breathed into the phone. His words came out slow and shaky, "Um, yeah, of course, thank you for, uh, letting me know. I'll, uh, I'll let you know what my plan is. I'm having surgery Sunday morning. Is it, uh, is Sunday too long to put it off?"

"No, Mr. Casey," Sandra's polite voice sounded reassuring, "The dialysis treatments should give her time, but the disease progressed quickly through stage four. Your mom's condition is severe, but she's willing to fight as long as she can." She was silent for a few beats, "I know your relationship with her is...*complicated*, but she really would like to see you."

Complicated. Yeah. That's one way to put it.

Quinn chewed the inside of his cheek before nodding. Upon realizing Sandra couldn't possibly register his nod on the other end of the phone he cleared his throat and spoke, "Thanks, Miss Burke, I'll be in touch." He hung up the phone and dropped it into his lap. Falling back onto the couch, he pinched the bridge of his nose, then pressed his palms into his eyes, as if blinding himself would make this go away.

After a long pause, Zoey leaned forward, placing a gentle hand on Quinn's shoulder. "Is everything okay?" she asked.

He sighed and stared up at the vaulted ceiling above him. "What a fuckin' day." Quinn grabbed the plush accent pillow from behind his head and pulled it over his face, wishing he was alone so he could scream into it.

CHAPTER 3

1998

Sun was bursting through the sheer lavender curtains in seven-year-old Raelyn's bedroom. Much like a Disney princess, she padded over to the window and threw the floor-length curtains open with a flourish. Raelyn smiled out at the beautiful view of her family's vineyard which seemed to go on for miles. This was always an amazing view, but today it really seemed to sparkle just a little more because it was Raelyn's seventh birthday. She just knew seven was going to be a good year- no, a *great* year. Lucky number seven, as the adults were always saying.

Staring out the window she thought about the day ahead. She would get to see all of her close friends and family members. Her grand-mére and grand-pére from her mother's side would be visiting all the way from Bordeaux. She always loved to hear them speak French with everyone; Raelyn could speak French decently but was better at listening and understanding the words than actually making the throaty sounds herself. Raelyn's father's side of the family was French-Canadian, which was apparently just not the same as really being from France, and there was always light teasing about which was better.

Birthdays were a big deal in the DeRose household. On June 21, Raelyn's was the longest day of the year- except for those pesky years when the Summer Solstice fell on the twentieth or twenty-second. To her, this meant that she got more time to spend with her friends and family than she would any other day of the year, and it was the dawn of her favorite season.

She took in a deep breath and the scent of bacon filled her nostrils. Smiling, she took off running down the stairs, not bothering to change out of her light blue and yellow ducky pajamas. She followed the scent of bacon into the kitchen, realizing that that wasn't all that was cooking in there. When her eyes fell on the kitchen island they grew wide with excitement.

Her mother and father were in the kitchen pouring each other mimosas made with champagne from their own vineyard and winery. They must have been up for quite some time with the maids to put together the display between them: Raelyn's very own personalized breakfast buffet with all her favorite breakfast foods. French toast, bacon, chocolate chip pancakes, blueberry muffins, a variety of flavored syrups, scrambled eggs, fried potatoes, and a giant fruit bowl with pineapple chunks, strawberries, kiwi, blackberries, and raspberries covered the surface of the large kitchen island.

"Wow," Raelyn breathed, eyes unblinking and scanning the buffet in front of her. "Thank you!" She rushed over to give her parents each a hug.

"Happy birthday, sweetie," her dad said, handing her a piece of bacon from the serving tray.

"Raelyn, please get a plate, you are not an animal," her mother chided, her accent always thicker when she was making reprimands.

"Oh, Margaux, it's her birthday," her dad said, smiling down at her and sneaking her another piece of bacon. Raelyn smiled back up at him but caught sight of her mother's face and thought she had better just grab a plate.

Raelyn's big sister, Camille, entered the kitchen, looking just as wide-eyed and awe struck by the smorgasbord in the middle of the room. The two sisters filled their plates and scurried giddily into the formal dining room. Their parents met the girls at the dining table once their plates were also full, and each set a glass of orange juice in a fancy champagne flute in front of the girls. Camille and Raelyn exchanged wide grins and clinked glasses before digging into their plates. In that moment, Raelyn knew without a doubt she was the luckiest birthday girl in the world.

Raelyn's birthday party was not just a party, it was an extravaganza! Because the only way she could think to describe it was "extravagant." "Over the top" didn't quite cut it, though it would not be inaccurate, and outdoorsy as it was, "lavish" didn't quite make the mark either. As usual the event was on the beach of Lake Michigan. There was a park with a playground and large play set for the kids, but it was empty because the beach itself was full of different activities. The theme here was clearly carnival; there were face painters, one of those giant hammer swinging games to win a stuffed animal, ski ball, a giant slide, pony rides- *pony rides!*- and even a few dunk tanks with clowns waiting to be dropped into the water below. There were concession stands with elephant ears, cotton candy, nachos, deep-fried *anything*, and an ice cream truck was parked in the shade past the sand.

Raelyn could not believe that this was her party. She was once again glad that her birthday was the longest day of the year because she was sure she would never get to all the events if it weren't. She had done her best so far, having ridden the giant slide several times, taken six pony rides, and she had beat both her sister and their older cousin, Paul, at ski ball- twice! Now walking around with a stuffed elephant the size of, well, her, in one hand and a fried corn dog in the other, she thought she needed to take a minute and breathe, and maybe let up on the junk food once this corn dog was gone.

Raelyn found her grand-pére who gladly took the stuffed elephant and tucked it away for her so that she could roam the beach more freely. She was walking by herself when she passed the three dunk tanks with clowns still dry, waiting to be dunked. She really didn't like clowns and wondered if her parents put them in the dunk tanks because of that, or if they simply forgot that she did not like them.

These clowns all had different make up and wigs. One wearing mostly yellow with a bright green wig seemed less intimidating than the other two. Not realizing the line had moved and Raelyn was now at the front of it, the man tending to the dunk tanks tossed her a baseball. She looked at the ball in her hand and back up at the clown, with its creepy oversized smile, trying to appear friendly but still scaring her a little.

"The birthday girl, yes?" The man had golden tan skin and dark hair, and she didn't recognize what kind of accent he had, but she found it enjoyable to listen to. Raelyn nodded in response. "We will give you some extra throws, of course! However many you want. None of these clowns has been in the water yet."

Raelyn concentrated, let out a breath and threw the ball as hard as she could.

Missed.

The man tossed the baseball back to her and this time she focused more on aim than force.

Missed again.

She caught the ball in her hand once more, closed her eyes, and concentrated. She opened her eyes and saw the clown waving her hands around by her head in a teasing manner. Raelyn sent the ball flying one more time.

Ping!

The ball had just grazed the end of the metal circle and bounced off, not hitting the button hard enough to send the clown into the water. The clown mimed a big, hearty laugh. Raelyn shook her head, but still smiled.

"I'll come back," she told the man. "May I keep one of the baseballs?" Baseball and softball were not sports she played much yet, but perhaps they should be. Maybe she needed to practice throwing a little so the next time there was a clown that needed to be dunked she could do it with ease.

The man nodded and tossed her one of the baseballs out of his bucket. She caught the ball and headed down the beach, tossing it in the air and catching it until she realized she had wandered a little farther from the party than she had meant to do. She turned to look back at all her friends and family having fun and smiled. Thinking she should probably head back before someone thought she was missing, she caught sight of a boy skipping rocks a little farther down the beach. Giving another glance back toward the party, she made up her mind and decided to walk toward the boy.

She stood back and watched him throw several rocks, sending them skimming and hopping gently across the surface of the lake. Raelyn noticed the boy's intensity gradually increasing, his arm throwing the rocks harder and harder until he was no longer skipping them, but simply seeing how far he could throw them. She thought maybe he sounded out of breath or like he was breathing heavily for some reason, and before she could stop herself she spoke.

"You can really throw."

The boy startled, whipping around and looking at Raelyn with his brow furrowed. He almost looked angry or sad, or maybe both. He was breathing heavily, his chest and shoulders rising and falling with harsh breaths as though he were about to scream or cry. His features softened when he took in Raelyn's presence. She was wearing purple shorts with a white tank top and a sash that said "Birthday Girl" in sparkly gold letters, her long blonde hair a windblown mess around her head.

When the boy didn't say anything to her she looked around and asked him, "Are you here by yourself? Shouldn't your parents be with you?"

The boy looked down, seeming to notice what he was wearing for the first time. An oversized t-shirt that had the *Budweiser* logo across the front and a pair of jeans that had large holes in both knees. His hair was dark brown, except when the sun hit it just right there was a hint of auburn, and it was untidy, sticking up in all places. Raelyn thought he must be around her age. He was standing barefoot in the sand, still holding a rock in one hand.

"Shouldn't yours?" the boy finally said.

Raelyn turned and gestured toward the big *extravaganza* down the beach. "They're over there. Along with my grandparents and aunts and uncles and cousins." They stood in silence for a short moment and Raelyn approached him further, taking a few more steps toward him. "I'm Raelyn DeRose. That's my birthday party, I'm seven today."

The boy looked over her shoulder at the beach carnival, then back at her skeptically. "That's a birthday party? It's a whole carnival."

"My family likes birthday parties," Raelyn said smiling. She took in the boy's appearance again and could have sworn she heard his stomach growl once or twice. "Do you want to join us? I'm the birthday girl so I can get you free food or whatever you want."

23

"I don't need your food," the boy said, not looking her in the eye this time.

Raelyn considered for a moment. "Well, here's the thing," she took another step closer, "there are three dunk tanks with clowns just waiting to be dropped into the water, but no one has dunked them yet. I really don't like clowns and I can tell you can throw." She tossed him the baseball that was curled in her hand. He dropped the rock he'd been holding and caught the baseball, looking down at it as though it were some valued treasure. Raelyn smiled and held her hand out for him to take. "Come on, let's go dunk some clowns."

The boy stared at her hand for a few beats before the corners of his mouth turned up in what was almost a smile. He said, "I'm Quinn...Quinn Casey," and took Raelyn's hand, letting her lead him back to her birthday party.

Quinn wasn't sure what to think of this girl who had dragged him away from his solitude; he'd gotten so used to being alone, but she seemed friendly enough, if a little spoiled to have a whole carnival set up for her birthday. He hoped she wouldn't ask too many questions about where his parents were. He didn't like to share about his mom's issues, or the large, dangerous looking men who came into the house wreaking of stale cigarette smoke, beer, and something more bitter. He would always slip out his bedroom window when he heard the low, scratchy male voices coming through the front door. His mom wouldn't notice his absence, and even if she did, by the time he got home she would be too far gone to care.

Raelyn stopped in front of the dunk tanks and spoke to the man who seemed to be in charge, "I told you I'd be back!" Still holding Quinn's hand, she pulled him to the front of the line. "This is Quinn. I'm giving him my unlimited throws."

Raelyn smiled brightly at him and then pointed to the line that marked where to stand when throwing. Quinn glanced up at the clown waiting to be dropped, the target that he needed to hit, and back at the girl who was smiling encouragingly at him. He felt himself smile back at her. He knew this would be easy enough. Turning back to the target, he rolled the ball in his hand a few times before he wound up and took his shot.

Ping! Splash!

There was a brief look of surprise on the clown's face before she was dropped into the water tank. Raelyn cheered and jumped up and down next to him, and there were claps and sounds of encouragement and interest among the small crowd of party guests who had gathered behind him. A warm feeling filled Quinn's chest as he heard this crowd of strangers cheering for him, making him feel a sense of pride and a rush of adrenaline he was sure he'd never felt before.

The dark-haired man standing next to the bucket of baseballs smiled and clapped his hands before tossing him another ball and gesturing toward the next tank. "If you can dunk all three like that, we'll let you choose any prize you want," he said as they moved over. This clown had bright blue pig tails and a black and white polka-dotted suit with bright blue clown shoes.

Quinn tossed the baseball up in the air and caught it, and with a glance and a small smirk in Raelyn's direction, he wound up and threw the ball for the second time.

Ping! Splash!

An even more enthusiastic roar of applause and cheering erupted behind him. He turned and smiled uncertainly at all the unfamiliar faces, and then moved down the line to the next and final dunk tank. Catching the ball again, he glanced up at this last clown who, if Quinn wasn't mistaken, looked like he was bracing himself. This made him smile even more, a surge of an unfamiliar emotion- *confidence?*- filling him up. He gave the ball a few tosses into the air, looked over at Raelyn who gave him an encouraging nod, and this time he really smiled. He wound up and sent the ball flying into the very center of the target once more.

The outburst of applause and cheers he received had him smiling wider than he was sure he ever had before, a few people had given him a pat on the back. He heard a few *wows* and *good jobs*. Raelyn cheered and pumped her arm in the air before giving him a high five.

"That was so cool," Raelyn said, watching as the clowns all got out of their tanks and began to dry off. "But I think the running face paint might make them even scarier."

Quinn looked over his shoulder at the drenched clowns, wigs askew, face paint and make-up running. She wasn't wrong. When he looked back at Raelyn, there was a tall man with sandy blonde hair, a perfectly manicured mustache, and bright blue eyes that matched the girl's, standing behind her with his hands on her shoulders. Quinn didn't know much about having money, but he could tell this man was drenched in wealth, from his haircut to his easy white button-down shirt with the sleeves rolled up and beach-patterned swim shorts that had likely never been in the water. This man's look said that he was pretending to be casual, but *why yes, this outfit cost more than your mom's monthly rent.*

"Who is this young man?" The tall man asked. He was clearly Raelyn's father, with a smile that crinkled his eyes.

"This is Quinn Casey," Raelyn said, smiling her friendly, bright smile again. Quinn wondered if she ever looked anything but perfectly happy. "He dunked all those clowns on his first throw! I think he's my new best friend."

Quinn paused, looking at the girl's face for a few moments. He'd never really had a best friend before. He wasn't sure why someone like her would want to be friends with someone like him, but he'd only known her for a half hour and already he'd experienced feelings of pride and confidence that he never had before. He returned her smile and for the first time was filled with hope that his life just might brighten up with a friend like Raelyn DeRose.

CHAPTER 4

Driving down the familiar lakeshore drive of his hometown with the top off of his rented new Ford Bronco, Quinn took in a deep breath, letting the unsalted air fill his lungs. Living in California was great, known for its breathtaking views, but the air up here in Northern Michigan was fresher and cleaner, more crisp. Quinn gripped the steering wheel with his left hand while his right arm hung in a sling across his chest.

This time yesterday he was getting discharged from one of the best surgical units in California, and now he was cruising down M-37 toward his childhood home. His gut lurched and knotted at the thought of the old, run-down bungalow that contained no happy memories. He hadn't seen it in years but remembered the flimsy chain link fence that wrapped around the yard, having jumped it countless times sneaking in and out of his house when his mom had company. The thought of his mom still sitting in that ratty chair facing the window made him tense.

Quinn wondered what the last words were that they had spoken to each other. Had he just told her "I'm off to Arizona, don't forget to eat"? Did she say anything to him? When was the last time she'd spoken to him at all? He and his mother had been passing strangers. They'd never had any kind of relationship, but were just sort of there, living in the same house, breathing in the same misery.

On the plane, Quinn had taken to Facebook to look up his two best friends from middle and high school who he was pretty sure were still in the area. Last time he'd talked to them, they were in the process of opening their own sports bar right in their hometown. He was happy to see that not only had they succeeded in opening a place of their own, but it was thriving. Traverse City was home to several breweries, distilleries, and wineries, and was famous for craft beer, with the best bar hops and brew tours in the state. With so many craft bars to choose from, Jett Miller and Chris Watson- *the third*- went for a classic sports bar featuring a variety of domestic draughts, local brews, and local ciders. It was the best of both worlds. While many of the bars in Traverse City boasted a very hipster vibe, Trojan Horse Sports Bar was a veritable man cave.

An idea began to form at the thought of the bar and his old friends. Quinn pressed the button on his steering wheel and spoke to Siri through the Bronco's bluetooth, "GPS to Trojan Horse Sports Bar, Traverse City, Michigan." The screen in the center console brought up the directions in maps. Only eight minutes away, it was worth the detour. Quinn wasn't much of a drinker, but he knew he needed something to ease his nerves and loosen up the knot in his stomach. Plus, the idea of seeing Chris and Jett again after so many years brought a much-needed smile to his face.

About ten minutes later he found himself parked in front of Trojan Horse. His nerves turned to excitement and he was having a hard time keeping the grin off his face, wondering what his old friends would say at the sight of him walking through the door. He made an awkward attempt to smooth his ever-unruly hair with one hand and threw on his aviators, he hopped out of the Bronco and sauntered into the bar.

The space was longer than it was wide, with large flat screens available at every angle, playing a variety of sports channels. The bar itself ran almost the entire length of one side of the building, with trendy bare-bulb rustic lights hanging down from wood beams. The place was done in dark wood tones, and where there weren't flat screens on the walls there were photos of sports teams, posters, jerseys, and various sports equipment hung up. Quinn scanned the walls and the bar again, the liquor bottles backlit on their shelves. There was a section of wall behind the bar that didn't have shelves filled with liquor, but instead boasted the white and blue number twelve LA jersey, with CASEY emblazoned across the top. He couldn't help smiling, swelling with pride and appreciation that his two friends had made a special spot for him on their walls.

The bar was pretty much empty, which wasn't surprising as it was 2:30 on a Monday afternoon. There were two men at the bar, one sitting on a bar stool with a laptop and notebooks on the bar top, and the other behind it, counting liquor bottles. Fair-skinned Jett Miller was pulling out bottles of Hendrick's from beneath the bar, his light brown hair as curly as Quinn had remembered. Chris was tall with coffee-colored skin, his black hair shaved short.

Quinn took a deep breath and let it out, "Jesus, boys, I heard business was thriving. Maybe if you took down that hideous number twelve, you'd get some business."

Both men looked up immediately as Quinn took his sunglasses off, their eyes doubling in size as they realized their old friend was standing in their bar. They erupted in exclamations of disbelief and surprise that he'd shown up unannounced, stopping what they were doing and coming over to greet him with manly, back-slapping hugs, though careful of the obviously injured arm.

"What the fuck is this? You're not really benched, are you?" Jett gestured to Quinn's sling. "Shit, I can't believe you came back! How long has it been?"

"Fuck, I couldn't tell you." Quinn looked around. "This place is fuckin awesome, guys."

"Quinn *fucking* Casey." Chris shook his head, taking in the sight of him. "Seriously though, what's the injury? It's not serious, right? Y'all won't keep your winning streak if you're out!"

"No, no, it's not serious. Just had surgery yesterday. I'm hoping I can find a decent PT while I'm here, but I should be good to go by the middle of next season," said Quinn, running his free hand through his hair again.

"How long are you in town?" Jett asked, then ushered Quinn toward the bar. "Fuck, man, let's get you a drink- on the house!"

Quinn slid onto a bar stool and Chris resumed his spot in front of his laptop. "You don't need to buy my drinks for me, guys." He shook his head as Jett grabbed a rocks glass from behind the bar.

"I do, actually," said Jett. "Then you can just leave us a good tip."

Quinn laughed, resigned. "Okay, that's fair. I'll have a Maker's on the rocks."

Jett tapped the bar top before turning around and grabbing the bottle of Maker's Mark off the shelf and pouring a glass.

"So, what brings you back?" Chris asked. "I would've thought your guys would have you set up with a physical therapist out there already."

Quinn took a sip of the amber colored liquid. It had been a long time since he last drank whiskey, but he felt the occasion called for it. Maker's was smooth, but still gave him the much needed burn to spark his senses. He took a moment before answering the question. Jett and Chris were two out of the three people who really knew what his life was like growing up with his mom. They'd been into his house and seen the worst his home life had to offer. It had been a long time since he'd been able to be honest about it.

"Well," Quinn sighed, "my mom's dying. I guess I should say goodbye or do what I can to…" he hesitated, thinking, "clean up any loose ends."

"Shit," Jett muttered while Chris grimaced and gave an "Oof."

"Yeah…" Quinn paused. "I wasn't sure how to take the news. I was on my way to the house but I thought you guys deserved a visit first. The bar was a happy coincidence, huh?"

Chris looked like he was considering what to say and then said, "Do you need us to go with you? I mean, I'm sure you'd be okay, but you don't have to face it on your own."

Quinn appreciated the offer, and was glad he could sit here and talk to his two friends as if their lives hadn't been completely flipped upside down in the last ten years, but he wanted to go alone. At least this first time. He had no idea what he'd be walking into and had a hard enough time preparing himself for his reaction, he didn't want to have to worry about theirs too.

"Thanks, man, but I think I should go alone. I have to meet with the nurse and go over all the boring medical stuff, ya know," Quinn said. "But seriously, thanks."

Jett and Chris seemed to accept this response and only took a few moments before changing subjects.

"Did you seriously sleep with Isla Merrin and Adriana Silva?" Jett asked, with the enthusiasm of a fifteen-year-old boy asking a buddy if he finally got to third base.

Chris laughed, putting his hands over his face as though embarrassed for his friend, "Jett, you're an idiot."

Quinn laughed, too. "You are, and uh, yes, I did."

"Damn." Jett looked off in wonder, then back at Quinn. "When did you and Paula Harris break up?"

Glad to have another topic besides his mother and tragic childhood, Quinn accepted that this was the conversation now. They discussed his various flings and hook-ups for a while; long enough for Quinn to start feeling...ashamed? A little self-conscious, at least. He rarely felt anything about the way he lived his life and he wasn't sure what it was about being here with his two old friends that brought on this sudden uncertainty. It wasn't that he was actually with a new woman constantly, it was just that he had a way of intentionally avoiding connections with any of them.

There was a beat of silence and Chris looked quizzical before asking, "Have you seen her yet?"

"Seen who?" said Quinn, oblivious to the heavy tone in Chris's voice.

"The long lost love of your life," Chris said, as if it were obvious.

Quinn looked at Chris, chewing on the inside of his cheek, the smile threatening to fade from his face. Leave it to Chris to bring up the serious stuff. Quinn refused to take the bait. "I don't know what you're talking about."

Chris looked challengingly back at Quinn, the two men having a stand-off, waiting for the other to break. Jett stood behind the bar, eyes going back and forth between his friends. Finally Quinn simply said, "I don't do love."

Chris laughed humorlessly. "You've never given it a chance."

Though he felt he could argue that point, Quinn didn't want to talk about her right now, but he was interested to know she was still in the area by the sounds of it. He had no intention of letting either of them know that his mind went straight to her at the mention of a long lost love.

Quinn was reaching for his drink again when Chris shrugged. "Not that it matters, I guess. She got engaged."

The rocks glass tipped over and ice and whiskey spilled onto the bar. "Shit…" Quinn began to reach across the bar at the stack of napkins to clean it up, frustrated that his hands were shaking and betraying his plan to keep it cool. "Engaged? When?"

"Oh, that's right," said Jett, using a much more effective bar towel to clean up the mess. "Sometime last February, I think. Some big shot corporate lawyer."

At that moment, Quinn was completely unaware of his facial expressions or actions. All he knew was the knotted feeling in his stomach was back and he really needed another drink. A double.

"Name's Emerson Yates," said Chris. "He's a big, Thor-looking dude."

Quinn's face twisted in disgust and he scoffed. "*Emerson Yates?* Is he fucking sixty years old? Does he smoke a pipe in his fucking study with, what, leather-bound books in his…his fucking plantation? The fuck kinda name is that? *Emerson Yates?*" He shook his head. "You guys are shitting me. There's no way the Rae I knew would marry a guy named fucking *Emerson Yates.*"

Chris and Jett exchanged triumphant looks and Quinn realized his mistake too late. With a grin, Chris said, "I don't remember mentioning Rae. Do you remember me saying that name?"

"No, I don't, Chris," said Jett in the same obnoxiously aloof tone. "That *is* interesting though."

"Fuck you guys," said Quinn, taking a refill from Jett. Well played, they got him. Since there was no taking it back he asked, "So, you guys were messing with me?"

"Technically, no," Jett said. "They did get engaged last February."

Chris paused before providing the last piece of information, "It only lasted a couple of months though."

Quinn let out the breath he'd been holding, feeling both relieved and annoyed at how relieved he was that Rae really wasn't getting married. "What happened?"

"The guy was an asshole. He cheated on her," Jett replied, leaning against the bar top.

"More than once, from what I heard," Chris added. "I don't know the details-"

"I do!" Jett piped in proudly. "I know it all."

Quinn turned a curious eye on Jett. "Oh yeah?"

Chris snorted. "You know Jett; all the ladies go to him when their love lives come crashing down, but not for anything else."

Jett glared before snapping the bar towel at Chris. "Dick."

Anger simmered momentarily in Quinn's stomach as he found himself caught between being outraged for Rae that someone would do that to her, and yet grateful that it meant she at least wasn't getting married.

Satisfied that they'd gotten Quinn to admit he did in fact think of Rae as his One That Got Away, the conversation transitioned into discovering what Chris and Jett had been up to since they'd last seen each other. Jett was still a bachelor, and according to Chris, had absolutely no game.

Chris was happily married, which Quinn had known. He remembered feeling awful about not being able to be there for the wedding, but had sent a generous check to the newlyweds, hoping to make up for his absence. They'd already started a family and had a two-year-old daughter, Sophia. Chris shared pictures in the way all proud fathers do, with a beaming smile at each image of his daughter doing literally anything- striking a pose with her mother, eating a birthday cupcake, or dancing in the kitchen.

"Wait, do you think you could be my wing-man?" Jett pointed at Quinn. "I mean, you're Quinn *fucking* Casey! If they see me with you-"

"They'll take one look at you and go home with him," Chris said, cutting him off.

Jett took the bar towel and whipped Chris in the shoulder while Quinn laughed. His face was sore from laughing so much and he couldn't remember the last time he'd enjoyed just sitting down with two people and talking about life.

"First of all," said Quinn, "Stop calling me Quinn *fucking* Casey, it's just weird from you guys. Maybe you should start calling yourself Jett *fucking* Miller, the confidence will come and you'll finally get a little action."

"I told him it's all about confidence. It's like he clams up and forgets how to speak when there's a pretty girl in front of him," Chris said.

Quinn finished his drink and slid the empty glass across the bar. "I should probably get going, but I'll come back tonight when you've got some girls in here and observe. Worst case scenario, nothing changes for you and *I* get to take someone back to my hotel room."

"Fuck you, man," Jett said, unable to hide his grin.

"Good luck," Chris said, giving Quinn another back-slapping hug. Jett came around the bar to give Quinn a handshake, pulling him in and slapping his back, too.

"Oh, before you take off..." Chris ripped a half piece of paper out of his notebook and wrote something down. "Rosewood Medical Group. They offer a ton of different services, but their sports medicine PT is the best around. Athletes from all over the state request appointments there."

Quinn looked down at the piece of paper and back up at his friend, "Thanks, man. I didn't bring any of my people to schedule shit for me, so this will save me some time doing research." He grabbed the wallet out of his back pocket, opening it awkwardly with one hand, fumbling between holding the piece of paper and opening the wallet. "Jett, just grab something out of my wallet for your tip and put this in its place," Quinn said, giving up the task and handing it over.

Jett opened the leather wallet and let out a low whistle. "All I see are hund-o's." He slid a blue-tinted one-hundred dollar bill out and waved it in front of Quinn.

"Take two if you want, just don't lose that paper," said Quinn. He felt it was the least he could do for these guys after being absent for so long.

With his wallet back in place, Quinn told the guys he'd see them again soon, put his sunglasses on and stepped back out into the sunshine and seventy-five degree weather, the bright sun shocking after the dimly lit bar. He felt significantly better after seeing his friends, letting some truth off his chest for a change. He hadn't even been perfectly honest with Mitch and Zoey about why he had to come to Michigan, and why he needed to come alone. Knowing that he had real friends in his corner who knew about the skeletons in his closet made the prospect of entering his old house a little less daunting.

CHAPTER 5

Quinn drove on auto-pilot it seemed to the house of his childhood, trying to think of his time just now at the bar rather than the task that lay directly ahead. He came to a smooth stop, parking on the street outside the house, but he hadn't allowed himself to look up just yet. He stared at his hand still on the steering wheel which was now beginning to shake with nerves, thinking maybe he should've had a second drink. Taking a deep breath in, holding it for a few seconds, and then slowly letting it out he steadied his nerves. He removed his sunglasses, placing them on top of his head and willed himself to look up at the house.

The bungalow sat back in a small yard, still looking old, but not run down and haunted like it did the last time he had seen it. The battered chain link fence had been replaced by a short white picket one and there was a garden with actual flowers in bloom on either side of the stairs leading up to the front porch. The house had been repainted, and was no longer a dirty yellow, but a calming blue.

Quinn stared at the house for several moments wondering if this really was the right place. He knew it had to be; the neighboring homes didn't look that different. The structure and design were the same, the size of the yard, the sidewalk out front, the front window where his mom used to sit were all the same but had simply been upgraded. He looked through the front window expecting to see his mom still there, staring out into the street.

He didn't get a chance to see if she was there because a middle-aged woman with curly brown hair and glasses opened the front door to wave. Quinn noted the light purple scrubs and knew this must be

Sandra Burke, his mom's nurse. Quinn never really knew what kind of work Sandra had been doing with his mom; she was still an addict when he left the house all those years ago. As much as he had wanted to just leave everything behind, he knew she needed someone to look out for her, or at the very least, to check in and make sure she didn't kill herself, whether through overdose or forgetting to eat.

Quinn realized he was just staring back at the woman, these thoughts and a million other questions running through his head. He lifted up his one good hand in a feeble wave, then got out of the Bronco and made his way toward Sandra, taking in all the small changes on his way up to the house. He noticed solar lights lining the walkway, a small stone frog statue in the garden, and- he had to do a double take-another small statue of a little boy sitting on a bench with a blue baseball hat, a bat swung over his shoulder, a glove and ball on the seat next to him.

"Hi, Mr. Casey," Sandra's voice was just as soothing and friendly in person. "Molly is really excited to see you."

Quinn shook Sandra's hand but didn't know how to respond to this so he simply nodded. Sandra and her mention of Quinn's mother's name seemed to be the only indication that the same woman still lived here. He was looking around at every little piece of the house, trying to find things that were the same and things that were new. The front window looked like it had been washed, so that was new. The screen on the storm door had been fixed, or maybe it was a new door all together. He could feel Sandra watching him and decided it was best to just go in and get the hard part over with. He looked back at Sandra and let out a sigh, then gestured for her to lead the way inside.

If the outside appearance of this house was disorienting, the inside was flat out unrecognizable. The carpet had been removed and hard flooring had been put in. It was the kind that gave the appearance of wood floors without the expense, but the light gray wood texture was clean and refreshing. There was a blue farmhouse patterned area rug in the living room with a coffee table. There was no ratty green chair, and all the furniture looked clean, or at least like she hadn't dragged it inside after it sat out in someone's yard with a 'Free' sign on it, like all the furniture that had previously occupied this space. There was a television mounted to the wall above the small fireplace.

Quinn turned around to look at all the other new changes that had been made but stopped when he saw his mom standing in the kitchen. She was looking at him with tears welling in her eyes, but when they made eye contact the tears overflowed, spilling out onto her cheeks. She was wringing her hands nervously as she stared at him through the tears. She looked younger than he had expected, but then again she really wasn't old at all. He remembered suddenly that she was only just into her fifties, which seemed way too young to be setting up end-of-life care with doctors and nurses.

His mother had always been thin as a side effect of all the drug use. Her hair was once the same color as Quinn's but was now a mousy brown. She was wearing a floral patterned t-shirt and blue jeans. His eyes took in every detail of his mom's appearance, and he had the sudden pang of sorrow in his chest that this wasn't fair, that she was too young to be dying.

Then his eyes traced from her nervously wringing hands and up to the track marks covering her arms. Painful memories resurfaced: Locking himself in his bedroom and climbing out the window just in time because one of her boyfriends suddenly felt violent and would rather take it out on him. Keeping latex gloves in the bathroom cupboard so he could safely clean the needles out of the sink before he brushed his teeth. His mother selling the baseball jersey Mr. DeRose had bought him for his birthday to get money for a fix.

Quinn looked up from the track marks, the reminders of the childhood that was stolen from him, and back up to her face. He knew the look he gave her was not friendly, it was not a look most mothers would receive from their son after a long absence, but he remembered too well all the pain he had been through. He remembered, and that's why he wouldn't return her smile. The pity and sorrow were gone as the realization hit him hard; she had done this to herself.

"Quinn..." his mother's voice was an airy squeak, as though she hadn't spoken in quite some time. He stared back at her waiting for her to say something else, explain everything she had put him through because there must be some reason for it. She took a few steps toward him and he felt himself tense when she was just out of reach. She started to put her arms out for an embrace, but he really needed her to stay back.

Finally he broke his eyes away from hers and found his voice, though it came out hoarse and shaky, "The place looks nice, Mom." He suddenly wanted to focus on something tangible, rather than messy things like feelings and bad memories.

His mom let out a small sob and attempted to smile, and he was sure she could sense by his tone and posture that he wanted her to keep her distance. She looked around the room where the living room, the small kitchen, and the hallway leading back to the two tiny bedrooms were all visible in one sweep. "It took some time."

He didn't know if she was referring to the house or herself but sticking with his plan to focus on the tangible he said, "I'll bet," but before he could help himself, "It can't be easy to paint and put down new floors when you're so juiced you can't see half a foot in front of your own face."

To his surprise, his mother simply nodded and looked down at her feet, then looked back up at him and said, "I deserved that."

Quinn let out a low, humorless laugh. "I don't think you want to talk to me about what we do and don't *deserve*, Mom." His mom winced as if the words were a physical stab.

He had almost forgotten the nurse was still in the room watching the exchange until she stepped up next to his mother and put an encouraging hand on her back, which seemed to pull the woman back together.

Molly looked back up into her son's face again and said in a shaky voice, scratchy from long term cigarette use, "I know this is going to be hard. I know it wasn't easy for you to come back here." At this, Quinn let out a derisive snort, but let her continue, "I'm sure you've got a lot of anger and hurt that you're holding in and I think the faster you just let me have it, the faster we can maybe begin to...heal this."

He couldn't help the humorless laugh that escaped him once again. "Is this a fucking joke? We're supposed to heal twenty-nine years- oh wait, let's make it twenty-six since I can't remember the first three damn years of neglect, and thank fucking God for that!" The anger that had been sitting stagnant somewhere inside for so many years was boiling right at the surface now.

His mom stood there quietly for a moment, then walked into the living room and took a seat on the cream-colored sofa. She waved her hand in front of herself as if to say "please continue." Something about this calm, accepting response to his hurtful words made his anger feel hotter in his chest until it was just an eruption and he couldn't hold back.

"Okay, *Mom*, let's do this then. Let's talk about all the ways you've failed me. Let's bring up every little detail of the past so I can remind myself how you were NEVER THERE FOR ME and then sure, maybe I'll want to be friends. That makes a lot of fucking sense."

When she simply continued to sit there on the couch, taking slow shaky breath after slow shaky breath, looking calm and ready to take the verbal beating, Quinn stared at her incredulously. How was he supposed to just stand there in the middle of the living room and yell at this tranquil, frail woman? Didn't that make him the bad guy? Is that what she was trying to do? Make him look like the bad guy in front of the nurse?

No, she didn't have that right. She deserved to hear everything that he'd been keeping in all these years, and she had no right to sit there calmly and listen. He was going to make this hurt. He was going to get some sort of reaction out of her other than this serene, accepting stranger sitting in front of him.

So, with one slow steadying breath, he let it all out. All of the anger, all of the hurt, the memories that he knew only he had because she wasn't present enough to remember any of it. He was shouting, even with the windows open, and he didn't care who heard it. He was shouting about the needles, about having to tuck her into bed when she'd passed out, about making sure some of the money got put towards groceries so they didn't starve, about the strange and dangerous men who wandered in and out of the house at all hours, about once putting not just him, but his friends in danger when they'd stopped by to check on him.

He yelled about having to shop for himself at local thrift stores because she couldn't bother to buy him clothes, and the things of his she had sold to get her fix, and how once he'd gotten a job of his own in high school he'd caught her stealing out of his wallet because she just needed a hit. He asked why she had never even talked to him, never gone to a single one of his games, never taken even the slightest interest in his life, why she ever had him in the first place, and the list went on and on.

By the end of his complete outburst, he was physically shaking. He swallowed around a hard lump in his throat and glanced briefly at his mother who was a sobbing mess on the couch. Averting his eyes, he clenched his shaking fists, clenched his jaw. He needed to leave. Everything he'd been holding in for ages had just been released into this room and it felt tainted and toxic. It was as if he were going to be sucked back in time and forced to relive every one of those moments if he stood there too long.

When he spoke again, it came out hoarse and restrained, "I…" he cleared his throat, "I need to go." Quinn turned and made a beeline for the door.

"Mr. Casey," Sandra's voice was softer as she followed him toward the front door.

Quinn paused with his hand on the doorknob. He shook his head, unable to take any more, "I can't. Maybe…maybe some other time. I have to go."

He drove back to Hotel Indigo with the radio turned off, just listening to the sounds of the wind and the city passing him by. Leaving his sunglasses on once inside and grabbing a baseball hat to pull over his face, he made his way to his King suite. The last thing he needed was someone to recognize him and ask for an autograph right now. Inside his room, which was equipped with a full-size living room, spacious bedroom, glass-railed balcony with a view of the lake, and a fully tiled bathroom with an extra-large shower, he strode past the living room into the bedroom, and pulled the black-out curtains shut. After awkwardly stripping down to his boxer briefs with only one hand available to undress himself, he collapsed onto the bed.

Quinn stared up at the ceiling, replaying the scene that had just exploded at his old house. With a shuddering breath, he felt the burning behind his eyes release, the tight knot in his throat win out. The tears overflowed, running off his cheeks and onto the pillows. It was like he was a little boy again, crying in his room from the hunger in his stomach, the fear he always felt, the constant uncertainty of what the next day would bring.

He was unaware of how long it took for the tears to subside, and he didn't care. He wasn't sure when he would go back, but the loosening feeling in his chest told him he would. First thing tomorrow, he would go to the physical therapist's office that Chris had suggested and then go from there. He'd take it one step at a time.

As he fell asleep, Quinn caught himself wondering if he'd stay long enough to see Raelyn DeRose, and thinking that if he did, he'd bring her with him next time he went to see his mother. He remembered the soothing effect Rae's presence always had on him, and if he wanted to avoid flying off the handle like that again, he needed her with him.

CHAPTER 6

2004

Face up and sprawled out on his worn mattress, Quinn closed his eyes and waited to feel the breeze blow over him through his open bedroom window. It was late August and there was no air conditioning at the Casey house. Only the occasional faint breath of wind through the screens could attempt to douse the summer heat. Michigan summers could be brutal, even this far north. The sun beat down all day and the humidity was merciless. Feeling a bead of sweat drip down his bare back, he let out a sigh and, drifting off, let the exhaustion he felt drop him right back into the dream he'd been having the night before.

He was laying on the beach listening to the waves. This wasn't the beach of Lake Michigan that he was used to, but somewhere the weather was this sunny all year, like Jamaica or Cancun. He propped himself up on his elbows to look out at the peaceful blue ocean. Rae was next to him on a beach towel, lathering up with suntan lotion. She was wearing a sparkling purple bikini he was sure he'd never seen before and Quinn couldn't help noticing she was all legs and golden sun-kissed skin, her usually straight blonde hair wavy with the salty ocean air.

Rae turned to face him, holding out the bottle of lotion she'd been applying to her legs. It was then that Quinn noticed how she glowed. She seemed to be emitting her own bright light, as if the sun were directly above her, its sole purpose to light her up. Quinn's gaze dropped from her face down her smooth neck, to her chest where two small, rounded breasts had blossomed sometime over the last few months. Even in his waking life this hadn't gone unnoticed, but were they really so perfect?

"Can you get my back? I can't reach," Dream Rae's voice was light but sultry, and let loose a needy growl in his stomach.

"Yeah, of course," his voice came out far more confident than he felt, and Rae moved so her back was to him, scooting back until she was close. Unusually close.

He squeezed the lotion onto his hands and paused for just a moment before resting them on her bare shoulders. *Oh wow.* Her skin was soft and hot from the sun and felt like satin beneath his palms. He began rubbing the lotion in and could swear he heard her let out a pleasured moan.

"Quinn?"

"Mmm, yeah."

"Quinn…"

"Mhmm, yeah that's good," he muttered, eyes closed.

"*Quinn!*" Rae's voice was sharper suddenly and lacked the sultry quality that had ignited the dormant monster in his chest. Missing the sweet sound to her voice, he scrunched up his face and let out a grunt.

Whack!

Quinn felt an abrupt blow to the chest, though whatever had hit him was soft. His eyes opened and he was no longer on the beach. The blue walls of his bedroom came into focus, as did the face above him. Rae was standing there, looking down at him where he lay on his bed. She was no longer glowing, and her hair was straight again. He realized she was holding a squishy pillow in one hand and had her other rested on the small curve of her hip.

Her face transformed from a look of concern to a sly grin. "Were you about to have one of those wet dreams they talked about in sex-ed?"

"No!" Quinn shouted defensively, grabbing the pillow out of her hands and swinging it back at her. She turned and the pillow caught her lower back.

Giggling she replied, "Are you sure? The little guy downstairs might disagree."

Quinn felt the color drain from his face as he glanced down to his crotch where, visible through his boxer shorts, he was indeed sporting an erection. "Shit," he muttered, using the pillow to cover up his arousal. "Don't call it 'the little guy', Rae, *Jesus*."

"Right, sorry, the big guy then." Rae shrugged, still smirking playfully.

"I'm glad my embarrassment is amusing to you," Quinn said flatly, rolling to sit up and put his feet on the floor, careful to keep the pillow in place.

"Oh, Quinn, it's a natural part of growing up," said Rae, mocking their health teacher's squeaky voice and clasping her hands together. Then in her usual voice, "I mean you're going to be fourteen in a couple weeks and I hear puberty's a wild ride."

Quinn merely grunted. He looked around, then asked, "How did you get in here?" He hoped she hadn't gone to the front door expecting to be let in by his mother who was likely still passed out in her room. Quinn had come home to find her face-planted on the living room floor, and after checking her vitals to confirm she hadn't overdosed and was simply drunk, he'd carried her to her bed.

"Your bedroom window is literally wide open," Rae said simply. "I just climbed in, like you're always saying you do."

Glancing at the alarm clock on his night stand he saw that it was ten o'clock in the morning. Rae was already put together, dressed in a simple light blue tank top and- "Are you wearing a skirt?" Quinn asked, finally taking in her full appearance.

"It's a skort, actually," she replied with a smile. She tugged up one end of the skirt and Quinn felt that monster in his chest stir again before he realized there were shorts underneath. "So I can still look cute while we do batting lessons."

"Why do you need me to teach you to bat? You play tennis at your country club, don't you? I'm sure it's not much different. You're a natural athlete," Quinn said, rubbing his eyes. Images of teaching Rae to bat while she wears that short *skort* buzzed in his head and it felt like dangerous territory.

"But I want to learn from the best," said Rae. "So get dressed, take care of...whatever you need to take care of, and I'll meet you out front."

"Take care of..?" Quinn looked at her confused.

Rae put a hand to one side of her mouth and whispered, "*Masturbation*."

"Oh my God!" Quinn shouted, horror-struck that the girl he'd just been dreaming about told him to jerk off if need be. "Rae, just go wait outside!"

Rae giggled once more, paused to grab one of Quinn's many baseball caps off his dresser and pulled it on over her long, sun-bleached locks before hopping out his bedroom window with ease. Quinn was left in his room, hands on his head as he threw himself back on the bed mortified, but grateful she hadn't been able to see into that dream.

That dream.

What had that been about anyway? Rae was his friend. Just a friend. Best friend, actually. And obviously she had no misconceptions of how their relationship worked. She was like one of his guy friends he could talk to about anything. I mean, hell, she'd talked about masturbation in front of him, and *that's* not something you mention in front of girls you want to...what? Go out with? Kiss?

It didn't matter. That dream version of Rae was not the real one anyway. It was probably just because they hung out all the time and he didn't see many other girls unless they were at school. They were on summer break and he'd seen Rae nearly every single day for the past three months, so it made sense that she would pop up in his dreams.

Quinn tried to shake off the weird feeling the dream had given him and got dressed. He threw on a pair of athletic shorts, a Nike t-shirt he'd scored at the thrift store, and his white Nike sneakers which were possibly the only non-thrift store item he owned. These had come in a donation box from one of the local charities, providing new clothes and shoes to "underprivileged" kids.

He resented the term, but there was no point denying it. When he spent all day with Rae and kids in similar neighborhoods- okay, maybe not *quite* like Rae's, but middle-class ones- their privilege and his lack thereof was clear as day. He'd met a few of the kids in Rae's neighborhood and, honestly, they were all little pricks. Quinn wasn't sure how Rae had turned out the way she did; even her sister, Camille, was sort of a spoiled brat at times.

Exiting his bedroom, he stopped to peek inside his mom's room where she was still sleeping face down, one arm hanging off her small twin-sized bed. "Mom, I'm going out," Quinn called into the room. When she let out an audible grunt, he pulled the door shut, satisfied that she was still alive, and headed down the hall toward the front door. He paused with his hand on the screen door, looking out where Rae was waiting for him on the sidewalk.

She was squatting down to pet a dog whose owners were taking it for a walk. It was a small spotted mutt, and it was going crazy for the attention. Rae giggled as the dog jumped up and licked her chin, the owners apologizing. She brushed off the apologies, explaining that she'd always wanted a dog.

Quinn felt that growl in his stomach again as his eyes traced the outline of her long, summer-tanned legs in that damn skort. Had he never realized how effortlessly pretty she was? He'd noticed that everything else had seemed easy and effortless to her, but this was the first time he'd seen her like this. He swallowed hard and shoved those feelings away. Nope, he couldn't risk their friendship with these stupid puberty-based emotions. Once he felt he'd gained control of himself, he pushed on through the screen door and met her out on the sidewalk like he had so many times before.

After a short walk, Quinn and Rae came to a stop at a two-story cape cod on Oak Street where Chris Watson, his little brother, Tyler, and Jett Miller were in the front yard playing catch. The pair waved and greeted their friends, Quinn jogging up the driveway and into the garage where he knew the spare sports equipment was kept. He grabbed two gloves and a bat, tossing one of the gloves to Rae as he walked back out and joined the circle.

"What's the plan today?" Chris asked, throwing the ball overhand to Quinn.

"Apparently Rae thinks she needs batting lessons," Quinn replied.

"I do," said Rae. "We've set up how many neighborhood games now, and I've had like two decent hits. I need practice."

"Uh, my question," Jett chimed in, "Why are you wearing a skirt? Isn't that gonna be weird when you slide into home base and flash everyone your panties?"

"Charming, Jett." Rae threw the ball hard to him, "and it's a skort."

"A what?" Chris and Jett both looked confused.

"It has shorts under it," Quinn explained, blinking the image of his best friend's panties out of his head.

"Aaah, smart," said Jett. "It's a diversion. The other team thinks they're about to get a peek at girl panties, so instead of watching the ball they're waiting for you to slide. Clever strategy, Rae. I like it."

"I'm not wearing it to create a diversion," Rae said, defensively. "I'm wearing it because I think I should be able to play sports and still be a lady." She gave a dainty curtsy.

"Ladies don't make guys think they're gonna see their panties," Jett said.

"Can we please stop talking about Rae's *panties*?" Quinn groaned, wincing at the last word.

"Thank you, Quinn," Rae nodded in his direction. "I guess you're the only one I can trust around here to respect my privacy."

Quinn swallowed guiltily, averting his eyes from Rae and throwing the ball to Tyler instead.

"Does this mean we need to go to the park then?" Chris offered. "If so, we should probably get going."

The group agreed and, after letting Mrs. Watson know where they were going, they set off toward the public ballpark. Once there they set up positions, Rae getting to bat first to get her practice she insisted on, Chris pitching, Quinn catching, and Jett and Tyler between bases. Before squatting down to catch, Quinn helped Rae get in her stance near the worn piece of ground that was recognized as home plate.

"You don't want to be too close or too far from the plate." Quinn placed his hands on Rae's shoulders, looking down at her black and white low-rise Chuck Taylors, positioning her to the right spot, "It's easier when there actually is a plate, I guess." He looked up at Chris on the pitcher's mound and determined this was the right spot, "Okay, let's see your stance."

Rae held the bat up and behind her right shoulder, with her left elbow up and her right elbow pointing more toward the ground.

"A lot of people do this." He got behind her and gently moving her right elbow up higher. "The tip of your bat should be facing up, not behind you. And you're leaning too much to the back. You want to load all your weight onto your right leg just before the swing, but you don't want to stick your butt out." He placed his hands on her hips and shifted her right hip slightly.

Why were his hands shaking?

"You two need a room?" Jett shouted from second base.

"Don't be jealous, Jett!" Rae hollered back. "You'll get to put your hands on a girl when you bring your cousin to the homecoming dance next month!"

Quinn let out a snort of laughter, his tension and nerves easing up significantly. "Okay, so I shouldn't be able to push you off balance." He walked around and gave her pushes from different angles, on her shoulders, back, and just for fun he pushed in next to her hip bone where he happened to know she was extremely ticklish.

Rae jumped back with a squeal, not able to stop herself from giggling. "Hey! That's cheating!"

"Sorry, sorry, I couldn't help it," Quinn said through a light laugh. "Okay, for real now..." Rae got back in her corrected batter's stance and Quinn got behind her again, now positioning her hands low on the bat. He held his hands over hers, his arms wrapped around her. So much for his nerves subsiding. Her butt was up against his crotch where only an hour or so ago he'd been sporting some wood.

Swallowing, he tried to focus on the game and not on how good she smelled. Tangible things. Baseball. The bat. All of his friends watching. *Her thighs resting against mine...*

No! No, no. Not that.

We're swinging a bat. Just swing...the bat.

Guiding her path through the swing, he helped her get a feel for the motion of it. "The beginning of your swing, you load onto your back leg, and the power of your swing should come from your legs and your core, and you want to hit *through* the ball. Your swing doesn't stop when you make contact."

After a few more guided swings he had her practice a few on her own. Once her swing was looking good, he called to the boys in the field who had started playing catch again, to let them know they were ready. He squatted down behind Rae and got his glove up, ready to catch. Before volunteering to catch he hadn't considered how much more distracting her skort would be from this angle.

Come on, man, we just got past this.

Quinn shook any unwelcome thoughts about her lean, sun-kissed legs or her new curves that seemed to fill out her clothes a little better out of his head and focused on the game. He couldn't have the ball come flying and hit him in the face because he was gawking at his best friend's...assets.

Chris sent in a solid pitch, Rae swung, but the ball ended up in Quinn's glove.

"Early," Quinn said, throwing the ball back to Chris, "but the swing was good."

Again, Chris wound up and sent in a close pitch this time. She pushed her hips back and jumped away from the ball to avoid taking a hit to the side, and Quinn missed the ball, distracted by the shape of Rae's butt as it stuck out when she hopped back. His face burned scarlet, wondering if anyone had noticed where his focus had been. He found the ball and threw it back over to Chris, shouting out "Ball!"

Focus, Quinn. She's your friend. Friends don't think about each other that way. Friends don't check out each other's curves, no matter how good they look in a skort.

"I think Jett was right about that skort," Chris chortled.

"Head in the game, man!" Jett exclaimed as he and Tyler laughed in the field.

Rae turned and looked at Quinn over her shoulder curiously, "You gonna be okay back there?"

Trying to stifle his guilty grin, knowing he'd been caught, he shrugged, "It's not a bad view back here."

Oh my God, did I really just say that?!

To Quinn's relief Rae just shook her head with a breath of laughter, "Boys..."

Chris sent in the next pitch.

Crack!

The bat hit the ball hard and sent it over the guys' heads, far into left field. Rae took off sprinting toward first base and dropped her bat on the way. Quinn stood up to watch as Tyler chased the ball into left field. An excellent runner, Rae was already approaching third base before Tyler had the ball to throw to Jett. Quinn broke his eyes away from Rae, knowing the ball would be coming to him- it was going to be close. He watched as Jett threw the ball, as it arced over Chris from second base, simultaneously aware of Rae advancing in his periphery. The ball was falling toward him now as he heard the *whoosh* of dirt rush toward his feet. Rae had slid into home base a fraction of a second before the ball landed in his glove.

"Safe!" Quinn shouted, arms out to his sides, signaling the call.

Rae leaned her head back onto the ground, eyes closed in a sigh of relief. Her signature bright smile lit up her face as she extended her hand out to Quinn and he helped her up to her feet. She pulled him into a tight hug and he immediately wrapped his arms around her, too. He liked how she felt in his arms and concentrated on every sensation. Her warm skin, dewy with summer heat and sweat, her hair that smelled like coconuts and vanilla, her breath was hot on his neck as her breathing came in heavy after her run around the bases.

When she pulled out of the hug he was struck by how beautiful she was up close with her blonde hair whipping around underneath his baseball cap. He liked her wearing his hat. It made him feel like she was his. Just as he registered this last unexpected thought, Rae planted a kiss on his cheek and whispered, "Thank you."

Quinn thought his heart must have stopped. His voice caught in his throat and upon realizing that he'd failed to respond he gave a quick and indistinct nod. She turned to face the guys and let out a triumphant cheer for herself, pumping her fist in the air. As he watched her walk over and pick up the discarded bat, he knew. It hit him with a resounding *thud* in his chest. He was falling for his best friend.

CHAPTER 7

Four days. Four painfully long days had gone by and still Raelyn could not seem to get a grip on this sudden onset of sexual frustration. Every night since Friday she'd ended her days with a glass of red wine and seven minutes in heaven with a new selection from her pleasure box- yes, that's code for a discrete hidden box with an assortment of sex toys. On her morning drive to work she told Amira she was considering getting a pair of vibrating panties for the workplace. She even dressed more feminine, with form-fitting dress pants that cut off at the ankle, a low-cut top, and heels. What kind of physical therapist wears heels to work? Clearly it was a not-so-subtle cry for attention from any male partner who could give her some sort of sexual release. Just one earth-shattering orgasm that wasn't self-induced. Was that really so much to ask?

Amira and Raelyn parked next to each other in the shared parking lot and walked around their vehicles to greet each other in person. Amira handed Raelyn a grande sweet-cream cold brew, as was her routine on Tuesdays and Thursdays.

"No Harry today?" Amira looked around and noticed the furry friend missing.

"Camille picked him up this morning," said Raelyn. "Her kids want a dog, so I'm letting them borrow him so they can get a feel for the responsibility of it. I'm having lunch with her and my mom today though, so I'll bring him back with me."

"That was nice of you. Also, I brought you these," Amira said, shoving a stack of magazines into her friend's arms.

With a quizzical expression, Raelyn looked down at the top magazine. She saw the signature red *Men's Health* logo and the black letters, bold and capitalized "HARDER, FASTER, STRONGER." Raelyn read the next headline out loud, "Quinn Casey's secret to bed-breaking sex: How and where she wants it." She glanced up at Amira. "How charming."

The picture on the cover was of Quinn, shirtless in his white baseball pants, one arm hanging by his side, the other grabbing his shoulder, looking at the camera with his famous handsome-devil grin. Raelyn looked back up at Amira after taking a few too many seconds to appreciate how fine he looked in those pants. "What am I supposed to do with this? Break my own bed?"

"If you do, let me know and I'll give those secrets a try," Amira said with a grin. "I didn't think it was a coincidence that your sexual frustration kicked in the same day you see his picture and talk about the last time you guys almost went out. I figured a visual might help with that perfect orgasm you're looking for."

"That's thoughtful," Raelyn said, rolling her eyes, "but he was my friend. I'm not going to go old school and stare at a magazine cover with his face on it to get off."

"You weren't *really* just friends though, were you?" Amira asked with a knowing smirk. Now really wasn't the time to unpack that particular box. Raelyn gave her friend an incredulous stare and Amira added, "There's a whole photo shoot I think you'll like, actually."

Clearly she wasn't getting the point.

"Whatever, I'm not taking these." Raelyn tried to shove the magazines back to her friend but Amira ducked inside her Mercedes and grabbed her own coffee in one hand and put her phone to her ear in the other.

"Oh, no! My hands are full and I really need to take this!" She winked and laughed as she turned and headed toward the women's center, shouting a quick "Love ya, bye!" over her shoulder.

Raelyn groaned and threw her head back in frustration. Her car keys were tucked away in her purse and she didn't see a way to get them without potentially losing her caffeine supply, so she let out a dramatic and loud sigh, then headed up the walkway to her office. Struggling to do the math on how she was going to get her building key without dropping anything, she was relieved to see a man sitting on the bench outside her office door. He had his head down looking at his phone, and his right arm appeared to be in a sling.

Already regretting the heels she was wearing, though they admittedly made her ass look amazing in these pants, she called out to the man on the bench, still bustling up the walkway, heels clacking, "Excuse me, do you think you could hold onto these while-"

"Rae?" The man looked up and his eyes went wide when he saw her.

Holy shit, it's Quinn.

In one stunned moment she was registering the familiar face, and in the next she dropped all the magazines- no, all the *Quinn Casey sex magazines!*- all over the sidewalk. She stared at him in disbelief. Okay, were her sexual fantasies really getting that bad? Not that she fantasized about him...ever. She must've been gawking long enough to be weird because Quinn was walking toward her now. He smiled, then bit his bottom lip looking shy, as if trying to bite back a wider smile.

Damn, that was a good look on him.

"Quinn..." she stared up into his golden brown eyes, absolutely hating the way her pulse was betraying her by increasing so rapidly. "What are you doing here? In Traverse City, I mean...obviously you're at a physical therapist's office- *my office*, obviously- because of your arm...but you're, ya know, back. Here. Home."

Girl, stop babbling, you are not a star-struck bimbo. You two are old friends. Kind of.

"Uh, yeah," Quinn let out a little laugh. "I'm back. For therapy. For other things, too. But I came here for you- to see you, I mean. As a doctor. In a professional capacity." He attempted to smooth his hair over, and the familiar gesture eased Raelyn. He was always trying to smooth down his unruly hair, but it had a mind of its own. It always had. "Actually, I didn't know this was your office. Chris gave me the address yesterday, so I'm just as surprised as you are."

Leave it to Chris Watson to try and play match-maker. Raelyn remembered the last time he tried doing that when they were in college- that night had been a disaster.

Quinn was now looking down at the mess of magazines on the ground. He bent down to pick one up and smirked as he glanced at the cover. He cocked an eyebrow up, turning the front of it to face her. "Some of your favorites?" Another shirtless Quinn smiled at her from the glossy cover.

Raelyn paused, mouth open as she struggled to come up with an explanation that had absolutely nothing to do with her adding these to her new wine-and-pleasure box nightly routine. "I was taking them to my friend, Amira. She's a gynecologist and needed examples in her office of people with sex addictions and the diseases that may come with such an affliction."

Quinn snorted. "Uh-huh, well I can assure I'm perfectly clean, so you might want to find a new example." He tilted his head to the side as though studying her. "Was that just your way of fishing for information in case something happens here? I'll show you all my medical records, test results, whatever you want."

Raelyn scoffed, squatting to finish picking the rest of the magazines up. "Not all women turn to mush when they see baseball stud *Quinn Casey*, you know." She said his name in a mock-dreamy tone. Of course she would never admit how much her own legs were currently feeling like Jell-O under his intense gaze.

Letting out a quick breath of laughter, Quinn helped her pick up the last few magazines, stacking them and grabbing the pile with his one- notably large- free hand. He shook his head. "Oh, I know. The one woman impervious to my charm is the only one that's ever mattered."

Raelyn's eyes flashed to his and her breath caught for a split second.

He's a player, Rae. He sleeps with supermodels and actresses and never calls them again. It's just a line.

With that reminder to herself she rolled her eyes and walked past him to the door and swiped her key to get inside. She held the door open for him, as his one hand was full and the other was incapacitated. He dipped an exaggerated gentlemanly nod as he passed through the door. She answered the gesture with a look of exasperated contempt.

Pulling the door shut behind them, however, she couldn't help noticing how his blue jeans fit his ass in all the right places. She scolded herself for the thought but made a mental note of which vibrating toy she'd definitely be needing that evening.

The office was empty, as it usually was this time of day. Raelyn typically liked to get there early a few days a week to get caught up on paperwork. On Tuesdays she didn't have any patients until ten o'clock, so getting to the office early gave her extra time to catch up. Of course, it didn't look like that would be the case today.

"Did you make an early appointment?" Raelyn asked Quinn as he looked around the office.

"Uh, no. I just figured I'd show up early and see if I got lucky." He winked at her. Raelyn thought this must be out of habit, constantly turning up the charm in the presence of anyone who could sufficiently fill out a skirt and a bra.

She decided to ignore the comment, once again reminding herself that he wasn't acting in any special way for her. This was just who he was now, and there was no point giving in. "Well, I'm here early, too. I was going to get caught up on paperwork, but I guess I can check you out. Your arm, I mean," she added quickly. "You can set those magazines on the desk," she pointed to Alexis's work area.

"You sure? You don't want to keep them all to yourself?" This last line came as a low, gravelly whisper in her ear.

Raelyn whipped around to find Quinn standing directly behind her, their bodies so close they were almost touching. She could feel the heat radiating off him, and the look he gave her sent a pleasant ache down between her legs. He was staring down at her, eyes bearing into hers. She'd forgotten how tall he was. She was tall compared to a lot of women, nearly 5'8", and he still had at least seven or eight inches on her. His Adam's apple bobbed with a swallow.

Is he nervous?

He licked his lips and she realized she was staring at them, wondering how they'd feel on her own lips, her neck, that new ache between her legs.

She blinked and looked up at his eyes, wondering if that golden gaze could see inside her mind. Her face went hot with a blush at the mere thought and she quickly turned back around and made her way to her office, Quinn following closely behind after dropping the stack of magazines on the front desk.

Part of her wished that he'd give her a little space to cool off, while the traitorous, sexually starved part hoped he might just push her up against the office door as soon as it shut and take her right there. This sexual frustration was killing her, and his presence was decidedly *not* helping. It was no secret he photographed well, but in person he was much more intense and his raw, sexual magnetism was palpable. Or maybe it was just that she hadn't shared her bed with a man in over a year.

Once Raelyn set her bag down, she leaned back against her desk and focused her attention on Quinn's arm in the sling. "UCL sprain, huh?"

"So you *do* read those magazines." Quinn's cocky smile flashed across his face and Raelyn had to actively stifle her own smile in response.

"I read *Sports Illustrated* because I'm a doctor of sports medicine and I enjoy sports," she said, the smile threatening to cross her lips. She was determined not to give him the satisfaction of knowing she was thoroughly enjoying his flirtatious behavior.

Quinn nodded. "Right, a doctor…" He looked around, his gaze falling on her framed degrees on the wall behind her desk. "So, you were engaged to a lawyer?"

Raelyn's gaze jumped away from his sling and up to his face. "Who told you that?" But before he could respond, she gave a knowing nod, "Ah, Chris…right."

"How long were you two together?" Quinn wasn't meeting her gaze as he asked the question, and for the first time she felt his overly-confident demeanor falter.

"Oh, just a few years." Raelyn waved her hand dismissively. "The engagement didn't even last three months though."

"What happened?"

Raelyn wasn't in the habit of airing her dirty laundry. Traverse City had a network of well-connected housewives who loved any piece of juicy information that had ever caused anyone emotional pain or embarrassment. Her mother and sister were well-established members of this network. But this was Quinn, her once-best friend who had opened up to her about all his biggest secrets and sources of trauma when he'd had no one else. What had happened to her paled in comparison to all of his demons.

"Well, about two weeks after the engagement I thought I saw him kissing another woman outside a bar. Amira and I were having a girl's night, he was out with the guys and we ended up at the same bar. I don't know, he explained it away like it was some misunderstanding. Like I didn't see what I thought I saw or something like that." Raelyn chewed her lip nervously and looked down, still embarrassed that she'd been so gullible. "Looking back I don't know how I was dumb enough to accept it. I guess I just really wanted to believe he was a good one. He was my first long term relationship...I don't know, it's stupid, I guess."

"It's not," said Quinn. "And you're not dumb. You're far from it. At least you were willing to trust him and take a chance, right?"

"A lot of good that did." Raelyn let out a hollow laugh. "About four weeks after that, I went to surprise him at his office. He'd been working late a lot, and I thought it would be fun to show up in a long coat with nothing but sexy lingerie underneath...but I guess someone else beat me to it."

Quinn winced. "The chick from the bar?"

"No, this was a different one, actually. So...isn't that cool?" Raelyn looked down at her feet again. "It was humiliating. And I'd worn like five-inch stilettos, so I almost rolled my ankle on the way out."

"The guy's an idiot," Quinn said, and it was a statement of fact. "Any man who has *you* and thinks for a second he can do better is just fucking stupid...he never deserved you."

Raelyn looked into Quinn's eyes, searching, and after a few beats she gave a nod and a small smile. "Thanks." She felt the need to lighten the mood so she mused, "I'd ask about your lovers, but I have a patient in," she looked at her FitBit, "three hours. I don't think we'd even make a dent in your little black book."

Quinn dragged out a big "Ha!" then shrugged. "What can I say? I don't want to give anyone the impression I'm capable of a functional relationship when I have absolutely nothing to model it after."

"Aw, you poor, broken little soul." Raelyn gave an exaggerated pout, pushing herself away from her desk and approaching Quinn to take a look at his arm.

He stiffened suddenly when she reached for the strap of the sling around his shoulders. She was close to him, maybe unnecessarily close, and she could feel the heat of him again. She slid her fingers underneath the strap and smoothly moved them up his muscular shoulders- okay, *that* was unnecessary. There was a slight hitch in Quinn's breath as she did this, and then she pulled the strap over his head with one hand and steadied his elbow with the other. She pulled the sling off, exposing the heavily bandaged arm, and began a light palpation from the top of his absurdly lean and muscular bicep down to his wrist with gentle squeezes.

His muscles wrapped like thick ropes around his arms, and those forearms, *holy shit*. She was silently praising the baseball gods for creating the sport that sculpted him.

"How does that feel?" Raelyn asked, continuing to test his arm for soreness or tenderness while wondering just how inappropriate it would be to do these palpations with her tongue. *Highly inappropriate. Wildly, absurdly...sensually inappropriate.*

"Feels good..." Quinn's voice cracked slightly, and he swallowed hard.

Raelyn looked up at him. "I mean is it tender? Sore? I need to know where it's most sensitive before I change the bandage."

Quinn cleared his throat. "Oh, right." A slight redness blossomed in his cheeks. "Yeah, it's a little sore on the...inside. Just under the elbow joint."

"That's normal," said Raelyn. "Normally I wouldn't unwrap this yet, but I think I'm going to trade the sling in for a splint. It's just better protection and you'll actually be able to move your shoulder. You'll still have to wear it until Monday or Tuesday, but it's sort of a pain in the ass to have to hold your arm across your body for that long."

"Whatever you say, Doc," Quinn said, his voice still low and husky.

Raelyn tried to ignore the tell-tale signs and sounds of arousal in his voice and led him out of her office and into one of the patient rooms where her supplies were stored. She willed herself to avoid looking down at his crotch in case there was a sign of arousal there, too. She was sure she wouldn't be able to contain herself if he'd gotten hard from her simply touching his arm and shoulder. Her body had certainly reacted to the touch, the ache between her thighs now accompanied by moisture.

Reminding herself that she was a professional and he was a model-seducing womanizer, Raelyn managed to put a smaller bandage over the scar on his elbow and get his arm into a hard-cased splint without having orgasm. Who knew it could be such a sensual task? It probably didn't help that she was sure he kept shifting his lower body to disguise the significant bulge stretching the denim of his jeans. These efforts were futile on his part; some things just don't hide well.

"So, what do you have going on when you get out of work?" Quinn asked as Raelyn walked with him back out to the lobby. "Or are you taking a lunch break? I could pick you up and we could catch up some more."

"Actually, I have a lunch date already," Raelyn replied. It was selfish to put it this way, but she had been observing his reactions when telling him about Emerson and thought she'd seen a bit of that green monster that is envy shadowing his face. The same shadow fell across him again at the mention of a prospective date, so she finished, "With my mom. And Camille."

Quinn's features immediately brightened as he looked up. "Oh, right. How is the queen of the grapes?"

Raelyn smiled at this. "And her apprentice? They're good."

A memory bloomed in the forefront of her mind: An aw-struck, eight-year-old Quinn stood in the driveway of Raelyn's family's French Provincial home, wearing ripped mud-covered jeans and a T-shirt that he was quickly outgrowing. "Remember when you came to my house for the first time and were convinced it was a palace?"

He laughed, evidently revisiting the memory, too. "That place *is* a palace, Rae. It literally looks like Malfoy Manor."

"That's a bit of an exaggeration," Raelyn chortled.

"I told you I didn't think they let peasants enter the castle so I couldn't possibly go in," Quinn mused.

"You called me Princess Raelyn DeRose of the Vine for a month."

"Until you challenged me to a backyard volleyball game." Quinn nodded. "If you won, I had to stop calling you Princess, and if *I* won, you had to start calling me King Amazeballs."

Raelyn let out a burst of laughter, having forgotten his terms of the deal.

He turned to face her in the middle of the lobby. "I let you win, you know." He was close to her again, and though the heat was still evident between them, the air was somewhat lighter, and she felt a sudden flare of joy blossom in her chest.

"You did not." Raelyn playfully pushed his good shoulder, an unwavering look of defiance on her face.

Quinn mock-staggered back. "It's not polite to shove cripples, Rae. And yes, I did. You're a great athlete but," he shrugged and sniffed arrogantly, "I'm better."

Raelyn shook her head, "You may be Mr. Baseball Man-"

"I prefer King Amazeballs, but continue…"

"But I know I won that game. Fair. And. Square," Raelyn finished, poking him in his hard and toned pectorals with the last three words.

Quinn leaned in next to her ear and paused briefly before whispering, "No, you didn't." When Raelyn scoffed derisively he added, "I just wanted to make you happy."

She halted, caught off guard by the sexy but sincere tone of his voice. She looked in his eyes, and this close up she could see how they softened when they looked back at her. There was a tug in her chest, an aching sensation picking at an old wound, threatening to bring so much of their past to the surface. Things she wished she'd said, things she wished she could take back. The raw intensity of how she'd felt after he left all those years ago, like he'd taken the most crucial piece of her with him. *God*, she had missed him. And…here he was.

A pull like a magnet was attracting her lips to his. Her eyes swept over his mouth that was now so close to hers and she could feel his breath on her skin as she self-consciously licked her bottom lip.

"Good morning!" A bright voice came singing through the door, snapping the sexual tension in half as Raelyn and Quinn each took a step back from each other. Alexis stood just past the doorway, impeccably dressed as always, her sharp green eyes darting back and forth between her boss and the stunningly handsome stranger in front of her. "Oh, I interrupted something intense."

"No, no, he was just leaving," Raelyn said, trying to look as though her heart weren't beating out of her chest, and the ache down below hadn't started to throb.

"Please, I could cut the sexual tension with a knife," said Alexis, walking past them to her desk, waving a hand in the air as if warding off evil spirits. "I feel a little dirty just walking through here."

Raelyn and Quinn both looked down awkwardly, and then around the room. Anywhere but at each other as if catching each other's eyes would reignite the spark between them. Quinn finally looked back at her with an almost shy grin. "Well, I'll be at Trojan Horse this evening if you want to join." He put his hand on her shoulder and let it brush down the length of her arm. "Thanks again, Doc."

Raelyn watched him walk out to the parking lot and get into a shiny charcoal colored Bronco and let out a breath that she hadn't realized she'd been holding in. Alexis stepped up next to her and looked out the window, then back up at her boss with a sly grin. "I'll give you a few minutes if you need to take some *alone time*."

Trying to laugh, Raelyn let out a groan and turned around to walk back into her office. Yes, she definitely needed those vibrating panties.

CHAPTER 8

That evening after his surprise run-in with Rae, Quinn stopped at the bar to tell the guys all about it, and to thank Chris for setting it up. He wasn't sure if he'd have had the guts to go if he'd actually known it was Rae's office. He'd spent the whole day buzzing with new energy- and okay, maybe he'd rushed back to his hotel to relieve some of that insane sexual tension- a few times. Fuck, who knew some purely clinical arm palpations and proximity to Rae's lips could leave him reeling like that?

It wasn't just him either this time. He could see it. Rae had definitely been feeling the tension, too. The way she had licked her lips and concentrated so hard on his. The uptick in her pulse was visible in the soft curve of her neck.

Quinn relayed each detail of the interaction to Chris and Jett from his seat at the bar where he ate a grilled turkey club. "...and then before I left," he paused for dramatic effect, "we *almost* kissed. I think."

Chris snorted and shook his head as he buffed a tumbler. "You almost kissed, you *think?*"

Jett poured a tall beer for another customer down the bar. "Wow, twenty years of foreplay and you *almost* kissed. I'm scandalized."

"You guys weren't there. It was intense," said Quinn defensively. "If that receptionist girl hadn't walked in and killed the mood, who knows what would've happened?"

Chris and Jett both snickered and Quinn's defensive tone heightened, *"What?"*

"You would've chickened out like you always do when it comes to Rae," Jett replied, sliding a Jack and Coke down to a server.

"I don't chicken out. I've been with a lot- *a lot*- of hot women guys only dream about, okay? I don't strike out when it comes to the ladies," Quinn said around a large bite of sandwich.

"Maybe not ladies you have no intention of seeing again," Chris said with a shrug, "but Rae?"

"You've never exactly been able to step up to the plate where she's concerned," Jett added.

"Baseball puns? Is that what we're doing?" Quinn asked flatly, sidestepping the- admittedly fair point his friends were making.

"All we're saying is you couldn't tell her how you felt back then, and now you've got the perfect opportunity to make up for it," said Jett.

"And don't forget you've got a bad rep," Chris said, pulling a tray out and filling it with drinks for a lingering server. "She's already been played and I don't think she's looking for another Emerson."

"I would never do that to her." Not a chance. Though he had screwed up in the past and hurt her before without ever meaning to.

"You just need to show her that you're serious," Jett said. "Assuming that's what you want. If all you're trying to do is sleep with the girl you couldn't get in high school, I'm going to kindly ask you to fuck off. But if you still think you want her for real, you've got some work to do."

Of course he still wanted her. He knew to some extent that he'd still been crazy about her all these years, even if he had been drowning himself in one meaningless hook-up after another. He could still remember the day he realized he was falling for her. It had hit him like a physical punch. He knew they were too young to start anything serious, but the longer he waited the more nervous he got, the task seemed astronomically daunting. And then when he'd finally felt ready, some other guy got there first. By the time they'd finished their short-lived fling, Quinn had already fucked up. And when he got the second chance he probably didn't deserve, he'd managed to fuck it up again. And now he was back, asking for another undeserved swing for the one woman who'd never left his thoughts, and it suddenly seemed critical that he get it right this time.

Looking up at his friends, he met their meaningful gazes and they each gave silent nods as though they knew exactly what he was thinking.

A rush of fresh air entered the bar as the front door opened. A grin tugged up the corner of Quinn's lips as he spotted Rae entering, blonde hair blowing back slightly as the door closed behind her. She met his gaze with a reserved smile. His heart was hammering as a flood of old memories washed over him. He swallowed hard. This was it. He was in the bottom of the ninth with two strikes.

Three strikes, you're out.

"You guys are dicks," Quinn grumbled, sitting on a beach towel as Chris and Jett tossed a football back and forth on the beach of Lake Michigan. It was only a short walk from here to where he'd met Rae for the first time, and he couldn't stop glancing down the shoreline toward that fateful spot.

"Sorry, hot-shot," Jett said with a grunt as he jumped to catch the ball out of the air. "You've had it pretty good the past few years; I think you can handle sitting out for a change."

Quinn was not particularly pleased that the guys were playing ball in front of him and, thanks to his bum arm, he had to sit on his ass and watch. He wasn't a fan of sitting around, and he was even less excited about his inevitable awkward tan line he'd get from the splint on his arm so he hadn't taken his shirt off yet.

It was warm for the middle of June in Northern Michigan, sunny and high seventies, but Quinn had spent the past several years in a much warmer climate, between his previous time in Atlanta and his current position in Los Angeles. With the breeze coming off the cool surface of the lake, he was grateful for the thin layer of clothing. Chris and Jett had lived up here their whole lives, so they broke out their shorts when the temp hit the mid-fifties.

The previous night at the bar when Rae had shown up, she'd taken a seat next to Quinn and it hadn't taken long for the group of four to get back into their old rhythm. Jett had suggested they all come to the beach for the day and hang out like old times. Quinn really wanted to find a way to get Rae to himself, but when she enthusiastically agreed to meet up with them after work he wasn't going to say no. Seeing Rae in a bikini again was absolutely a good option.

There were three towels laid out in the sand, a large cooler filled with a variety of beer and a slightly smaller cooler of snacks. The guys had all arrived around 4:30 and Rae was supposed to be getting out of work and heading straight to their meeting place.

"Come on, just one throw," Quinn pleaded. "Toss me the ball, I'll catch left handed."

"No way." Chris shook his head. "The doc told us your restrictions. Besides, we don't have the precise aim you do. What if we just throw it into your bad arm?"

"I don't want that bill," Jett said, then signaled for Chris to go long for his next pass.

The sound of tires on gravel caught Quinn's attention and he whipped his head around toward the small parking lot beyond the sand. A silver Jeep Wrangler came to a stop and Quinn saw Rae's bright blonde hair catch the sunlight through the window. The trip of his pulse sent his whole body into acute awareness. *Shit, she's not even out of the car yet and I'm a fucking mess.*

This was familiar and completely unfamiliar all at once. Quinn knew how to act around women. He knew how to flirt and charm and get them to come home with him. And once they were there he could pretty much get anything he wanted. But this wasn't some woman. This was Rae. Everything he knew about charming or seducing women somehow flew out the window and got run over by a semi when she was near. Because he actually cared. Because she was...it.

He hesitated as he watched her get out of her Jeep and sling a large blue and white striped canvas bag over her shoulder. She held the door open and a mass of fluff- brown, white, and some black- hopped out of the vehicle.

Quinn smiled as the huge animal wagged patiently at her side. *So, she finally got a dog.*

He wasn't sure if he should get up and greet her. Would that be weird? Was it rude to just sit here and wait? Chris and Jett weren't going anywhere. But Chris and Jett weren't trying to make her fall in love with them. If this was just some girl he was trying to hook up with, he'd stay put. She could come to him. He wouldn't put in any special effort. But again, this was Rae.

Yes, I should definitely get up and meet her. Walk down here with her. But wait…should I? Would that be too obvious?

Shit.

Fuck.

God dammit, Case! Figure your shit out!

Making the last second decision to get up and greet her, he didn't realize she had already crossed over half the distance between them. He was standing when she approached with an amused grin.

"You know, Case, I'm not *actually* a princess. You don't have to stand up in my presence," Rae teased coolly.

Quinn let out a short puff of laughter. The sound of her voice when she said the nickname all his high school teammates and coaches had used made his heart squeeze. He'd heard it hundreds of times at practices and games, though not recently. In LA he was just Quinn. But hearing Rae say it so fluently made it feel like the years they'd spent apart had suddenly evaporated. He was here. In his hometown. On the beach where they'd first met. And she looked fucking beautiful.

She had on a long skirt cover-up that tied at the side and split so her long, toned and tan legs were still available for eager eyes, such as his own. Her white tank top was simple, and he could see the yellow straps of her string bikini top underneath. The contrast of white shirt against her golden sun-kissed skin was evidence of just how much time she spent out here. Quinn couldn't help the thought that she looked like she belonged in California. In LA. With him.

The big, furry dog finally found Quinn and greeted him enthusiastically. He bent down to pet him and looked up at Rae, "I see you finally achieved one of your life's dreams."

"Yes, I did!" she exclaimed. "We dream big here. This is Harry."

"I see that," said Quinn, now playing with the dog's ears.

"His *name* is Harry, you smart ass," Rae said, the eye roll audible in her tone.

"As in Harry James Potter?"

"The very same," she nodded. "Once a Pott-head, always a Pott-head."

Quinn flattened his expression for his best *Professor Snape* impression, *"Always."*

Rae giggled and Quinn's heart jolted at the sound. She pulled her own beach towel out of her striped bag and laid it out on the other side of Quinn's.

"You're not joining, Rae?" Jett asked, making another dive for the football.

"Nah," she said, taking a seat on the towel. "Not unless we're actually playing and I can tackle you and shove your face in the dirt again."

Jett paused before releasing the ball, flashing Rae a brief scowl. "That was a long time ago. We hadn't really hit puberty yet so we were all basically the same size."

"You were definitely bigger than me," Rae said, "and you still went down like a little bitch."

Quinn let out a burst of laughter at the memory. It was the first time Rae had met Chris and Jett. They were in sixth grade and their gym classes were separated by gender. Chris and Jett had asked Quinn if he wanted to meet up and play a game of football after school, and Quinn agreed, saying that he'd bring along his friend, Rae. He'd failed to mention, however, that Rae was a girl and both boys were shocked when he arrived at the park with her, and that she was fully willing to play tackle football with them. Quinn assured them several times that they didn't have to go easy on her just because she was a girl, but they'd been hesitant regardless. Jett had paid for his hesitation. Twice, if memory served him correctly.

"Oh, are we playing this game?" Jett was worked up now, throwing the ball hard to Chris's chest. "Okay Rae, how about the time we all played racquetball at your fancy-ass country club? You swung like you were trying to murder an intruder with a baseball bat and screamed for a solid thirty seconds when the ball went off and wouldn't stop. We were trapped in a fucking human pinball machine. With lots of girly screaming."

Rae threw her head back laughing and Quinn exclaimed, "Oh my God! I remember that! I thought they were going to ban you from that place!"

"I'm honestly surprised they didn't," Rae breathed through her continued laughs. "I remember playing doubles on the tennis court in high school and this guy tried to cop a feel under my skirt and I literally just went at him with my tennis racket."

"He deserved it," Quinn shrugged. "Did they ban him?"

"No," Rae snorted derisively. "Country clubs are ultra-conservative places that worship the patriarchy. They don't give a shit about that kind of stuff."

"Good thing I wasn't there for that," Quinn said with a slight twitch of one eyebrow. He'd had quite the temper back in the day. Especially where Rae was concerned. Well, other guys and Rae and said other guys disrespecting her.

"Oh, you would've been banned for sure," she agreed with a knowing grin.

Harry was now sitting between Quinn and Rae and began giving long licks to the side of Quinn's face.

"*Harry!*" Rae exclaimed. She pulled a tennis ball out of her bag and threw it down the beach toward Chris. The dog immediately took off after the bright, highlighter yellow ball. "I'm sorry, he doesn't usually do that. You must just taste good."

Quinn tugged at the back of his shirt, pulling it up and over his head, and looked at her with a meaningful quirk of his eyebrow. He used his shirt to wipe his face clean of dog slobber and one corner of his mouth pulled into a mischievous grin. He was pleased to see Rae's cheeks flush and her gaze drop to sweep over his bare chest and stomach. Oh, there were so many ways he could respond to that.

"I mean, um…" she sputtered. "You know, he must like your…face or something."

"Well, I kind of figured that's what you meant. That's where he was licking," Quinn said, grateful he was no longer the only one here who seemed completely flustered. "Where else were you thinking might taste good?"

Rae tried to bite back a wider grin and her nose scrunched up like it always did when she was caught in an awkward situation. She looked away toward the water. "Nowhere…I was just… thinking about your face."

"And how good it must taste?" He pressed further, loving her adorable discomfort.

She playfully shoved his face away. "Something like that."

Quinn and Rae sat together exchanging pleasant conversation and reliving old memories while Chris and Jett tossed the football around. He passed Rae a drink from the cooler and they took turns throwing the tennis ball for Harry, even though Quinn could only throw left-handed.

"Hang onto this for a sec," Rae said, holding her drink out toward Quinn. He grabbed it from her and was caught off guard when she pulled her tank top over her head.

Oh...fuck. I am fucked.

Rae's skin was all golden, with various tan lines on her shoulders from the time she spent outside. Her torso was long and lean, with a flat, toned stomach. She had small breasts tucked inside her triangle bikini top. Small, but perfectly rounded and they fit her shape just right. Quinn's cock stirred in his board shorts.

Rae reached for the tie holding her skirt together on the side and unknotted it, pulling the skirt away from her body and folding it into her bag. Her bikini bottoms were the same sunshine yellow as the top and he could see where they cinched in the middle of her ass, making them *very* cheeky.

He was unaware of how long his eyes roamed up and down her body, from her pink-painted toes all the way back to the swell of breasts just barely out of sight. He did know that he was staring, however, and he couldn't stop. He just wanted to look at her like this...admire her form and the work she must have put in to sculpt every inch so precisely. It wasn't until he realized his mouth was actually watering that he snapped his gaze up to hers.

"Don't get a lot of girls in bikinis in sunny Los Angeles?" Rae asked with a smirk.

"Um…" Quinn's throat was dry as he tried to form words. "No. I mean, yes. There are. Lots of them. Just no…" He did another slow sweep of her body, gaze hovering over her thighs, imagining all the ways he'd like to see them- around his waist, thrown over his shoulders, up close with his head between them. Now he'd completely forgotten what he'd been planning to say. He felt his eyes glaze over as he stupidly muttered, "legs."

"They don't have legs?" Rae questioned, her eyebrows pulling together in confusion.

"What?" Quinn looked up at her again, nearly drooling. He cleared his throat and smoothed a hand through his hair. "Oh, um...shit. I mean, yes they have legs...obviously. That was dumb. I just meant..." The quirk of Rae's eyebrow told him he'd been caught. He let the smile break across his face, "I'm busted. I was staring at your legs and...zoned out." He laughed shyly and handed her drink back. "You look great, Rae."

She looked away with a quiet laugh and muttered, "Thanks." She seemed to muse to herself and bit her lip. After taking a long pull of her summer shandy she said, "I wouldn't think someone who has one-nighters with supermodels would be speechless at the sight of some legs."

Oh. Ouch. He didn't know why that felt like such a blow, but coming from Rae it did. With his teammates he'd have something cocky to say, something that would puff up his ego. But he suddenly found himself wanting to do the exact opposite of that with her.

Luckily he was saved from having to come up with a response when Chris stopped by the cooler to grab a drink and took a seat on the towel on Quinn's other side.

"I know you're not giving our boy shit about *his* sex life, Rae-Rae," Chris said, popping the tab of his beer can. "Rumor has it you could've given him a run for his money in college."

Quinn turned slowly toward her, giving her a look as if to say "oh really?"

Her mouth hung open as she tried to force her smile back and she gasped, "You traitor!"

"Yeah, Rae," Jett said, taking a swig of Labatt Blue as he plopped down on the last beach towel. "You are still in the *double* digits, right?"

"Okay, that's enough," Rae said, just as Harry dropped the slobbery tennis ball in front of her. She picked it up and threw it at Jett. "I have *not* slept with a hundred guys. That's gross."

"Oh, what are you at then? Ninety...eight?" Jett laughed, whipping the tennis ball down the shoreline.

"*No.* We're not having this discussion," Rae said. "I'm surprised you'd even want to bring it up seeing as how embarrassing it is for you, Flower."

73

Quinn wanted to laugh at the jab toward Jett but was caught off guard by the sick churning feeling in his stomach at the thought of her being with other guys. *A lot* of other guys, apparently.

He reminded himself he had absolutely no right to feel that way. She was completely right about the one-nighters and probably any other impression she'd made of him, so he couldn't reasonably feel upset by what he was hearing.

But that was the thing about his lifelong attraction to Rae- it wasn't entirely *reasonable.* It wasn't reasonable that he'd always felt like she was his when he'd never done anything to make it so, and it wasn't reasonable to think that she'd been pining after him all this time like he had for her.

"Okay, I don't know where this bullshit about me being a virgin started, but you guys all know I have sex," Jett snapped, angling his beer toward them. "As a matter of fact, I hooked up with a woman less than a week ago, thank you."

"Sure you did, Flower," Rae said with a wink. She turned and grabbed a bottle of tanning lotion out of her bag and started lathering it all over her arms and chest, working her way down to her- *yes, we've already established this-* notably stunning legs.

Quinn was reminded then of a memory much like this one, only he'd been seventeen, nearly eighteen, and had teenage boy hormones running rampant throughout his body. It was the first time he'd ever felt like he was actually going to make a move on his best friend before he was swiftly interrupted. The fact that he was now twenty-nine should have meant that he'd have better control over his impulses, but he just knew if she were to ask for his help rubbing the lotion into her back, he'd likely be even more of a horny, dick-brained mess than he'd been all those years ago.

He barely had time to complete that particular train of thought when Rae passed him the bottle of coconut-scented lotion. "Could you get my back?"

He had no choice but to nod and take the bottle of lotion from her. He spread his legs and patted the space on the towel between them, "Your throne, Princess. I am but a lowly servant."

Shaking her head with a sigh, she relented, "I'm going to have to come up with a new consequence for that game I won forever ago. Clearly you're never going to stop calling me that."

"I lost on purpose, Rae. Now that you know that I think I need to call you Princess to make up for lost time," said Quinn, as Rae settled herself between his legs with her back to him. He swallowed hard again, taking in the sight of her sleek, toned muscles, the dimples on the small of her back, and the amount of asscheek visible with her cinched bikini bottoms. His cock began to stiffen as Rae lifted her hair up, piling it into a messy bun on top of her head and tying it up with a scrunchie. Her back bowed slightly with the motion and his pulse kicked up a notch. *Yeah...I'm fucked.*

With tanning lotion on his left palm, he realized he would have to awkwardly bend his right arm with the splint to be able to feel her with both hands. It was worth it. If he was reliving this fantasy, he was going to rub her down with both hands. He wanted to feel her soft, warm skin as much as possible.

He massaged the lotion into her shoulders, then smoothed his way down. Mischief tugged at his lips when he imagined untying the back of her swimsuit top accidentally-on-purpose. Maybe if it was just him here he would tease and pretend to do it, but he couldn't see that going well with the other guys watching. Now onto her lower back he pressed each thumb on either side of her spine and massaged outward. Rae's back arched and he repeated the motion.

A pleasured moan escaped Rae's mouth and Quinn could have fallen to pieces. Just that one little sound from her and he was done. He *had* to hear that again.

Rae had gone suddenly still. Quinn could feel the tension in her muscles as she paused, breathing halted. He would've given anything to see her face. To try and get an idea of what she was thinking.

"You okay?" Quinn asked, voice low.

A nervous laugh brought on an exhale and her body relaxed slightly under his touch. "Sorry, this is the closest I've gotten to sex in a while. I forgot what a man's hands felt like."

"I didn't mind," Quinn replied, smiling. His heart leapt at the thought that she hadn't been with another guy recently. Of course, based on what Chris and Jett were saying about her sex life, teasing or not, he was curious. "What's...a while?"

She laughed nervously again, "Well, let's just say that walking in on the man you think you're going to be with forever while he's balls deep inside another woman is sort of a headshot to the confidence. And self-esteem. And the will to even have a sex life."

Quinn's hands stopped, simply resting on her waist as her words sunk in. "But didn't that happen like…?"

"About fourteen months ago? Yeah," Rae said, and he could hear the tightness in her voice that clearly stated her discomfort with the topic.

"Oh…" Quinn was at a loss for words. He suddenly felt even more sleazy having just hooked up with some random woman whose name he couldn't remember *less than a week ago!* He also felt the urge to knock Rae's ex-fiance in the jaw for making her question herself. The girl was a twelve out of ten, easily. For someone to be able to destroy her confidence...it didn't sit well with Quinn.

Sensing the need for a lighter mood Rae joked, "So just keep doing your thing. Just be aware I'm like a land mine. I guess if I go off, that's just a bonus for both of us."

"You're saying you might have an orgasm from just this?" Quinn asked, kneading his hands into her lower back again. Her back bowed again and she groaned softly, making his cock harden even more.

"I'm saying put your hands to work, Case, and we'll see what happens." The smirk was audible in her voice, and when she turned her head to peak over her shoulder, he had to bite his lip to keep his own groans caged in.

"Yes, your highness," Quinn replied smoothly, and he continued working his hands across her back, her shoulders, her arms. He wanted so badly to reach around and feel the small mounds of her breasts and run his thumbs over her top where he knew her nipples were.

What he really wanted was to clear the beach of anyone but the two of them, strip her down, and give her a full, sensual body massage from head to toe. He'd make it a challenge to make her come with his touch alone. His hands, his lips and tongue brushing over her skin. She deserved it. She deserved more, and he was determined to give it to her. *Fuck*, he wanted to give her everything.

76

Pressing his hands into the small of her back, lowering...lower...*lower...* he dipped his fingers into the waistband of her bottoms and teased, though he wasn't sure if it was working more on him or her. His cock was hard, aching to feel more, touch more. Rae let out another sigh that mingled with a moan, and her body relaxed even more beneath his palms. He leaned forward, eyes closed, chest to her back getting lost in her. His lips just barely brushed over her shoulder near her neck as he slowly moved the tips of his fingers from her back dimples and down into her bikini bottoms again...and again...and...

A cough and the clearing of throats made Quinn snap his eyes open, squinting against the bright reflection of the sun off the water. Reluctantly he backed away from Rae and turned to see Chris and Jett looking at them with amused interest. Chris took a drink from his beer, cocking an eyebrow, and Jett was trying not to grin as he scratched the side of his head.

"Do you two...need us to leave?" Jett asked, tilting his head, still failing to suppress a smirk.

Yes.

Quinn cleared his throat and ruffled his hair, looking down into his lap where his hard-on was evident. "Uh...no." He cleared his throat again. "Sorry, I..." His apology was more directed to Rae; he'd been a fraction of a centimeter away from kissing her neck, tasting her hot skin.

Peering at Rae over her shoulder he saw her chest rising and falling steadily, as though she'd been getting lost in him, too. Her skin was flushed, her pulse thrummed, betraying her forced slow and steady breaths and the calm demeanor she was at least trying to give off.

"It's fine," Rae said, her voice breathless. She grabbed the scrunchie wrapped around her messy bun and pulled, letting her hair fall down her back with a swoosh.

Standing up, Rae brushed a few grains of sand off her legs and stretched. She dropped her empty bottle back in the cooler and picked up the discarded football. She ruffled Jett's curly hair. "Come on, Jett. Let's see if I can still kick your ass."

Jett heaved himself up, finished his drink, and tossed the can into the cooler. "If you can I'm blaming it on having a head start on drinking."

Quinn and Chris watched from their beach towels as the other two walked toward the shore where the water just covered their feet.

"You look like you could use a dip in that water right now," said Chris, tipping his beer to take a drink.

Quinn let out a heavy exhale, attention still focused on Rae. Harry was now following at her side, jumping at the football when it was thrown and chasing it down the beach. "Yeah...I kind of lost myself for a minute there."

"A minute?" Chris chuckled. "We weren't sure if we should stay or just leave you to it."

New heat crept into Quinn's cheeks and he grinned into a swig of beer. He wanted to feel bad for putting his friends in the awkward position of witnessing his and Rae's...expression of passion, but he was too pleased with himself.

"I'm sure it'll be slow and sensual when it finally happens. A celestial experience, when all the stars align," Chris said, gesturing grandly with his hands and arms.

"You're that confident in us, huh?" Quinn's smile was wide and he didn't even try to hide it this time.

"Just don't fuck it up this time, man."

Quinn watched as Rae ran at Jett, shoving him with her shoulder and sending him off balance, toppling into the incoming waves. It had always amazed him how someone so slender and feminine had so much force. She was still his Rae that he'd known and loved for half his life. Tough, feisty, and fucking gorgeous. He wanted her, and he was willing to wait if it meant he could show her just how much she meant to him. If showing her that meant she finally could be his, and not just in his own head. She needed to see that he wasn't some playboy who was just looking to score. This was it. She was the one. He wasn't striking out this time.

CHAPTER 9

Every evening since her first run-in with Quinn, Raelyn had seen him, Chris, and Jett in one way or another. Mostly they hung out at the bar, with the exception of their spontaneous afternoon at the beach, and perhaps that was for the best. At the bar, the four friends were light-hearted and fun, joking around and teasing as though no time had passed between them and they were back in high school. Over the years, Raelyn had still seen Chris and Jett frequently, having made a habit of stopping into Trojan Horse any time she and Amira went out for drinks, even if that's not where they were planning on spending their whole night. Having Quinn back though was...well, it was a lot of things.

Overwhelming? At first.

Unexpected? Absolutely.

Just what she needed? She was beginning to think so.

After the way they'd left things Raelyn had always assumed seeing him again would be awkward, or maybe that they'd bicker and be confrontational, but that was definitely not the case. She had tried holding her walls up at the office when he'd come in unannounced, all shy smiles and rippling forearms, but she couldn't help tearing them down. He was still Quinn. For years he'd been her safe place, her person, her best friend. Maybe he had a bit of a reputation these days, but she could tell he was the same guy. The one who'd always defended her and protected her; the one who'd gotten suspended when he'd taken the blame for something she had actually done, and again when he'd overheard boys making indecent comments about her and reacted rather aggressively.

Now, after that sensual tanning lotion rubdown, she was feeling all sorts of hot and bothered every time she got herself ready to meet up with him again. If she thought she was sexually frustrated before, it was absolutely nothing compared to how she felt after having his large, sturdy hands cover her body. The warmth of his bare chest pressed against her back was imprinted in her mind that night as she rushed into her bedroom, unable to flip the lid off her pleasure box fast enough.

Yeah...it was intense.

It was Friday night and Raelyn had asked Amira to come along to Trojan Horse this time so she could finally meet Quinn, which her friend was absolutely dying to do. Amira offered to drive and was practically bouncing with excitement when she burst through Raelyn's front door and into her kitchen.

"Who's ready to get their drink on?" Amira sang, drawing out the last two words. She stopped abruptly upon finding Raelyn in the kitchen, filling Harry's food and water bowls. "*That's* what you're wearing?"

Raelyn looked down at her white t-shirt, ripped skinny jeans, and sparkly sandals. "What's wrong with this?"

"Seriously? It's a Friday night and you're trying to make your old flame wish he'd never even looked at another woman." Amira shook her head and grabbed Raelyn's wrist once the dog bowls were on the floor. "No, absolutely not. You don't go to the gym five days a week and build up a booty like that to wear *blue jeans* on a Friday night out."

Amira dragged Raelyn down the hall to her spacious bedroom and swung open the French doors to the substantial walk-in closet. "All of these clothes and you wear jeans and a t-shirt," Amira sighed then clapped her hands together as if to say "and now, we begin!"

Clothes were getting shoved at Raelyn to try on; skirts, dresses, and sparkly tops that she hadn't worn since before meeting Emerson. Before then, she'd been a casual dater, a regular weekend bar-goer, and had always gotten dressed for the occasion.

She must have tried on a dozen different outfits before Amira clapped her hands together again and gawked with wide eyes. "Yes, this is it! You are going to *slay* tonight!"

Raelyn stepped in front of the full-length mirror in her closet and even she had to do a double take, looking from herself in the mirror and down at the clothes on her body. She had on a black cold-shoulder top, a form-fitted, camel-brown leather skirt that fell just above mid-thigh. Her feet were encased in a pair of black peep-toe booties that gave her an extra four inches of height. Raelyn spun and checked her reflection from several angles.

"Damn, okay." She nodded. "I don't show off my hard work enough, do I?"

Raelyn had always been slim, but it was more a result of her athleticism. She wasn't a twig and she never had been. She simply had toned and defined muscles from all the sports she'd played when she was younger and kept up a relatively strict workout plan as an adult. And she really loved leg day at the gym.

"Now let's pull this hair down..." Amira grabbed the pins holding Raelyn's messy bun up and let the hair cascade down her back. "Oh yeah, he's gonna wish he could wrap his fingers in that and give it a tug."

After grabbing their bags and giving Harry a few goodbye pats and ear scratches, the girls set off, hopping- or more accurately, *scooting*- into Amira's Mercedes, and cruising downtown. They were lucky enough to find a parking spot available only two blocks away from their destination, and the walk gave Raelyn some time to get reacquainted with her heels. It wasn't until they were crossing the street toward the Trojan Horse sign that Raelyn's heart sped up.

"Oh God, I'm nervous," she said out loud as she recognized the emotion swell in her chest and stomach.

"Haven't you seen him every day this week?" Amira asked, looping her arm through Raelyn's in a comforting gesture.

"Yes, but not like this." Raelyn motioned to her outfit. "I mean, I look hot - *we* look hot. It's like I'm expecting him to make some sort of move."

"You are." Amira shrugged. "And not just him, either. Any guy in there with a functioning set of eyes is going to be goggling that ba-donka-donk!" She slapped her friend's ass and the leather made a resounding *smack!*

Raelyn giggled, not used to this kind of attention, but expecting nothing less than this level of support from Amira.

"Listen, you need a plan," Amira said, stopping just outside the bar entrance. "Quinn is used to getting attention from women *obviously*, but I think it's also obvious that he thinks you're different. You need to own the situation. Take control of it before he has a chance to charm you. Be overly confident...it'll throw him off his game. He can't control you if you let him know *you* are the prize here, not him."

"Prize?" Raelyn questioned. She didn't like being viewed as some object to win.

"You know what I mean." Amira shrugged. "He needs to think there's no way even he can have you. Because you're the best."

Raelyn nodded. She'd never had real issues with self-confidence before, but ever since getting played by Emerson, her ego may have been knocked down a few pegs. Quinn wasn't Emerson, though.

Well...okay, he was also sort of a player, and had previously been able to make Raelyn feel special while not really ponying up to how he claimed to feel about her in return.

She really didn't like that she was able to make this comparison, but nonetheless, it stiffened her resolve that she needed to do exactly what Amira had suggested. *She* was the one who needed to be impressed here, not him. She wasn't about to let another Emerson get the better of her, and she sure as hell wasn't going to gawk at him like some star-struck fan girl.

Raelyn pulled her shoulders back, standing up straighter. With their arms still looped, she gave a quick nod to Amira before they walked through the door.

Unsurprisingly, the bar was more packed than usual. Friday nights in Traverse City, particularly in the summer, came alive with all sorts of partiers: Regulars, sports fans, hipsters looking for the latest craft brew, college students, and bachelorette parties from out of town.

Among the buzz of the crowd, it still didn't take long to spot the head of dark, untamed hair at the bar. A woman with a trendy, silver-blond bob sat on the bar stool next to him, leaning in with obvious intent in her posture. She was leaning toward him, placing a flirtatious hand on his splinted arm.

A primal growl rumbled deep in Raelyn's chest, taking her by surprise. She really had no right to be possessive over Quinn but couldn't help feeling like she needed to stamp "Mine" in permanent ink all over his obnoxiously handsome face.

Finally, when she was about halfway between Quinn and the entrance, he turned and looked in her direction.

His jaw literally dropped.

Raelyn felt Amira's little elbow nudge of encouragement and had to look down to keep from smiling directly at Quinn. She couldn't have him feeling too confident just yet. When she'd contained her smile into a sly grin she looked back up at him, catching as he unsubtly eyed her from head to toe, mouth still wide open, having fully turned his back on the woman at the bar.

Stopping in front of her apparently wonderstruck admirer, Raelyn swept one hand out and cupped his chin in her palm. "Let me get that for you," she said as she pushed his jaw back up to meet the rest of his mouth. She noticed his eyes seemed stuck somewhere between her knees and the top of her skirt. In a fully alpha-female moment, Raelyn gave a challenging glance over his shoulder at the blonde woman who immediately recognized that she was being dismissed.

She turned back to focus on Quinn who, after what seemed like an unusually long amount of time, met her gaze seemingly unable to speak.

"This is my friend, Amira," Raelyn said, gesturing to the woman on her arm.

Amira stuck her hand out for Quinn to take and he did just as she said, "Wow, you are absolutely gorgeous."

Raelyn whipped her head in Amira's direction and shot her a look that she hoped was read as 'what happened to *he* doesn't impress *us?*' but was simply met with a lame shrug in her direction and then a beaming smile back to Quinn.

Apparently that was only *her* mantra tonight.

Quinn cleared his throat and looked up at Amira, giving a reserved grin, "Ah, yes, the *other* best friend."

"I'm sorry, *I'm* the other best friend?" Amira asked defensively. "Strongly disagree. I have been by this lady's side for the last ten years."

"That's cute, I was there for *eleven* years before that," said Quinn, keeping a sarcastic yet playful tone.

"We lost our virginity on the same night," Amira countered.

Quinn's playful demeanor faltered for half a second, flicking his gaze to Raelyn for a beat before grinning mischievously. "Was it...with each other? Because I wouldn't mind the details."

Amira hesitated, appearing flustered, "Well aren't you naughty? You handsome...beguiling specimen..."

Raelyn glared at her friend, shouting with her eyes, *Get a grip, woman!*

Leave it to Amira Jones to lose her senses at the sight of a handsome-devil grin, immediately after giving a pep-talk on female empowerment.

Once again, she told herself to take control of the situation. "Do you think we can find a booth in here? Not sure my skirt's really made for bar stools."

Quinn's eyes dropped back down to the tight skirt embracing little more than her ass and thighs and then back up to her face. The slow lick of his bottom lip accompanied by a small bite didn't go unnoticed.

He nodded and slid off his bar stool, "Yeah, I'll go find us a spot." His glance back down her legs didn't go unnoticed either and she turned to Amira once he'd walked away.

"Why don't you dress me more often?" Raelyn asked, feeling her confidence boosting significantly.

"I'll start coming over to set your clothes out before bed each night." Amira leaned over the bar where a tall girl with light brown skin and long braids was pouring drinks, "Can we get two shots of tequila with lemon and two cosmopolitans?"

"Tequila?" said Raelyn. "How the hell am I supposed to own the game if I'm table dancing?"

"Oh, sweetie, that's exactly how you own the game."

Quinn returned just as the bartender handed the girls their drinks. He watched as they drained their shot glasses and bit into the lemon slices with matching winces, and tried to conceal a grin. "Come on, I saved us a spot over here."

The girls left the empty shot glasses on the bar and followed Quinn back to a large corner booth that was sized for up to six people. Amira and Raelyn slid into one side and Quinn sat down across from them. He tipped his glass in a greeting to a group of college-age guys walking by who had pointed, recognizing the MLB all-star at once. He was bound to get a lot of recognition at a place like this, frequented by sports fans, and Raelyn was sure that wouldn't be the last, nor would it be the most enthusiastic greeting Quinn would get from passing fans that night.

"Rae told me you're getting married at the end of next month," Quinn said to Amira. "Congratulations."

"Oh, thank you," Amira beamed. "Brody might actually be stopping by later. He's out with the guys tonight, but I told him I was meeting baseball's most notorious bad boy and he threatened to come swooping in with his damn sword if need be."

"Sword?" Quinn raised a curious brow, "As in…?"

"As in a sword," said Raelyn. "Like an actual weapon made from metal, designed to slice off various appendages."

"It was his way of incorporating my heritage into his outfit on our wedding day," Amira said, sounding slightly annoyed, but adoration was present in her voice. "He couldn't pull off the whole Indian groom look, but he couldn't pass up the sword."

"That might be the coolest wedding accessory I've ever heard of," said Quinn, awestruck.

"It was a bit of an argument. I tried telling him he'd look like an idiot in a tux with a sword, but then I realized it might come in handy if I needed to slice off the best man's balls," Amira reasoned.

This comment earned a look of wide-eyed shock from Quinn, "Do we not like the best man?"

"We do not," Amira and Raelyn said in unison.

When Quinn gave Raelyn a curious look she sighed and took a sip of her cosmopolitan before explaining simply, "Emerson."

"And before you let that color the character of my idiot future husband, let me just say that they were friends and roommates in college and Brody just hasn't realized yet that he's completely outgrown him," said Amira.

Quinn seemed to understand the explanation, giving a nod. He looked intently at Raelyn then, "Does that mean you're walking down the aisle with your ex?"

"Thankfully, no," said Raelyn. "Amira's mom insisted she make her little sister maid of honor, so I was rescued from that horrifically awkward situation."

Quinn's responding smile seemed both genuine and relieved, "I know a guy who's got nothing going on if you're looking for a date."

"Yes!" Amira exclaimed before Raelyn had a chance to respond. "Yes, she would love to flaunt her super hot, major league *stud* in front of that pompous asshole!"

"I don't need to make Emerson jealous," Raelyn protested. "His opinions of me and who I sleep with are completely inconsequential."

"You think we'd sleep together if I was your wedding date?" Quinn asked, eyes glinting mischievously.

Raelyn returned his mischievous charm, "I'd give you the opportunity to beg."

Across the table Quinn shifted in his seat, eyes darkening with lust as he took a steadying breath. His gaze momentarily dropped to Raelyn's lips and he licked his own. Again.

"I think we need another round of shots," Amira grinned before slipping out of the booth and heading up to the bar.

Two hours later there was a collection of empty glasses on the table in front of them and Chris and Jett had joined them in their booth. Raelyn and Amira had taken three shots of tequila each and were now finishing up their second mixed drinks. Chris and Jett had handed responsibility of the bar over to the bartender and the assistant manager in the kitchen so they could join their friends for a couple of drinks. Quinn finished his first beer and had down-sized to a pint for his second.

Jett had started a new game of Never Have I Ever, in which those who *had* done what the speaker hadn't would take a sip of their drink.

"Okay, uh, never have I ever..." Chris pondered, "slept with an actor or actress."

Quinn pressed his lips together as if to keep from saying too much and simply sipped his beer.

Raelyn gasped, "Was it George Clooney?"

Giving in to a laugh he replied, "Even I couldn't score Clooney." He looked thoughtful for a moment then said, "Never have I ever sucked a dick."

"Come on, Quinn, let's get a little more creative," Raelyn sighed. She and Amira both took small sips of their cocktails. "Never have I ever had an audience to a wet dream."

"Hey!" Quinn exclaimed as the other three at the table laughed. "I was maybe fourteen, you just climbed through my window, and...invaded my privacy. It was traumatic. One moment I was on the beach, lathering sunscreen on a hot babe, and the next I'm being whacked with a pillow, my best friend pointing out that I'm getting an erection. I will never sleep with an open window again." Everyone laughed at this and he added with a flirtatious grin in Raelyn's direction, "You were impressed. Don't deny it."

"Ah, so you have a *thing* about lathering sunscreen on hot babes," Jett nodded, clearly referencing their day at the beach.

Raelyn and Quinn made brief eye contact across the table, both smiling and blushing a little before looking down into their drinks. Not only had they shared a sensual, passionate, arguably monumental experience, but they'd had witnesses. Raelyn recalled the sensation like sparklers igniting all over her body as she'd felt Quinn's mouth so close to her skin and heard those primal groans and harsh breaths like secrets whispered in her ear.

"Never have I ever lost my virginity to a cowboy," Amira said with a pointed stare in Raelyn's direction.

She shrugged, conceding, and took another drink.

"A cowboy, Rae? Really?" Quinn asked, disbelieving.

"True story. He came to our dorm every day for like a month and would antagonize me and try flirting, and I couldn't stand him. And then one day I thought," Raelyn gave a quick shrug, "eh, he's attractive enough, why not?"

"Why not?" Quinn said flatly. "You didn't even like the guy but, hey...why not?"

"It was a magical experience, I assure you." Raelyn tilted her glass toward him. "Never have I ever posed nude on a magazine cover!"

"You would not believe how much shit my teammates give me for that."

"I thought it was exquisite," Amira cut in, sending an exaggerated wink across the table at him. "Never have *I* ever had a threesome."

Raelyn narrowed her eyes across the table at Quinn who was holding back a guilty grin. He took a quick gulp of his beer, not breaking away from her gaze. She arched one eyebrow in challenge as she also took a deep drink from her glass.

Quinn's eyebrows raised in apparent surprise before pulling together as he chewed the inside of his cheek, shooting her a curious, scrutinizing look across the table.

Jett let out a low whistle, "Damn...We had our suspicions about you, Rae-Rae, but I wasn't sure."

"College is stressful, and sometimes one dick just isn't enough," Raelyn replied, keeping her tone entirely nonchalant.

Quinn set his beer back on the table hard, it sloshed as he coughed, pounding his chest. Amira had thrown her head back with a delighted laugh while Chris and Jett stared at Raelyn, appearing both astounded and mildly impressed.

"Wow, I was sort of imagining you two, but," said Jett motioning between Raelyn and Amira. "I'm not really sure where to go from here now."

"I think I need another drink," Raelyn said, pressing her hands to the table. When she stood up she stumbled a little before finding her balance.

Up at the busy bar, she leaned and waited for an available bartender to take her drink order. She hadn't been waiting long when she felt the light pressure of a hand on the small of her back. She'd expected to see Quinn when she turned but was instead face-to-face with a stranger.

He was handsome enough, with light brown hair and bright blue eyes, a square jaw and, from what she could see, he was physically fit. He was also young. College-age young. That explained the level of confidence it took to come up behind a stranger and touch her like they were already together.

"Hi," he smirked, brushing his gaze down her body and back up to her face. It was *not* a subtle gesture. "I'm Carter," he said, cocky smirk still in place as he extended his hand to her.

"Raelyn," She shook his offered hand and turned to face him so that his hand fell away from her back.

"I'll buy this round if you come back to my table with me. You could share your life story or…" he dipped his head in what Raelyn was sure was a practiced move so that he could offer the perfect smolder. "We could skip all that and you can just come back to my place."

It took some effort to not laugh derisively in this guy's face, "What makes you think I need someone to buy my drinks for me?"

"Oh, I don't," Carter said, his eyes making another slow sweep down her body. His eyes were still down, gaze hovering over her thighs. "But I needed a reason to catch you before you went back to your table."

Raelyn nodded slightly to one side, deciding it was a reasonable enough response. Still, there was no way she was going anywhere with this guy. She wasn't going to let him buy her drinks either, but she couldn't deny the unexpected male attention was nice. At least until…

"You've got some legs on you. I can't help wondering what those thighs would look like wrapped around my neck."

Before the laughter could burst out of her, a large and imposing figure had inserted himself between her and her admirer.

Quinn's arm wrapped around her waist and he slammed a twenty dollar bill on the bar top, "I've got this round, babe." His voice was low and there was an edge to it that she knew well, though she hadn't heard it in quite some time. This was angry, protective, possessive Quinn. And it was quite possibly the sexiest thing she'd ever seen.

She would've given anything to see the fire in Quinn's glare that made Carter back down and cower like a nervous puppy. Carter slunk away from the bar and Quinn watched, not taking his eyes off him until he was back at a table with a few of his bros.

Quinn looked back at Raelyn whose face was caught somewhere between amusement and arousal. "Whatcha doin' there, Case?" she asked. "You called me babe."

He gave a short nod, "I did." He looked her over, and though he was also taking in her full appearance, his attention fell heavily on her lips. His gaze flicked up to her eyes and he smirked as if to tell her she knew *exactly* what he was doing. "Did you order another drink?"

"Not yet." She suddenly felt breathless under his intense gaze.

"You're already a little tipsy, why don't we call it a night?" He started lightly trailing his hand up her back and over her shoulders, stopping to push a stray piece of hair back behind her ear, then sliding his hand back down slowly.

"Amira's in worse shape and she drove us here," Raelyn managed to say, mesmerized by the rhythm of his strokes up and down her back.

Quinn lowered his voice, ducking so that only she could hear him, "Let me take you home."

Staring into his golden, honey-brown eyes, it was as though they were exchanging secrets and trying to read each other's minds as well as they once had. They used to be able to read each other so well, know what the other was thinking or feeling, know how to make the most minute adjustments to make the other comfortable. It was like they had known everything about each other. Or at least she thought they had.

She searched his face for any sort of nefarious intent and, unsurprisingly, saw none. The bartender appeared in front of her and asked for her order. Raelyn considered, gaze fixed on Quinn for a moment longer before turning, "I'll take an eight ounce glass of DeRosé." She faced Quinn again, "*One* more, and you can take me home."

CHAPTER 10

Rae's last drink of the night turned out to be a highly potent sparkling rosé from her family's vineyard that left her a giggling, flirty, beautiful mess that Quinn had to usher out of the bar in his arms. Amira's fiancé, Brody had found her and after she'd introduced them, he was helping her walk back to her car so they could get home.

Once they made it to Quinn's Bronco, he realized he was going to have to awkwardly lift Rae into the passenger seat with his left arm, avoiding the use of his splinted arm as best as he could. Rae was able to do some of the work, but it didn't stop him from having to fully grasp her ass to push her up into the seat. Tipsy as she was, she simply giggled at this and made a comment about how he'd clearly been waiting to do that all night. She wasn't wrong.

Following Rae's slurred and giggled directions to her house was easier than he'd anticipated. While the city had grown since he'd last lived here, the roads still had a familiarity that he had never felt during his time in Arizona, Georgia, or California.

He pulled into a driveway and parked in front of an attached garage. Rae's house was a dark blue ranch-style home with a walkout basement, and a wrap-around porch that turned into a balcony overlooking the lake. It was a beautifully built home, but Quinn couldn't help noticing how different it was from the massive French manor-style home she'd grown up in.

After helping her out of the lifted vehicle, ensuring she didn't sprain an ankle, she keyed in the garage passcode and he partially followed, partially carried her inside.

Rae pushed the door open and Quinn followed her into what appeared to be a mudroom and laundry room. They were greeted by a wagging mass of long hair, and Rae sat down on a small bench to avoid being knocked over by the large dog.

"'Ello, Harry," Quinn squatted down to pet the dog.

Noting the British accent, Rae giggled, "That's how I talk to him, too."

Quinn stood up and looped his good arm under Rae's and across her back, pulling her to her feet. She leaned into him and he was reminded of the first time he fully realized how much he loved the feel of her in his arms.

"Where to?" He asked, gesturing ahead, through an archway that looked like it led into a spacious kitchen.

Rae directed him through the kitchen and living room, down the short hallway to her bedroom. The wall where her king-sized bed was situated was painted a deep stormy blue, while the rest of the walls were a much lighter shade. Apart from the crystal chandelier in the middle of the room, it was a very simplistic space. Artistic photographs and small shelves with different knick-knacks adorned the walls. Quinn didn't miss the Ron Weasley *Funko Pop* figure or the House Stark plaque, acknowledging them with a fond grin. There were two sets of white French doors on opposite walls, and a set of glass doors on another leading to the balcony.

Quinn led her to her bed and sat her down gently, taking a seat next to her as he lay her back on the pillows. He pulled her legs up into his lap and began slipping off her shoes, then found himself slowly tracing up and down her legs with his fingertips.

With a long sigh, attention fixed on the twinkling chandelier overhead, Rae said, "This. This is why I don't drink tequila. I just have to lay here and wait for the room to stop spinning."

"Are you going to be sick?" Quinn asked, hoping he sounded more concerned than alarmed.

"No, no, I don't get sick," she shook, or rather lulled, her head from side to side.

"Never?"

"Nope," she made a cute face with pursed lips. "Except for that one time."

"The time with the two guys?" Quinn let it slip out unable to help himself. Though he'd reminded himself that he, of all people, had absolutely no right to be upset about anyone else's sex life, he hadn't liked the video that played in his head upon discovering that dirty secret from her past.

A drunken giggle bubbled out of her lips as she looked up at him through narrowed eyes, "That bothers you, doesn't it?"

"No," he lied quickly. "It's just a lot to take in."

"*Yeah* it was," Rae said, bursting into a fit of laughter.

Quinn pushed his tongue to the inside of his cheek and gave a nod, "Okay, I asked for that one." He wiped his hand down his face. "I just never would've thought, you know, you would have let...I mean, you just seem like you like to be in charge. I can't imagine you being...tag teamed by some college guys."

"How do you know I wasn't dressed in a sexy leather catsuit with a whip and they were on leashes being my obedient man-servants?"

Raising an eyebrow he looked down at her, "Were they?"

Another giggle, "No." Rae sighed. "Let's just say I had a bit of a...sexual liberation my junior year of undergrad....and then again in grad school."

"You go girl." Quinn rolled his eyes with a sigh. Looking up at the ceiling he wondered where the hell he was while she was going through this *sexual liberation*.

He was still brushing his fingers up and down Rae's bare legs. "Where are your pajamas? I can get you some and let you change." He let his fingers stop just short of the hem of her skirt before sliding them back down toward her ankles.

Rae pointed to the white doors closest to her bed. "The dresser is in there."

Reluctant to move, Quinn forced himself up and opened the doors, discovering a large walk-in closet with a dresser on the right-hand side. He pulled out the top drawer which was clearly her underwear drawer. He noticed a purple box and, though knowing he shouldn't look inside, made a quick glance to confirm that Rae could not see him before he lifted the lid.

Yep, vibrators. All different shapes and styles. He always found it interesting that they came in bright pinks, blues, and purples, rather than flesh tones. He grinned, then caught an image in his mind's eye of one of the larger pink toys sliding into Rae's wetness, making her shake and rock with an orgasm. He felt blood rush to his groin and quickly slipped the lid back on the box, moving on to the next drawer before he forgot what he was supposed to be looking for.

He found a pair of shorts and a matching black shirt and took them back over to the bed and set them next to her.

"I'll turn around so you can get dressed." Quinn faced the door that led to the hallway. He felt her hand catch his and pull him back around.

"There's no way I'm getting out of the skirt by myself unless I stand up, and I think we both know that's not happening."

Quinn swallowed and watched as Rae slowly pulled the zipper down the side of her skirt. Maybe she wasn't really moving that slowly, but everything in Quinn's mind was suddenly going in slow motion, the rest of the room had gone fuzzy, and all he could see was Rae undressing in front of him.

She slid her fingers under the waistband of the skirt and tried pushing it down over her ass. She let out a small laugh, "Yeah, you're going to have to pull from the bottom...I think it's become one with my skin."

Quinn slid his trembling hands up the bottom of her skirt, feeling where it had stuck itself to her skin. He smiled and shook his head, "The things you women wear to make a man's jaw drop." Once he'd successfully un-stuck the material from her legs, taking his time to feel her thighs and making his blood that had already rushed itself downward throb even harder, he gently tugged the skirt down. First revealing her navel set into a flat and toned stomach, then the sweet and surprising curves of her hips and ass, and her lacy lavender colored thong. He slipped the skirt down until it fell onto the floor at his feet.

His heart was pounding as he took in the sight of this woman laying here next to him and a rush of breath escaped him. As many times as he'd fantasized about her over the years, never was she this striking. His fantasies didn't account for her constellation of freckles across the bridge of her nose, nor did they remember the small birthmark on her left hip, just above the band of her thong. Quinn wanted to devour her like an exquisite and essential course he'd been starving for after a long day on the diamond. One he knew he should savor, but *goddamn*, he wanted her all at once.

She was too tipsy to make a move on, that was for sure, but his cock didn't seem aware. He felt his erection press hard against the zipper of his jeans, begging to be let out. He couldn't stop staring at her. And then she pulled her shirt over her head, revealing a sheer and lace bra, and he heard the growl escape his throat.

"Nothing you haven't seen before, right?" Rae's voice came out low and sultry as she watched him drink her in. She laced her fingers with his and pulled him on top of her.

Quinn looked down at this goddess beneath him, swallowing hard, "Your body's changed a little since we were seventeen. Good changes, though," his eyes swept over her body under his. "*Really* good."

He hesitated for a moment with his lips hovering over hers. Their eyes met, and with another look down at her full, wanting lips, he let his brush hers briefly, pulled back to meet her eyes once more, before crushing his mouth to hers.

Quinn wasn't just kissing Rae, he was tasting her, consuming her. He parted her lips with his tongue and swept into her mouth with insurmountable force. He climbed on top of her and she tore his shirt over his head. He swore he never wanted their lips to part as his tongue conquered hers. He pressed his hips down on hers, holding her hard against the bed. A groan escaped the back of Rae's throat as he grinded the length of his cock between her legs, and her body's response told him that it was exactly what she wanted. Her hands slid up the hard planes of his chest and around the back of his neck, pulling him deeper into the kiss.

He was dizzy with how much he needed this, needed her. He needed to claim her *now*. He had to know that she was his- and he was going to make sure she knew it, too.

To hell with his damn elbow, Quinn tore Rae's hands away from where they were tangled in his hair and thrust them above her head, pinning them there. Her sexy little grin she gave in response told him she needed to be dominated by him. *Fuck*, she was going to let him make his claim on her and take her any way he wanted. Quinn kissed her hard again, covering her mouth with his and drinking her in. He could practically hear his dick screaming to be let out of its cage or else it was going to tear itself out.

He let go of Rae's wrists and began unbuttoning his jeans and she used this moment to swiftly unhook her bra and toss it to the side. *Mother of fuck.* He growled again, urgency filling his veins to get these fucking pants off faster so he could worship those breasts. Hastily, he kicked his jeans off, along with his boxer briefs and held himself above Rae and watched as her eyes widened with hunger at the sight of how hard his cock had gotten for her. She reached a hand down toward his stiff dick, but Quinn grabbed it and shoved it back up over her head, pressing himself back onto her.

"Not now, baby," Quinn whispered hoarsely. "I've gotta make you mine first, then you can have me."

Rae let out the most perfect moan of pleasure from his words and he almost lost control- if he hadn't lost it already. Quinn was grinding down on her over her soft, lace panties, and knew he was rubbing her clit just right with his cock. Rae threw her head back, arching her neck and back, and letting out another moan. Quinn felt the wetness of her pussy as she soaked through her panties.

Oh fuck, this was fucking happening. Rae. Rae DeRose. My Rae is under me and she fucking wants me. Bad.

Giving her mouth a break from his, he trailed his lips and tongue down her jaw and neck to her perfectly rounded, pink-tipped breasts, licking and sucking a nipple into his mouth. Rae let out a whimper and he continued to rub his rock hard length against her clit, sucking and gently scraping his teeth across her bare nipple.

Quinn felt high on the sounds of her ragged breathing, her little whimpers and moans as he did everything to please her, and the feel of her bare skin against his. Even against his hips that were holding her down, Rae was raising hers to match his rhythm, to get the most out of the sensation of his now wet cock against her clit, and he felt her body tense for a split second as she gasped. The release came wave upon wave, and she threw her head back with an impassioned cry of his name.

Holy fuck, that's the only way I ever want to hear my name again.

Her muscles jerked and quivered as the orgasm ripped through her, and Quinn watched, studying every detail, storing this moment in the deep crevices of his memory to play over and over again. Rae's chest rose and fell with her heavy breathing, and as it slowed her muscles began to relax, until she was lying under Quinn, gazing up at him with a satisfied expression and a glint in her eyes he'd never seen before.

Raelyn DeRose, you are the most beautiful creature on this earth.

As Quinn's eyes swept over her again, drinking in the delicious sight beneath him, he was hit with an infuriating truth, and he sent an apology to his cock before saying through his own harsh breathing, "Rae...you have no idea how bad I want this. *Fuck* do I want this, but..."

"What's wrong?" Rae's expression changed so immediately and he inwardly cursed himself for making her go from looking like a sex goddess to startlingly insecure so quickly.

"No, nothing, you're perfect. *So fucking perfect*," Quinn closed his eyes, "but you've had a lot to drink. I don't want to do this... *like this*. You deserve more...I...I want to know you want this, *want me*, and it's not just alcohol and bad decisions on your part."

Rae's eyes flicked back and forth between his, and he felt like she was holding her breath, surely remembering the last time he'd interrupted what should have been a perfect, intimate moment between them. He swallowed and tried to communicate with his gaze how much he wanted to make this up to her. Make *everything* up to her. Finally, she let out a breath, the corner of her pink lips pulling up in a slight smile and nodded, "Okay."

The tightness that had formed in Quinn's chest loosened so he continued, "Let me take you out. On a date. A *proper* date. And if it leads us here, I will fucking worship you."

Rae narrowed her eyes looking up at him and chewed her bottom lip as she considered, then at last, she sighed, "Fine...You're probably right. Besides, I want to be fully sober when I enjoy *all* of this." She dragged her hands over his shoulders and down his sides, grabbing his hips and pulling them tighter onto hers, "But you don't have to stop kissing me."

Quinn's smile spread across his whole face and he was filled with the most genuine happiness he'd felt in ages. His lips pressed down to hers again, more gently this time, and then placing a kiss on her forehead, he rolled onto the bed next to her, wrapping her in his arms. God, this had to be the best feeling there was. Raelyn DeRose here with him, her skin against his.

They dressed, Rae in the pajamas he'd picked out for her, and Quinn in his boxer briefs. They exchanged kisses, talking and laughing into the darkness of her bedroom. Rae fell asleep in the early hours of the morning, and curling his body around hers, Quinn fell asleep to the sound of Rae's slow, steady breathing.

CHAPTER 11

Oh God, my head. My poor, stupid little head.
Raelyn winced as she opened her eyes into her bright, sunlit bedroom. None of the curtains were drawn, and the glass door to the balcony hadn't had the shades pulled before she got in bed.

How had she gotten into bed? She remembered Amira dressing her in a tight leather skirt and heels to go to Trojan Horse. She remembered meeting up with Quinn and getting a booth. Chris and Jett joining them an hour or so into the night. The booth littered with empty glasses.

The buzz of a blender came from the kitchen and Raelyn's eyes shot open wide.

Quinn.

She'd let Quinn take her home. And he'd...stayed the night?

Raelyn quickly felt her body over for the absence of clothes. Looking down she saw the scarlet and gold *Gryffindor* lion on her black shirt with the matching red shorts. With a sigh of relief and then a groan she closed her eyes trying to remember what had happened once they'd arrived at her house.

Quinn had practically carried her through her house and to her bedroom and then...

Oh mama.

She'd thrown herself at him. Or...she'd thrown him on herself? Flashes of Quinn's hard, corded muscles rocking over her invaded her mind. She could still hear his primal groans emanating from deep inside him as he kissed her so fiercely, and his long, full erection pressing into her until she climaxed.

Raelyn let her heartbeat slow before quietly sliding her feet onto the floor, bracing herself for stars as she rolled up out of bed and silently padded across the room to her bathroom, closing the doors behind her. She started at the sight of herself in the mirror. Mascara and eyeliner had smeared under her eyes and her hair was a tangled mess. She sent up a silent prayer that when Quinn had woken up her face had been in the pillow and he'd missed this ungodly sight.

Needing to press refresh on her morning appearance as soon as possible, Raelyn reached into the shower and turned it on, brushing her hair while she waited for the water to heat up. She stripped down and stepped into the shower, standing under the consistent spray of the shower head while trying to remember each and every detail of what had gone on in her bed with the man now apparently making breakfast smoothies in her kitchen.

They'd both been naked. No, *he* had been naked. The memory of Quinn's perfectly sculpted, muscular naked body was something she was sure no amount of tequila could make her forget. The sensitive throb between her legs from his hard length grinding into her clit certainly wouldn't let her forget. She hadn't had an orgasm like that in *months*. But why hadn't they had sex?

Not able to come up with an explanation after simply standing under the hot water, she proceeded to wash her face, hair, and body, until she felt somewhat alive, though the pounding behind her eyes was still present.

Having dressed and brushed her teeth thoroughly, with her hair still wet but at least combed, she headed out to the kitchen where Quinn had made himself at home. He was sitting at the kitchen table, drinking what looked like a protein shake and reading one of her physical therapy journals. Harry had made himself comfortable at Quinn's feet and it struck Raelyn as funny how perfectly domestic this picture was.

Raelyn took a deep breath before saying, "So...I might need some reminders on what happened last night."

Quinn snapped his attention up to her, a flash of alarm crossing his face, "You don't remember?"

"Oh, I remember some of it...I'm just a little fuzzy on the details," Raelyn said, trying not to feel too embarrassed. "I don't typically drink that much and I'm quickly remembering why that is."

Quinn looked as if he were trying to read her before responding, "Well, you got super horny and insisted on doing anal. It's not usually my thing, but when the princess makes a request, I must oblige." He gave an indifferent shrug.

Raelyn let out a dry laugh and returned his tease, "Um, well, that's a lie, because every time I do anal my breasts swell the next day. It's the weirdest thing." She grabbed her breasts and looked down at them. "They feel normal today, so that can't be true."

Quinn looked as though he were going to say something, but it got lost and instead he just stared with his mouth open.

"I know we didn't have sex, ya dummy," she chortled, walking over to the fridge and opening it to look for some hangover food.

"So...your boobs don't swell when...?" Quinn began, then laughed when Raelyn shot him an incredulous look. "Right, well, I can't put anything past you now, Miss Sexual Liberation- getting liberated two dicks at a time."

Raelyn paused, staring into the fridge as she remembered that topic of conversation. She felt her cheeks color and a slightly embarrassed grin crept across her face, "Right. That."

"I made you a smoothie," said Quinn, getting up from the table and grabbing it off the top shelf of the refrigerator. "It's a miracle cure for hangovers. I didn't know how long you were going to sleep, otherwise I would've made you French toast with sliced strawberries."

"Thank you," Raelyn smiled appreciatively as she took the glass out of his hands. "You remember my favorite breakfast, huh?"

"French toast with butter and a little bit of powdered sugar, topped with sliced strawberries," said Quinn, a slight rose color blossoming in his cheeks. "Your dad made it all the time when I had to...stay over."

Quinn's brown eyes were almost too intense this close, Raelyn found herself having to drop her gaze as she felt the warmth of his words spread through her chest. Those nights he stayed over when they were kids were some of the most fun nights she could remember of her childhood. The blanket forts, movies, and conversations about anything and everything into the early hours. Raelyn's dad loved having Quinn over for family dinners to talk baseball and other "guy stuff" that he didn't typically talk about with his two daughters. Unfortunately the reasons Quinn *had* to stay at their house some nights were less than fond pieces of Raelyn's memory.

"Is that why you're back?" Raelyn asked, feeling her brows pull together in concern. "Is it your mom?"

Quinn nodded, looking down at his feet, "Kidney failure."

"She got sober, you know." Raelyn felt like she blurted this out.

"I...How did you know?"

Raelyn bit her lip, not knowing if he'd think she had overstepped, "When you left I stopped and checked on her a few times. I knew you'd be worried she'd overdose or starve or...pass out and drown in her own vomit without you around to take care of her. So I did for a little bit. And continued to every now and then until I met that nurse you'd hired."

He didn't say anything for a while and she could feel him looking at her. "You didn't have to do that. You shouldn't have. It was dangerous. Anyone could've been there."

"I know, Quinn, I remember," she said, losing the hesitant tone. "Believe me, I remember. But...despite everything, you still always looked out for her."

Quinn sighed and then said, "I need to go back there. I went Monday, before I saw you again and I haven't been back. It's just...so different. I thought I'd be angry to see her still using, but it's like I was even more mad that she'd waited until I left to get sober."

"What happened?"

"I screamed at her," Quinn let out a huff of humorless laughter. "I stood in the middle of the living room and yelled at this frail dying woman about all the ways she'd failed me. And then I left."

Raelyn considered for a beat, nodding her head from side to side, "Did it feel good?"

Quinn winced, "Am I horrible if I say yes?"

"Of course not," Raelyn placed a comforting hand on his shoulder. "She was never a real mom to you. She didn't take care of you or take any sort of interest in your life. She put you in danger on countless occasions, and honestly she just never deserved you." It was the first time Raelyn had spoken openly about her opinion of Molly Casey, but she felt like it was overdue. "Don't get me wrong, I'm glad she had you and that you still managed to be like, pretty okay."

Quinn smiled half-heartedly, "Gee, thanks, Rae."

"But seriously," Raelyn continued, "she had no right to have a son who cared so much when she gave you nothing."

There were a few beats of silence before Quinn brought Raelyn into him, embracing her in his long, muscled arms, and held her there for several moments. When he pulled out of the hug, he dropped his arms to her hips, his forehead pressed to hers.

"Come with me," he said, his voice sounding tight as though a lump were caught in his throat. "Come with me when I see her again."

"Okay," said Raelyn, and it came out almost a whisper. She tilted her head up and searched his intense brown eyes before touching her lips to his.

Quinn kissed her back with force, sweeping his tongue into her mouth. He let out a low groan filled with longing and her body responded instantly. Warmth crept up her thighs and pulsed between her legs and she pressed herself against him, finding that his body had also responded. Raelyn could feel Quinn's hardness through his jeans and she rubbed herself needily against it.

Wrapping one arm around her bottom, he lifted her up onto the kitchen counter and pulled her legs around his waist. His hand cupped the side of her face as he took control of the kiss. Who knew a kiss could be so demanding? But *damn*, if he didn't command the attention of her mouth and tongue.

The room was filled with the sounds of their breathing, Raelyn's moans, Quinn's growls. Chests heaving, breaths coming in harsh and heavy, Raelyn couldn't believe she was getting so worked up over a kiss. She could feel the moisture between her legs as she pulled him closer, fingers grasping his shirt so tightly, as if she'd simply float away if she let go.

It was like nothing Raelyn had ever felt, every sensation taking her to the edge: His scent, the feel of his lips, his stubble scratching her skin as they kissed deeper, the taste of his tongue, the way his hands felt against her cheek, her neck, and then holding her hips, pulling her in close.

Raelyn had no idea how long they'd spent making out like horny teenagers before finally parting. Their lips were swollen from prolonged contact and her heart squeezed as Quinn let out a shuddering breath. He rested his forehead back on hers with his eyes closed. Raelyn brushed her fingers lightly down the side of his face, concentrating on those magnificently talented lips.

"Remember," Quinn began, his voice low and husky, "when we made blanket forts at your house in the basement?"

"Mhmm…"

"Why didn't we ever think to do this then?" Quinn asked, the hint of a smile in his words.

Raelyn pondered for a moment, remembering the many different forts that were built and all the activities that *had* taken place. "Probably because…we were ten and thought we might catch cooties."

Quinn's laugh was silent but she'd felt his breath on her lips, "I don't think I ever thought you had cooties…I thought you were a princess, remember? Princesses don't have cooties."

"I guess I didn't think you were all that interested in kissing me," Raelyn shrugged. "I almost suggested it once. For science, of course. Just so that when we finally did have a boyfriend or girlfriend we knew what we were doing."

Quinn took a breath, paused, then let it out shaking his head.

"What?" Raelyn pressed, knowing he'd wanted to say something.

"When did that thought cross your mind?" he asked. "To kiss for practice?"

"Oh, I don't know, when we were twelve? Thirteen, maybe?" Raelyn replied, "Camille was fifteen or sixteen and was always talking about boys and kissing different boys so I thought maybe I should get a leg up on it."

There was another silent pause before Quinn spoke again. "I definitely would've kissed you for *science*."

Raelyn giggled, "If I ever get a time machine I'll go back and let twelve-year-old me know that you would happily be a test guinea pig for kissing."

"If it had felt this good, I doubt we would've ever wanted to kiss anyone else though," Quinn said, finally looking up. His look was searching; Raelyn could feel him reading her face.

So it wasn't just her imagination. Or her lack of any sort of action in the fourteen months. It really had been that good and he'd felt it, too.

She smiled, almost shyly, letting him know that she'd experienced the same surprising flood of emotions and sensations during their countertop make-out session.

Looking back at Quinn, she got the feeling he was holding back. She kept getting the impression he wanted to say something, but he would drop his gaze to her lap instead or bite his lip. Biting back whatever was on the tip of his tongue, as if it would jump out if not caged in.

"What are you thinking?" Raelyn pressed again, bringing her hand up to cup the side of his face.

Quinn shook his head and cleared his throat, "Just all the things I'd do differently if I had the chance."

Raelyn raised a curious eyebrow, "Really? You're Quinn Casey, Major League All-Star. You're being considered for *People's* 'Sexiset Man Alive' which I'm pretty sure is a title that usually just goes to singers or actors. You date Victoria's Secret models and probably have like a crazy huge LA mansion from your multi-million dollar Major League contract, and you're telling me you would've lived your life differently?"

"I've never dated a Victoria's Secret model, I was photographed with a couple of them and people just assumed we were hooking up," Quinn corrected. "And yes, I've made a lot of great achievements, especially considering where I started from, but," he shrugged, and gave that look like he was going to say something, then changed course, "yeah, there are some things I would change."

"You're holding back, Quinn," said Raelyn, giving him a quizzical look. "I can tell there's something you want to say...I'm your oldest friend, you don't have to hold back with me."

His intense gaze held so much behind it. She searched his face and he looked as though he were finally going to let it out, but again shook his head, "It doesn't matter. We're here now."

Raelyn decided to accept that he wasn't going to say whatever was troubling him. At least not yet. It was just under the surface and they had another six weeks of physical therapy to get through. She didn't know how long he was planning to stay, but knew he'd have to go back to L.A. eventually to train once his elbow was healed enough to throw a ball and swing a bat.

The thought of him leaving again already tugged uncomfortably inside her chest. It had been years since they'd last seen each other. Less than a week in and he was becoming a constant figure in her life again. She'd been aware of missing him, but she hadn't realized just how much had been taken away by his absence.

"Do you remember me saying I wanted to take you out on a date?" Quinn asked, breaking the silence that had settled over them.

"A *proper* date, I believe were the words," said Raelyn, nodding.

"Yes, well," Quinn sighed. "I don't have a lot of experience with those. So you might have to excuse me for a while so I can Google what to do on a real date."

"Oooh, Dates by Google," Raelyn teased. "While you do that, I am going to finish this wonderful anti-hangover breakfast smoothie and give Amira a call. She's probably dying to hear all the fine details that I'm struggling to remember about what happened between us last night. I might have to make some of it up so it's juicy enough for her liking."

"Seriously? You're going to tell her *all* the details?" Quinn looked mildly concerned.

"I mean, mostly we just talk length and girth, width of the head, that sort of thing. You know, girl talk," Raelyn said nonchalantly, only cracking when she saw the look of horror on Quinn's face. "Kidding. Of course you really have nothing to be nervous about in that department."

"Girls really are worse than guys about that stuff, aren't they? Guys just want to know like…'did you fuck?' 'Yeah', 'Would you tap it again?', 'Meh, probably'," Quinn said, going back and forth as though two different people were speaking.

"'Meh, probably'?" Raelyn glared.

"That wasn't in reference to you," Quinn said quickly, "Or anyone else in particular…just a general example. We haven't had sex, so obviously it wasn't...but I'm sure when we do- *if* we do, I mean- I'd definitely say yes, I'd do it again."

"I'm truly charmed," Raelyn said breathlessly, putting her hand over her chest as she mocked swooning.

"Well, there's more where that came from, babydoll," Quinn said with a wink.

Raelyn giggled and hopped off the kitchen counter. "Go plan our date, Rico Suave." She reached up on tip toes and gave him a light peck on the lips. They walked to the front door together and Quinn gave her one last long, deep kiss on the porch before sauntering to his car and driving away, leaving her feeling blissfully lightheaded.

She stood on the porch and watched him disappear from view with a million different thoughts and memories flashing through her mind. She thought of the night before, and the kisses in the kitchen. She wondered about the secrets that he was just barely keeping in. She thought about graduation night and how he'd been so sweet and perfect until the truth came out. She thought about the girls swarming him at the bar in college when they'd planned to meet up for the first time in years and how he'd completely blown her off.

Letting out a long sigh, Raelyn looked down to where Harry sat at her feet. She scratched and massaged his ears with another sigh, "Oh, Harry, what am I getting myself into?"

CHAPTER 12

2007

Quinn rested his back on the cold metal of the lockers after a quick shower. His hair hung into his eyes, wet and overgrown, and he ran his hands over it attempting to tame it now before it could dry too wild. As he contemplated the task ahead- a task he'd completely pussied out on every chance he'd gotten that day- he wondered if there was something about being seventeen that made every decision seem so dire.

"You all right, man?" The sound of Chris Watson's voice came from a few lockers away.

Not realizing he'd been closing his eyes, Quinn shook his head, trying to wake up his brain, then gave Chris a small nod. "Yeah man, I'm just...thinking."

"Good practice today, huh?" said Chris. "Think we'll have a shot at playoffs this year?"

It was football season, and although Quinn's heart didn't beat for the sport the same way it did for baseball, he appreciated the rough contact and aggressive nature of it. Dealing with his mom's habits required an outlet, and as her addiction and the company she kept continued to become more dangerous and intense, Quinn always seemed to be in the mood to shove or punch something.

He really was a decent player, but it was more Chris's sport. As a junior, Chris was the team's star quarterback, and he lived and breathed for Fall and everything that came with it.

"I think we should see how the homecoming game goes and then we can worry about playoffs," Quinn said as he dressed.

"I asked Lana to homecoming," said Chris, pulling his Traverse City Trojans t-shirt on. "We're both up for homecoming court and I think we've got a good shot."

"Yeah…" Quinn trailed off, his mind distant.

Chris sat on the bench in front of the lockers, closer to Quinn now. "You finally gonna have a *real* date this year? Or are you and Rae sticking to the *just going as friends so we don't have to acknowledge our real feelings* routine?"

This quickly snapped Quinn out of his haze. "What do you mean?"

Chris shook his head and laughed dryly, putting up his hands as if in surrender. "I'm sure it's none of my business."

"No, but you seem to have an opinion on it, and you've never been one to hold back on those."

Needing no more encouragement, Chris let it out, "Why the hell do you pretend to be fine just following her around like a lost puppy waiting to be loved?"

"The *fuck*, man?" Quinn bellowed, taken aback by Chris's bluntness. Chris was always direct, but he'd never commented on this particularly touchy subject before now.

"Sorry, dude, but you've obviously been into her for like, what? A year now?"

Three years.

When Quinn remained silent, Chris continued, "All I'm saying is it's time to put up or shut up. If she ain't into you after nine years of friendship, she ain't gonna be. At least you can get your answer and try to find someone else who is."

Of course that was exactly Quinn's fear. If he told Rae how he felt and she didn't reciprocate those feelings, then what? Sure, he could find other girls to spend time with and make out with and probably have sex with if he wanted, but Rae was different. She was his best friend. She had been since her seventh birthday when she spoke it into being.

"This is Quinn Casey… I think he's my new best friend."

If he put his feelings out there and it backfired, he wasn't just getting rejected by some girl. He'd be putting a strain on their friendship, changing it, and making things awkward between them. The way his home life was with his drug-addicted mother, never having money, and never knowing what the next day might bring, Rae had been his one constant. She was the only part of his life that was unchanging. *She* was the one thing he could count on and the one thing he'd been able to count on for nine years. Telling her he'd been in love with her since he was fourteen seemed like too big a risk. Nevertheless…

"I'm gonna ask her this time. For real," Quinn said before he could stop himself. It was a decision he'd already made earlier that day but saying it out loud to someone seemed to solidify it.

Chris beamed and clapped Quinn on the back. "It's about damn time! You'd better do it now before you have a chance to puss out."

"Yeah, I'm meeting her out in the parking lot when she's out of swim practice." Quinn felt a smile finding its way to his face. "We're supposed to go get something to eat."

"Perfect! Ask her before you get in her car though," said Chris. "The less you put it off, the better."

Quinn nodded, a movie reel playing in his head: Being cool and calm as he asked her to go to the dance, her giggling and pointing out they always go together, him taking both of her hands in his and explaining he meant *for real, as dates*. Then Rae would act surprised, but say yes, and they would get into her car, except she'd tell him to drive because they were on a real date now so *he* should chauffeur *her* around. They'd get to the restaurant to eat, but before getting out of the car, he'd turn her towards him and lean in, their lips would meet for an innocent kiss, but then she would want more. So he'd kiss her harder. They'd start breathing heavier, start peeling layers off each other until…

"Case!" Chris snapped his fingers in front of Quinn's face.

Quinn blinked and shook his head and, noticing his mouth had gone dry, he took a long swig from his water bottle.

"Did you just imagine some sort of scenario in which asking Rae to the dance leads to you guys having sex in the parking lot?" Chris asked, an amused look on his face. "Because I totally did that before asking Lana."

Quinn was only slightly embarrassed. "And how *did* she react?"

"Well, all our clothes stayed on, so it wasn't exactly what I had in mind. But she did say yes," Chris said with a shrug.

Quinn and Chris finished getting dressed, slung their bags over their shoulders and walked out of the locker rooms and back toward the school parking lot. Quinn stopped when he spotted Rae next to her silver Beamer. Her hair was wet from a shower, and she'd squeezed herself back into a pair of tight skinny jeans that always made that beast in his chest stir.

"Go get your girl, Case," said Chris as he gave him another clap on the back, then walked toward his own car.

With a deep inhale, Quinn continued walking toward Rae, heart racing and hands shaking with anticipation. He was one row of cars away when he paused, watching another figure approach Rae and lean coolly against her car next to her.

His heart dropped. Not just into his stomach; he was pretty sure it actually fell out of his body and onto the pavement beneath him.

Liam Hamilton's body language was easy enough to read from where Quinn was standing. He had one side of his body leaning on Rae's car, angled toward her, head dipped low as he spoke, looking at her hungrily with a cocky grin on his face. He was asking her out.

Fuck.

Quinn was undecided whether he wanted to stay back and give them space to have their conversation or if he should barge in and interrupt. Maybe he could get to them before Liam got his question out. Or maybe he'd get there just in time for Rae to say yes, and he was sure he didn't want to hear that.

Liam Hamilton was a senior on the varsity football team with Quinn. He was a typical jock in most ways: Over six feet tall, short blond hair, one of the few high school seniors who could successfully grow facial hair that wasn't patchy. He had that confident look of a person who had always been well cared-for, wanted for nothing, and had absolutely no idea how lucky he was for it. He strutted around as if everything his parents had been able to provide were his own personal entitlements. Quinn was sure Liam's family was nearly as well off as the DeRoses. A silver spoon baby, so unlike himself.

A possessive growl rose in his chest as he saw Liam put his hand on Rae's arm. He made up his mind to interrupt the moment with hopes that Liam would get the message that this was Quinn's territory and he needed to take his business elsewhere.

"Ready to go, Rae? I'm starving," said Quinn, acting as though he hadn't even noticed Liam standing there in his brand new Under Armour sweats and a white t-shirt that was purposely a size small to showcase his possibly steroid-enhanced muscles.

"Oh, hey, Quinn!" Rae turned and smiled at him. Her smile fell for a second and she looked as though she were carefully crafting her next sentence. "Um, yeah, I'm starving, too. But, hey, uh...Liam just asked me to go to the homecoming dance with him." She gestured toward the blonde jackass next to her. "We hadn't really talked about it yet. I know we usually go together in like a big group, but..."

Shit, is she asking my permission? How the fuck do I do this without looking like a damn territorial caveman?

"Oh, right..." Quinn paused, looking back and forth between Rae and Liam. It suddenly struck him how much they must have in common. They were from the same world. Liam was the kind of guy Rae's parents probably wanted her to end up with. Quinn had been so sure Rae would've gone with him, but here she was, interested in this other guy who seemed so... obvious for her. "I mean, that's up to you, isn't it? I can't tell you who to go with."

What the fuck, man?

Rae looked confused for a few beats and didn't say anything as she just stared at Quinn.

Feeling like he should say something and seriously despising the situation he'd been put in he spat out, "I mean, if you go with Liam it's not like I can't find a real date."

What. The. Actual. Fuck.

Rae's eyebrows shot up in surprise at his remark, not that Quinn could blame her. Why was he acting like such a dick? She was giving him an incredulous look he was sure she'd never given him before and then let out a hollow laugh and turned back to Liam. "I'd *love* to go with you. I'd hate to hold Quinn back from his numerous other prospects."

113

"Great!" Liam flashed a megawatt smile at Rae and gave her a kiss on the cheek. "I'll see you this weekend at the club, right? Tennis tournament, I think. We can go over the details then."

The subtle mention that their families were members at the same country club felt like a slap to Quinn's face. Rae gave a nod to Liam with a "see you then". Quinn fully understood the meaning of Liam's smirk as he bumped his shoulder unnecessarily hard into Quinn's when he walked by. *Checkmate*. Quinn felt his nostrils flare as he physically bit his tongue to keep from saying anything else.

Rae turned around and assessed Quinn briefly before blurting, "What the fuck, Quinn?"

"What?" It was more a clipped statement than a question.

"You're being an ass," Rae said as she tossed her bag in the back seat, holding the door open for him to do the same.

Apparently I am an ass. A fucking stupid one.

Quinn let out a sigh, though the anger he felt didn't fade. He walked around to the passenger's side of the car. "It's just been a long day."

They got into the car and Rae started the engine. "Maybe you're hangry. I'm sure food will help. I'm always ravenous after swim practice."

"I'm really not that hungry," said Quinn, unable to take the attitude out of his voice.

"You just said you were starving," Rae pointed out. She paused then sighed. "If you didn't want me to go with him, you should've said something."

This annoyed him further. "You didn't have to say yes...and I don't see why it should be my choice who you go with." He could feel himself glaring at her. "You're telling me if I'd made the decision for you and told him to back the fuck off because we were going together, you wouldn't have punched me in the balls for being a controlling dickhead?"

"Is that what you wanted to do?" Rae asked, seeming genuinely curious.

"No," Quinn lied. After a beat he finished, "I wanted you to choose for yourself."

Rae considered him and his response for a few moments before turning her car out of the parking lot. She let out another sigh, "Don't say *dickhead*. It makes me think of that creepy thumb guy from *Spy Kids*, but instead of thumbs he's just all dicks."

Quinn let out a quick snort of laughter and shook his head, though there was little humor to his clipped laugh. Leave it to Rae to be able to make him laugh even when he was fuming. He turned his attention to the window and ran a hand through his now cold, half-wet, full-messy mop of hair. He thought about what Chris had said in the locker room about his and Rae's routine. Well, apparently they weren't going together this time, but they were definitely sticking to the routine of ignoring their actual feelings for each other. Only for the first time Quinn felt like he wasn't the only one putting on an act.

The Trojans won their homecoming game 56-28, which meant everyone was ready to really celebrate at the after-game mixer and of course at the dance the next day. Chris was flying high, loving all the attention he'd gotten from his plays. Jett, who was an offensive linebacker on the team, had made some solid tackles that had received him a lot of recognition which he was basking in. Jett loved all sports, but hockey was his number one. It wasn't often he received the same high praise and admiration he got on the ice, and he was loving it.

As Quinn got ready in Chris's room, the guys talked about some of their better moments the previous night. It was strange to Quinn that they were still going to dinner and the dance in a group, but Rae wasn't part of it.

He'd ended up asking Britney Garrett, a sideline cheerleader who'd been flirting with him in several of their classes after Rae had made the decision to go with Liam. He wondered if Britney had always flirted with him like this, but he'd been so focused on his crush on Rae that he hadn't noticed before. She was pretty, Quinn thought. She was short, a flyer on the cheer team, with long blonde hair, blue eyes, and she seemed to have a sun tan year round. He was starting to think he had a type.

"Did Britney make you coordinate with her?" Jett asked, tying his necktie for the fourth time.

Quinn was dressed in navy blue dress pants with a matching blazer and a white dress shirt. It was a simple outfit for homecoming, but he had to admit that now that he'd surpassed the six-foot mark and his muscles had really filled out over the last year, he didn't look like the raggedy kid he'd always felt like.

"I think she said her dress was white, or off-white." Quinn replied.

Jett snorted. "Way off, by the sounds of it."

"What's that supposed to mean?" Quinn asked.

"Usually a girl in a white dress is a symbol of purity," said Jett. "And Britney, well, let's just say that's not the word I'd use to describe her."

Quinn paused, looking at Jett in the mirror. Turning to Chris he asked, "Is that true? Am I the only one who didn't know this?"

"You miss a lot when you let one girl become the center of your world," Chris replied. "I mean, they're only rumors, but I've definitely heard she gets around. So, I wouldn't be worried about what you're wearing. Probably won't be for too long."

Looking at himself in the mirror and fixing his hair, Quinn wasn't sure how to feel about this. He'd sort of always imagined his first time would be with Rae, and hers would be with him. Okay, so maybe that was more of a fantasy he liked to play on a loop in his head when he was alone. Regardless, he couldn't admit his feelings to her, and if she had any toward him- which he highly doubted- she hadn't stepped up either, so it seemed unlikely that fantasy would ever come true.

He told himself to just treat homecoming as any other night and not think of it as a big deal. Life would go back to normal on Monday and he'd have his chance to tell Rae how he felt then.

Now with the prospect of sex looming over his head, he was both heart-racing excited and brick-in-his-stomach nervous. What if he did have sex with Britney? How was he supposed to handle his feelings with Rae then? What if she had sex with Liam?

Oh, fuck, don't go there.

Quinn shook his head of the thought. No, he and Britney were *not* having sex. Rae and Liam were *definitely* not having sex. He told himself again that it was just one night of dancing and then he'd go straight to Rae's house tomorrow morning and tell her the truth. Why wait until Monday? That way he wouldn't have the whole weekend to talk himself out of it. He'd tell her that he'd been planning to ask her, but Liam got there first, and that's why he'd been such an ass, but with homecoming behind them, they'd be able to start something for real. Homecoming was just a big show, anyway. He didn't need to see Rae in a fancy dress to know she was all he wanted.

Quinn, Chris, and Jett finished getting ready and hung out until Mrs. Watson called them down to let them know their ride was out front. They'd pitched in together and rented a limousine for the occasion. It was a splurge for homecoming, but it was the best way to fit six of them in a vehicle, and now it felt like their way of celebrating their big win the night before.

Lana, Britney, and Jett's date, Melanie, were all picked up at Lana's house where they'd gotten ready. The girls all had their parents there waiting to take pictures before heading to the restaurant for their dinner reservation.

At the table, Britney insisted on sitting next to, rather than across from Quinn and he'd barely started on the free bread when he began to suspect the rumors Chris and Jett had heard about her were true.

He felt her hand on his leg and looked down briefly to confirm that it was in fact Britney's perfectly manicured hand grasping his right leg. Not thinking anything of it, he dipped his Italian bread in the olive oil mixture in the middle of the table and took a full bite.

Britney's hand slid slowly up his thigh and back down, adding pressure. This was not simply trailing a lazy hand up and down in an affectionate gesture. This was a massage. An upper thigh massage. An upper, *inner* thigh massage. And then- yep. She found it. Not that it was a difficult task. He had little control over how his body responded to a sensual inner thigh massage- he *was* a seventeen-year-old boy, after all- and once it decided it liked something, there wasn't anything he could do to hide it.

Quinn was grateful to have a mouthful of bread when he groaned, eliciting curious looks from the rest of the table. He gave a muffled, "So good," pointing to his mouth.

Everyone quickly got back to their conversations, and Quinn leaned his forearms on the table as Britney continued rubbing the length of his hard cock through his dress pants. A few times he had to stifle a moan or turn it into a cough. He made the mistake of briefly catching Jett's eye as he looked around the table self-consciously to see if anyone was watching. Jett quickly figured out what was going on and had to bite back a laugh, turning toward Melanie and becoming suddenly very interested in her earrings.

Running out of ways to disguise his obvious arousal at getting an over-the-pants hand job at the table, Quinn found himself immensely relieved when Britney stopped abruptly, though he was throbbing and his balls were aching for release.

"Oh my gosh," Britney said in a sweetly innocent voice. "Quinn, I think I left my clutch in the limo. Will you come help me look for it? It has my retainer case and I need it before our food comes."

Quinn cleared his throat and gave a quick nod. Well, there was no hiding it now. He'd just have to make a quick exit through the restaurant so no one saw his hard-on. Letting Britney lead the way out to the limo, Quinn was completely oblivious to what he was in for. It's cute how naive he once was.

Britney climbed into the limo and Quinn followed and began to look for a clutch, whatever that was. Some sort of purse?

Too late, Quinn realized the search for the bag was a ruse. Britney pushed him onto the long bench seat of the limo and kissed him full in the mouth, slipping her tongue between his lips and into his mouth. He couldn't help the groan that escaped, even though he was sure he really had no idea what was happening. The moans coming from Britney were having a surprising effect, intensifying his arousal, which he'd thought had already reached its limit.

Her hands were unbuckling his belt, unbuttoning his pants, pulling the zipper down. He wasn't entirely sure how to handle this situation unfolding before him. He didn't think he wanted this. Well, he didn't want *her* to do this. They hardly spoke on the way to the restaurant, and apparently her way of making dinner conversation was to start rubbing one off under the table.

She began kissing down his neck and slid down his body until she was on her knees on the floor of the limo and his erection had been freed from its navy blue prison.

"Oh fuck," Quinn groaned as she put her mouth on him. The times he'd pictured this happening, he thought he'd be able to lean his head back and relax, but he found himself straining to not burst too soon. He wrapped a hand in her hair, the sensations he was feeling completely blocking out all other thoughts. She worked her mouth up and down, tongue licking, hands pumping, and before long he was letting out a low, guttural moan. His hips jerked and thrusted, emptying himself inside her mouth. "*Goddamn.*" Quinn threw his head back on the leather head rest of the seat, chest heaving, trying to come back to reality after this celestial experience.

"Oh, look," Britney's bright voice cut through the fog filling his brain. "There's my clutch." She picked up a small white purse off the far end of the seat that couldn't possibly contain more than a few cards and, likely, a retainer case. Britney gave him a wink and slid toward the door. "Come on, you'll need to eat if you want to keep up later."

Britney dipped out of the limousine and Quinn simply stared after her in shock.

What...the fuck *just happened?*

He had no real recollection of deciding that it was something he wanted Britney to do. She'd just sort of...started, and his body responded. Not that he'd had absolutely no say in what had just happened, but he did feel a little like he'd been attacked. By a mouth.

Once he'd pulled his boxers and pants back on, and had successfully tucked his shirt back in, Quinn slipped out of the limo and followed Britney back into the restaurant. He hoped he didn't look too disheveled, although he was sure Jett at least had an idea of what had just happened out there. Quinn was sure he'd be forced to give him a play-by-play once they got to the dance but wasn't entirely sure he wanted too many people knowing about it. If everyone except him had known about Britney's reputation, how long would it take for this to get back to Rae?

They made it through dinner and arrived at the dance without any more spontaneous attacks. The weight of what happened didn't hit him until he saw Rae enter the gymnasium on Liam's arm, looking like an elegant and alluring goddess in her light blue and lace dress. Quinn couldn't take his eyes off of her and he was suddenly hit with the same feeling of regret, or more likely self pity, that he'd felt a couple weeks ago when he'd witnessed Liam asking her out only moments before he'd planned to ask her himself. He wondered what their night would have been like if he was with her instead. He was almost certain he wouldn't have gotten a blow job in the back of a limousine, but he was sure he would've found a way to survive.

He saw Liam step away from her to greet some of his buddies and Quinn decided to take this chance to talk to her. It had only been two weeks since he'd struck out with Rae and in that time, things had seemed a little strained. He wanted to make sure that once this night was over, things would go back to normal.

"Hey," Quinn said as he approached Rae. "You look...amazing."

Rae turned and looked up at him, smiling her familiar, bright smile. "Hey! Thanks." She looked down at her dress before looking him over. "You look handsome. You got a haircut...and you tamed it somehow."

"Don't try to run your hands through it," said Quinn. "They'll get stuck. I think I'm ninety percent gel right now."

Rae looked curiously amused, then touched the top of his hair. "Oh, yeah, that's crusty." She giggled and looked at him, biting her lip. "Who'd you come with?"

"Uh, Britney Garrett," Quinn replied hesitantly.

Eyebrows shooting up in surprise and her face twisting into a suggestive smirk, Rae said, "Trying to lose the V-card, are we?"

Quinn groaned and put his face in his hands. He looked up with a wince, "I had to be the only person who didn't know that about her."

Nodding, unconvinced, Rae said, "Sure, just make sure you wear protection. And I'm not just talking about a condom. I mean, full body armor. She will attack you like a grizzly bear in heat."

"Are you trying to scare me so I don't do it?" Quinn asked, one eyebrow raised.

"Maybe." Rae shrugged. "I'd hate for you to catch the herp at the fragile young age of seventeen."

"Is that all?" Quinn's head was down, voice lowered so that only Rae could hear him.

Rae looked at him, her eyes searching briefly before falling on his mouth. He wondered if she was going to kiss him and wasn't sure how he'd feel having his first kiss with Rae on the same night he'd already been mauled by a sexually ravenous cheerleader. That suggestive smirk returned and she raised a thumb to wipe under his bottom lip. "Lipstick," she said, showing Quinn the dark red color that was now on Rae's thumb.

Heat flushed Quinn's cheeks. "It was a narrow escape."

Rae's gaze was piercing and Quinn counted the seconds before she spoke again. Thankfully when she did there was a smile and a bit of a laugh in her tone. "Well, I can't say I blame her. You clean up pretty good, Quinn Casey."

"Thanks." Quinn grinned down at his feet. While he was here talking easily again with Rae he thought maybe he didn't even have to wait until tomorrow to tell her the truth. Part of him wanted to wash off what had happened earlier in the limousine before getting sincere with her, but he wasn't sure he could wait. "Listen, I'm sorry...for being such a dick the other week."

"Don't say dick," said Rae. "I thought we talked about that."

"You told me not to say dick*head*," Quinn said pointedly. "You say 'dick' all the time. Why can't I say it but you can?"

"Because 'dick' sounds better coming out of my mouth than yours."

Quinn looked up at the ceiling trying to stifle a laugh, but failed. "Yeah, I would imagine dick sounds way better in your mouth, that's a good point."

Rae straightened and Quinn saw her blush when she caught his clever quip. "Quinn. Casey. Casey."

Laughing, Quinn pointed a finger at her. "Don't use my middle name out loud. People will *know* my mom was on drugs when she named me."

Rae clapped a hand over her mouth, trying to cover up her laugh.

"Are you laughing? You're laughing because my mom is a drug addict? That's really insensitive, Rae, wow," Quinn pressed, amused. She was really the only person he could joke like this with, and it felt good after the strain that had been put on their friendship over the last couple of weeks.

They continued joking around and talking like they always did. It was as if nothing had changed, and they really had come to the dance together. Quinn asked Rae to dance during a slow song and they stayed on the dance floor for a few more upbeat songs after that. He wasn't sure at what point he remembered that he actually had come with a date, thinking she must be around here somewhere. Although, he wasn't particularly interested in another savage attack. Unfortunately, Liam had *not* forgotten that he'd come with a date.

The DJ put on another slow song and Liam cut in, glowering at Quinn before he and Rae could couple up again. At first, Quinn felt slighted, but the friendly, even flirty, banter between him and Rae was still making him buzz. Plus, he couldn't really blame Liam for wanting to dance with his own date, especially when she looked like that.

Quinn wandered over to the beverage table, where he was sure someone had spiked the punch, as was some sort of tradition at these things. Jett was holding a plastic cup in each hand, sipping from one of them when Quinn approached.

"Britney was looking for you," Jett said with a sly grin. "Looking for a little more back seat limo action probably."

Quinn groaned and rolled his eyes. "I can't fucking believe that happened."

"And what happened exactly?" Jett asked, wiggling his eyebrows suggestively.

"I was viciously attacked," Quinn replied, searching the room for his date. He wasn't interested in another round, but he'd need to keep tabs on her location so he could successfully dodge her.

"You looked pretty relaxed for being attacked," Jett said. "*Sounded* pretty relaxed, too."

"Shut up," Quinn grumbled. "I should've stopped her. Jesus, I got a fucking blow job in the back seat of a limo and all I can think about is what Rae's gonna think if she finds out."

"What if she does?" Jett shrugged. "She doesn't own you, dude."

More than I'd like to admit.

Sighing, Jett handed one of the cups of punch to Quinn. "Like you said, she didn't *have* to say yes to Liam. But she did and she's here with him and you're going to have to deal with it."

Quinn winced, but still didn't speak.

"Got it that bad, huh?" Jett said, studying his friend. "Well, for what it's worth, I think the guy's an asshole. Rae's smart...she'll figure it out."

Quinn gave an indistinct nod, unsure if he should feel better or worse that Rae was out with a guy who everyone seemed to think was a complete ass. Thinking he wouldn't mind some fresh air, he downed the small drink in his hand and headed toward the door to the gymnasium that led outside to the courtyard.

He stopped at the door, turning and scanning the crowd of coupled bodies, some dancing an awkward distance from their partners, others practically squeezed together in a close and intimate embrace. Quinn hoped to catch a glimpse of Rae again before stepping outside, just needing to see her face again, and silently sending up a prayer that she was looking around for him, or at least looking miserable and annoyed to be stuck with Liam Hamilton.

He had to do a double take when he saw her. He'd seen the light blue and lace of her dress, the sparkling headband in her glossy blonde hair that was cascading down the bare back that her dress showed off so elegantly. She was not looking for him or looking annoyed at being stuck with *not* Quinn as her date. Rae's arms were wrapped around the back of Liam's neck, pressing their mouths together in a fervent kiss.

Quinn's breath rushed out of him so suddenly, as if he'd been punched in the stomach. A squeezing pain in his chest made his legs lock and a rolling sensation in his stomach had him feeling sick. He looked away and swallowed, then looked back, focusing his sights on Liam rather than Rae. Anger was easier to deal with than whatever this other feeling was. Jaw clenched, hands balled into fists at his sides, Quinn shoved the door open and walked out, past the courtyard, away from the school, and into the chilling night air.

CHAPTER 13

The silence of Quinn's hotel suite was too quiet. He'd been lying on the couch with his iPad trying to plan out his date with Rae, but everything he came up with sounded weak and underwhelming. This was the date that would make or break his shot with her. This wasn't about just having sex, although that was certainly a point he was looking forward to. This was about having her. Getting her. Keeping her.

At last, when he was about to resign himself to the bar to ask for Chris and Jett's advice, his phone rang. Quinn sat up to see the name Mamacita appear on his phone, a smile tugged at his lips and he got an idea.

"Hola, Mamacita," Quinn said after swiping to answer the call.

"Oh good, I wasn't sure I'd be able to get in touch," Zoey's voice came across the other end. "How are you? How's your mother doing?"

"I'm fine, mom's fine. I need your help," Quinn rushed all in one breath.

"Um, all right, is everything okay?" Zoey asked, now concerned.

"Yes, everything's great," said Quinn. "Except I need your creativity. You're good at coming up with stuff. You've managed to get me out of some tight spots and keep my appearance a hell of a lot cleaner than it should be."

"This doesn't sound promising..."

"Zoey, I have a date tonight and I need it to be big," Quinn stated.

"A date? Quinn, you go out with women all the time," said Zoey, and Quinn could hear her eye-roll from across the line.

"Not like this, Zo," said Quinn. He braced himself for the admission. No doubt Zoey would freak out. She'd been trying to get him to tell her about Rae since she'd started working for him two years ago. "This is the girl. The one I always pretend doesn't exist when you ask about my mysterious past love. The one that got away. The..." he paused, taking a deep breath. "This girl is probably the love of my life and I really, really, *really* need to not fuck it up."

Silence.

Quinn waited a few beats. "You still there?"

More silence.

Checking his phone to make sure the call hadn't dropped, "Zo-"

"Oh my God. Oh...my God. *Oh my God!*" Zoey exclaimed, followed by a high-pitched shriek. Quinn winced and pulled the phone away from his ear briefly. "Quinn! Are you serious? How? When? Ohmigod, Quinn...is this a joke? This had better not be a joke!"

"It's not a joke. I'm completely serious," Quinn replied.

Another shriek of excitement.

"So are you going to help me or not?" Quinn asked. "I have no idea how to do this date, but it needs to be the best."

"Yes! Yes, I will help you! Oh, Quinn, I'm so happy for you!" Zoey squealed again. "What's her name?"

"Raelyn DeRose. I just call her Rae, though."

"Oooh, Rae..." Zoey cooed. "Quinn, I can't believe it. I mean, I knew there was a girl in your past, but I thought it was like someone who'd broken your heart or rejected you. I didn't realize you still thought of her as the *love* of your *life!* And you're actually going to do something about it!"

"I've spent the last six years thinking I'd blown my last chance with her. And then I ran into her again and it was like...this is it. I *have* to make this work, Zoey. I need to," said Quinn.

"Aw, Quiiiinn, that's the sweetest thing. And it came from *you!*"

"Yes, I have feelings and a past. Everyone's shocked," Quinn huffed. "Now can you help me? It's tonight. I have an idea but I don't know if she'd like it."

"First tell me about her," Zoey said. Quinn could hear her settling in on the other line like she was getting comfy on the couch, ready to gossip with her girlfriends. "How'd you meet? What are some of your favorite memories? How did you screw it up?"

"Why are you assuming *I* screwed it up? Maybe it was just poor timing. Maybe *she* screwed up and I've had enough time to get over it." It was stupid to get defensive when he had in fact been the one to mess everything up, but he didn't appreciate the assumption.

"Quinn, please."

There was a moment of stubborn silence before Quinn sighed, "Okay, yeah I fucked up."

"Tell me everything. Start from the beginning, and don't leave out the messy parts."

Feeling as though Zoey might simply be satisfying her own curiosity by asking for the full story, Quinn hesitated. However, the idea he had for the date *did* have a lot to do with things that had happened in the past. Deciding that some background information wouldn't hurt, he began.

"Okay, well, we met when we were seven..." He told her everything. The story of how they met and how embarrassed he was when Rae's dad insisted on dropping him off after the party. The first time he ever saw Rae's house and how he couldn't figure out why in the world a girl who lived like this wanted to be friends with him. The first time she stuck up for him at school when some of the rich kids teased him for his thrift store clothes. The sports they always played. Rae insisting her parents take her and her friends to a Tigers game for her eleventh birthday because she knew Quinn didn't get birthday parties. That day at the local ballpark when he started falling for her and how that was one of his favorite memories.

Then came high school. Playing seven minutes in heaven their freshman year and reluctantly making out with some other girl when the bottle did *not* land on Rae. Getting even more upset when she also did not land on him. Going to homecoming as friends, then junior year getting beat to the punch by Liam Hamilton. Rae and Liam's short-lived relationship after the dance, and Quinn avoiding being around them as much as possible. The big locker room fight when he'd overheard Liam bragging about how far he'd gotten with her. Senior homecoming and prom. Even graduation night. Then the last time he saw Rae in college, thinking he was finally getting another shot and screwing it up in less than a few hours.

"... and then we almost had sex last night, but it just didn't feel right. To do it like that, I mean. She, and *us*, felt more right than anything, but..." Quinn trailed off, hoping she understood what he meant.

"Wow..." Zoey said after a pause. "That's a lot to unpack."

"Yeah, I know," Quinn said, running his hand nervously through his hair.

"Quinn, I feel like this girl is your soul mate. You need to not screw it up this time."

"Yes, I'm aware." Quinn didn't appreciate the reminder of just how much was riding on this date going well.

"And I want you to know that you're an idiot. Actually, I think you both might be idiots. Why the hell did you not just tell her how you felt in high school? She obviously was into you, too," Zoey added.

A large sigh escaped him again. "It seemed like it sometimes, but then she'd just...I don't know- like homecoming. She just kissed Liam after I was so sure we were getting on the same page."

"You got a blowie that night in the back of a limousine," Zoey said pointedly. "I don't think you can get too upset about a kiss."

"That's different. That girl attacked me. I was innocent- yes, once upon a time, I was the innocent one being taken advantage of. That was all her," Quinn said defensively.

"She was probably a foot shorter than you. Did you try to stop her? Did it ever occur to you to shove her hand away under the table?" Zoey asked, and Quinn could just imagine her with her hand on her hip and a sassy eyebrow raised in challenge.

"Right, well...I didn't want to be rude," Quinn mumbled.

Zoey's laugh was hollow, "What a gentleman you are. But you're lucky I'm a complete sucker for things like this. Let's hear your idea."

The date would require a few phone calls, and help from Chris and Jett, and he might have to get Amira involved, too. Throughout his conversation with Zoey, she noticed his longing for a chance at a do-over, a chance to do some things differently, or to simply go back and relive some of those favorite moments, and that's exactly what this date would be about.

Once everything was set, Quinn showered, shaved, and got dressed in a pair of dark blue jeans, a gray slim-fit button-down shirt, and a navy blazer. The black Chuck Taylors were intended to give the look a nostalgic touch. He'd lost count of how many pairs he'd run through before finding his first pair of Nikes, but whenever he thought of those days playing ball with Rae, he'd thought of these shoes.

At seven o'clock on the dot, Quinn pulled into Rae's driveway and the nerves returned in full force. When was the last time he'd shaken this much? After taking three steadying breaths, he hopped out of the Bronco and walked up to the front porch where he'd kissed Rae just that morning. He knocked on the door and heard Harry's boom of a bark on the other side.

The door swung open. Rae was standing there in an ice blue dress that landed above the knee. It had a halter neckline and when she turned to the side, Quinn noticed the back was almost completely open, stopping just past her waistline. She wore strappy sandals, and her long hair was cascading down to the middle of her back in waves. He was staring again, taking in her appearance, sweeping his eyes over her from head to toe.

The nervous shaking had disappeared with the familiar sight of his best friend, although his heart must have skipped a beat. He had to remind himself to breathe and looked up to meet her gaze. Feeling himself smile, probably like an idiot, Rae let out a shy laugh. He couldn't believe this was the first time they were doing this. Fuck, what would his fourteen-year-old self say if he saw Rae standing here looking like this? Guarantee, he wouldn't still wait fifteen years to ask her out.

"You look perfect," Quinn finally said, after searching his brain for words that he remembered.

"You're not so bad yourself," Rae replied with a smirk. Her gaze dropped to his shoes. "I know you switched to Nikes at some point, but I always imagine you in those anyway."

Quinn gave a satisfied grin and inwardly high-fived himself for at least doing this much right.

Looking down at her own dress she said, "I hope this is okay. Amira was over here earlier and said I needed a nice dress."

"It's perfect," Quinn said, drinking in her full appearance once more before offering his arm. "Are you ready?"

With a nod, Rae looped her arm through his, gave Harry a few pats and pulled the door shut. Quinn walked her to the Bronco, opened the door and helped her up into the vehicle before walking around and getting in the driver's seat. This formal behavior with Rae seemed so strange. Tonight needed to be different, but he couldn't help feeling like being too formal was really not the way to go. They always felt most comfortable when they were teasing and joking, just having fun with each other.

"Ready for me to romance your pants off?" Quinn said brightly, deciding he needed to stop overthinking everything that he did or said.

"I'm not wearing pants," Rae said, looking down at her bare legs.

"Okay, ready for me to romance your panties off? At least that's something I know I'm good at."

"Who says I'm wearing panties?" she asked, raising an eyebrow as she looked at him, eyes twinkling.

He blinked and dropped his stare to the skirt of her dress, then back up. "That's cruel. Now I'm just going to be wondering all night."

"Oh, I'm sure you won't have to wonder *all* night," Rae said with a wink.

A low groan mixed with a laugh as it escaped him. "I put a lot of thought into this night. You're just going to have to hold onto your panties or...whatever. We're not cutting straight to the sex. We can do that next time."

"That's awfully presumptuous, Mr. Casey," said Rae. "You seem to be quite sure of how this night's going to go already."

Approaching a red light, Quinn took his eye off the road to look at Rae with his most seductive smolder. "Trust me, baby doll. If I wanted to cut right to the hot and sweaty stuff, I wouldn't have any trouble getting there." He reached a hand over and gently caressed her upper thigh. Rae's skin flushed under his touch and she took in a quick breath. He took his hand away and noticed her chest decompress as she let out her breath. "I just want you to know you're worth more to me than that. I want to make up for being such an idiot in the past, and I need you to see how much I mean that."

Quinn watched her breathe in the passenger seat for a few moments. The twin swells of her breasts gently moved up and down in a slow, steady rhythm. The sexy smirk returned to her face and Quinn was overcome with the urge to kiss it when the light turned green and the car behind them honked at them to get moving.

"You're going to make up for your past mistakes in just this date?" Rae asked curiously. "Which mistakes would those be?"

"You'll just have to wait and see." Quinn took her hand in his, grateful that she'd switched his arm into this splint so he actually could hold her hand.

After a short drive, the Bronco pulled back into the parking lot of Hotel Indigo and Rae looked skeptically at Quinn. "I thought we weren't starting with sex?"

"We're not," said Quinn. "There's a rooftop restaurant and I hear the food up there is the tits."

"Isn't this the hotel you're staying at?" she asked.

"Yes, but I've mostly been eating the protein shakes I brought and the burgers at Trojan Horse. I was waiting to bring you here with me to lose my food virginity to this place."

"We're losing our virginity together?" Rae questioned, eyeing him knowingly, and he instantly wished he'd phrased it differently. That brought up bad memories. *Guess I better just roll with it...*

He turned the car off. "Yes, and I've been waiting a very long time for this. I'd better get you up there before you change your mind." Practically jogging around the car to get the door, he scooped her out of the seat and threw her over his good shoulder. She shrieked and Quinn was sure several people were turning to watch, but he didn't care.

"Quinn! I'm wearing a dress!" Rae squealed through laughter.

Strategically, he slid her back down to the ground, careful to keep his hand under her skirt. A finger caught the lace band of her panties and he snapped it against her skin. "Just had to check."

He held his arm out for her again and she took it as they walked into the hotel lobby and to the elevator.

Outside the rooftop restaurant, Quinn wrapped his arm around Rae and held her close to him, thinking how incredibly lucky he was to have this chance. He probably didn't deserve it, but he was going to make the most of it. Rae leaned into his side as they waited to be seated and he let out a calm breath, squeezing her closer into him.

"Hey!" A man's voice came from somewhere beside Quinn. "You're Quinn Casey, right? You play for Los Angeles?"

Quinn turned at the sound of his name and faced a college-aged man whose arm was around the shoulders of a curvy woman with bronze skin and long black hair. He gave a polite nod and a wave with a smile.

The guy's girlfriend seemed to recognize him suddenly and her bronze cheeks were tinted with red. "Oh, my gosh, you are!" She looked from her boyfriend back to Quinn. "You're on my hall pass list! I can't believe you're actually like...right here."

Quinn looked down at Rae to see her reaction. She was trying not to laugh as she turned to the young woman. "That's actually why I'm here with him. My husband's at home probably puking his guts out, hoping I don't actually go through with it."

The woman looked mildly horrified before turning her attention back to her boyfriend.

Quinn held Rae close to him and had to fight the urge to run his hands all over her body. Instead he slid his hand down to her hip and squeezed her ticklish spot which elicited a squeal and a jump, followed by an involuntary giggle. Rae swatted Quinn as he chuckled to himself and pulled her back toward him again. He gave her a kiss on the side of her head and nipped playfully at her ear. "Don't forget, I know your weakness," he whispered. Rae straightened and color blossomed up from her chest, into her neck and face, and fuck if he didn't love being able to do that to her.

They were seated at a table where they were read the specials and given a drink menu which Rae politely declined after the previous night's events. She ordered a sparkling water while Quinn ordered a pint of Two-Hearted Ale. The food was indeed the tits, but it didn't come close to the high he felt just sitting there talking with Rae, teasing, flirting, picking up their witty banter that seemed to come so easily. Quinn had never been able to talk to other women this way. It wasn't that he hadn't met any intelligent girls who were capable of conversation, he just always felt like he was miles away during those interactions. Some part of him must have known he was meant to be here with Rae instead.

The table was cleared except for their glasses at nine o'clock. Almost an hour and a half had flown by as they caught up, going more in depth than what they'd been able to during their meetings at the bar with Jett and Chris that week. They talked about college, and everything that had happened in the time they'd spent apart. Their dating horror stories, professional achievements, Rae talked about her family, and then they circled back to the nightmarish world of casual dating.

He gathered their lives were both filled with flings and one-night stands. Quinn began to realize that, although he'd done what he could to avoid his predisposition for addiction, she had become his. Rae was a strong shot of whiskey that burned all the way down and stuck with him, and all the other women he'd been with were like chasers. He tried watering down the burn that Rae had left behind, but none had been strong enough to make him forget.

The wait staff were pulling tables back and creating a dance floor. The hanging lights that were strung up all around the roof flickered to life and the music was turned up to a significantly higher level that clearly gave out the message that it was time to dance.

Quinn held his hand out to Rae as they stood to allow a couple of waiters to move their table. The music registered in her ears and she smiled to Quinn. "Is this T-Pain?"

"Yeah, I think it is." He observed her as she mouthed some of the words to *Buy You a Drank*. "I paid the DJ to play songs only from 2009 and earlier."

Rae looked at him curiously. "Why 2009?"

"I figured it would make up for junior and senior homecoming, and senior prom," Quinn explained.

The look Rae gave him was everything he could have asked for, a beaming smile that brightened the blue in her eyes to turquoise. She reached up on her tip-toes and planted a kiss on his lips and took his hands. "Let's go dance like horny teenagers!"

They lost count of how many T-Pain songs they danced through, along with The Black-Eyed Peas, Ne-yo, Beyoncé, Maroon 5, and Sean

Paul. They joked about the content of the songs and how cool they probably thought they were dancing along to such adult material when they barely knew what a G-spot was. By the time they left the rooftop, they had aches in their sides from laughing so hard and their legs were sore from trying to pop, lock, and drop it through the entire song by Huey. Though Quinn had only had his one beer at the beginning of the night, he was sure they looked drunk as they stumbled out of the hotel to his car, clutching onto each other to hold themselves up from laughing.

"Onto part three," said Quinn, starting up the vehicle.

"Part three?" Rae asked, buckling her seat belt as Quinn pulled out of the parking spot.

"Part one was dinner, part two was the homecoming-slash-prom do-over, and now we're onto part three," Quinn couldn't wipe the smile off his face. This night had already gone so perfectly. He couldn't wait to see the next part unfold.

"How many parts are there?"

Quinn shrugged. "That all depends on how much energy you have." The combination of Rae's mischievous grin and the warm summer air blowing over them as they drove by the lake with the Bronco's top off filled his chest with such joy, he felt like he was flying.

The sound of gravel under his tires brought back more memories and he was afraid he'd float away when he got out of the vehicle. He had driven to the ballpark where they'd played so many games, held countless practices, and where he'd officially recognized that he was falling for his best friend. He turned the vehicle off, hopped out, and grabbed a ball and a bat out of the back seat before helping Rae out of her side of the car.

"Quinn, you can't play ball right now," said Rae, tapping his splint under his sleeve. Quinn tossed his blazer in the back seat and pushed up his sleeves.

"No, but you can," Quinn replied, tossing the ball underhand to her with his good arm.

Rae caught the ball and looked at him uncertainly. She looked down at the ball, then back at him. "Which memory are you making up for here?"

"Not making up for," said Quinn. "Re-doing. It's one of my favorites."

"Oh, so this one's about you."

"Yes, I'm being selfish. Come on." Quinn grabbed her arm and pulled her into the ball diamond. He handed her the baseball bat and placed his hands on her shoulders, positioning her in the right spot at the home plate, which he noted actually had a plate now.

"I know where to stand now," Rae said.

"That's not the point. Just let me have this." Quinn finished putting Rae in position, walking behind her and grabbing her hips. Rae stuck her butt out, straight into his crotch, giving a little wiggle, and Quinn half laughed, half groaned. Placing his hands on her hips, he reluctantly shifted her weight forward and away from his body.

They ran through this whole scene the way he'd remembered, although with some extra touching, and Quinn was surprised by how much of it Rae remembered, too.

Without a pitcher, there was no real point in squatting down into the catcher's position, but Quinn still did. The view, once again, was not disappointing.

"You don't happen to have another athletic skort, do you?" Quinn asked from behind Rae.

"I might," she replied, giving him that sexy smirk again over her shoulder. "You gonna be okay back there?"

Feeling pleased that she'd remembered her line perfectly, Quinn flashed a grin. "It's not a bad view back here."

"You don't expect me to actually slide into home base in this dress, do you?" Rae asked.

"I was actually really hoping you would," said Quinn with a shrug, "but I suppose we can improvise."

Rae shook her head then turned away, facing the field. With the baseball in her left hand she tossed it into the air and took a swing.

Crack!

The ball flew far into the outfield again and Quinn couldn't help being impressed. Something about this woman wearing this beautifully feminine dress, being able to still play ball better than some guys he knew was such a turn on. Rae took off running, not quite the sprint she'd had all those years ago since she wasn't actually racing the outfielders this time around. Quinn stood just behind home plate and watched as she hit a full sprint after passing third base, heading toward him. He angled his body and stretched out his left arm. This time, instead of sliding into home base, Rae jumped into his arms- or arm, rather- and wrapped her legs around his waist and her arms around his shoulders.

The sound of Rae's laugh as she held onto him put him on cloud nine. He couldn't remember ever feeling this happy. It was more than happiness. It was euphoria.

Rae gave him a kiss on the cheek and pulled back with a smile. Gaze dropping to his mouth, she wrapped her fingers in his hair and pressed her lips to his. Quinn's chest filled once again, with air and with something else he felt he needed even more. Heart pounding and light-headed, this was a moment he wanted to play over and over until he was ninety and couldn't catch her anymore.

Chests heaving, their lips parted but kept close together. With a smile, Quinn kissed Rae's lips again. This was going to be his last first date, and he wanted to put it all out there.

"Ask me why this is my favorite memory," Quinn said, so close his lips brushed Rae's when he spoke.

A smile formed on her lips and he kissed it again. "Why is this your favorite memory?"

He was really swinging for the fences now. "Because this was the moment I realized...I was falling for you."

CHAPTER 14

This was the moment I realized I was falling for you.
The words rung in her head like the loud chime of a clock. Like the Big Ben, only...bigger. Time was all she could think about. All that time. This memory they were reenacting had happened almost fifteen years ago. There was no way.

The smile faded from her face and she looked at Quinn with stunned disbelief. A nervous laugh bubbled out of her lips, "Quinn, we were thirteen."

"I know," he breathed.

"No, there's no way that's when it started." Raelyn was sure she would have noticed. Or at least sure he would have made some kind of move in the last fifteen years.

"Maybe not for you."

"Why didn't you..." The words caught in her throat as she racked her brain for some sort of sign she must have missed.

Quinn's breathing had gone still, as if he were holding his breath, wondering if he'd made a mistake in telling her.

It wasn't a mistake. Just a shock. Why hadn't he told her before? Sure, her feelings for him hadn't started at thirteen, but by fifteen she was at least becoming more interested in the prospect of boys as more than friends. She was a late bloomer in that regard. Most of her early friendships were with boys, so it had taken her a while to see them in any other way. It was the summer before their sophomore year before it hit her how physically attractive he was becoming, but even then she'd tried her best to have strictly platonic feelings toward him. There were plenty of other girls interested in him and she didn't feel like inserting herself into that competition only to come out on the other end having lost a friend. Of course, if he'd expressed interest earlier, there's a good chance she would've taken the risk. Perhaps that's why *he* hadn't tried harder. Their friendship was worth too much to risk. But to hold it in *that* long?

Quinn slid her back to the ground while her brain swam with thoughts of their childhood, their history, and now. She found herself looking up at him, trying to figure out what to say. The pleading look he was giving her told her that she needed to say something. Was he waiting to hear she'd felt that way all that time, too? Words were failing her. What was the correct response here? If words wouldn't work, she knew one language that would be sure to let him know exactly how she felt.

Her arms flew around his neck and she pulled him back in for another kiss. She pressed her mouth harder to his this time, slipping her tongue through his lips and meeting his, making him growl deep in his chest. Goosebumps popped up onto her skin, while simultaneously feeling hot and flushed all over.

Quinn pulled her back up so she could wrap her legs around his waist again. Tangling her fingers in his hair, she pulled him further into her kiss and rocked her hips against him. She wanted him. And she was sure she'd never wanted anything or anyone else more in her life. This amazing, sweet, talented, sexy man had wanted her since they were both just kids. He'd never wavered in that, and tonight he made that perfectly clear.

It felt like there were years of lost kisses and touches and heated moments to make up for. Maybe it wasn't possible to pack fifteen years' worth of missed opportunities into one night, but she was certainly going to try.

Raelyn's eyes were closed as Quinn carried her back to the Bronco, lips never parting. Dear God, she was already wet and they'd only been kissing. Hard metal pressed up against her back as Quinn pushed her against the passenger door. Their lips were pink and swollen from kissing so hard. Raelyn let out a gasp as Quinn began kissing down her jaw to her neck. His hot breath covered her jaw before he switched sides, licking and kissing and sucking at her skin. He held her steady with one strong arm and slid the other up her skirt, massaging and caressing her thigh.

Head lolling back onto the window of the truck, Raelyn savored the feel of Quinn's mouth moving from her neck down to the swell of her breasts. He lay a few soft kisses across her chest before returning his attention to her lips. As he slid his tongue between her lips, she felt a practiced finger slide into her lace thong and she gasped again, letting out a small whimper.

His finger traced down her wet sex and he whispered in her ear, "*Jesus, Rae*, you're so fucking wet for me already."

Heat radiated up her neck from her chest as her nipples went taut. She loved the sound of his voice when he said those words. Her breathing was coming in shallow and fast, eyes closed, face turned toward the sky.

He slipped his finger inside her and another pleasured moan escaped her. His thumb found her clit and began rubbing it in circles. Raelyn's legs tightened their grip around his waist, needing him further inside her.

"Look at me," Quinn's voice was low and smooth, like a purr in Raelyn's ear. "Rae, baby, I want you to look at me while I make you come."

Oh my God.

Raelyn opened her eyes and looked into Quinn's. They had darkened from gold to bronze as he held her gaze, making her feel like she could melt in his arms.

Oh God, he knows what he's doing.

Quinn's finger slid in and out of her as he worked her clit, then two solid fingers filled her.

"*Oh my god*, Quinn," Raelyn breathed, struggling to keep eye contact as her eyes fought to roll back.

"Mmm, you like that, baby? Just wait until it's my cock filling up this tight pussy." Quinn nipped playfully at her ear.

Raelyn rocked her hips against Quinn's hand, determined to be taken over the edge. His filthy mouth was doing almost as good of a job as his fingers at getting her there. He pulled his fingers slowly out then back in, pressing them further, finding her G-spot as he put more pressure on her clit. His pace quickened and she was there, just on the edge of ecstasy.

"Yes, Quinn, oh, fuck yes," Raelyn cried through harsh breaths.

"*Goddamn*, I love hearing my name like that," Quinn groaned.

A smirk played across Raelyn's lips as she touched them to his ear and moaned, "*Quinn*...you're gonna make me come...yes, *Quinn*."

With a growl, Quinn's fingers worked harder, faster until Raelyn cried out, yelling his name into the night air as she shook with her orgasm. She clung to him, digging her nails into his back, moving her hips as the waves kept coming. She rested her forehead to his as her breaths shuddered through her, finally letting her eyes flutter closed.

When Quinn put her back on the ground, her thighs were still shaking and she needed to lean up against the door for support.

With a sweet kiss to her lips Quinn grinned and said, "Part four awaits." He opened the passenger door and gestured for Raelyn to get in.

"There's more?" Raelyn asked, breathless.

"I wasn't exactly planning to fuck you in a baseball field." Quinn's smirk was accompanied by a mischievous quirk of the eyebrow. Raelyn returned his look with a bite of her bottom lip, then let him help her back into the front seat.

Quinn drove them back to her house. In the driveway, the engine shut off and Raelyn was sure Quinn could hear her heart beating through her chest. He'd already given her two toe-curling orgasms without even taking all of her clothes off. She couldn't imagine what the real deal was going to be like. Just kissing him got her all hot and sweaty and wet. What was she going to do with his naked body on top of hers? Under hers? Hell, how was he handling the suspense? She'd at least had two releases of her own. Quinn was saving up for this. And he'd been waiting years longer than she had.

Raelyn's arm fell naturally through his again as they walked toward the house, but when she started heading toward the front porch Quinn stopped, gesturing to go around the garage. There was a small brick paved walkway that led around the garage to the basement entrance in the backyard. It was lined with solar lights, otherwise it would have been completely dark. Quinn led her to the French doors that would take them into the finished basement and paused in front of them.

"Okay, I don't know exactly what this is going to look like. I may have had some help." Quinn reached for the doors and pushed them open.

The doors led directly into her living room that was fully equipped with a mounted flat screen television and sound system, a sectional and a recliner, as well as a bar that was typically kept stocked with her family's wine. Tonight it was transformed. There were blankets and sheets hanging and draped from the ceiling to create a large fort. There was a sheet pulled back like a tent door and she could see inside where the sectional and chairs had been pushed back to make room for a mattress with a ton of blankets and pillows. The mattress faced the TV which was currently featuring *The Sandlot*, an old favorite of theirs.

"When did you do this?" Raelyn asked, jaw dropped.

"Chris, Jett, and Amira snuck in after I picked you up." He looked down at her, hopeful. "Do you like it?"

"I *love* it." Raelyn was still taking in all the details. There were at least a dozen condoms sprinkled on top of the blankets, which was certainly a nice touch. Twinkle lights had been strung up inside the fort, which was something she had always tried to get Quinn to put in their old blanket forts. He had always protested, saying he was not going to hang out inside a "princess fort for sissy girls." Raelyn giggled at the memory and turned to Quinn, "Did Amira have permission to put those lights up?"

Quinn smiled as he replied, "Yeah, I actually insisted."

"You're not going to feel like a sissy girl princess?" Raelyn teased.

Quinn eyed her up and down briefly, "Trust me, nothing that's about to go down in there is suitable for sissy girl princesses."

Oh mama. And just like that my panties are wet again.

Raelyn swallowed as she met Quinn's intense gaze. After kicking his shoes off by the door, he took her hand and ducked into the fort, pulling her in with him. A brief sensation of deja vu flooded her as they stood facing each other by the foot of the bed holding hands, hearts racing. She was seventeen again and about to have sex for the first time.

With her best friend. The pulse visible in Quinn's neck quickened just like it had that night. This wasn't just about the nostalgia of the blanket fort. This was another do-over.

Fingers trembling slightly, Raelyn began unbuttoning his shirt. She wanted to take her time. It didn't matter if they stayed up all night. Raelyn wanted to see all of him. Memorize him. Inhale his warm scent of pine and spice. Run her hands along the hard planes of his stomach. Learn every piece of him with her hands and then her mouth.

She pushed his unbuttoned shirt off his muscled shoulders and let it fall to the floor, drinking in the sight of his bare chest and abs and arms. Dark hair peppered his chest and a trail down the middle led somewhere still hidden. She reached for his belt and was aware of him intently watching her undress him. He didn't try to hurry her along. It was like he knew exactly what she needed and was letting her have it. He'd have his turn soon enough.

The sound of metal clinking as his belt and pants fell to the floor was all Raelyn heard as Quinn stood in front of her in a pair of black boxer briefs that were not doing a good job disguising his arousal. Her breath quickened as she slipped her hands into the waistband of his boxers and tugged them down. He was now standing in front of her completely bare. A Greek God statue...with a massive erection.

A cocky smile tugged at one corner of his lips as he watched her study him. Her eyes slowly made their way up his body and back to his face. She hoped her jaw hadn't dropped like a dope, because she was sure if her mouth were hanging open, she'd be drooling.

Quinn stepped in closer and slid a hand to the back of her neck where he unfastened the buttons holding her halter dress in place. The top half of her dress fell easily and exposed her breasts. His eyes darkened with lust, and he tried to bite back his groan. He stepped behind her and finished unzipping her dress, letting it drop to the floor. His hard chest pressed up against her back as he slid his fingers into the lace band of her thong and slipped it down, joining the pile of clothing at her feet.

He appeared back in front of her, standing close enough that their bodies were touching. Raelyn savored the sensation of her nipples against his bare skin as it sent goosebumps up her arms. Letting her fingers lightly skate up and down his sides, she saw the same chill ripple across his skin. Their eyes met again. Quinn seemed to be waiting for her to make the first move.

She reached for his hand, lacing their fingers together and tilted her face up to meet his lips in a deep, slow kiss. His free hand slid up from her hips until he was palming one breast, massaging gently, lightly teasing her nipple as he circled it with his thumb.

Needing to feel him, Raelyn unlaced their fingers and ran both hands up the flat, hardened plane of his stomach and chest, feeling his warm, rippled muscles beneath her palms. Her hands wrapped around the back of his neck and fingers plunged into his hair, urging him to kiss her deeper, more fiercely.

Quinn soon had both hands firmly grasping her hips as he began walking her backward toward the bed. The backs of her legs met the mattress and she lowered herself onto it, sliding herself up toward the pillows. She took Quinn's hand again and gently pulled him onto her, breathing a sigh of relief at the comforting weight of him once he was laying on top of her. God, his skin was warm and smooth, his cock hard against her thigh so close to where she was wet and aching for him.

For a moment she was equally relieved and terrified at how natural it felt for the two of them to be like this together. She remembered feeling this with him before and it sent a shock of nervous energy through her body. Her eyes flickered back and forth between his, searching for some indication he might feel the same. His golden eyes like liquid amber stared back into hers and she could see everything he felt reflected in them: Fierce admiration, adoration, longing, hopefulness, and yes, lust. Deep and burning.

Though her whole body was humming, pulse practically vibrating, so ready to get the release it had been deprived of for far too long, there was the slightest notion of hesitation. The faintest bit of tension. She needed to relax, she needed reassurance that she could fully give herself over to him this time.

It must have been written all over her face, or he could feel it in the way her body refused to go pliant. Quinn cupped her face with his hand

and traced his thumb lightly over her bottom lip. "Rae, I know I've made mistakes...I won't do anything you don't want me to, but you need to know that *this*...this thing between us...it's not going away. I've wanted you over half my life and that's not changing. I'm all yours...if you want me."

His voice was steady as he spoke, but there was a vulnerability in his eyes that Raelyn couldn't ignore. She knew he meant every word. And it was everything she needed to hear.

She exhaled a breath she hadn't realized she'd been holding and smiled softly up at him, her oldest friend, and curled her arms around his neck. With his mouth covering hers she sighed, relieved, giving herself and her body permission to give in to him. She wanted to trust him as intensely as she once had; her heart, her mind, and her body felt he deserved this chance.

Their kiss began slow and deep once again, but after one...two...three thrusts of her hips against his hard length, Raelyn's moans mixed with Quinn's needy grunts and groans, and they became impatient. They were both needy and demanding, and their bodies, their heart rates, their breathing sped up at once. Raelyn grasped at his hair, clawed at his shoulders, while Quinn explored her body with his hands.

His tongue wrestled with hers, the rough stubble of his jaw scratching her chin, teeth scraping, consuming her pleasured gasps and moans as they mingled with his. He slipped a hand down her body, between her legs to feel her wet crease again, slick with need.

"*Fuck*, Rae," he whispered, bowing his head to look down their bodies where he was touching her. "I love how wet you get for me...*my God*."

She knew she was even wetter than she had been at the baseball field when he made her come. God, she needed this. Needed him. *Fuck* she needed him. "Quinn..." she breathed into his neck as he rocked over her, rutting against her, pressing against her clit.

Holy hell, I'm going to come already...

"Quinn, please," she whimpered. "I want you inside me when I come again."

A primal groan tore out of Quinn's chest and sent a wave of heat all the way up Raelyn's entire body from the ache between her thighs.

He reached for one of the nearby condoms scattered on the bed, then pulled the corner of the comforter back, gesturing with his head for Raelyn to get beneath the covers. She hurried and slipped beneath the sheet and comforter and Quinn settled himself back on top of her, already rolling the condom down his hard length.

She felt his long, firm finger slide into her while another brushed over her clit. He kissed and licked and sucked at her neck. It felt so good. *So fucking good.* All of it. All of him.

"Please, Quinn," Raelyn breathed. "You can't make me wait. Quinn, I fucking need you *now*."

He let out an open-mouthed groan against her skin, placed a steady, bracing hand on her hip and raised his gaze to meet hers. His eyes were glazed over, lids heavy with lust and need and desire. He looked back down their bodies, and her gaze followed. She watched as he held the base of his cock and guided himself to her opening. As the head pushed into her, Quinn bit his lip and the rise and fall of his chest grew heavier. Their eyes flicked back to each other as he pushed himself slowly, deliberately, inch by inch into her.

Oh. My. Godddddd.

Raelyn's eyes rolled back as her head pressed into the pillow, arching her back, his cock filling her up so completely. It was impossible to know whose moan of relief was louder as they meshed together. Their bodies and sounds became one, and when Quinn began his deep, measured thrusts, the room became a symphony of moans and grunts, primal growls, and ragged breaths.

"Oh my- *fuck, Rae*, you feel so good," Quinn groaned, nearly breathless, burying his face in her neck, teeth scraping against the long curve of her throat. "*So good*, oh my God."

Unable to form words, Raelyn's pleas and cries for more came out in gasps and moans and whimpers. She was so wrapped up in the feel of him, the sensation of his skin sliding against hers, his words, his hands on her, so firm and sure, but gentle. Their tongues slid together again, moving with the rhythm of their bodies. Quinn's thrusts into her quickened, pumping harder...faster. Hungry and restless.

And *oh God*, it was exactly what she needed. *More...more, oh my God, it's been too fucking long.* Raelyn slid one hand between them, feeling his stomach, his abs contracting, skin hot and sweating, working so hard to give her everything. She was wrapped so tightly around him, but so wet she felt it on her thighs.

Quinn pressed his forehead to hers, and it was the most intimate experience she'd ever been a part of. His eyes bore into hers and she felt his hot, heavy breath on her lips. He was inside her, but he was also *part* of her; he was inside her head, reading her thoughts, her body's every reaction to each touch, each thrust, each and every kiss and exhale of words. She liked when he kissed her on the mouth, groaned into her lips, felt his words of pleasure vibrate down to her core.

With every movement, he praised her. *Jesus, Rae...yes baby, oh God...it's so good, baby. That's it, yes, oh fuck yes...I know you're gonna come for me...that cock feels good inside you, doesn't it, baby? So...so fucking good.*

She felt the moment her body flushed, from deep between her thighs and all the way up into her face. Goosebumps covered her skin, but she felt heat and sweat all over. She gasped and began grasping desperately behind Quinn's neck, tangling her fingers in his perfectly untamed hair. She was there. She could feel it...*oh God, yes!*

Raelyn pressed her hips up to meet the thrust that would send her straight over the edge, "Oh, yes Quinn...yes, *yes* I'm coming!"

Another growl ripped through his chest and she wanted to capture it, his sound of triumph when he pleased her, satisfied her to her core. He pressed his mouth to her neck just below her jaw, still thrusting, and pumping into her, never letting up as she squeezed around him. And oh God, it felt like it was going to last forever. She was coming and gasping and letting herself fall completely into him, pulling him, begging him to fall with her.

Again, he watched as her body shook and quivered, wrapped so tightly around him. Her sex squeezing him as her orgasm continued to crash through her, legs encircling his waist, not ready to let go. She wasn't sure that she'd ever be ready to let go.

His mouth found hers again and he groaned into a kiss, "So fucking gorgeous when you come for me, Rae...tell me what I need to do so I can see that ten more times before we go to sleep."

Raelyn smiled against his lips. "Ten? I'll pass out after three more like that."

"Then three it is," he grinned. "You're a fucking goddess when you come like that. I love watching you…" His hand slid up her waist and he focused his attention to where he was touching her, gently caressing the side of her breast. She felt the goosebumps sprinkle her skin again and her nipples both went hard once more at his touch. He was looking at her as though he'd never seen something so amazing…so awe-inspiring.

Raelyn's breaths had slowed, but her chest was still rising and falling in a gentle, steady rhythm as she lay beneath him. Quinn dipped his mouth to her breast and swirled his tongue around its perked pink tip, eliciting a small gasp from her. His eyes flashed up to her, keeping his mouth there, sucking and hot and wet. Raelyn arched her back, pushing her chest toward him, urging him to continue.

When he lightly scraped his teeth across her nipple she moaned.

"You like that?" Quinn rasped before doing it again.

"Yes," Raelyn whispered, laying her head back and enjoying his gentle teases.

His cock was still rock solid and full inside her, moving with slow, steady strokes. He may have been planning to take his time, but after fourteen months Raelyn felt like they were playing dominoes with a lit fuse. One earth-shattering orgasm would lead quickly to the next, and again, and again, until she physically couldn't withstand anymore.

Of course she had no idea how long he was capable of holding out, but despite his urgency when he was pumping into her, Quinn had this controlled calm about him. She sensed he was stubbornly disciplined. His God-like form and sculpted muscles were certainly a result of discipline; she wouldn't be surprised if he had the same control over his bedroom performance as well.

He groaned around her breast in his mouth, hips slowly stroking into her, pressing her down into the mattress. She liked that he was in control, she trusted him to make her feel good. He was six feet three inches of solid muscle and he could do whatever he wanted with her, but his movements were so steady, so gentle, perfectly measured and precise.

She let her legs come down, but her pussy was still wrapped tight around him, and she could feel the slide of his cock entering her, then pulling out...entering, then pulling out, but never fully separating his body from hers. Raelyn met his motions, urging him to increase his pace, his intensity as her hips moved fluidly against his.

Finding her voice, she pleaded breathlessly, "Quinn, please...more."

He obliged instantly, sending his thrusts deeper, harder, a little faster...*yes...yes, oh God yes.*

"Oh yeah, baby," Quinn whispered. "Yeah, you like that. That pussy is so wet...so hungry for my cock...feels so fucking good."

"*So* good," Raelyn exhaled.

"You want me like this again, baby?" He nibbled and tugged at her ear with his teeth.

She needed his body on top of hers, needed him to be in control. She rolled her hips into him again, wanting to feel him as deep as she could.

Before she had the chance to express this need, Quinn smirked, flashing his one-sided dimple, and pulled her legs one at a time onto his shoulders. "You want me deep, don't you?"

"Oh God, yes," Raelyn breathed. With her fingers she lightly traced his face, his sharp jaw, his full bottom lip. Quinn captured her hand in his and kissed it. "Please, Quinn...*yes.*"

Both his hands held her hips firmly as he gave three long strokes. He sat back on his heels, hands still in place and he began snapping his hips into her harder...*harder...faster.* Raelyn's hands fisted the pillow next to her head and she again allowed herself to give her body over to him. She watched him as he reached his hand between them, gently petting her clit with two practiced fingers and she felt her walls clench around him at the sensation. And the wave came so suddenly, crashing over her again without warning.

"Jesus, yes...fuck, Rae, you're coming, oh fuck," Quinn rasped, his face again looking as though she were something he would never be able to get enough of. He looked in awe of her, that she was here with him, that they were really doing this. Finally.

Raelyn bucked into him, throwing her head back, eyes squeezed shut as she screamed his name, panting, gasping, whimpering. Another explosion had just gone off in her chest and her skin tingled, nipples hardened, heat flared all over her body. She was light-headed and dizzy as she looked up into Quinn's eyes. He kissed her ankle and brushed his lips up her leg to her knee and back down.

"That was so good, Rae," Quinn said, lips pressed to her calf. "You're so goddamn beautiful when you come...I swear, baby, there's nothing like it."

"And you?" Raelyn asked, chest heaving as she struggled to catch her breath.

"What about me?" Quinn smoothed a hand up her thigh, lightly sweeping his fingers over her clit as he pumped into her again. He returned to his maddeningly slow pace and she could feel each hard inch of him slide in and back out. Sweat dripped down his chest, making his skin glisten in the low lighting, and Raelyn's eyes followed a bead of sweat as it trickled down his abs and got lost in the trail of hair below his navel.

"Aren't you going to come for me?" Raelyn asked softly, her gaze flashing back up to his with the slightest quirk of an eyebrow.

Quinn smirked, one corner of his lips curving upward. "When I'm ready."

She swallowed hard and felt her pulse kick up a few notches again. *Yep, he is stubbornly disciplined and is planning to fuck me until I literally pass out.* "Okay," she whispered.

His palms massaged the insides of her thighs and she let her head fall back again, ready for him to plunge into her until she was shaking and coming again. His hands slid around to her hips. "Roll over." Quinn's voice was low as he gave his command and Raelyn's eyes snapped open. Before she could help him, he was flipping her over onto her stomach and pulling her hips back, her ass up toward him.

"This ass, Rae," Quinn growled, and his warm palms smoothed over her skin. "I've always wanted you like this."

She backed into him, the wetness between her legs throbbing, still needy, still wanting him. She didn't know if she could get enough of him. They were making up for years of missed touches and kisses and raw, carnal sensations, and her body craved it. Feeling the head of his cock press up against her slick crease, she bit her lip with a moan, "So take me like this, Quinn."

The guttural groan Quinn let out was pure need. His hands grasped her hips with force, and he slammed himself into her. There was no slow build this time. He'd been unleashed, fucking her with hard, impatient, frenzied strokes. His chest covered her back as he leaned over her, their bodies were slippery with sweat, sliding against each other. He grunted and groaned into her ear. *So fucking good...Jesus, so wet...so fucking...oh fuck, baby.*

He ran his palms down from her shoulders, her back, her hips, over her ass. His hands settled, grasping her ass full in his hands and began snapping himself into her, thrusting hard, pulling her back onto him harder. His cool calm had evaporated, and he was completely wild and ravenous. Her ass slapped into him over and over...the room filled with sounds of skin against skin, gasps and groans, her pleas for more...*more...oh God, yes, more!*

Quinn was hard and she was wet down her thighs. She was getting close, but she wanted to keep feeling this. She wasn't ready to be done, but her body was about to completely unravel. The sharp smack of his hand on her ass made her gasp and she fisted the sheets.

"Yes, Quinn, oh God." Raelyn felt herself coming undone. She wanted to be just as wild and unrestrained as he was. She wasn't going to hold back anything. "Yes, Quinn, you feel so...*so* fucking good."

"Come for me again, Rae," Quinn rasped. "I know you're there, baby, I can feel it."

"So close...Quinn, *oh God.*"

All at once, she felt his hands, the heat and sweat of the two of them moving together, his cock, stiff and unyielding, pumping inside her, his groans and words vibrating into her skin, deep into her bones, and she was there. The slide of his cock in and out of her from behind hit her so deep and in all the right spots. She tightened around him again, thighs quaking as the tidal wave rushed through her. It ignited from her chest, and she felt it explode into her toes that curled so hard they threatened to cramp up. Raelyn screamed his name again, begging, pleading, and desperate for the way he made her feel.

Before she had the chance to fully come down from the riptide that had come over her, she was being flipped onto her back again. Quinn spread her legs wider, settling between them and he plunged into her, and she was so grateful. She wanted to see him when he finally let go, wanted to study him the way he studied her.

There may not have been anything more satisfying than the weight and comfort of Quinn's body on top of hers, and leaning over her again, they were chest-to-chest, skin sliding slippery and smooth. Raelyn tangled her fingers in his hair and pulled his mouth onto hers, tongue against tongue, tasting, panting, kissing, fucking.

Oh God, it's all of him. Fuck, it's all so good.

Quinn moved over her, into her. Thrusting harder, faster, deeper...and *yes, yes, yes!*

Raelyn screamed again, body flushed, tight, wet, and squeezing his cock hard and he came with her.

"Oh *fuck*, Rae...*fuck me, oh God*, I'm coming," Quinn groaned, thrusting in quick, impatient jabs as he came.

Quinn's breath came out shuddering, his body shaking, muscles rippling and gorgeous. He buried his face in Raelyn's neck, still groaning, emptying himself in a fervent rush. His mouth pressed soft kisses against her skin, and he tried to catch his breath, collapsing on top of her.

After a few moments of nothing but their breathing filling the room, he pushed himself up to look at her again. His eyes were glazed, chest still slowly heaving. He pressed his forehead to hers and kissed her nose sweetly. "Mother. Of. Fuck..." he panted. "That was worth the wait."

Raelyn smiled as she sighed, "I guess this means you win." Quinn looked at her, curious. "I officially have to call you King Amazeballs."

A breathless laugh emanated from him, and Raelyn briefly saw the joyful, triumphant smile that lit up Quinn's face before he collapsed on top of her again.

CHAPTER 15

There were absolutely no accurate words that came to mind to describe how gloriously perfect that night was. Quinn was elated that he'd managed to pull off what might go down in history as the best first date ever. No number of one-night stands or meaningless lovers could have prepared him for what had happened in that fort. The high he thought he'd been getting from those countless other women couldn't begin to touch what he felt with Rae.

After chugging a tall glass of water or three from the kitchen, Quinn and Rae had come back down to the fort to lay in each other's arms, restarting and actually watching *The Sandlot*. At least until Squints tricked Wendy Peffercorn into giving him mouth to mouth and Rae's hands started to roam his body again. Their second round of love-making had put Quinn to sleep almost instantly, with his arms wrapped around Rae and holding her all night.

The following morning, they couldn't seem to keep their hands to themselves. In bed. In the shower. At the breakfast table. Quinn declared there should be a rule against all clothes when they were together.

"Do you have anything to change into?" Rae asked from beneath him on the couch.

"In a bag in the Bronco," Quinn said, trailing his mouth over that birthmark on her hip he'd noticed the other night.

"Seems like a good place for it." Rae ran her fingers through Quinn's hair and massaged his scalp. "You know, I've always loved how untamed your hair is."

"I love how untamed your hair is after I throw you on your back and take you for a ride." Quinn noted her quick intake of breath and grinned. "I also love how you're still surprised when I say dirty things to you."

Rae bit her lip. "I guess I just really like how it sounds coming out of your mouth."

"Don't get me started on how much I like the sounds that come out of your mouth." Quinn kissed and nibbled at Rae's hip some more. He raised his voice to imitate hers, *"Faster, Quinn...please, Quinn."*

The fingers in his hair tightened their grip and pulled as Rae giggled, "Stop, you're making me blush."

He laughed into her stomach and continued his exploration of her body with his mouth. Silence stretched out for a few beats as they lay together like this. Then suddenly Rae said, "When are you going to see your mother again?"

Quinn paused, mouth hovering over soft skin. He looked up. "Why?"

A look of apprehension flitted across her face, but she regained her composure. "You wanted me to go with you...it's Sunday, and I can't go during the work week."

The thought that he'd have to go back eventually was constantly at the back of his mind, but this last week he'd been so consumed with seeing Rae again and his chance to finally get it right this time around. Now that he'd at least had last night, he supposed it was time to try visiting his mom again.

For the first time in several hours he felt tense. Quinn's jaw clenched at the memory of the scene that had unfolded at his old house almost a week ago. How was he supposed to just show up after that? Then again, how had his mom expected him to react? She hadn't seemed surprised in the least. She hadn't argued with him or tried to defend herself. She simply let him rant until there was nothing left for him to say. This time he would have Rae with him and he knew that would make a world of difference.

"Yeah, we can go today," Quinn sighed. "But since you're the one who's making us put clothes on, I get to decide what we do later when we take them back off."

"Ready?" Rae asked as she parked her Jeep on the street in front of the blue bungalow.

Quinn peered through the car window at the old house that would now look inviting to anyone else who passed it on the street. To him, however, it still held all those nightmarish memories. The soft warmth of Rae's hand over his made him take a deep breath and look away. He looked down at their hands and back at her and gave her a nod. She held his hand on the way up the walkway and as they stood on the porch. Quinn glanced down at Rae while he stood in front of the door and she gave him an encouraging smile. It was all he needed. With a deep breath in and out, he knocked on the door.

After a few heartbeats the door opened, and Quinn's mom stood in the doorway. Her eyes widened in surprise at the sight of her son, only briefly flitting to Rae on his arm before her face broke into a teary smile.

"I came back," Quinn said.

"I thought you probably would," she replied as she gave a half-hearted smile.

Quinn tensed, jaw clenching, squeezing Rae's hand tight in his own. His mother just assumed he was going to be a good boy and come back for her. How did she have that right? Rae seemed to sense his tension- or had she simply heard the hot breath he let out of his flared nostrils?- and placed her other hand on his forearm, shifting her body toward his.

Molly Casey was a tall, thin woman who had the appearance of someone who was likely very pretty before various forms of abuse. When he was little, Quinn remembered thinking that she looked far younger than his friends' moms. She had even been mistaken as an older sister or an aunt on the few occasions that they had actually gone out together, usually for groceries.

His mother held the door open and ushered them into the new, clean living room where they all took seats; Rae and Quinn on the sofa, Molly across from them in a matching overstuffed chair.

"Good to see you two are still together," his mother said, as her gaze traveled between the couple sitting on the sofa.

Quinn and Rae exchanged brief and awkward looks, letting out uncomfortable laughter.

"We weren't-"

"I mean, we were together a lot, but-"

"And *now*- um- well-"

"We were always friends," Rae stated, and they settled with that. Their friendship had come first, and it was something Quinn felt they both valued above whatever else may have happened between them. It was probably the best way to put it without having to get into the *What Are We Now* discussion.

Molly eyed them with a curious smile. "Well, you could've fooled me."

Another awkward laugh in each other's direction told Quinn they were likely thinking the same thing: *If everyone else had seen it, why hadn't they done anything about it before now?*

"I remember the first time you came over here to see Quinn," Molly mused. "You were both so little. Six? Seven?"

"Seven," said Quinn, looking curiously at his mother. "You actually remember that?" He'd always had the impression his mom was too high or simply didn't care to notice what was going on in his life.

"Of course," Molly said, then turned toward Rae. "Your dad drove a black BMW. I thought it was some government lawyer or someone coming to ask around. But instead a little blond girl came up to the door and asked if my son could go swimming with her and her family at their country club."

Quinn and Rae exchanged grins at the memory. Quinn said, "I had no idea what a country club was, but it was like a hundred degrees and swimming sounded like a good option."

"I saw the car and heard the words 'country club' and thought, 'hey, my son got in with the right people on his own'," Molly said. "After that I didn't worry too much about where you were going when you snuck out."

This new information rolled around in Quinn's head for a few moments. He wasn't sure when he'd taken Rae's hand in his again but was suddenly hyper-aware of her presence as she rubbed her thumb back and forth across his knuckles.

Where would he have been without her? Who would he have been friends with? Before she came along he had been an angry kid. He got into fights and was called into the principal's office a few times a week. The teachers and other school staff had labeled him "troubled" and he'd received several home visits from concerned staff members.

There had been people throughout his life who had looked out for him in ways that his mother never had. Teachers who had taken a particular liking to him, coaches, school social workers. But what Rae and her family had done almost seemed like too much. She had insisted on being his friend- for some reason. Mr. DeRose never asked too many questions, but Quinn had always suspected he knew on some level what he was dealing with at home. Regardless, he'd made it clear that their house was always open if he needed it.

That day Rae had showed up on his doorstep asking him to go swimming only a few days after her birthday party, he'd been in shock. When Mr. DeRose had insisted on giving him a ride home from the beach, refusing to let him walk home in the dark, Quinn was sure someone who could afford *that* birthday party and *those* clothes and *that* car wouldn't want to be his best friend once they saw the run-down little structure he called his home.

But she had shown up. She could have asked any of her friends to go with her that day, but she had picked him. And then she continued to pick him after that day.

Quinn looked at Rae, sitting there on the sofa next to him, and suddenly felt so overcome with gratitude. She had done everything for him just by choosing to be his friend. He wanted to wrap his arms around her, shower her with kisses, and never stop giving her any and everything she wanted or needed or asked for.

"Why are you looking at me like that?" Rae asked, a curious smile on her face.

Quinn cleared the lump in his throat and shook his head, "Just thinking about how lucky it was that I went to the beach on your seventh birthday."

Rae's smile brightened and she leaned into him. Quinn put his arm around her and planted a kiss on top of her head.

He looked across to his mom. The woman who had failed him in so many ways. He was a long way from forgiveness, but in this moment he wondered if he would have connected with Rae on the same level if he hadn't been so lonely. If her bright, sunny persona would have attracted him so much if he hadn't been starving for some light in his life. Would he have valued her friendship as much? Would he have allowed himself to see what kind of person she was if he hadn't needed a friend back then?

Clearing his throat again he asked, "So… when did you decide to get sober?"

Molly smiled, eyes tearing up again, and she wiped away the tears before they could fall onto her cheeks. She stood up and gestured toward the hall. "Come on, I have something to show you."

There were three doors down the hallway and Molly pushed open the door that led to Quinn's old bedroom. The last time he had been in this room was to pack the rest of his things after coming home for a couple of weeks during the summer before his sophomore year of college. The paint on the walls had been peeling, the carpet was worn and scratchy, and the furniture was all second-hand from Goodwill or Salvation Army. He'd still had a twin bed even though he'd outgrown it in high school- his feet would just hang off the end. His wooden ceiling fan was old and squeaked, and there had been a Detroit Tigers poster on the wall his bed was pushed against.

Despite the changes to the rest of the house, Quinn still found himself expecting to see the exact same space he'd left behind. Untouched. It would make sense that his mom would have ignored his room just as much as she had seemed to ignore his own existence.

He was wrong.

The bedroom had not only been repainted, it had new floors and new furniture. Even the window he'd snuck in and out of so many times looked new. But the thing that really caught his attention was the long wall that had once sported his only piece of personal touch. In place of the Tigers poster, the wall now featured a poster of him in his white and blue LA uniform, along with all of his jerseys. His number seven Traverse City Trojans jersey, the number twenty-one he'd worn for the Arizona Sun Devils, and his number twelves for both Atlanta, whom he'd been drafted by right out of college, and of course his current team in Los Angeles.

On the adjacent wall, his varsity jacket had been placed in a shadow box along with local newspaper clippings featuring the Trojans baseball team. The headlines announced their two consecutive state championship wins, another announced a no-hitter that Quinn had pitched his senior year, and the last one featured a front-page picture of him at the end of a good swing, a cocky grin across his face as he watched the ball fly over the fence.

He remembered that game. It had been during his sophomore year and he was fully aware of the college recruiters in the stands. He'd hit four home runs in just that game and had pitched another no-hitter. The next day his coach had called him out of class and into his office to play him messages from the recruiters wanting to set up meetings with him.

Molly was pulling down what looked like a photo album off of a bookcase he'd certainly never had when he was a kid. She set the album on top of the new full-sized bed and opened it. The front page was a school picture of Quinn, probably ten or eleven years old, then began a chronological collection of his baseball career and successes. Little league pictures, photos from the local ballpark that Mr. DeRose had taken and had developed for him.

He put his hand on one of the pages, wanting to look more closely at the photograph. It was after one of the many neighborhood games they'd put together- and won. Chris, Jett, and Tyler were in the picture cheering. Quinn had a baseball bat slung over his shoulder and his other arm was around Rae's waist. As usual, she'd been wearing one of Quinn's hats, and a black skort with white stripes on the side. She was pumping her fist in the air and cheering along with the boys. But Quinn was smiling at her.

Rae tucked a piece of hair behind her ear as she leaned over the photo, a smile spreading across her face. She looked up at Quinn who was watching her, as he'd apparently always done, and there was the same twinkle in her eyes now as there had been the previous night before she'd kissed him on the baseball field. If she hadn't believed what he'd said last night about falling for her so long ago, he was sure she knew now.

"We should make a copy of this picture and put it next to your jersey at the bar," Rae said.

"I like that idea." Quinn smiled back at her. He liked the idea of people knowing this was where he'd started, and these were the people who'd gotten him where he was. He didn't even mind the thought of other women seeing he was clearly taken and had been for the last fifteen years. And probably would be for the next fifteen...or fifty.

They continued to flip through the pages of the photo album, through middle and high school team pictures and onto more newspaper and magazine clippings during his college and Major League career.

"You came home one night from a game," Molly began, "in high school. You were so excited. You'd even brought friends with you, which you never did. And you certainly never used the front door." She glanced for a moment from Quinn to the window and back. "You boys were going on about college and recruiters and scholarships, and one of them said that you would definitely be getting a full ride offer from somewhere, if not multiple schools. And then you had made a comment about if you didn't get a scholarship to play ball, you probably wouldn't go to college. That you'd have to rely on... 'pity scholarships', I think you called them, for people who were never meant to go to college."

That sounded like something he would've said.

Quinn heard Rae's scoff and looked up from the album. "What?"

She was looking at him with disbelief. "Quinn," she shook her head, "you always thought you were less than or unworthy of college. You were always making snide comments about how *people like you* weren't supposed to go to college or do great things. Like you were completely incapable of any achievement off the ball diamond. Which, by the way, was and still is complete bullshit."

"I really don't have any achievements outside of baseball," Quinn stated.

"Seriously?" Rae's eyebrows shot up. "Do you realize how many people grow up like you and become psychopaths? Your achievements go way beyond the field." She gestured around the room. "Yeah, you're an amazing ball player, but how many people on your team had to overcome everything you did? You were never willing to accept that your life couldn't be everything you wanted and then some. Do you realize how rare that is? Do you know how many people would have used the cards they were dealt as an excuse to never amount to anything?"

Quinn swallowed, searching Rae's eyes as he tried to figure out what to say. He wasn't used to praise outside of the ball field. Well, okay, or the bedroom. Being acknowledged for his character was entirely new territory. "Rae, I can throw a ball and swing a bat. It's not like I'm a *doctor* or anything."

Rae shook her head with an incredulous smirk. "Yeah, becoming a doctor is pretty easy when you're funded by a miniature French empire." Quinn looked back at her, unconvinced, so she pressed on, "Quinn, if I'd had half your ambition I could be the princess of my own damn nation by now."

Quinn shrugged. "You'd hate being called princess though."

"Queen, then," Rae rolled her eyes. "Do you get what I'm saying though? Everything you have was earned. By you. No one else got you there."

"Your family paid for me to be on teams," Quinn said with another shrug. She didn't seem to realize how much *she* had actually done for *him*.

"Yeah, they could've paid for every kid in Traverse City to play, but you're still the one who got yourself where you are," said Rae.

"She's right," Molly piped in. "I know I didn't do...anything to help make your life easier. What you've done with your life was all because of who you are and the choices you made."

Quinn sort of understood what they were saying but couldn't help focusing on the way Rae's family had supported him. Paid his team fees. Bought him decent equipment. Housed him, fed him, clothed him when he'd outgrown everything he owned in one summer.

"When I heard you boys talking about scholarships," Molly said, "I knew you played ball, but I didn't realize you were so good. I didn't know you were taking yourself somewhere with your talent. I saw the newspapers after that game you all talked about and couldn't believe *my* son was going somewhere. Every other parent in town knew how talented you were, and I'd been such a horrible mother I didn't even know how remarkable my own son was."

"You never said anything." Quinn looked at his mom uncertainly. This was the most she had ever said to him, he was sure of it. But she'd noticed him. She'd been interested to know about his talent, and maybe was even proud of him. But she hadn't spoken up.

Molly sighed, "I went on sort of a self-pity bender."

Quinn raised an eyebrow and looked down curiously at her. "Just the one?"

"No, I suppose not," Molly said. "I realized how much I had failed. And if you were leaving it was too late to fix it, so it didn't matter."

"I was leaving for college. If I'd known you wanted to fix things…" Quinn trailed off. If he'd thought his mom wanted to fix things and get sober, what would he have done? Would he have even believed her? Would he have been able to focus at all at school, constantly wondering about his mom's inevitable relapse from hundreds of miles away?

Another image popped into his head: Red and blue flashing lights, the old Toyota Corolla crashed nose-first into a big oak tree, his mom being pulled out by paramedics through the window. Feeling completely numb as he watched it all unfold, standing above the ditch in a tux and black Chuck Taylors.

Not how most high school seniors spend their prom night.

He'd had to call Rae and tell her he wouldn't make it to the dance, but that she should go and have fun. It had felt like a sign. He'd finally gotten the balls to ask her to one of the dances, she'd said yes, and he'd come across the accident on the way to pick her up.

Of course Rae came to the hospital instead and spent the night in the waiting room with him. They hadn't even spoken to each other. She'd just shown up in her prom dress looking like a dream come to life, given him a hug, and sat with him all night.

"Is that why you were so drunk when you crashed the car?" Quinn asked, "Because you were upset that you'd failed me?"

Molly nodded, chewing her lip.

"Did you know that was my prom night?" Quinn wasn't looking at anyone now, just staring out the window wondering how differently that night could have gone if she'd just said something.

"I didn't," Molly said. "At least, not until you came into my room in a tux."

Anger was bubbling at the surface again. He hadn't cared much that he'd missed his own prom. What made him mad was that it had ruined Rae's, too. She had been looking forward to it and had seemed genuinely excited when Quinn had finally asked her to go with him. Rae must have sensed his change of tone or registered his expression, because she reached for his hand and laced their fingers together, leaning into him. Her weight pressing into his calmed him instantly.

"I suppose surviving that accident gave me a new perspective," said Molly. "I figured if it wasn't too late to keep disappointing you, by ruining your prom night or a number of other things, then it wasn't too late to try to do better."

They spent at least another hour looking through the photo album, bringing it out to the living room. They talked about the first time Molly really tried to give up her vices. She started with the drugs, and instantly knew she would need help. She went to a support group and looked into all of her options, found out all about the detox phase, relapses, and what to expect. She admitted that the first several meetings scared the crap out of her, and she nearly gave up right then. But then she'd turn the TV on to a baseball game when she got home and had to constantly remind herself why she was going through it.

After four years, she had made some progress, though not as much as she would have liked in that time. But when Sandra had visited the first time, explaining that Quinn had hired her, it renewed her ambition to try harder, knowing that he was still trying to take care of her. She said it felt like he was rooting for her from a distance. It wasn't easy and it didn't happen all at once, but now she had three years and five months of complete sobriety to be proud of.

When Quinn and Rae got ready to leave, he felt the knot in his chest that he'd kept with him at all times loosen just a little bit more. The first time he'd been here he needed to get all his emotions out there, all that pain off his chest. With Rae, he felt stronger and braver, like he could ask his mom the hard questions and hear the answers without losing his head.

There was an awkward moment before he and Rae left when he felt like his mom was going in for a hug. They'd covered a lot of ground, but he couldn't quite get there yet. He put a hand on her shoulder instead and told her he'd be back soon, then walked out the door with Rae's hand in his.

CHAPTER 16

"How does that feel?" Raelyn was stabilizing Quinn's elbow gently after putting him in a soft sleeve brace that still kept a bend to the sensitive joint. The hard splint was gone, and he no longer had to carry his arm at a sharp ninety-degree angle at all times. They were both relieved about this- the hard-cased splint was a pain in the ass to maneuver around in bed.

"So much better," Quinn sighed. "You thought we'd been having good sex- I've got use of both arms now, baby. Better get ready for what's comin'!"

Raelyn laughed. "You still can't fully extend your elbow for another three weeks. Please don't go injuring yourself further to prove anything to me."

"I'll always be trying to prove something when it comes to you, Rae." He smiled shyly and his eyes went soft and adoring, and Raelyn's heart could have melted right there.

They were so disgustingly crazy for each other. A month ago, if Raelyn had seen a couple act the way she and Quinn acted around each other now, she would have scoffed, rolled her eyes, and made some snide comment about wondering how long that would last. But here she was being obnoxiously cute and doe-eyed over this man. Her best friend.

She frequently found herself wondering how she'd kept herself from attacking him when they were teenagers. He was all male and muscle and boyish charm with that goddamn sexy dimple. His hair was always that perfect level of untamed, making him look like he'd just rolled out of bed after having heart-pounding, toe-curling, earth-shattering, multi-orgasmic sex. Which, at least lately, had been the case most of the time.

Having to scold him upon coming at her with grabby hands at work was one of the most difficult tasks she'd had to perform in quite some time. She'd had to explain that she was not allowed to make out with her patients in the therapy rooms and that while they were at her office they had to maintain a strictly professional relationship. He had argued this, of course, and tried staring her down, tried pulling her close and whispering his filthy thoughts in her ear. Had it made her panties go damp? Of course it had. Had she given in? Reluctantly, no. No, she hadn't.

Raelyn showed Quinn a few different finger, wrist, bicep, and shoulder exercises he could do without having to extend his elbow and he got to work repeating one of the wrist movements.

"Tomorrow's your birthday," Quinn stated suddenly. "Any plans? Carnival at the beach? Trip to Paris? Fancy yacht party with two hundred of your closest friends?"

Quinn had always been astounded at the ways her family had celebrated her and Camille's birthdays. Admittedly, her parents were absolutely nuts for doing those things. Raelyn would have been satisfied with a pool party in their backyard or a slumber party with her closest friends.

Raelyn shook her head. "No, I usually just have dinner at my parents' place anymore. Although, I would totally be down for another trip to Paris."

"That was one hell of a Sweet Sixteen," said Quinn.

"Would've been better if you hadn't *refused* to go." Raelyn gave him a pointed look.

"Your parents did enough for me. I wasn't about to let them buy me a two-thousand dollar trip to *Paris*." Quinn looked stubbornly at Raelyn, and when she returned his stare with a raised eyebrow- he knew damn well two-thousand dollars was nothing to her parents- he added, "The funny thing about having money is you never have to think about it. When you have none, it's all you think about."

Raelyn nodded, conceding. This wasn't a topic that usually went over well between the two of them. She had no idea what it was like growing up the way Quinn had. Sure, she'd watched it from the sidelines, but she had no way of really knowing what it was like. She did know enough to recognize that this was one of the reasons she'd been so interested in him as a friend. Not because he was poor and she was rich, but because his perspective was so different from her own and she felt like it helped her grow as a person. She liked knowing there was more to life than designer brands, country clubs, and the other many luxuries her family was so familiar with.

"I could take you to Paris now if you wanted," Quinn said.

Raelyn had been admiring the thick, corded muscles of his forearm work as he flexed his wrist but shot her gaze up to his face. A thought hit her that she'd never even considered before now. Surely he didn't think the only reason things were going well between them now was because he had money? He knew she wasn't that shallow, right? Her brow furrowed, disliking this thought, then blinked it away. "Or you could just come to dinner with me tomorrow," she offered. "I'm sure Dad would be thrilled to see you."

Quinn met her eyes and smiled, giving a nod. "Yeah, I could do that."

She had to remind herself not to lean in and kiss him and forced her attention back to his wrist and forearm. This may not have helped. Smirking, Raelyn lightly traced her fingertips down his unbelievable forearm.

"I thought we were to remain professional in this room, Doc," Quinn said smoothly, lips curved into a grin.

"Just making sure everything's how it should be," she replied innocently, though she couldn't hide her mischievous smile. "Sometimes these muscles get sore during these exercises. You might want to massage them out afterwards."

"That so?" Quinn asked, breath catching in his throat as he watched Raelyn's hand rub the length of his forearm, down to the wrist, and back up below the elbow. Her hand pressed gently into his muscles, wrapping around the width and admiring the strength of his as she remembered how they felt holding her, pulling her in tight so her body was flush against his.

He reached for the hem of her skirt. "And what was that you were saying...about *finger* exercises? I feel like I might be able to come up with a pretty good one."

Raelyn hummed, telling herself she needed to back away, but instead staying put. "I'm sure you would be very good at those finger exercises."

"Should we give them a try?"

"You know we can't do that here," Raelyn said, but she found her body moving a fraction of an inch closer.

"You don't really want to wait until we get home," Quinn said, voice low, husky, and nearly breathless.

Until we *get home.*

Raelyn blinked up to him and it appeared he had also caught the slip. He had a hotel room he was paying for, yet he planned to stay with her as he had been since Saturday night. Was he already thinking of her home as his, too? The thought made Raelyn feel like there was a balloon inflating in her chest, and it wanted to burst at the sight of Quinn's pink blush that crept into his cheeks.

"I don't," she agreed. His breath rushed out of him, relieved, and he moved closer, slipping his hand beneath her skirt. The moisture between her legs had steadily increased since she'd joined Quinn in the therapy room. Her body seemed to physically miss him, yearning and aching for him, pulling his toward hers like a magnet. But she was at her office. And this was...wildly inappropriate.

But, dear God, I want him so bad.

His large palm was smooth against her thigh as it slid toward her core.

Just a little...light petting. That's okay, right?

Of course it's not! You. Are. At. Work!

Quinn moved her panties to the side and his fingers hovered, teasing.

Please...yes. Touch me.

No! This is completely unprofessional...not okay.

His fingers slid lightly down her crease and he groaned, biting his lip, eyes closed.

"Quinn..." Raelyn whispered. She wasn't sure if she was going to tell him to stop, insisting they wait until they get home, or if she was simply enjoying his touch. Maybe both. "We really should wait."

"Is that why you're already wet through your panties? Because you want to wait?" Quinn's touch was light, still teasing, barely touching her. She had to resist bucking into his hand.

Raelyn bit through an agonized groan, "I didn't say I *want* to wait- I said we *should* wait." Her eyes began to flutter shut and she felt ready to give in. She sighed, body relaxing, and opened her eyes. Catching the sight of his arm pushed up her skirt- *in her therapy room*- she straightened and snapped her legs shut, pushing his hand away. "No! Dammit, Quinn- you are a bad influence. You're going to get me in trouble."

Quinn's laugh was a low rumble in his chest, "You almost let me finger fuck you in your office." Obnoxious pride made him puff up as he grinned wide. "You think I'm irresistible."

Raelyn gaped, blushing, "I was not! I was just..." she sputtered. Frustrated, she scrunched up her nose, knowing he had the upper hand here. She grabbed a stress ball off a nearby table and threw it at him. "You're a butthead."

Turning his head and letting the stress ball hit his cheek before it fell into his lap, he laughed again. "I can't believe you were about to break your sacred oath of doctorhood."

"It's not an oath, and *I* stopped *you*!" Raelyn said defensively. "Tread carefully, Quinn Casey, or you'll end up with a new physical therapist."

"I'll be on my best behavior from now on," said Quinn, putting his hands up in surrender.

"That seems unlikely," Raelyn said, eyes narrowed, doing her best to stifle her smile.

He lifted one hand in a three-finger salute. "Scout's honor."

The session wrapped up with a few more exercises and Quinn made her blush again as he left, calling over his shoulder that he couldn't wait to try out more of those finger exercises at home. What a jerk. But Raelyn still couldn't help the smile that blossomed on her face, no matter how much of an irresistible tease he might be. She had no doubt he'd make it up to her when she met him later...at *home*.

CHAPTER 17

"Happy birthday, gorgeous," Quinn said, enveloping Rae in his arms in the entryway. He'd come to pick her up to take her to dinner at her parents' place and let himself in. As always, Rae looked beautiful, although Quinn thought she was most beautiful when she was in her real birthday suit with her blonde hair splayed all over the pillows. Today she wore a light pink strapless sundress that was shorter in the front than the back and heels that were only a few shades lighter than her sun-tanned skin. She met his greeting with a long kiss, then smiled as she wiped a smudge of lipstick off his lips.

It had only been a few hours since they'd seen each other. Quinn had stayed with her again the previous night and had woken her up before her alarm with birthday morning sex. The image of her slowly waking up as he touched her, kissed her neck, collar bone, and breasts, had been playing on a loop in his mind all day. Once she'd woken up enough, she rolled on top of him, grinding down on him, using his body like an instrument for her pleasure. He would gladly be any and everything she needed him to be if it meant getting to watch her lose herself to those beautifully intense, dizzying orgasms.

Quinn pulled a small, gift-wrapped package out of his pants pocket and handed it to her.

"You didn't have to get me anything," Rae said, though she beamed as she took the small present out of his hands. Quinn watched anxiously as she unwrapped and opened the small red box. Her eyes went wide at the site of a diamond tennis bracelet and a pair of matching princess-cut diamond earrings. "Quinn...*Cartier?* These must've cost..." she trailed off, gaping at him.

Quinn shrugged. "I've got a lot of birthdays to make up for." Showering women in gifts wasn't something he'd ever done before, but it was something he'd always wished could do for Rae.

"They're beautiful, Quinn," she said, looking into the box at the glittering jewelry before pressing her lips to his again. "Thank you."

"I didn't know what *princess cut* meant, but it sounded like it was the right fit for you." Quinn smirked as he took the bracelet and gestured for Rae to hold her wrist out so he could put it on her.

"I thought that might have been intentional."

Once the bracelet was clasped and she began switching out her earrings, Quinn pulled an envelope out of his back pocket, "One more thing."

"More?" Rae gave him an incredulous look before taking the envelope. "Well I know it's not a card. I've heard enough rants from you about how dumb it is to spend money on cards and gift bags."

"It is. I already bought the gift; why pay to dress it up? And what do you do with cards anyway?"

Rae opened the envelope and pulled out two plane tickets. Quinn watched, studying her as she read them. "Two tickets to Paris?!" she exclaimed. Looking down at them again she noticed the date. "For December?" She looked up at him unable to contain her obvious excitement. "So does that mean you plan to stick around? Or am I supposed to take Jett?"

Quinn laughed. "If Jett got my romantic French getaway with you I would be about as happy with him as I was that time he licked frosting off of you from *my* birthday cake at *my* eighteenth birthday party. Or the time he walked in on you changing out of your bathing suit."

Rae's giggle met his ears and made his heart squeeze. "It's starting to sound like you want me all to yourself...and for a while."

"I do," said Quinn, now meeting her gaze, his expression turning from playful to sincere. "That's exactly what I want, actually." He was used to stating outright what he wanted, just not when it came to Rae. But he knew he didn't want to go another seven years without seeing her. Hell, he didn't want to go seven days or hours. He struggled with not being able to see her while she was at work. "Is that going to be a problem?"

Rae briefly seemed surprised by his straight-forwardness but smiled her sunshine bright smile, "No, it's not a problem."

"Okay...good," Quinn nodded, taking Rae's hand and kissing it.

She glanced back down at the tickets in her hands before smiling back up at him. "Quinn, this is amazing. Thank you...I guess we get to re-do my sixteenth birthday, too!"

"I would've made it your next birthday, but I might be playing again by then. I just know you love it there."

"I'm going to have to teach you French now." Rae wiggled her eyebrows.

"I know croissant, so I'm off to a good start," he replied, in what even he knew was a thick American accent, enunciating all the wrong letters.

Rae pulled her eyebrows together in a pained smile. "We'll work on that."

They piled into his Bronco- him, Rae, and Harry, since Camille's two kids were always begging for more time with the large animal- and started the familiar drive to Rae's parents' house. The smile refused to fade from Quinn's face as he reveled in the fact that Rae had agreed to be *his*. Inside his head he was doing a ridiculous happy dance, cheering and screaming at the top of his lungs, but on the outside he was only smiling, probably like a dork, as he drove down M-37.

When he glanced over to the passenger seat, he saw that Rae was also smiling, though it was a cute, reserved smile. She was clearly doing a better job concealing her joy than he was. He wanted to see her bright smile light up her face again. "Did you know," he started, "I used to love when you'd wear my baseball hats."

Rae's smile widened a little further as she looked over at him. "You did?"

"Yeah..." Quinn bit his lip, feeling shy about what he was going to say, but he'd spent long enough holding his feelings in, so fuck it. "I, uh...it made me feel like you were mine."

There was the smile he was looking for.

Seeing her smile at this made him continue, "I would, I don't know...I'd think other guys would see you wearing it and they'd just know like 'Oh that's Quinn's girl'."

Rae opened her mouth to say something, but couldn't seem to form the words. She ran her fingers through her hair as though she were nervous, but her smile said it all. "I guess you'll have to give me one of your new ones, then."

His chest felt so full with triumph and joy and outright exhilaration that she *wanted* to be his and she *wanted* people to know it. He'd been waiting for this moment, this feeling, for so long. He wanted to hold onto it and never let it go.

"I've got a few. You can have your pick," Quinn said, and he reached over to lay a possessive hand on Rae's leg. She rested her hand on top of his, brushing her thumb back and forth over his knuckles.

It had been about ten years since Quinn had been to the DeRoses' massive French manor home, and when he pulled in, past the tall wrought-iron gate into the long driveway, his excitement turned anxious. Even though he now had his own mansion back in Los Angeles, it was obvious that his home and this one were from different types of money. Quinn's sleek, angular, beach-front house with its floor-to-ceiling window-walls was an obvious show of new money, meant to impress and brag about his success. The DeRoses' manor, however, with its stone accents, large pillared fence, perfectly landscaped stone walkway and massive arches spoke of money that had been there for generations.

All of the upstairs rooms had balconies and large windows, the steep roof gave away the high, vaulted ceilings. The front doors were tall, with a huge stone archway over the porch, and there were multiple elaborately decorated chimneys. Quinn remembered his first time here, covered in mud from playing baseball in the rain with Rae. He'd wondered why in the world someone would need more than one fireplace, and why- *why* would a family of four need such an enormous house at all. On the left-hand side, there was a section that looked distinctly like a tower or a turret, which had given his eight-year-old self the impression that this was some type of castle, not just a house.

"Does it still look like a palace?" Rae's light voice cut through the memory he was reliving as he stared back up at the impressive structure before them.

"Oh yeah," he replied, gaze traveling to the front door. "What did they say when you told them I was coming?"

She looked briefly uncomfortable, like a little kid with her hand caught in the cookie jar as she scrunched her nose. "I thought maybe we'd just surprise them. It's not like there won't be enough food."

Nodding, Quinn bit his lip and felt his pulse kick up a notch. No, he didn't have to worry about her family being unprepared with food or accommodations. They'd always had maids, some that cooked, others that cleaned. Hell, they'd had chauffeurs to drive Rae and Camille to school or soccer practice when they were kids.

Accommodations were the least of his worries. It was just that the last time he'd been here he'd been a mess, begging to talk to Rae nearly every day for the entire summer after graduation. Mr. DeRose had done his best to get Rae to come down and talk to him, but she had refused until the very last week before he moved to Arizona for college.

"You have nothing to worry about, Quinn," Rae said, taking his hand. "My parents love you. They're going to be ecstatic to see you, I promise."

Nodding again, Quinn let out a deep breath, "Let's do this then."

For the first time in years, Quinn stood in the foyer with its grand arches and vaulted ceilings. The decor had been modernized since he'd last stood here, but it still kept the feel of a grand French palace in his mind. Everything was white or cream colored, the vases and picture frames and mirrors were all ostentatious and ornamental.

There were three arched windows ahead in the living room that took up the entire wall, floor to ceiling, brightening the space with natural light. Looking through the large windows, Quinn could see the patio that had been updated and redecorated, but still held the same grandeur as always.

Every intricate piece in the house had no doubt been perfectly placed by an interior designer and was kept immaculately clean by the crew of maids. Quinn wondered how many of the items, like the white grand piano, ever got any use, or if they were simply placed there to fill out the massive space. There were small touches of gold accents throughout the foyer, and the theme continued into the living room. He wondered if any of these accents were real gold. He knew there were similar-looking decorations in gold color that the average person could buy from the home decor section of any local store, but he wouldn't put it past Margaux DeRose to insist on the real thing.

"Is that you, Rae?" A familiar voice Quinn recognized as her older sister, Camille, called from the other room.

"Yeah, it's me," Rae called back as she grabbed Quinn's hand again and began pulling him toward the sound of voices and clinking dishes. Harry was leading the way, likely sniffing out his young niece and nephew. "I brought someone with me, too."

Just around the corner from the kitchen now Quinn heard the bracing sigh of Rae's father as he muttered, "Oh boy, here we go again."

Stifling her laugh she continued around the corner into the large kitchen with Quinn at her side. "Family, this is my new *boyfriend*," her eyes twinkled into his as she emphasized the word, making his heart flip and his stomach do a cartwheel. "I'd introduce you, but I don't think that's necessary."

All eyes were suddenly on Quinn as everyone eagerly craned their necks or snapped around to see who the mystery guest was.

Anyone else's reactions to seeing Quinn beneath the archway of the kitchen were immediately drowned out by the startling and excited cheer from Mr. DeRose.

"Yes!" Mr. DeRose pumped both fists in the air and looked as though he were about to praise Jesus. "Yes, finally!" He got up and rounded the kitchen island to embrace Quinn in a massive bear hug.

In the past ten years, Mr. DeRose had aged very well. He still had a full head of hair, which was now mostly gray, and instead of the mustache that he'd sported when Quinn was a kid and the clean-shaven look he'd remembered as a teenager, Mr. DeRose now had a short beard which suited him well.

Pulling back, he placed his hands on Quinn's shoulders and looked at him very seriously as he said, "I have been waiting for this moment my entire life."

"Dad, you haven't even known him your entire life," Rae managed through a fit of giggles. Quinn's face was stuck in a stupid grin, not having expected this type of reception.

"I don't care," Mr. DeRose said and glanced briefly at his daughter. "Oh, and happy birthday, sweetie. Although you just gave me the best gift I could ask for."

"Gee, Dad, thanks," Camille drawled from behind her father. "I thought you were supposed to say Mom gave you the best gift ever by birthing your two amazing daughters."

Mr. DeRose waved a hand dismissively. "Yeah, that too, whatever." He turned back to Quinn and his familiar eye-crinkling smile spread across his face. "It's good to see you again. We've missed you around here."

Quinn returned the friendly smile. "It's good to see you again, too, Mr. DeRose."

"Please, I think you can call me Charlie by now," he replied, giving Quinn another quick back-slapping hug before moving on to his daughter. Charlie wrapped Rae in a tight hug and said quietly, "You know, I might be a little premature on this- I've only known him about twenty-two years- but I like this one. You should keep this one around."

"I kinda like him, too," Rae said, smiling and reaching out to Quinn to loop her arm through his.

Charlie raised a finger animatedly and gasped as though a lightbulb flicked on over his head, "Oh! I have an idea! I'll be right back." With that, he quickly made his way out of the kitchen, leaving Quinn to greet the rest of Rae's family.

Margaux pulled him into a hug and gave him a short peck on each cheek. She told him how wonderful it was to see him and that she was proud of him.

Camille smirked, glancing between him and Rae before making the announcement: "You two are definitely having sex. It's really good, too, isn't it?"

Quinn coughed and felt his face turn hot, chancing a glance at Rae. He expected her to look equally called out, but simply returned her sister's sly grin, "Yep, lots of it."

"Girls!" Margaux snapped, gesturing toward the little boy and girl giggling around Harry, perfectly oblivious to the adult discussion. "There are children in here." She flicked her eyes between Quinn and Rae briefly before surprising the hell out of him

when she added, "But if I'm speaking honestly, I have to say it's really not surprising you two are so good together- you've had amazing chemistry since you were children."

Camille's husband, Josh, was not at all what Quinn had pictured in his head. He had always imagined she would end up with some hot-shot lawyer or business executive, but Josh was a nerdy guy who worked for some big tech company. He was tall and lanky, and admitted to not having a single athletic bone in his body. Their two children, Peter and Chloe, were almost a fifty-fifty split of their parents, and were rather precocious little kids.

Quinn was talking with Josh about the kind of fitness regimen a professional athlete has to keep up with when Rae caught their attention.

"What the hell is Dad doing out there?" Rae was peering out the kitchen window to the patio.

Camille leaned next to Rae and looked outside, "Oh boy...he's putting up that movie projector. A hundred bucks says we're about to relive your childhood. He's going to point out every moment he knew you and Quinn were meant to be."

"Oh God, I think you're right," Rae sighed. She peered back over her shoulder at Quinn whose stuck-on smile had returned after such a welcome greeting from her family. "I hope you're feeling reminiscent."

They ate dinner out on the patio where there was a long farmhouse table decorated with ornate place settings, crystal vases spilling over with greenery and blue flowers. It was something Quinn would expect to see on the head table at a wedding. The silverware was real silver, the plates and bowls were pure white and Quinn felt like he was supposed to somehow fill his plate without getting anything messy on it. They all had large goblet-like wine glasses in front of them, and two maids in knee-length black dresses circled the table when necessary to offer different wines, no doubt from the DeRoses' own vineyard.

This wasn't the first time he'd eaten with the DeRose family, but he never thought he would get used to their lifestyle. It wasn't always this formal; he remembered eating pizza from the local pizza joint at the kitchen island with Rae, Jett, and Chris, or taking whatever food was made for them into the living room to watch a big game or play video games. But their special occasion dinners were fancier than some of the finest restaurants he'd visited in LA.

After stuffing themselves with the delicious four-course meal, Charlie called them all to the other end of the patio which was set up like an outdoor living room. He had indeed put up the large projector screen and Quinn had no doubt the videos he planned to show would be all about Rae's childhood, and by extension his own. The good parts, anyway.

Sitting down in the middle of the sectional next to Rae with his arm around her, he grew excited to see some of his best non-baseball moments relayed on screen.

"Dad, this is insane," Rae shook her head as Charlie fired up the projector. "Where have you been keeping all these videos anyway? Did you really get them all converted to DVDs?"

"Of course I did," Charlie said, now taking a seat next to Margaux. "I knew this day would come eventually and I would have to point out how ridiculous it is that you didn't see it before."

"Uh-huh, I'm sure you just knew," Rae said, leaning into Quinn, now turning their attention to the large screen in front of them.

The screen was black and the words *June 21, 1998* popped up. Already grinning, Quinn knew exactly what was special about that date, though he had no idea any of it had been captured on film. Charlie's voice came over the speakers now and the video showed an excited Rae standing next to his seven-year-old self. He was scrawny and looked like a scrubby little kid, in his oversized t-shirt and ripped jeans, through which you could see both scraped and skinned knees.

They were standing in front of the skee-ball machine and Quinn was holding a fried corndog and not paying much attention to Rae as she explained the game to him, too absorbed in actual food to think about anything else.

"I think I ate like four of those that night," Quinn said, watching as young Rae took her first throw, sinking it into one of the 100-point slots and turning to young Quinn with a smirk. Young Quinn looked stunned, nearly dropping his corndog before taking his own turn. The pair went back and forth scoring in the 100 and 50-point slots, the game becoming increasingly competitive with the sound of Charlie's commentating until they were both teasing and laughing together. Even when Rae won.

The video flashed ahead to the two of them standing in front of the dunk tanks again, this time with Rae throwing and Quinn giving instruction until she finally hit the target and dunked a clown. Rae jumped up and down cheering herself on as Quinn stood by laughing and enjoying her victory.

When the screen went black again, the date *September 4, 2000* popped up followed by a video of Quinn's first-ever birthday party that was thrown in this very house. Next was a baseball game at the local ballpark shortly after they'd met Chris and Jett, then a shaky video from 2002 in which the four of them were constructing one of many blanket forts in Rae's basement.

"Rae, no way are we putting those girly lights in here,"
A twelve-year-old Quinn stated, arms crossed over his chest as Rae brought in a string of white lights. "This isn't some princess fort- you're outnumbered."

"But we need light in here and these are pretty!" eleven-year-old Rae protested. "We already have all the Christmas lights up we're going to use, Mom said we can have these."

"No," Quinn said firmly again. "We already have your girly purple sheets."

"Uh-oh, Mom and Dad are fighting again," Jett said, training a video camera back and forth between Quinn and Rae. Chris, hanging another light purple sheet snort-laughed, but looked away quickly at the sight of Quinn's glare.

"Shut up, Jett," Rae snapped. Turning her attention back to Quinn she corrected, "They're not purple, you caveman. They're lilac."

"That's it, take them down," Quinn said, throwing his arms up. "I can't sit here and read Sports Illustrated or

watch Monday night football surrounded by lilac sheets."

"How old are you?" Rae asked, now crossing her arms over her chest, one eyebrow raised.

Quinn ignored her and looked at Chris, "Seriously, take them down. We'll go to Jett's place and get new ones."

"Uh, no way!" Rae interjected. "I'm not going to sit here and watch you guys flip through Sports Illustrated swimsuit edition- because I know you're not actually reading, Quinn- surrounded by Jett's wet-dream-stained sheets."

"Hey!" Jett called out defensively.

Rae glared at the camera. "Tell me I'm wrong."

There was a hesitation before Jett replied, "My mom washes my sheets..."

"That's gross. You shouldn't make her wash them. Your mess, you clean it up."

A derisive laugh sounded from where Quinn was moving the couch around, "Says the girl who has a whole crew of maids cleaning up after her."

Rae scoffed, "I don't make disgusting messes in my bed sheets."

"Of course not, Princess, what was I thinking?" Quinn replied, a playful smirk to his tone now.

"Don't start."

"I say if her highness requests the lilac sheets and twinkly lights, we should do as she says," Chris chimed in.

"I hate you guys," Rae dropped her arms to her sides in defeat. "You're monopolizing this. I'm the one who started these forts and you guys just want to come in here and take over with your gross boy smell, your swimsuit model magazines, and your stained sheets. You know what you are? You're all chauvinists. All of you."

All three boys were on the brink of bursting out laughing.

"Who said anything about playing Monopoly?" Chris cocked an eyebrow.

Jett asked curiously, "What's a show-van-ist?"

"Is it like a peasant?" Quinn asked, tilting his head to the side. "Rae, we don't understand your fancy rich-people lingo. Gotta bring it down to our level, Princess."

"It means you think you can take over because you're boys!"

"I think we can take over because...well, you're outnumbered by boys," Jett said, then quickly added, "Princess."

"Stop calling me that!" Rae shouted. She turned toward the stairs and yelled, "Daaaad!"

This brought all the boys' held-back laughter out and Rae turned and glared at the three of them.

The sound of footsteps made their way down the stairs and a younger Mr. DeRose poked his head into the room, "What is it, Princess?"

At this, the boys all doubled over or collapsed with laughter as Rae sighed heavily, "That was the epitome of being unhelpful. Thank you, Dad."

On the couch next to Rae, Quinn was again bursting with laughter, as was her entire family. "I'm sorry, but that's gold."

"I forgot what jerks you guys were to me all the time!" Rae exclaimed, though she was also laughing.

"I don't know why you put up with us," Quinn said, pulling her closer. He wanted to plant a kiss on her lips but knew everyone was watching.

"She knew you would all do anything for her when it counts," Charlie cut in. "But see, even your friends could tell you two were like an old married couple."

"If I remember correctly, we let you keep the purple sheets up," Quinn said. "Which is what an old married man would've done for his wife."

"You all knew I was right about Jett's sheets," Rae said with a laugh.

"You'd probably still be right about Jett's sheets," Quinn replied, grinning.

After the video presentation which contained several videos through middle and high school, Quinn ended up sitting around the small fire pit on the patio with Charlie and Josh while Rae, Camille, Margaux, and the kids took Harry out into the yard to play.

"I couldn't believe you two never dated in high school." Charlie shook his head. "I waited for it and waited. This is going to make me sound crazy, but I was expecting to come home and find you two making out on the couch like teenagers do. I had it all planned out: I was going to act mad and yell at you guys and then tell Rae I needed to talk to you in private, and then once she'd left I was going to congratulate you and tell you to hold onto her because all the other guys she met back then," Charlie made a face. "Do people still call them *tools*?"

"I think the term people use now is *fuck boy*," Josh cut in, looking about as amused as Quinn felt.

"What? What the hell is wrong with kids?" Charlie chided. "Anyway, I didn't like any of them. I wanted to grab her by the shoulders and just point her in your direction and tell her 'There! There's your guy, that's the one!' But Rae's got a mind of her own and she does things how she wants."

Quinn laughed, but looked at Charlie with disbelief. "I had no idea. I mean, I was crazy about her back then, but... I just didn't think I could compete."

"With what? Pop-collared polo shirts and khaki cargo shorts?" Charlie retorted.

Both Quinn and Josh snorted at that. "I remember that look," Josh nodded. "I was more of a 'skinny jeans and a band t-shirt' kind of kid, though."

"I was just a whatever-thrift-store-rags-would-fit kind of kid," said Quinn, looking back at Charlie. "I guess that's why. I had nothing. I came from nothing, my mom was a damn train wreck, and I just...I just knew I wasn't good enough for her."

Charlie shook his head, "No, Quinn, that's crap. You were the *best* thing that's ever happened to that girl. You let her be *her*, and she didn't get that with anyone else. You showed her how to care about people for who they were, not what they wore or the cars they drove or what kinds of things they could buy her. For ten, eleven years, you were her favorite person, even though all you could give her was yourself."

These were the words Quinn needed to hear, he just hadn't known it until now. It was as if they hovered at his surface like slowly sinking honey, and they began melting into him until they hit him at his core. Once he felt the words and knew them to be true, Quinn wasn't sure if he should jump for joy or kick himself for taking so long to catch on.

Feeling the grin creep across his face, Quinn looked up and met Charlie's gaze. He couldn't get out the words to say thank you, but somehow he felt Charlie knew that's what he'd wanted to say. Charlie nodded briefly and changed the subject before it could get too heartwarming, "And thank every God there is or ever was that I don't have to put up with that asshole, Emerson, anymore."

On their way back to the house, Rae teased him with her fingertips skating up and down his thigh as he drove. She had a light wine-buzz and was playing with fire, thinking he wouldn't pull the vehicle over and finish what she started. Somehow he made it into the entryway before shoving her against the front door to close it, slipping his hands beneath her dress and yanking her lacy panties down to her ankles.

"Is that what you wanted?" he asked, breathing into the soft skin of her neck. "Trying to get me wild for you so I couldn't control myself when we got home?"

"I'm not complaining," Rae said, breathless already, with a mischievous grin as she nipped at his jaw.

"How do you want it?" Quinn ran his mouth down her jaw, her neck, her collar bone. With his hands he cupped her breasts and pushed them up and together so he could trace his tongue along the swell of them.

"It's my birthday, surprise me," Rae replied, gasping as he pulled the strapless dress down, exposing her bare breasts.

"Goddamn, I knew you weren't wearing a bra under this." Quinn dipped his head and took a hardened pink nipple into his mouth. He pressed against her hips and knew she could feel his erection against her stomach. All that teasing in the car had made him solid as a rock. "You can't do that anymore...not in public, baby. Gotta have more than a thin layer of cotton between these beautiful tits and the rest of the world."

"You think so?" Rae wrapped one long leg around him, urging him closer.

Quinn hummed, tongue circling one nipple while his hand teased the other. He channeled his inner caveman and practically grunted, "Mine now. I don't share what's mine."

"Possessive, are we?"

"You have no idea," he breathed heavily. Wrapping his left arm under her ass, he lifted her up and she easily circled her legs around his waist so he could move her further into the house.

In her living room, there was a large sliding glass door that led to the wrap-around porch-balcony overlooking the lake. Her neighborhood was secluded, with plenty of distance, trees, and privacy fences between houses. He slid the door open and stepped onto the covered balcony.

"You're contradicting yourself, Case," Rae teased. "I'm far more exposed now," she moaned the last word, arching her back as Quinn's teeth met the side of her breast.

"I'll make an exception to the rule," said Quinn, "if there's no doubt you belong to me, I'll allow it." He sat down on a cushioned chaise lounge, bringing Rae on top of him. "And if there's no doubt *I* belong to *you*, then I can be exposed, too."

Rae kissed him hard, tongue sweeping into his mouth, flicking against and tasting his. She pulled back and looked in his eyes. "There should never be a doubt that I belong to you." Her hands shoved into his hair, forcing him to kiss her back with the same ferocity. He wanted to breathe her in, consume her, never let her go. Rae's mouth moved along his jaw as she whispered, "I'm your girl, Quinn."

And he was hers. Fuck, he'd *always* been hers.

"Ride me," Quinn demanded hoarsely. "I want you to ride me like you did this morning. Use me. I'm yours, baby, I'm all yours."

Her wicked grin sent a shock down to his cock and she began undressing him. She pushed his jacket off his shoulders to the floor and unbuttoned his shirt. With his shirt undone, she spread it open, splaying her hands over his chest, and he groaned at the hungry look in her eyes as she dragged her fingernails down, down, *down* his abs to his belt. He worked his pants and boxers off as she finished unzipping her dress and letting it fall, exposing all of her.

Taking his cock in her hand, she stroked him gently and he watched with a heavy-lidded stare. Rae was watching her own hand move up and down his shaft, whimpering, biting her lip as though she were enjoying it just as much. Her eyes slowly looked up from beneath her eyelashes, meeting his greedy stare. She looked so hungry for him, needy. He braced himself, taking in a sharp breath before she lowered her mouth to his cock. Her tongue licked the length of it, from base to tip, before her lips wrapped around and she took him inside.

"Oh...oh *God*," Quinn groaned, eyelids threatening to close, but he fought it. He didn't want to miss a second of this. She groaned as his tip came in contact with the back of her throat and it rumbled through him, making him begin a slow thrust.

Quinn grasped a handful of her hair as she took him deep again touching the back of her mouth into her throat, and back up to lick around the tip before taking him fully again. Groaning, muscles in his stomach and thighs flexing, his breath became louder, more ragged.

"Fuck, baby that mouth feels so good." He leaned back, chest heaving slowly as he tried to keep control. "Dammit, Rae, what are you trying to do to me? *Fuck...*"

Just when he thought he was going to lose control, Rae sat up, still holding the base of his throbbing cock in her hand. He was aching so badly for release but needed to see her let loose on top of him, go wild and take what she needed from him first.

Quinn reached for his pants on the floor and hastily pulled a condom out of the pocket. Preparing to open it and roll it on himself, Rae snatched it out of his hands and slowly tore the package open with her teeth, keeping intense, heated eye contact with him. He watched as she slowly rolled it down his length, then leaned over him, kissing between his jaw and his ear.

"You taste so good, Quinn," she whispered, pressing another kiss to his now sweaty skin. He groaned at her words, and outright growled as she slid herself down onto him.

"You can taste me any time," he groaned, grasping her hips and helping her move up and down on his dick. "I fucking promise there's never a wrong time to have your mouth on me."

She grinned playfully. "What if you're up to bat and I want to taste you then?"

"I'll fake an injury...the team can manage without me."

Her mouth came over his again, her body moved with his, their skin sliding against each other, so in tune, such a perfect fit, and he was already close. He watched as her pace quickened, her eyes closed, head lulled back, mouth open with silent pleas and cries of pleasure.

"Yes, baby...fuck," Quinn gritted out, thrusting up and into her. "Use this cock, baby...take what you need from me." He slid his hands into her hair and guided her to him, needing her mouth, her lips. He wanted to feel her cries and moans vibrate into him, take them as his own.

"*Oh God,*" she moaned. He took her bottom lip between his teeth and felt instantly when she got there. Rae gasped and rode him harder, riding out the pleasure, letting her pussy squeeze tight around him, daring him to stay together.

Quinn gripped her hips tight, turning needy and selfish as he finally took his release from her. Fewer than ten strokes into her wet, squeezing sex and he was shaking, sputtering out a guttural groan of sounds and curses and praises to some deity. Rae collapsed on top of him, her hot breath blowing against his neck, and he wrapped both arms around her, wanting to hold her like this all night. Chest-to-chest, her lips on his neck, sleepy and satisfied.

Fingers tangling into her hair, Quinn closed his eyes and let his breathing come down. Things were so perfect. Everything was perfect. Was it too soon for the types of feelings welling up inside him? They'd been there to some degree for ages, but having her, holding her...they were so much more concrete. Clear and startling and true.

I love her.

I am absolutely, irrefutably hers, and I love her.

CHAPTER 18

2007

The night of homecoming had been a complete disaster. It turned out that Britney had *not* forgotten that she'd come with a date and *had* in fact noticed that he'd ditched her at some point in the evening. Even though she ended the night hooking up with a sophomore in the back of his F-150 in the parking lot, she had still taken it upon herself to spread rumors about Quinn throughout the school. He wondered how it did anything to benefit her reputation for everyone to know that she'd given him a blow job and then been ditched, but apparently Quinn's treatment of girls was a far more interesting topic to Traverse City West's gossip network.

As if the colorfully evolving rumors about Quinn being an ungrateful oral sex recipient and womanizer weren't enough, he also had to deal with the second-most talked about topic: TC West's newest power couple, Raelyn DeRose and Liam Hamilton. The buzz of their budding relationship had reached Quinn's ears just in time to see the two of them making out at Rae's locker that Monday morning after the homecoming dance. There wasn't much he could do to avoid it, as their lockers were assigned alphabetically and *DeRose* was only nine lockers down from *Casey*.

Football practices had also been hell, having to put up with Liam as a teammate and listen to him talk about spending the weekends with Rae. Chris and Jett had the habit of looking up at Quinn every time Liam mentioned her. He wasn't sure if they were simply showing their support or if they were trying to gauge how long until Quinn snapped and punched the guy in the face. The practices themselves and the locker room talk weren't nearly as bad as walking out after practice where he had to witness Liam and Rae locking lips up against her Beamer or his Audi. Quinn had been catching rides with Chris and Jett after practices instead and avoiding Rae as much as possible during the days. Liam was *always* with her and couldn't possibly keep his hands or face to himself.

It took about two weeks for the rumors to die down, and the judgmental stare-downs he'd been receiving from several of his female classmates had somehow turned into looks of curious interest or flirtation. This made no sense to Quinn, of course, but he'd take it over the glares and scoffs he'd been getting every time he dared to look at a girl.

It was Friday afternoon and Quinn was aggressively shoving his books in his locker after sixth period, mentally preparing himself for their home game that evening when a smooth, silvery voice met his ears.

"Is it true that you fucked Britney Garrett from behind, only turning her around in time to blow your load in her face?" Alaina Costello was leaning up against the locker next to him with a playful expression that showed she clearly did not believe the rumor.

"Is that what people are saying now?" Quinn asked. He wondered where his classmates came up with this shit.

"Well, I heard it in the locker room after gym class," Alaina replied with a shrug.

Surprised to feel a smirk tug up the corner of his mouth, he returned the flirtatious banter, "Well, then it *must* be true. Everyone knows locker room talk is practically gospel, kinda like anything you read on the internet."

"Etched in stone," Alaina nodded, biting back her smile slightly.

Quinn grabbed his backpack, slung it over one shoulder, and shut his locker. Alaina fell into step beside him as he walked down the hall. "So, you're approaching me because you're into that kind of thing and wondering how much I charge?"

Alaina laughed, "Ew, no! And don't go saying that so loud. The way rumors circulate around this place, who knows what kind of freaks I'll be dealing with next week."

"I know what you mean," Quinn chuckled. "I swear, the weirder these rumors get, the more girls I have giving me attention. As a girl, can you offer any possible explanation for that?"

"*As a girl*," Alaina said, "oddly, yes. Part of it may be that girls now know- or at least think- that you're sexually experienced and they find that attractive. Others just want a guy they know their parents won't approve of."

Looking down, Quinn raised an eyebrow, puzzled, "Is that supposed to make sense? I mean, I guess the first part sort of does, but why would you want to be with a guy who ditches a girl after getting cum all over her three hundred dollar homecoming dress?"

"You got cum on her dress?" she looked up at him, seemingly amused.

"No, just a rumor I heard," Quinn said. "I got called an asshole for not replacing the dress I ruined, and then another girl who'd been listening in asked me what I was doing this weekend."

"And what did you tell her?" Alaina asked, tucking her long, dark curls behind one ear.

"The usual." Quinn shrugged. "Plotting new forms of sexual humiliation and looking for available masochists willing to test my wicked methods."

"Okay, wait," Alaina stopped walking and turned toward Quinn, putting her hands up. "The rumors of you being a sexual sadist are completely untrue- from what I heard of the *real* story, she sort of attacked you- but you're *perpetuating* the rumors anyway?"

"Fighting it seemed like too much work," Quinn said simply.

"You just like that you're getting all this attention," said Alaina with a smirk.

Quinn considered this assessment, "I guess it's not all bad being known as more than 'that poor kid who's really good at hitting a ball'."

"Or Raelyn DeRose's sidekick?"

That stung a little. Partially because he wondered if that's really how people saw him, and partially because he'd actually been enjoying this interaction that had yet to poke at that still-sore wound.

When Quinn failed to respond, Alaina said, "When I got to school and everyone was talking about you and Raelyn, honestly I was sure you two had finally got together. I was surprised to learn they were two separate rumors."

"Yeah, well," Quinn sighed heavily. "You were at least right about *her* getting together with someone." He began walking again, not particularly interested in this new topic of conversation.

Alaina caught up with him and continued anyway, "You guys never really made sense to me anyway."

"Why would you say that?" Quinn asked. His tone was flat, though he was mildly curious.

"Isn't it hard to connect with someone like her?" Alaina questioned. "A trust fund kid whose entire life has been handed to her on a sparkling silver platter? She has no idea what people like us have to deal with."

People like us?

Quinn gave her a sideways glance. Her dark brown hair hung in loose curls past her shoulders which were bare in her off-the-shoulder sweater. Her olive-colored skin looked soft and flawless, and he found himself focusing on the nape of her neck. He'd never considered what kind of life Alaina Costello might have had and he began racking his brain for everything he did know about her. She was artistic, he remembered. She was an excellent painter, sculptor, and sketch artist. He remembered the school making a big deal about one of her sculptures being displayed at the Grand Rapids Art Prize festival, in which artwork was displayed all over the city. She was one of the youngest artists chosen that year. Quinn wondered if art gave her the same feeling of calm and relief from her life as baseball and other sports did for him.

Maybe he did have more in common with Alaina than he did with Rae.

"What makes you think you know anything about what I have to deal with?" Quinn asked, looking ahead and avoiding eye contact.

"You called yourself a poor kid like two minutes ago, so that's something," Alaina said.

"Something we have in common?"

"Among other things," she replied.

"Like what?" Quinn glanced sideways at her again. "You gonna tell me you've got a single mom who's a complete train wreck, too?"

"No, but I *do* have an alcoholic father." Alaina's tone was conversational and casual. "My mom might as well be a single parent, as much parenting as Dad does."

Quinn wasn't interested in explaining as much about his own situation. "I'm sorry, that can't be easy to watch."

"I can't ever decide if it's better or worse that I have a little brother to go through it all with," Alaina continued. "I mean, it's nice to know I'm not alone, but I'm also the one who has to calm him and take care of him when Dad goes off."

"Goes off?" Quinn hadn't meant to press- it really wasn't his business.

"Usually just yelling," Alaina clarified, "He can get pretty mean and belligerent...sometimes he'll break something or throw shit."

"I'm glad I don't have siblings," Quinn said. "I wouldn't want anyone else to have to experience the same shit I do. I've got enough with having to take care of my mom when she...can't take care of herself."

There was a small pause before Alaina forced a shy smile. "I'm sorry, this conversation took a turn for the depressing," she said. "Sometimes I feel like we're just so surrounded by these rich assholes here, it gets exhausting trying to act like my life is just as perfect as theirs."

"Yeah, I guess it does," Quinn said, realizing he really didn't have anyone to talk to who could relate to his own situation. While he wasn't glad that others were suffering, it did feel a little less lonely knowing that he wasn't the only one without a happy family. "Are you coming to the game tonight?"

"Oh, no," Alaina replied. "I don't do sports. Participating, watching...not my thing."

"You sure? You'd look pretty cute in that cheer uniform," Quinn teased.

She raised an eyebrow and her look became almost threatening, "*Don't.* Just don't even go there. I'm not even going to be flattered that you think I'd look cute. I don't want anyone imagining me as a damn sideline cheerleader."

Quinn snickered, "Got it."

They had reached the doors and walked out toward the parking lot together. Chris and Jett were standing by one of the benches outside the door and greeted Quinn as he walked out, and he noticed their matching looks of intrigue when they saw he was walking and laughing alongside Alaina.

"Hey, Quinn and *Alaina*," Jett said, very unsubtly.

"Hey guys." Alaina held up her hand in a wave.

Quinn's focus had gone elsewhere at the sight of long blonde hair over a white, green, and gold football jersey, and those skinny jeans he swore she wore just to torture him. Rae was wearing Liam's jersey. Clearly this was more significant than her borrowing Quinn's baseball hats all the time. He was caught between feeling sick to his stomach and wanting to fucking level that smug bastard. When Liam wrapped his arm around Rae and grabbed a handful of her ass, that feeling became far less mixed. Quinn watched as Liam pulled Rae to him and kissed her, both hands now hanging onto her butt.

Quinn groaned in disgust, "Do they have to fucking do that in front of everyone?" At first he hadn't realized that he'd spoken out loud. When Chris, Jett, and Alaina all turned their attention to him, he added defensively, "Seriously, every time I turn around they're practically eating each other's faces. It's fucking gross."

"Those people are making out," Jett pointed to a couple pressed up against a Jeep who were essentially dry humping. "Does that bother you?"

No. But if that were Liam and Rae it fucking would.

"Yes," Quinn lied. "It's gross. Why can't people just do that shit in their cars? Or their bedrooms? Not everyone needs to see that."

"Maybe if you were getting some it wouldn't bother you so much," Chris said, subtly nodding toward Alaina behind her back while looking meaningfully at Quinn.

"Or maybe if you suddenly discovered you had a multi-million dollar trust fund, you could finally get Raelyn's attention," Alaina said, eyes traveling back and forth between Quinn and Rae.

"That's not why she's with him," Quinn insisted. "That's not Rae. She's...she doesn't care about that."

"Are you sure?" Alaina asked. "You guys have been friends for years and she's never considered even trying to kiss you? Wasn't her last boyfriend Ryan North? His dad's like a big shot administrator at the hospital, right?"

"So?" Quinn looked to Chris and Jett for support.

"I heard they went to the Dominican Republic or something last year for spring break and he bought a hospital just so he could write the trip off as a business expense," Alaina said. "*Those* are the kinds of guys your girl is interested in."

Quinn shook his head, "You don't know her."

"Maybe not," Alaina said, "but maybe you don't know her as well as you think."

Chris and Jett stood awkwardly, looking down at their feet, not meeting Quinn's eye.

"See you around, Quinn," Alaina gave another wave toward Chris and Jett, who looked up just enough to give feeble waves of their own, before heading off into the parking lot toward her red Pontiac.

Quinn looked to Chris and Jett, arms out to his sides. "What the fuck, guys? She's your friend, too!"

Chris opened his mouth and paused while he contemplated his words, "She *is* our friend and I don't think she's that shallow. But..." he looked to Jett for assistance.

"But she's with Liam, Quinn," Jett finished. "She picked him. Granted, I don't think she knew you were an option, but for now, maybe you should try finding someone else. Or just find a way to accept that you lost this round."

"You're seventeen, dude," said Chris. "We're supposed to have fun, make out with a whole bunch of girls, try to get to third base or see how far they'll let us go. We're not supposed to be hyper-focused on one person."

Quinn squinted over his shoulder where moments ago Rae and Liam had been sucking face. Liam was no longer there and Rae was now talking to a group of girls he knew were on the swim team with her. As if sensing his gaze, her head swiveled around they locked eyes. In spite of himself, his mouth curved into a small but friendly smile. He wanted to be mad at her, though he supposed she really hadn't done anything wrong. Rae returned his smile with a much wider one and a wave.

Turning back around, he let out a long sigh, "You guys are probably right."

"Exactly! Yes!" Chris pumped his fist. "After we win our game tonight, we'll go to the mixer and *you* are going to begin your reckless adolescent phase."

"He's a late bloomer, folks," Jett said, slapping a hand to Quinn's back, "but I think he'll catch on quick."

Nearly two months after Quinn's declaration to really enjoy being seventeen, it had become abundantly clear that he had been squandering his potential simply holding out for one girl, amazing as she was. His classmates had forgotten all about the homecoming scandal and his new reputation as a badass lady-killer had reached, well, just about everyone.

At that first post-game mixer, he had danced with several girls, and had to be pulled away from a hot and heavy lip-lock session at the end of the gym corridor with a girl when Chris had told him if he wasn't walking home, they needed to get going. In most of his classes, he had girls asking to pair up with him for in-class work and asking him for help when they clearly didn't need it. Most of the girls would flirt shamelessly, giggling at everything he said and using any excuse they could find to touch his arms or shoulders. Frequently, Quinn would take advantage of these cues and ask the girl out.

By December, his confidence had been elevated to the point that he rarely *asked* the girls if they would like to go out with him but simply told them he was taking them out. The lines "Go out with me this weekend" or "Let me take you out tonight" were now regular and frequent pieces of his vocabulary bank, and they had yet to fail him.

Despite all the fun and female attention he was receiving, the reason for it was painfully clear every time he caught sight of Rae. She was still dating Liam, and Quinn couldn't help the tight squeeze in his chest every time he saw them together. It was a reminder that he was simply stalling, distracting himself until the girl he really wanted was available again.

Thankfully, Quinn had two classes with Rae in which he felt he could pretend nothing had changed. They talked and worked together whenever there was partner work or free time. It wasn't as if their friendship had collapsed because of her relationship or his flings, but they certainly spent far less time in each other's company in and out of school. No amount of third-base hook-ups could stop Quinn from missing Rae's companionship as much as he did.

It was the week before winter break, and Rae walked back to Quinn's locker with him after their shared chemistry class. There was a small group of girls huddled near Quinn's locker when they approached, but upon registering Rae's presence, they dispersed abruptly.

"Wow," Rae said as she watched the fleeing trio. "Sorry, Casanova, I didn't mean to cockblock you there."

Quinn furrowed his brow and looked at Rae with puzzled amusement, "I don't think *you* can cockblock *me*."

"What do you mean?" Rae asked, her attention still on the retreating girls.

"I could cockblock you by preventing you from getting some, but it doesn't work the other way around," Quinn explained.

"I thought it was like...blocking you from giving your cock to someone else," Rae said, her expression perplexed and adorable.

"Uh, no," Quinn chuckled, turning the combination lock on his locker.

Her eyebrows raised. "Huh, I guess I've been using that all wrong." She blinked a few times, then set her gaze on Quinn. "What are your plans for the holiday break?"

"Probably just hangin' with the guys," he shrugged. "And you? Spending Christmas in Paris with your new beau?"

Rae's eyebrows pulled together. "Why would you think that? And since when do you use words like 'beau'?"

"I was trying to appeal to your French side," said Quinn. "And I don't know. We peasants don't know what you fancy *power couples* do on your holidays."

"I think I'd take you to Paris with my family before I took my new *beau*," Rae replied with an eye-roll.

Quinn closed his locker after grabbing his gym bag. He cleared his throat, trying to sound more casual than eager. "Trouble in paradise?"

Rae gave a small shrug, falling into step beside him as they began their trek down the hall. "It's fine. He's not much of a conversationalist."

"Maybe you should try grunting," Quinn offered, biting his lip and failing to repress his grin at his own joke. "Pound on your chest a little bit."

Failing to conceal her own giggle, she pinched his arm. "He's not a caveman, Quinn."

"Could've fooled me," Quinn said.

"Well, you only see him, like, on the football field, or in the locker rooms, or weight room. You guys all sound like cavemen in that environment," Rae said. "We just run out of things to talk about and then it's like, guess we'll just make out or fool around. Honestly, Quinn, I think my lips are getting chapped."

"Spare me the details."

"Oh, sure, I have to listen to every last detail of your endeavors from every girl you've gone out with, but you have a right to complain when I talk about kissing Liam?" Rae said, incredulously.

"I don't have to hear about it. I can see it just fine."

Rae's cheeks flushed. "Oh, right." She seemed to glance around at their surroundings, figuring out where they were headed. "Are you going to the gym?"

"Yeah, I've got weight training. Your boy toy's in my class if you want to say hi." Quinn had no idea why he had suggested this, but he was getting the impression their relationship was approaching its expiration date.

Rae stopped walking. "No, that's okay. I didn't bring my Chapstick." She gave a *what can I do about it?* kind of shrug with her hands up. "I have a free period so I'm just going to head to the library," Rae placed her hand on his arm briefly before turning away. "*Á bientôt*, Quinn!"

"I don't know what that means!" Quinn called after her. She turned and glanced over her shoulder with a playful smirk in his direction then turned back around, hair swinging and swaying across her back as she set off for the library. Quinn found himself staring after her with a satisfied grin for a few moments before continuing to the boys' locker rooms.

Once dressed and out in the weight room, Quinn, Chris, and Jett found their places at the squat rack and deadlift platform and began loading bars with weights.

Jett gave a quick look around the weight room before saying in a low voice to Quinn, "Did I see you and Rae walking together in the hall? You guys were looking pretty friendly."

"Well, we are friends," said Quinn, loading the final fifty-pound plate on his bar. He caught the exchange of glances between his friends. "What?"

"I mean, I know the past two months have been a nice distraction for you, and obviously we're glad you took our advice," said Jett, "but I guess I just thought you were still into her."

"The past two months have been like a Rae detox," Quinn said.

It was a lie, of course, but something made him want to keep his feelings for Rae tucked away. After the whole homecoming debacle, it had almost seemed worse that his friends knew what kind of pain he was in watching Rae with Liam. He wasn't able to pretend he was fine because they knew he wasn't. There was something that made him want to go back to simpler times when the four of them were just friends and no one had any idea that he secretly pictured Rae as his own.

Now, he looked across the weight room to where Rae's boyfriend was performing chest presses and grunting loudly at the top of each rep. He wondered what she saw in him. Obviously the guy was ripped, but Rae couldn't just be into him for that. Quinn wasn't exactly scrawny, and there might be guys who could bench more than Liam. *Maybe.*

"It was just this long-held crush, and now I'm good," he shrugged. "I'd been missing out just focusing all my attention on her, and now look. I'm livin' the fuckin' dream."

Chris and Jett hesitated, looking at each other skeptically, then back to Quinn. Jett got in position to spot Quinn, and Chris finally spoke up, "And who do you have to thank for livin' the fuckin' dream?"

"Don't flatter yourselves," Quinn replied with a cocky slanted grin. "You probably wouldn't have suggested it if you'd known I'd be playing the field this good. You guys had no idea I'd take all your options away when I got in the game."

"Oh, but we're the ones flattering ourselves?" said Chris with a shake of his head. "Sounds like someone needs to let a little air out of that ego."

"It's only ego talking if it's not true," Quinn said with a grunt as he stood back up from his low squat.

"Yeah, yeah…" Jett rolled his eyes and Chris laughed as he set his deadlift bar back on the platform.

The rest of the weight training class went on with the guys joking around while they lifted, alternating stations and spotters, talking about the girls they were hanging out with over the weekend or ones they had seen recently. Jett admitted he was interested in a particular girl in his French class but had no idea how to ask her out. Quinn silently wished he'd signed up for French at the beginning of high school so he could understand when Rae randomly threw sexy little French phrases at him.

"What's…'ah bee-yen-toe'?" Quinn asked as they made their way back into the locker rooms to change. Quinn had completely sweat through his shirt and wasn't going to be able to avoid taking a shower.

"Á bientôt?" Jett repeated, but far more French-sounding, "It just means 'see you soon'. Why?"

"Oh, uh, just something Rae said before she left for the library," Quinn muttered, realizing too late he didn't want to get caught talking or thinking about Rae too much.

"Soon, huh?" Chris said. "Are you guys gonna start hanging out again outside of school? Now that you're really back to being *just* friends?"

Quinn thought he detected a flicker of doubt or skepticism in Chris's tone but ignored it. "I don't know. I guess I wouldn't mind it. It's not like I'll be having too many dates over the next two weeks while we're on break."

Raucous laughter and other male voices filled the locker room as a group of seniors made their way in. Among the new group was Liam Hamilton, who seemed to be the source of the laughter. He was about the same height as Quinn, but had more bulk, with a broad chest that he seemed to puff out when he walked.

Tall and lanky Wes Evans, with his floppy boy-band hair was peeling off his shirt on the way to his locker as he spoke to Liam,

"You're not seriously telling me you've been with her for two months and haven't hit that yet."

Quinn's eyes snapped up, but he kept his head low, still rummaging around his gym bag for his shower stuff. Chris and Jett both stopped what they were doing to subtly gauge Quinn's response. If he wasn't mistaken, Quinn could've sworn he saw both his friends flare their nostrils and go tense, too.

"Hey, hey, hey," Liam put his hands up defensively. "I knew it was going to take time going into it, all right? She's a virgin, remember? But it's not like I'm not getting anywhere."

"Oh yeah?" Wes asked, grabbing a towel before walking toward the showers, "Tell me you at least got *something* in those panties." He held up a hand and wiggled his fingers, raising his eyebrows suggestively.

Liam laughed wryly, "Oh, fuck yeah. Gotta prep that tight pussy for what's coming."

Quinn stood up, his jaw and muscles now clenched as he stared at the row of lockers, his back to Liam. Jett looked as if he were biting his tongue, and Chris shook his head at Quinn. He wasn't sure if the gesture was out of disbelief in what they were hearing, or if it was meant as a warning for Quinn to not let it get to him.

The voice of Nick Preston, a senior wrestler, joined the conversation, "There he is; we were starting to think you'd gone soft on us."

"Nah," Liam's cocky voice rang out. "I just like a little bit of a challenge, ya know?"

Fucking jackass…who the hell does this guy think he is?

He couldn't wait to tell Rae about this. It would be tough, and probably awkward, but she needed to know her boyfriend was a fucking creep who didn't respect her boundaries or privacy. He was sure she wouldn't hesitate to kick this asshole to the curb if she knew how he talked about her in a full locker room of eagerly listening ears.

Grabbing his towel, soap, and shampoo, Quinn turned and walked rather stiffly toward the showers, glowering at Liam over his shoulder as he passed by. He'd expected Liam to look alarmed or maybe concerned that Quinn had overheard, but instead the smug bastard smirked in response.

He fucking smirked.

Quinn was white hot. He turned away from Liam and let an aggravated breath out his nose like a bull getting ready to charge, and, with much effort, forced himself to his destination before he decked the son of a bitch.

His movements during his shower were robotic, eyes staring ahead, replaying the vulgar discussion of his best friend's intimate life. He squeezed his eyes shut tight, willing the sickening images of Liam having his way with her, touching her, out of his head. The memory of her cute grin as she walked away and her flirty French popped into his head, helping him breathe easier.

She's over him. He just doesn't know it yet. She's getting sick of him. That's what she'd been hinting at, right?

Quinn walked back to his locker after his shower, toweling off and getting dressed. Liam, Wes, and Nick started up their boastful discussions of female conquests again.

"I remember thinking I'd hit the jackpot when I hooked up with Candace Newman," said Wes, "but Raelyn DeRose, man. She's like a *prime* fuckin' piece. That pussy probably tastes like some gourmet *coq au vin.*"

The sardonic laughter that met Quinn's ears instantly made his muscles tense and he could practically hear his blood boiling. He looked up at Jett and Chris who had also gone rigid at these last comments; Jett met Quinn's stare and Chris was glaring up at the seniors who were still jeering and carrying on about Rae.

"The way she uses that mouth of hers- mm!" Liam moaned crudely. "Fuck, you'd think I was the gourmet meal."

The echoing bang of a locker door being slammed shut cut through another chorus of raucous laughter. Everyone looked in the direction of the loud noise, and Quinn was surprised to see it had come from Jett who was now staring down the guys across the room.

"You guys might wanna be fuckin' careful," Jett said, his voice low and threatening. "I don't think I need to remind you we've known that girl you're boasting about for a long fuckin' time, and I guarantee if *we* tell her how you're talking in here, it'll be game over for you."

"Aw, come on," Liam whined mockingly. "This guy knows what I'm talkin' about, right?" He gestured toward Quinn, who looked up but refused to respond. "This guy's got all the girls in the school eating out of the palm of his hand- kudos, by the way. That was pretty impressive how you were able to show Raelyn up after she picked me over you."

Liam's cronies stood on either side of him, watching with enjoyment. Their self-satisfied grins made Quinn want to level each one of them, but he remained calm- at least on the outside. He was glaring at Liam, still not taking the bait. He'd drawn himself to his full height and was standing with his shoulders back, feeling almost like he could stare down at Liam.

"It's too bad, really," Liam continued, the smug grin still plastered to his face. "You can have anyone you want *except* her. It must just kill you. All those years being her friend and she can't see you as anything more than that."

Chris and Jett had flanked themselves on either side of Quinn and the six of them were now standing across from each other, squared up and ready for one side to break first. The rest of the small weight training class had positioned themselves on the outside to watch.

"Your time's almost up, by the looks of it anyway," said Chris. He and Jett must have been watching Quinn and Rae's interaction in the hallway a little closer than they'd let on.

"After tonight, I'm not really worried about it," Liam said with a shrug. "We've got a *romantic* little night planned and I'll finally pop that million-dollar cherry. I'd say you can have her after that, but that'll never happen."

Swallowing hard, Quinn clenched his hands into fists, and clenched his jaw even harder. He'd be lucky if he didn't break a goddamn tooth. There was no way this douchebag was going to have sex with Rae. Not if he could help it. Quinn refused to believe she would let this guy just do whatever he wanted to her. He imagined that's exactly how it would be with Liam; he'd just take what he wanted without any regard to how it was for her. She deserved a hell of a lot better than this jackass.

"I'd actually be embarrassed if I were you," Liam continued, "between your crack-whore mother and being some rich family's charity case." At this, Quinn's expression must have faltered. "Oh yeah, Raelyn told me all about it."

"You don't know what you're talking about," Quinn said, and though his voice sounded sure, his insides were twisting. Rae wouldn't have told Liam about any of that, would she?

"Don't I?" Liam goaded, taking a step closer. As though flipping a switch, his voice went from goading to sweetly concerned, "'Come on, hun, you can tell me about it. He's an important person in your life, and that means he's important to me, too'." The malicious smirk returned to his face. "She'll never respect you as a man, Quinn. Her family took you in like a fucking stray dog."

Quinn felt himself take a step closer, closing the gap between him and Liam. They were nearly eye-to-eye, though Quinn was a fraction of an inch taller.

The part of him holding onto his and Rae's friendship was telling him Liam was just taking a good guess- it wouldn't be hard to figure out. But another part of him was absolutely furious that she would even talk about him, say *anything* to this asshole, that had to do with him. She knew how important it was to keep his home life a secret. She knew how much he wished he could refuse her family's help, and how much he wanted to make something of himself so he could pay them back one day. That she would talk about him, especially to this guy, felt like a stab in the back. It felt like an unforgivable betrayal.

"I know you think you wanna hit me, but think again," said Liam. "One hit, and I can have my lawyer take you for everything you own- which, I suppose, probably isn't much."

"You fuckin' rich kids," Quinn's steely glare bore into Liam, "with your lawyers and your parents' money always there to bail you out. I'd be embarrassed not being man enough to fight my own battles."

A spark flickered in Liam's eyes as his expression grew more delighted. "Go ahead, *Case*. Spend your weekend buried in legal fees, and I'll spend mine buried in balls deep in your girl."

And his blood boileth over.

There was a flash of red that flooded his vision before he threw his first punch. His fist connected with flesh, and there was a satisfying crunch. Next to him, Chris and Jett had begun their brawls with Wes and Nick. Fists were flying, bodies were falling to the floor. Quinn grabbed Liam's shirt and pulled him back up, shoving him against the lockers and throwing another punch to his already bloodied face. Liam grunted, then bent low, sending his shoulder into Quinn's ribs and throwing him backwards. He should've guessed the offensive lineman would use his football-tackle skills to his advantage.

The two were sent over a bench and wrestled on the floor. Liam was pinning Quinn down. He pulled his fist back to wind up for the punch, but Jett wrapped an arm around Liam's neck before he could take his swing, pulling him off of Quinn in a chokehold. As Quinn stood back up, a fist caught his jaw, sending him staggering sideways. Nick was shorter and stocky with a baby face, but *fuck*, he had a solid punch. Squaring up with his new opponent, Quinn attempted to blink the dizziness away before sending an uppercut to Nick's gut. With Nick doubled over, Quinn placed a hand on the back of his head and drove his knee into his face, then shoved him over, moving back to his original target.

Liam was throwing punches at Chris, who was dodging them like a champion boxer. Quinn prepared himself with a deep breath in, and quick out, setting his sights on Liam and charging. The side tackle sent Liam crashing through the crowd of onlookers and onto the locker room floor near the entrance. Quinn managed to get a few good shots at Liam's face, and when Liam held his arms up to block the blows, Quinn started on his abdomen. An elbow flew up and caught the bottom of Quinn's chin, then a fist met his cheekbone, making him sway slightly, but he didn't lose his superior position.

A whistle echoed through the locker room, piercing ears, but not halting the fight between Quinn and Liam. Two sets of arms wrapped around Quinn, pulling him away and off of Liam, who hadn't seemed to register the presence of the gym teacher and football coach, along with various other coaches. With Quinn's weight off of him, Liam heaved himself back up and charged back at Quinn. Coach Andrews and Coach Landon rushed forward to stop Liam before he could make contact and pulled him back several feet.

"What the hell is going on in here?" The football coach-slash-gym teacher's forehead vein was pulsing as he shouted and glared back and forth between the two students who were being held back. Both Quinn and Liam were covered in blood, both their own and each other's, and were glaring intently at the other, not speaking.

"Would anyone else who witnessed this like to give me an idea?" Coach Barlow shouted into the room.

There was an awkward shuffle as the boys in the room looked from one to another, waiting to see if someone was going to speak up. Chris and Jett stepped up next to Quinn and the coaches registered their injuries for the first time. Nick was leaning against a locker, covering his gushing bloody nose, and Wes was wiping at his lip which was both swollen and bleeding.

"Case, why don't you come with me and tell me your side of things?" the baseball coach's familiar voice suggested, and Quinn realized Coach Garcia was one of the men holding him back.

"Fine," Quinn answered gruffly. His arms were slowly released, though the two coaches still kept a hand on either shoulder as they escorted him past Liam and out of the locker room.

Quinn was not in the mood to talk. His adrenaline was still pumping, and his anger was still at the forefront of his mind. Not only had Rae chosen that fucking pig over him, but she'd confided in the guy. She'd told Liam things about *him* that he didn't want anyone else to know. What the hell had she been thinking?

He was sure their *romantic date* was likely off for the evening, so he wasn't going to bother rushing to tell her everything that had been aired out in the open for the whole locker room to hear, or that Liam was totally playing her.

No, he needed time to cool off before he talked to her. He wanted to know why she was running her mouth about him to people who have no fucking right to know anything. Even more, he wanted to know if what Liam had said was true. Is that really why she couldn't see him as more than a friend? Did she really see him as some charity case to help her rich family feel better about having more money than God?

Fuck that.

He didn't need anyone feeling sorry for him. What he needed was something, *someone* to get that thought off his mind. Someone who understood him. Someone he could bitch to about all these entitled bastards strutting around their school like they're a damn gift to the planet. He just wanted to escape. He thought this must be how drug addicts felt when they're dying for a hit of something. But no, drugs were off the table for him. He would have to find some other high.

Dark brown curls, olive skin, and coffee brown eyes flickered in his mind. That sassy fuck 'em all attitude, and her way of delivering a hard-to-swallow dose of reality. Once he was discharged from the nurse and no doubt sent to collect his things to go home with a suspension, he would find Alaina Costello and they would get the fuck out of this place.

CHAPTER 19

The weeks following Raelyn's birthday were complete bliss. Even though she had to work her regular hours, she still saw Quinn during the day. He would either bring her lunch or pick her up for lunch most days, and she would of course see him when he came in for his therapy sessions. After working hours, they were inseparable. Quinn would arrive at her house only minutes after she got home and either join her in the shower or start cooking them dinner so that they could eat once she was out and dressed and have the rest of the evening to themselves.

While much of their time was spent in Raelyn's bed or occasionally Quinn's hotel suite, they still made sure to get out and do things together on the weekends. For the Fourth of July weekend they had taken a trip to Mackinaw Island and stayed at the Grand Hotel, another weekend they joined Amira and Brody on a bike and brew tour around the city. Raelyn's dad invited them out on their pontoon, and they'd been on the lake the entire previous weekend, lazing around on the top deck and soaking up the sun.

The day of the bachelorette party arrived, and Raelyn was ready for a girl's day. They were meeting at Amira's house to go over the itinerary, play some drinking games and take some shots- it was a solid start. Amala passed out black tank tops for everyone with various *Game of Thrones* sayings on them, such as 'Hand of the Bride,' 'He bent the Knee,' and 'Hangover is Coming.' Raelyn had requested the 'I Drink and I Know Things' design and started her day off with a strong mimosa and a tequila shot.

They had a two o'clock appointment for a *Kayak, Bike, and Brew* tour, in which they started on bikes and rode to different breweries, then hopped into kayaks and kayaked to several more. As much fun as she'd been having with Quinn lately, Raelyn had forgotten how therapeutic it was to spend time with the girls and get a little rowdy. It nearly felt like she was revisiting her wild party days from college, minus the manhunt. A party bus which had been completely decked out in themed decorations picked them up for their dinner reservations on the Leelanau peninsula. Raelyn was grateful for the food after drinking such a wide variety of alcoholic beverages all day. Unfortunately, the large pasta dish hadn't quite seemed to absorb all the alcohol, so Quinn would likely be carrying her into her house again like he had several weeks ago.

The girls had been split into teams based on the family houses- Lannister, Stark, Baratheon, and Targaryen- for the themed scavenger hunt Amala had put together. The hunt featured tasks such as finding men with hair like Jon Snow, or someone with a dragon tattoo. They had to take a picture with a shirtless man- Raelyn suspected this was an ode to all the naked women in brothels that were featured in several episodes- and challenge someone to a sword fight with the fake mini-swords Amala had provided in their goodie bags.

Raelyn and Amira were completely killing the competition- Fifty points to House Stark! Or something to that effect.

The party bus dropped the loud, cheering and stumbling group of girls off at Amira and Brody's house around ten o'clock, where the guys already had the bonfire going in the backyard.

The previous summer, Brody had insisted on converting their unused garden shed into a mini-pub. It was a full-on Irish style pub crammed into the shed, with an outdoor walk-up window to order drinks. There were draughts on tap, a wine fridge, and fully back-lit liquor display with a wide variety of mixers. Of course this meant someone had to play bartender, but the guys always seemed to have fun with it.

Amira was holding up her House Stark banner as she hopped, quite successfully, off the party bus and ran toward the makeshift pub, where Brody was passing out drinks to the guys. In the dark with only hanging globe lights and the fire, Brody's bright orange hair made him easy to spot. Amira leapt into her fiancé's arms and gave him a sloppy, drunken kiss.

"We won!" Amira cheered, thrusting her mini-sword into the air.

"Oh shit, that thing's not actually sharp, is it?" Brody asked, alarmed. He grabbed Amira's hand and pulled it down to examine the sword. Upon discovering it was both plastic and had a mostly rounded tip, he sighed with relief and set her back on the ground.

Raelyn stood next to the bar window and looked around for Quinn. Disappointed that he hadn't shown up yet, she slunk back onto the small bar with a sigh. She snapped to attention and a tingle ran down her spine at the familiar deep, smooth voice that sounded from behind her.

"Congrats on the win." Emerson was inside the pub shed, behind the bar. He handed a drink out the window. "Tito's and tonic with lime? Or is it a wine night?"

As the sudden surprise of hearing her ex's voice again faded, she was pleased to note that Emerson's presence wasn't bothering her nearly as much as she'd expected it would when she'd first received the email about this night. And there was her new blissful happiness that she was finding with Quinn. That helped, too.

"Actually, I've been drinking since noon," Raelyn replied. "Any chance you've got some Tylenol and water back there?"

Emerson grinned his charming grin, all straight white teeth with a twinkle in his stormy blue eyes. His sandy blonde hair was short, as if he'd recently gotten a haircut, but his beard was the same perfectly trimmed length as always. "Actually, we stocked up on that for just this occasion." He ducked into the bar and came back moments later with a water bottle and a travel packet of Tylenol.

"Perfect, thanks." Raelyn grabbed the items off the bar ledge and ripped open the packet.

"No tip?" Emerson asked, a playful tone to his voice.

She wasn't drunk enough to not be annoyed by him trying to flirt. "Hmm...don't screw girls who aren't your fiancé on your office desk?"

"All right, I had that coming," Emerson said in an uncharacteristically humble manner. Then he attempted a charming flirt again, "Would it help if I said I'm sorry? Again?"

"Be sorry or don't," Raelyn sighed. "It's not going to change a thing now."

"Missssster Yates!" Amira slurred, bumping into Raelyn and slapping her hand down on the bar ledge. "Are you bothering my best friend?"

"Miss Jones," Emerson dipped his head. "I was just getting her what she'd asked for, with the side of an apology."

"Little late for that," Amira scoffed, then giggled drunkenly. "But it's fine because she's got a new man now."

"She does?" Emerson asked, clearly taken off guard. "That's news to me. Must be a new thing?"

"About a month," Raelyn shrugged, turning to scan what she could see of the road in hope of spotting a charcoal Bronco.

"Who's the lucky guy?" Emerson asked. He then set a shot glass on the bar, poured it full of Jameson and tossed it back. Emerson and whiskey were usually a bad combination. It completely negated his filter and he turned into a giant, testosterone-fueled mega-douche.

"He'll be here later," said Raelyn, watching as he poured himself another shot. "Don't you think you should take it easy on the Jameson?"

"Why?" Emerson asked. "You used to like when we'd drink like this. We'd end up fighting and then fuck like the world was ending."

Raelyn rolled her eyes, though she did indeed remember those nights. There was so much fire in their arguments, she often felt like Emerson would pick fights with her just for the steamy make up sex.

"Just try not to make an ass of yourself," Raelyn finally said. She looped her arm through Amira's and steered them toward the fire where the other girls were seated.

The fire pit was dug into the ground and there was a perfectly landscaped stone patio surrounding the now roaring bonfire. There were four tall posts on each corner of the patio with globe lights strung from one to the other, outlining the space. Raelyn and Amira sat on one of the live-edge wood benches that surrounded the fire. Amira put her arm around her best friend and rested her head on her shoulder.

"This was so much fun," Amira sighed, words still slurred, but dreamy.

"I needed a night like this," Raelyn replied, "and I'm so glad you had a good time." She put her own arms around her friend and gave her a squeezing hug. Unable to conceal what was on her mind, she asked, "So, Brody didn't tell him about Quinn, huh?"

"Apparently not," said Amira. "I know he told James and Ethan because they're *huge* baseball fans and they almost wet their pants when they heard a major league all-star was coming to our house."

Raelyn smiled. "I wonder how Quinn will react to that sort of attention. He always acts so shy and humble when people recognize him in public. Nothing like how he's portrayed in magazines and on TV."

Amira lifted her head up and looked perplexed, "That's true. I wonder if it's an act... I totally thought he'd be all, like, cocky and full of himself. But every time we've gone out he just, like, smiles and waves all nice."

"In high school, he was cocky on the field. Sometimes around girls, too. Maybe that's why," Raelyn pondered. "He's not trying to impress anyone because he knows he can be himself with me."

"Aww, that's so cute. That's why I can't wait for you guys to get married," Amira cooed.

"Oh my God, Amira," Raelyn chortled. "We've been together for a month."

"No, no, no," Amira held up and wagged her finger, "You've been together since you were seven and just now realized it. Everyone else knew it, by the sounds of it, but you finally just figured it out." Amira gasped suddenly, "Aww, Raaaaae! You guys are soul mates!" Amira nearly sounded like she was going to cry.

Raelyn grinned and shook her head, then glanced down at her phone. "Where is he anyway? I thought he'd be here by now." She turned and looked toward the house again, craning her neck in hopes of seeing that messy head of hair.

"Oh no," Amira said, turning to look as well. "Looks like my future hubby has hi-jacked him to show him off." Amira pointed toward the shed where, instead of the mess of hair, Quinn was sporting a backwards baseball cap. With the limited light, it was hard to tell from where they sat, but Raelyn thought it looked like his official LA hat. His casual t-shirt stretched over his broad chest and biceps, and Raelyn couldn't help the mischievous grin that tugged at her lips.

Oh, the things I am going to do to you later, Quinn Casey.

"Looks like Brody might have prepared him for meeting fans," Raelyn said, amused. "I haven't seen him wear a baseball hat since he's been home." She was surprised at how much this relaxed, baseball jock look was already making her body hum from a distance.

"Aren't you going to jump his bones?" Amira asked, excitedly.

"I think I'll let the guys have him for a few before I steal him away," said Raelyn, watching as Brody led Quinn into the mini-pub to meet the rest of the guys. "Also, I think it might be good if I'm not there when he meets Emerson. He's already had at least two shots of whiskey, and I don't want to give him an excuse to go full dick-bag on Quinn. Because he will."

"Good call, sister," Amira said, turning back to face the fire again. "If they're not out of there in five though, we should probably go run interference."

"Agreed," Raelyn nodded, and the pair returned their focus to the bonfire and the rest of the girls surrounding it.

Quinn arrived at Amira and Brody's house a little later than he'd expected. At the bar with Chris and Jett, he'd been trying to convince one or both of them to come with him. He was eager to see Rae, but anxious at the thought of meeting her ex-fiancé. This was the guy who just over a year ago Rae had been planning to marry. He wasn't just some ex-boyfriend with an expiration date approaching. To her, he was the one, even if it hadn't lasted.

"You're *Quinn Casey*," Jett had stated. He and Chris then went back and forth reminding him exactly what that meant. He was a Major League star player on, arguably, the best team in the league. He had a multi-million-dollar salary. He was featured in magazines and had proven he could get just about any woman he wanted. They assured him the one who should be anxious in this particular situation was Emerson.

Once his ego had been stroked enough and he was feeling good about himself, if even a little cocky, he left for the party.

He pulled into the driveway of the large modern craftsman, grabbed his LA ball cap out of his back seat and flipped it back on his head. Just to serve as a reminder of who Rae's ex was messing with. Hopping out of the Bronco and heading around back, he spotted Brody on the back patio and waved. Brody was standing next to two men who must be brothers. Both tall with red hair and freckles.

"Quinn!" Brody exclaimed. "Guys, I told you he'd be coming." He clapped his hand to Quinn's and slapped him on the back before stepping back and introducing his brothers, Ethan and James.

"We were just grabbing another case to restock the pub," Brody said, gesturing to the case of Labatt Blue in James's hand.

"The pub?" Quinn raised a curious brow.

"Yeah, you have to check this out." Brody waved his hand for Quinn to follow him down the yard.

There was a charcoal gray garden shed with white trim and a burnt-wood sign on the door stamped with "Kalahan's Pub." A large shamrock was burnt into the wood, and there was a long, open window next to the door that appeared to wrap around the side of the shed. There were bar stools set up along the outside near the window that had a small ledge, much like a very narrow bar top.

"Amira doesn't garden, but the house came with the shed," said Brody. "So I convinced her last year to let me convert it into our own pub."

"It's become the go-to spot to hang out," said Ethan, moving forward to open the door. Quinn looked around before following the guys inside and saw that all the women were sitting around the blazing bonfire. He wanted to go find Rae, but thought she was probably enjoying her girl time, and he didn't think it could hurt to get to know a few more of Brody's friends.

Stepping inside behind the three brothers, Quinn looked around at the impressive set-up. It really did look like an actual pub. The bar top was glossy, live-edge wood, the back wall behind the bar had a back-lit liquor display and there were four separate taps for draught beers. More stools with emerald green seats surrounded the bar, giving the place a very Irish feel. Quinn spotted another sign over the bar with the same "Kalahan's Pub" stamp as the door, and noted the signs for Guinness, Killian's, Bushmills, and Jameson posted along the walls.

There were about eight other men inside the pub and Quinn skimmed the faces of all of them, hoping to be able to figure out which one was Rae's ex.

Why didn't I ask the guys what he looks like? Why didn't I Facebook stalk the guy so I could be prepared?

Brody put his hand on Quinn's shoulder and announced to the room, "You may recognize this guy from *ESPN, Sports Center, Sports Illustrated*...or because you actually follow the game. Quinn Casey, everyone- Let's make him feel welcome."

Quinn was acknowledged with several friendly greetings, manly handshakes, and claps on the back.

"Don't forget *Men's Health*," one dark-haired man with thick-rimmed glasses said. "My wife bought that issue with your article on 'bed-breaking sex'."

Quinn coughed as he laughed. "Yeah, that was a popular one."

"Amira has your entire collection, actually," Brody mumbled quietly. "I swear I found them stashed in her nightstand like a teenage boy trying to hide porn."

Quinn remembered his first run-in with Rae in which she was holding an entire stack of magazines all with himself featured on the covers. "I think Rae ended up with them, though I don't know how badly she really wanted them."

Brody looked relieved. "Good. Now that we know each other it would be a little weird."

Behind the bar, a tall, well-built guy with sandy blonde hair and a short beard was setting out shot glasses. With a bottle of Jameson in each hand, he filled the glasses quickly and began passing them out.

"All right, all right," the guy boomed, his voice low and carrying through the chorus of the other male voices. "Everyone- back off All-Star for a minute and take a shot. He looks like he's going to need one before all you wanna-be A-listers bombard him with more questions." The man held a shot out to Quinn.

Sliding up to the bar and taking the shot glass, Quinn looked down into it and scrunched his nose. He wasn't supposed to drink at all. He was supposed to be Rae's ride home, but he suddenly felt like he needed to make an effort to bond with these guys. These were the guys in Rae's circle, right? She'd gone to school with Brody and Amira, and these were their friends. They would probably be here a while anyway, and what was one shot going to do?

Finally Quinn passed the shot glass back. "It's Maker's or nothing."

"Maker's?" the man chided. "We're taking shots, All-Star, not sipping whiskey and diet Coke like we're in a sorority."

Quinn laughed and shook his head, conceding, and took the shot with a wince. "Fuck, at least it's not Jim Beam."

"The All-Star's a diva, huh?" The man- whose name he still didn't know, he realized- raised an eyebrow. He seemed to be taking an X-ray of Quinn, taking in each and every detail in a split second before relaxing his posture, leaning back against the beer cooler.

"Nah, I just don't drink a lot. When I do I guess I'm particular," Quinn shrugged, and sat down on a cushioned bar stool.

"Well we do drink a lot around here," Sandy-blonde said, slamming another shot glass down on the bar and filling it with Jameson again. He pushed the glass toward Quinn. "So drink up, All-Star."

Quinn glanced down at the fresh shot glass in front of him, contemplating. When the guy poured himself another shot and held it up, Quinn sighed, clinked his glass and threw it back. With another wince, he set the glass back down and wiped his mouth with the back of his hand. "You're trying to get me drunk and I don't even know your name. Is this how Thor puts the moves on?"

The guy laughed heartily, "Ah, yes. Shots first- always." He switched to a booming and rather convincing God of Thunder impression, "And then you put the hammer down! That's how we do it back in Asgard."

"You're not actually trying to give Quinn Casey tips on how to pick up women, are you?" A blonde guy whose entire face just screamed "former frat-bro" chimed in, leaning up against the bar. "Seriously, *Thor*, when was the last time you tapped Giselle Frederick?"

Still not dropping the Thor voice, he replied, "Giving a woman shots isn't exactly a ground-breaking strategy." He poured two more shot glasses and slid one to Quinn again. "The secret is in the hammer. And if you don't have the hammer, you won't bring the thunder."

Quinn let out an amused laugh and, without much thought, brought the new shot of whiskey to his lips. Just as Quinn began tossing the drink back, the Thor impersonator muttered, "Fucked every single one of those Valkyrie bitches," causing Quinn to choke and spit half his shot back out as he laughed.

Rae would have my ass if she knew I laughed at something like that.

Blame it on the alcohol, the sea of testosterone residing in the shed, or the fact that he hadn't had a guy's night in ages, but Quinn was enjoying himself. This new company, and the spreading warmth the whiskey was filling him with were easily pushing aside the earlier anxiety he'd been feeling.

Thor the Bartender grabbed a towel and tossed it to Quinn to clean his own damn mess up before ducking beneath the bar. "You're right, All-Star. No more shots for you." He placed a rocks glass filled with ice on the bar and poured in a small shot of Maker's Mark and topped it heavily with Diet Coke. "Enjoy your scrapbooking party, you goddamn sorority girl." He plopped a small straw into the glass, adding, "Don't forget- I'd hate to see a sorority chick without something to suck on."

Quinn half-suppressed his laugh and snatched the straw out of his glass, flicking it back to the bartender. "Anyone ever tell you you're kind of an asshole?"

"All the time." He reached into the beer cooler and pulled out a Heineken. Leaning back again, he asked, "You're from around here originally, right?"

"Yeah," Quinn said. "Not quite this neighborhood, but in Traverse."

Fake-Thor eyed him curiously. "Some kind of 'rags to riches' inspirational story?"

With a sigh, Quinn shrugged. "Something like that, I guess. Not too inspirational. Just a kid who learned to hit a ball pretty well."

"Don't tell me Quinn Casey's humble in real life. Are all those rumors just for show?"

Quinn glanced out toward the bonfire where all the women were sitting, their drunken laughter echoing through the open window. He didn't have a clear enough view to see where Rae was, but he could distinguish her clear, vibrant laugh from the rest when he heard it.

He smiled half-heartedly. "No, those rumors are true. Or some of them. Maybe most of them. Just somethin' about being home again, I guess."

"Harsh reminder of where you came from?"

"It's not as bad as I thought it would be," Quinn replied. "How about you? Just around for the night or do you live up here?"

"I'm from Romeo, down state," he said, now snapping the top off his bottle. "The land of wealthy, entitled, trust-fund assholes. Like me."

"Must be a rough life."

"Yeah," Fake-Thor tipped the green bottle to his mouth and sighed after a long swig. "It's not all it's cracked up to be." When Quinn gave him a skeptical glance, he added, "I'm not saying it was worse or anything like whatever you might have dealt with. At least I never had to worry about food or money, but everything was still chaos. Carefully kept under the guise of being perfect and normal."

"Ah, yes, gotta keep up those appearances." Quinn nodded. "Not that I know anything about that exactly. I was just trying to keep CPS from putting me in foster care."

Whoa, where had that come from? Why am I sharing that with this guy?

"Okay, you win," Fake-Thor chuckled. "I just never saw my parents, and the turnover rate for my nannies all depended on how long it took for my mom to catch my dad in bed with them. Or in the car, or the office...the laundry room. Wherever."

Quinn considered for a few moments. "So, you had hot nannies? And I'm supposed to feel bad for you?"

With a hearty, low laugh, Fake-Thor nodded. "Fair point. I guess that's why I'm terrible at relationships. I had a mom who put up with my dad's shit because she didn't want to give up her lifestyle, and I was raised by a whole slew of my dad's side pieces." He took another pull of beer, then tilted the bottle to gesture toward Quinn, "What's your excuse?"

Before he could talk himself out of it, he replied, "I only ever wanted one girl, and I never thought she wanted me. I never thought I was good enough."

"Bet she'd think differently now. Come back successful, a shit ton of money in the bank, and every other woman in the world wants you apparently. I bet she'd think you're good enough now."

Quinn paused suddenly. He looked across the bar at this guy who for some reason was unnaturally easy to talk to. Had he considered this yet? All the guys Rae had dated in the past were wealthy, they were from the same life, they had the same experiences. Rae wasn't suddenly interested in him because he had money now, too?

No. Of course not. Rae was my friend back then because she wanted to be, and now we're together because we both want to be.

"We have reconnected, actually," Quinn said. "I took her out on this date and kind of made up for all my mistakes in the past. All the things I wished I could've done differently for the past, shit, hundred years, it feels like." He told the guy across the bar all about the date, about reliving the moment he'd known he was falling for her. Okay, and a little about how she'd reacted and how they'd spent the later part of the evening.

"Sounds like you got it all, All-Star," Fake-Thor took another long pull of his beer. "The dream job, the money, and now the girl who- if you don't mind me saying- sounds like she's got a pretty insatiable sexual appetite."

Quinn snorted with laughter. "Yeah, we're having a good time in the bedroom. Or the living room, or kitchen, or laundry room."

"Wherever." Fake-Thor rolled his eyes. "Yeah, the last girl I was with- in a relationship with, I mean- was like that. Shit, she just wanted to fuck all the time." He smirked and Quinn could tell he was remembering the good times. "I work late sometimes, and I'd get back to my place and she'd be there in sexy lingerie, or just naked on the couch, wet and waiting for me. There were nights I'd walk in and she'd just drop to her knees like she'd been hungry for me all day. Or I would..."

"Sounds like a fuckin' dream girl," Quinn remarked. "What happened?"

"Just my usual shit," he said with a shrug. "Like father, like son."

Quinn paused with the rocks glass to his lips. His brow furrowed as his blurred brain seemed to be making connections.

Like father, like son?

He cheated on her?

Fuck. Me.

Before he could even figure out how to respond, the door to the shed opened and Amira walked in followed by Rae. He smiled instantly at the sight of her in her black tank top and distressed denim skirt, cheeks still flushed from a long day of drinking. Then he cautiously drew his attention back to this guy who'd intentionally kept his name a secret.

Emerson. Of course. He was eyeing Rae as though imagining her...on the couch waiting for him after a long day? On her knees?

Fuck that.

Quinn glared, nostrils flared as he bit the inside of his cheek. He wondered if Emerson knew Quinn was with his ex or if he'd unintentionally mentioned their hot and heavy sexual connection.

That was until the previously friendly bartender's eyes met Quinn's again. Like flipping a switch, he'd gone from a potential new buddy to this smug, self-satisfied asshole. Emerson's mouth twitched as he suppressed a grin, but the challenge in his expression was undeniable.

Challenge accepted, motherfucker.

Raelyn stood in the center of the garden-shed-converted-Irish-pub and felt momentarily paralyzed as she spotted Quinn sitting at a bar stool in front of Emerson. She held her breath as she assessed the situation. There were no fists flying, no noses bleeding, no fat lips. That had to be a good sign. Maybe they were more mature than she'd been giving them credit for. Maybe Emerson was just as over it as she was and his earlier comments about their sex life were just part of his inability to avoid conflict or stir the pot even just a little.

"*There* she is." Quinn smiled at her and closed the space between them with two of his long strides. With one hand on her hip and the other gently on the side of her face, he pulled her into him and pressed his mouth to hers, sweeping his tongue through her mouth, breathing her in. When they pulled apart, a growl emitted from deep in his chest, "Damn, I've missed you."

The sensual kiss left Raelyn momentarily breathless. She blinked a few times and smiled, eyes focused on his chest as she regrouped. Quinn's finger tilted her chin up so that she was looking at him and she suddenly felt hot everywhere as he gazed down into her eyes. This wasn't a look he usually gave her when they were out in public. This was his possessive bedroom stare that he used to make her melt right before he plunged himself inside her.

"I missed you, too," Raelyn was finally able to get out before he kissed her again. His tongue played with hers in her mouth and she felt his groan rumble through her, and this time she thought she tasted whiskey on his tongue. Raelyn placed a hand to his very firm chest and pushed herself away gently.

"What's wrong, baby?" Quinn breathed, his lips brushing hers as he spoke.

"You taste like whiskey," Raelyn replied. "I thought you were going to be my ride home."

"Change of plans," Quinn said, before dipping low and whispering in her ear. "We may be finding another ride home, but I still fully intend on being your ride for the night." He kissed her neck just below her ear. "All night."

Feeling heat spread up her skin and the increase of her pulse, she curled her fingers into his shirt, nearly forgetting they were in a room filled with people. She was ready to call a Lyft or an Uber right then. Hell, she'd crawl home if it meant she could have him when she got there.

"Sounds like a damn good plan to me," Raelyn sighed, just before Quinn caught her mouth in another fervent kiss. Suddenly aware of all the eyes on them, Raelyn pulled away again. She didn't necessarily have anything against public displays of affection but couldn't help sensing the prickling tension in the room.

Over Quinn's shoulder she spotted Emerson whose jaw was clenched, eyes piercing into the back of Quinn's head. His steely gaze flicked to Raelyn and he drained his bottle of Heineken before dropping it into a bottle bin. Emerson walked out from behind the bar, past where she and Quinn were still in a close embrace and shoved out the door. When she looked back to Quinn, his triumphant smirk was undeniable.

Oh...that was just some show to get the upper hand then?

"Quinn," Raelyn pulled his attention away from the door that had just closed. "Quinn, can we talk for a second?"

"Sure." Raelyn was immediately annoyed at how quickly the heat that she'd thought was so genuine had evaporated from his demeanor. He placed a hand on the small of her back and led her outside and away from the makeshift pub. Turning to her, he asked, "What's up?"

"What the hell was that?" Raelyn snapped, gesturing over her shoulder toward the converted shed. "This isn't some kind of competition, and I don't exactly appreciate you using me like some object to prove a point."

"What? No. Baby, you wouldn't believe the kind of shit that guy was saying," Quinn said, looking past her, no doubt trying to see where Emerson had stalked off to. "He didn't even tell me who he was and then starts bragging about his ex who was all over him all the time. He knew I was with you and did that just to make me look like an idiot. Like we're just two buddies exchanging stories about our girls."

"*Exchanging* stories?" Raelyn questioned, rearing back. "You were talking about me- about *us*- to some guy whose name you didn't even know?"

"No, not like that. I told him about our first date. How I finally got the girl I always wanted." Quinn smiled at this and tucked her hair behind her ear, leaving his hand there to lightly brush his thumb across her cheekbone. His expression darkened just slightly. "I guess he knew it was you somehow and decided to make up some shit about this ex of his who just always wanted him, just waiting for him to come home so they could fuck. Must've known I'd put it together eventually."

Raelyn truly hoped the lighting was poor enough that Quinn didn't see her cheeks redden. Though she didn't know specifically what Emerson had told him, she doubted very much that he'd made it up. Their relationship had been very physical. There were emotions, too, but they tended to express their feelings for each other in a physical way. Almost aggressively so. She was that way with Quinn now, too, only the emotions and feelings were incomparable to what she'd felt with Emerson.

Being with Emerson versus being with Quinn was *want* versus *need*, heat versus fiery explosions all over her skin, being together versus being completely consumed by each other. It wasn't the same. Not by a long shot.

She must have been silent for several moments, because it took her a moment to register that he'd asked her a question.

"Hm?" Raelyn blinked up at Quinn.

His brow furrowed. "Was it true?"

Oh. That.

Raelyn hesitated. "Quinn, it really doesn't matter now what things were or weren't like. I'm with you now and we're happy, right?"

The humorless laugh Quinn let out was accompanied by an equally humorless smile. "So it was."

"I don't know what he said," Raelyn said defensively, "but it doesn't matter now. I don't want to be with him anymore. I want *you*, Quinn."

Quinn took his baseball hat off to swipe a hand through his hair, then scrubbed his hands down his face. He let out a sigh and gave a small nod, "Okay."

"Okay?" Raelyn raised an eyebrow. Replacing his ball cap, he turned away from her, but she caught his hand, pulling him back. "Hey," she wrapped her arms behind his neck and went up on her toes. "I mean it. I don't care what he said, and neither should you. You're the one I want. Nothing that happened in the past can change that." She snatched the baseball hat off his head and put it on her own. "I'm *your* girl, Quinn."

A reserved smile curved his lips up. She'd consider that a win.

"Let's give it another half hour and then set up that Uber," Raelyn suggested. "I'm sort of looking forward to getting you home."

Quinn grinned mischievously. "I like how you think. Let's make it fifteen minutes."

CHAPTER 20

Far more than fifteen minutes had passed when Raelyn thought again about setting up a ride for her and Quinn. She was sitting on one of the benches around the fire and Quinn was standing on the miniature patio off the pub-shed with another drink in hand as he laughed and made conversation with more of Brody's friends. She had just finished off her second bottled water when someone joined her on the bench.

"Raevyn Noir?" Emerson extended a wine glass filled with a deep purplish-red wine. It was her favorite wine that her family's winery sold-it was even named after her, or at least the spelling had been inspired by her name.

Raelyn glanced at the glass. Truthfully, it sounded delicious, but accepting anything from Emerson suddenly felt like accepting candy from a stranger in a white panel-van. Narrowing her eyes at her former fiancé, she asked, "What do you want?"

"Just saw the bottle behind the bar and thought I'd offer you some before it ran out," Emerson replied, innocently.

No, it was feigned innocence. Raelyn knew by now that this man didn't do anything selflessly. There was always an agenda, a goal in mind, something in it for him.

"Oh, is that all?" Raelyn asked skeptically. "You're not hoping to provoke Quinn? Hoping he'll look over here and see us talking like we're old friends?"

"What if he does?" Emerson shrugged. "He doesn't own you, Rae. He can't tell you who you can and can't talk to. You'd think *you* would be the jealous one. Dude's been with some solid tens."

Raelyn rolled her eyes and reluctantly took the glass of wine from his hand. "Why are you here?"

Emerson glanced around. "It's my best friend's house. I was invited-"

"No, I mean *here*. Next to me. What do you want? For real."

He sighed and faced the large fire now. There were only a few others sitting around the fire, and their seats were far enough back that their conversation remained private. "I just want to tell you I'm sorry. Again. I know it probably doesn't change anything, but I am. I shouldn't have...I wish things had gone differently. You deserved better."

"You're right," Raelyn agreed. "It doesn't change anything, and I *do* deserve better."

Emerson scoffed, "Is that why you're with All-Star? Because he's so much better than me?"

Well, that humble sincerity dissolved real quick.

"I promise he is."

"Oh please," he sneered. "That bullshit about falling for you when he was a kid? That's a fucking line, Rae. He's on vacation with his fucked up arm, comes home, sees the girl he always wanted to bang in high school is available, and is willing to say whatever it takes to get you in bed. That's all it is. It's called a revenge fuck, and when you've healed him up, he's going to fly back to LA and go back to banging twenty-two-year-old models."

"Not every guy is you. Not every guy just cares about fucking whoever he can get his hands on. And now that you brought it up, wasn't that intern of yours also twenty-two? Twenty-one? I think you might just be expressing what you'd be doing in his position. You two are not the same."

"I never meant for that to happen, Rae," Emerson groaned, pinching the bridge of his nose. As if *he* were the one who'd been hurt by his actions. As if *he'd* been wronged and was over having this conversation.

"Right, you just slipped on some legal documents and fell into her vagina- penis first." Raelyn took a gulp of her wine. "It doesn't matter either way. I'm over it. I've moved on." She tipped the glass back again, draining it completely, and handed it back to Emerson. "Thanks for the

Noir. Now if you'll excuse me, I'm going to get my boyfriend and take him home."

"Let me know when you find out I was right," Emerson drawled. "I promise to make you feel so good you'll forget he ever happened."

She wasn't going to dignify that with a response, and instead headed back toward the shed to find Quinn.

She was only a few feet from the huddle of six or seven men when she heard Quinn's voice. He had an arm around James's shoulders, and they were leaning into the circle as though sharing secrets.

"...gotta amp up the dirty talk. Seriously, it works," Quinn was saying as she approached. "When I do it, I'm just like talking to her like, 'yeah, this is what I'm about to do to you and you're gonna be fucking begging for more'. You should see Rae when I whisper shit like that," Quinn gave out a groan. "Fuck, does her body respond."

Raelyn stopped in her tracks and stared at his back, trying to ignore how great his t-shirt looked stretching over those muscles. *What the fuck did I just walk into?*

Another one of the guys chimed in, "Damn...I haven't mastered that yet," he admitted. "I feel like I think too much."

James added, "Everything just sounds dumb in my head."

Quinn waved his hand dismissively. "Just take charge. 'Babygirl, I'm gonna flip you over and take you for a ride.' I used that on Rae a few times and, I'm talking, *instant* waterfall."

Rae felt her face go red as she dropped her jaw and stared from a short distance. She had been getting ready to speak up but wasn't sure she wanted to draw attention to herself after that, so she waited and listened for the right moment.

"Full disclosure," Ethan, Brody's younger brother piped in. "The first time I met Raelyn..." he paused and gave a low whistle. "Let's just say you are one lucky man."

"That ass though," one of the men added.

How old are these assholes? Are we in a fucking high school locker room?

Quinn let out a mischievous and boastful sounding laugh, "Oh, I know. That view when I hit it from behind- *fuck*- it about does me in just seeing-"

"Seeing what, exactly?" Raelyn forced herself to cut in. She really didn't want to hear the rest of that sentence. She didn't want this entire group of men to hear the rest of that sentence. She stood with both hands on her hips, head tilted to the side, and an eyebrow raised in a challenging glare.

Raelyn thought he'd at least be humble enough to recognize he'd been busted and that talking about her like that was *not* okay. Not to a bunch of people he barely knew! However, when he was fully turned around, he was displaying his cocky, charm-the-pants-off-you grin. "Oh, hey baby. We were just admiring your...assets."

He winked.

This motherfucking, cocky son of a bitch actually winked.

Raelyn glowered at him for several silent seconds. His expression refused to falter.

"I'm sorry, do I *look* charmed to you right now? Is this shit supposed to be cute or something?" Raelyn stood her ground, staring him down. She wanted him to collapse to his knees and beg for forgiveness.

Apparently Quinn had no such intentions.

"It's really a compliment, if you think about it," he said, shrugging one shoulder.

Her jaw dropped once again, and she let out a hollow laugh. She rolled her neck as if she were getting ready to fight a bitch, then crossed her arms over her chest to control that urge.

"Oh, she's mad…" Someone in the group muttered.

"It's a compliment?" Raelyn kept her voice quiet and controlled. It seemed everyone except Quinn recognized her tone as threatening.

"Rae, come on," Quinn said, letting his head fall back as though exasperated.

You're fucking kidding me, right?

"Come on?" Raelyn repeated, incredulous. "Are you serious right now? If I remember correctly, this is exactly the kind of thing you beat the shit out of Liam Hamilton for in high school."

"I'll take a swing at him if it'll make you feel better," Emerson's deep drawl came from behind her.

"Fucking try it, Trust-Fund Ken," Quinn snapped, taking a step closer and puffing up.

"*Quinn!* You are not getting in a fight with your arm the way it is," Raelyn hissed.

"I don't need both arms to fight him," said Quinn.

Who the hell is this right now? This is not *my Quinn…*

"Just ignore him. What the hell are you doing? Bragging about our sex life?"

"Yeah, I'm sure he's got way more interesting stories to tell than the time he finger-fucked a girl at a baseball field," Emerson interjected.

Raelyn froze. Hadn't Quinn told her he hadn't gone into detail about that night? Hadn't he implied that he'd only told the story about how he'd finally got the girl he'd always wanted?

She was staring daggers at Quinn. "You actually told him that? About the baseball field?" Raelyn was livid. "What the *fuck*, Quinn? Am I really just some…" she searched for words other than Emerson's, but found none, "some *revenge* fuck because we didn't hook up in high school?"

"*Revenge fuck?*" Quinn's brows pulled together. Closing the gap between them, he reached out to take Raelyn's hand, but she pulled away before he could make contact. "You're not seriously going to believe what that asshole said, Rae." He glowered over Raelyn's shoulder at Emerson, "What the fuck did you tell her?"

"The truth," Emerson shrugged. "At least as far as I could see it."

"Rae, he doesn't know what the fuck he's talking about," Quinn said, still glaring over Raelyn's shoulder.

"I will say though, All-Star, you're definitely right about that view," said Emerson, smirking between her and Quinn. "Remember riding me reverse-cowgirl on the floor because you just couldn't wait for it?"

Quinn lunged forward, but Raelyn placed two firm hands on his even more firm chest to keep him back. "Quinn, don't. It's not worth it."

Wrapping an arm around Raelyn's waist, Quinn squeezed her against him as he continued to stare Emerson down. "You can fuck right off. She's *mine*, and you fucking lost," Quinn said through gritted teeth.

Raelyn pushed away and untangled herself from Quinn's arms. "I'm not some object to win," she snapped. "And just because *he's* a sociopath doesn't mean I'm not still mad at you. I expect that shit from him, Quinn. Not you."

"Well, *Princess*, maybe you should. I've only been letting you down since we were sixteen!"

Behind her, she heard Emerson laugh, "Oh God, this is so much better than I imagined."

Raelyn whipped around, her voice laced with venom, "Will you *shut up?* This has nothing to do with you!" Turning back to Quinn, she asked, "What do you mean? When we were sixteen?"

"Everyone knew I was into you, Rae. Everyone knew I was crazy about you, but you just refused to see it. Why? So you could date rich assholes like Liam? Like this guy?" He gestured toward Emerson.

"You're not exactly in a position anymore to be complaining about rich people, Quinn," Raelyn replied.

"Exactly," Quinn snorted derisively. "Why now? Why should I think you're interested in me now?"

Whoa- what?

Raelyn stepped back as though dodging a physical blow to her stomach. "I'm sorry- what exactly are you implying?"

"Do the math, Rae," Quinn growled. "All these guys you've been surrounding yourself with since we were kids. *Jesus*, I can't believe I didn't see it."

It didn't matter that she had been drinking since noon and had consumed more alcohol in twelve hours than the past twelve months. She was suddenly completely sober. That terrifying thought she'd had during Quinn's first physical therapy session had drifted so far out of her mind, but here it was slapping her across the face.

Just the other day when she was talking to Amira on her way to work she had admitted that she sometimes completely forgot that Quinn had a mega-million dollar salary, and that she still thought of him as her best friend from the proverbial wrong side of the tracks. Maybe she would've preferred him that way. Maybe that's why she hadn't been able to see this obnoxious, cocky, hot-shot version of him.

She swallowed around the lump in her throat once again, urging it to go away. She did not want to cry in front of all these people. She especially didn't want to cry in front of fucking Emerson and give him the satisfaction that he'd done exactly what he'd intended. Feeling her lip tremble and the tears start to fill in, she looked away from Quinn. He was her oldest friend. How the hell could he believe that? Her heart was in physical pain, but she couldn't let herself cry here. She had to get home.

Anger. Anger is easier.

Raelyn closed her eyes and channeled her inner rage. Finding it, she let out a humorless laugh. The kind that lets a man know that a woman is both angry and maybe a little crazy. "Quinn, I don't need your money. I don't know if you remember, but I've got a small fortune of my own, and one day I'll be getting an inheritance that makes your salary look like pocket change."

She met his gaze and noticed his whole mood changed drastically, sobering and realizing too late the weight of his own words. His golden eyes flared with panic. "Rae- no, I-"

She turned around, knowing she wouldn't be able to keep the tears at bay much longer. "I'll find my own ride home," she muttered, and made her way back up the lawn to the house alone.

CHAPTER 21

2007

Raelyn jumped as the librarian, Mrs. Combs, placed a hand on her arm. *The Curse of Curves* blared through her headphones and she had apparently missed the bell that signaled the end of fifth period. One more class to go.

Thanking Mrs. Combs for alerting her, Raelyn wound her headphones around her iPod and stuffed it away in her bag along with her books. Her last class of the day was an AP history course, which she shared with Quinn, so she had to move quickly if she was going to get upstairs in time to walk to class with him. She needed to talk to him. There was a lot on her mind, and she needed the support and encouragement of her best friend right before the end of the day. They might be able to talk in class, but she'd prefer to not have a bunch of eavesdroppers for such a sensitive topic.

Liam was planning to take her out on some big fancy date tonight. He had also been getting particularly handsy lately and dropping hints about getting time alone. Raelyn was able to put two and two together and figure out he expected to have sex with her tonight, which quite frankly, she was not ready for.

She'd been under no disillusions when she decided to start dating Liam. She knew he was sexually experienced. She was also aware that he wasn't the type to wait around very long. To be perfectly honest, she was surprised he had waited two months as it was. Their relationship was fun and flirty and, okay, it satisfied a lot of those hormonal teenage cravings, but it was not meant to last.

It wasn't meant to happen at all, really. For some reason, Raelyn had found herself exceptionally annoyed that Quinn had been so arrogant about being able to find someone else, someone *better*, than her to take to homecoming. So, in a particularly petty moment, she'd agreed to go with Liam. He was exactly the type of person Quinn would hate to see her with. Vain, arrogant, entitled. Quinn would probably tease her and say he's exactly the type of guy people expected to see her with.

Again, petty. And she had felt bad as soon as they got in the car and he pulled his brooding, grumpy attitude with her. But she felt a lot less bad when that hoe-bag, Britney Garrett, told everyone in the girls' bathroom how they'd been making out and it escalated into a blow job in the back of the limo.

Out on the dance floor, Raelyn had thought Quinn was being oddly flirtatious with her. She thought maybe he was making up for being extra moody and brooding in the weeks leading up to the dance. But no. It was the new-found confidence of a seventeen-year-old boy who'd gotten his first blowie and now thought he was hot shit. The following months had made that point perfectly clear.

Their walk together after chemistry earlier that day was probably their first interaction in weeks that they'd had a whole three minutes to themselves; no shameless flock of girls fawning over him, and no Liam trying to stick his tongue down her throat. It had been so refreshing- while it lasted.

The walk had made her reach a definitive decision, though. Between the stress of her and Liam's impending date and her three-minute reminder of how much she missed Quinn's company, she'd decided she needed to end things with Liam after school. There was no point going through the motions of whatever extravagant date Liam had planned only to ruin it by telling him that no, she would not be putting out tonight. Or worse, let herself get coerced into something she wasn't ready to do just yet.

Something told her Quinn might also be relieved to hear this news. Sure, he had all this new female attention that he was basking in, but Raelyn liked to think he missed their friendship, too. She was hoping things could go back to normal and she could start spending time with her three best friends again.

After pulling on her T.C. West Baseball crewneck and throwing her backpack on, Raelyn started her trek through the halls toward her and Quinn's lockers. In her head, she rehearsed what she was going to say to Quinn about her date and what she was going to say to Liam when she broke things off.

Once at her locker, she shoved her bag inside and grabbed the books she would need for her next class. With no sight of Quinn yet, she walked down to his locker and leaned against it, letting her eyes shut momentarily as she waited for him.

"Must feel pretty good to have the school's hottest womanizer defending your honor," an amused voice drawled somewhat sarcastically from a few lockers down.

Raelyn rolled her head to face the always-moody Alaina Costello. "Are you talking to me?"

"Obviously," Alaina droned. "Or do you not know yet?"

"Know what?" Raelyn snapped, really not in the mood for Alaina and her moody condescension.

"Wow, you really do just live in your own world," Alaina said as she shook her head in disbelief. "Must be nice never having to worry about anything other than what's going on in your own pretty little head."

"What's your problem with me?"

"Guess I'm the only one who doesn't understand what's so fantastic about *Raelyn DeRose*," Alaina's tone was airy and mocking as she said the name. "Although, I suppose I did hear a rumor a couple minutes ago about how you're *quite* the cocksucker."

"*What?*" Raelyn's eyebrows came together. "Where the hell is that rumor coming from?"

"Apparently your own boyfriend," Alaina smirked. "I guess he was telling everyone in his weight training class all about your 'talented mouth' and the various uses he's found for it."

Anger flared in Raelyn's stomach, though she wasn't exactly surprised. She and Liam had gotten pretty physical- certainly more so than any other guy she'd been with- and he was sort of a mega-douche. Locker room talk about sexual conquests sounded exactly like something he'd be into.

Oh God…Quinn's in that class.

Raelyn was temporarily horrified at the thought that Quinn- *and* Chris *and* Jett, *fuck!*- had heard whatever crude things her soon-to-be-ex-boyfriend had been bragging about. She should have seen this coming sooner or later. It was stupid that she'd even considered he might keep some things private when it came to their intimate life.

Not allowing Alaina to have the upper hand and think she'd somehow offended her, Raelyn simply said, "Well, everyone likes to hear they've got a natural talent."

"Oh yes, it's always good to know you've got career options," Alaina remarked. "I hear that's one market that just doesn't crash."

Well, fuck. That was good. I hate this bitch.

Luckily, Raelyn was saved from having to come up with a quick retort, because Quinn appeared around the corner. Both girls' attention went to him as he approached. His expression was angry, and the bruising along with the cut on his lip would've made him look menacing if he weren't so devilishly handsome.

Why does he look so hot right now?

Whoa- back up. Why does he look like he got into a fight? Focus, girl!

She pushed herself off from Quinn's locker and gaped at him. He had a darkening bruise along his cheek bone, another mark on his chin, and his lip was split, but not actively bleeding.

"Oh my God, Quinn," Raelyn reached for him and took his face in her hands to look him over. "What the hell happened? Are you okay?"

Quinn shook her off and moved around her. He opened his locker and began stiffly grabbing his things out, shoving items in his bag, and definitely *not* looking at her.

"Quinn…" She stood by and watched him clean out his locker.

Was Quinn mad because of the things Liam had said about her? About them?

Would Quinn get into a fight with Liam over that?

Of course he would. Quinn was big on respecting a person's boundaries and knowing when to keep your mouth shut about things that didn't need to be said. He was also big on letting his fists do the talking.

"Quinn, what happened?" Raelyn asked again, not wanting to jump to any conclusions.

"Ask your boyfriend," Quinn mumbled.

"What did he say?"

No response. Quinn's jaw clenched and Raelyn could see the muscles there move.

"You didn't seriously just punch him because you found out we do more than kiss, right?" Raelyn prompted, hoping to end the silent treatment.

Quinn paused for a brief second, hovering a notebook over his backpack. He looked like he wanted to say something. She *knew* he wanted to say something. But he just shoved the notebook in his bag and continued clearing out his locker.

"Okay, well, I'm confused. An hour ago we were fine, and now I hear there are rumors being spread about me and your face is covered in bruises..."

Quinn shut his locker with force and turned to face her finally. "What the hell are you doing talking to Liam about me?"

Raelyn raised one eyebrow. "What do you mean? I can't mention you around him?"

"I mean, why are you telling him about my life? About my mom? About home?" Quinn asked. "You think I'm some sort of charity case that your family took on? Is that seriously what you think of me?"

"Of course not!" Raelyn was completely taken aback by the accusation. "What the hell? Quinn, we're friends. Why would I say something like that?"

"Why does he know any of it?" Quinn countered. His eyes were dark and challenging- unforgiving.

"I don't know, Quinn. I didn't tell him anything," Raelyn insisted. Why was he glaring at her like this? How could he not know that she would never betray his trust like that? She suddenly realized she was also angry. She couldn't believe after nine years of friendship that he'd actually think she felt that way.

"The way this shit's gonna run around the school, I'm sure everyone will know by the weekend," Quinn grumbled. "I'll just be some crack-whore's kid. Fucking great."

Letting her anger get the best of her she seethed, "It's not like your mom never leaves the house, Quinn." The voice in her head was screaming at her to stop there, especially after Quinn's gaze pierced her further, but she forged on, "Anyone who sees her is gonna pick up on the fact she's strung out on something."

If she didn't think his glare could get more piercing, she was wrong. And it was worse. She could see the fleck of hurt that she'd inflicted in them, too.

Quinn wasn't exactly one of those guys who was protective of his mother, but he was protective of his reputation, how people saw him. He hated to think that anyone might see his situation and pity him. But how could you not at least feel a little bad for him? His home life was a wreck and he'd had to fend for himself until Raelyn's family had come along.

She knew he hated it. He hated accepting help, but Raelyn's dad had set him down when he was ten years old and firmly told him that it was completely unreasonable to expect a kid to take care of himself and his mother. It was completely unreasonable that he had to make sure the bills got paid, that groceries were bought, and that both he and his mother were safe. Charlie had told Quinn that he would accept help from them because it was the least they could do. He would accept their help because even with it, he'd still been robbed of so much of his childhood. Quinn had resisted at first, but over time learned that if he was going to remain in Raelyn's life, this was something he would have to put up with.

But for him to think she thought of him as a charity case? How could he think he meant so little to her?

She didn't expect Quinn to respond. He was far more the silent brooding type.

Instead, his gaze traveled behind Raelyn, and back one more time before walking around her without a word. Alaina was still standing in front of her locker, apparently watching their argument closely. If Raelyn had been given a million guesses as to what Quinn was about to do, she would never have guessed right.

Quinn snaked one arm around Alaina's waist and pulled her close to him. Tilting her chin up with his other hand, he kissed her. Right there. In front of Raelyn. With tongue.

I'm sorry, what am I witnessing here?

He pulled away from Alaina who looked mildly surprised, but mostly rather pleased with herself and the situation she'd been placed in. Raelyn heard Quinn say to her, "Looks like I'm suspended now... We should get out of here."

Trying her best not to stare, because she felt like *she* might throw a punch if Alaina gave her another smug little sneer, Raelyn looked down at her feet and once again wondered what the *fuck* was happening.

Quinn put his arm around Alaina's shoulders and they walked down the hall together, attracting stares from everyone they passed.

Raelyn watched as they walked around the corner together. Once out of sight, she rolled her eyes and gave a dramatic sigh-slash-groan, feeling as though her best friend had just figuratively bitch-slapped her by walking off with Alaina fucking Costello.

Instead of heading to class, Raelyn ran back down the stairs, past the library, to the principal's office. She figured the principal and counselors would be calling parents to come in and meet with them about the fight and hoped that Liam would still be down there. Quinn had likely been released to get his things because the school knew better than to expect Molly Casey to answer her phone, but Liam's parents would be there in an instant. His mom was a lawyer and his dad was a family court judge, which meant, depending on the series of events that had taken place in the locker room, things could get really ugly for Quinn.

Tearing through the door of the main office, she didn't expect to find Chris and Jett waiting with various bandages and ice packs. Raelyn stopped in her tracks and stared from one boy to the other, taking in their injuries. Jett was holding an ice pack to his eye, and Chris had bandages on his knuckles, as well as a fat, split lip. She noticed the blood on their shirts and wondered how much blood Quinn's sweatshirt had been concealing.

"Uh...what the hell happened?" Raelyn blurted finally. "Quinn wouldn't tell me a goddamn thing and then he just walked off all pissed. Oh! And he made out with *Alaina Costello* before walking out. What the fuck?"

"Language, Miss DeRose," Coach Barlow said firmly as he stepped into the office.

"Sorry," Raelyn muttered. Jett moved over one chair so she could sit between him and Chris while they waited.

"He didn't tell you *anything?*" Chris asked.

"Really? No reaction on him walking out with Alaina?" Raelyn looked back and forth between Chris and Jett, "Is this a thing? Are they a thing? He *knows* I hate that bitch-" She pointed to Coach Barlow who was giving her another warning look, "I'm not actually sorry about that one. I'm also technically skipping class so feel free to suspend me for the rest of the day if you want."

Coach Barlow shook his head and made a face that clearly stated he was giving up.

Jett stifled a laugh and Chris covered his face with his hands, trying to shield his own grin. Leaning forward, Jett looked at Chris, "Can you imagine if we would've talked to him like that on the football field?"

"Princess Rae says and does what she wants," Chris shrugged. "Apparently everyone's got that memo."

Raelyn snapped her fingers impatiently. "Hey- back to Alaina. What's going on there? Or was she just a random pawn Quinn was using to piss me off?"

Folding his arms over his chest, Chris eyed Raelyn, "Why would it piss you off to see him kiss someone else?"

Raelyn stared back, mouth half open as she contemplated, "It...wouldn't. He can kiss whomever he wants. I just want to know why he refused to tell me anything and then swept her away like he'd been dying to see her all day."

"It's hard to keep up with Quinn these days," Jett said. "But I've seen them together a few times. Maybe there is something there."

"Gross..." Raelyn muttered.

"He really didn't tell you anything though?" Chris prompted again.

"Nothing useful," she sighed. "Though I gather it had something to do with Liam."

"Your boyfriend is an asshole, Rae. Sorry, Coach," Jett held up a hand to an increasingly frustrated Coach Barlow before turning back to Raelyn. "He's quite possibly the worst person I have ever met."

"But he's so pretty when he takes his shirt off," Raelyn said dreamily, knowing the disgusted and animated reactions she would receive.

Chris and Jett both groaned. Chris's head fell into his hands and Jett scrunched up his face before making a barfing gesture.

Laughing, Raelyn craned her neck to look around the office and the boys understood she was looking for him.

"His parents already came and got him," Chris said. "His mom was furious and was throwing around words like 'lawsuit' and 'press charges'."

She groaned, resting her head back on the wall behind her. "What a mess...I'm sorry, I feel like this is my fault."

"It's not, Rae," said Jett, putting an arm around her shoulders. "You should've heard the way he was talking about you. I'm pretty sure you would've smacked us around if we *hadn't* done something about it."

"We were supposed to go on this date tonight..."

"We heard," Chris droned. "Please tell me you're not still considering it."

"Of course not," Raelyn assured them. "And I know he had it in his head that we were going to have sex-"

"Heard that, too," Jett cut in.

"-but I wasn't going to."

"Thank God," Jett sighed. "Although I doubt he's feeling up for it after having his nose broken."

"Quinn broke his nose?" Raelyn gasped. "Tell me everything."

After school, and after hearing Chris and Jett's version of events before both their parents came to pick them up, Raelyn drove straight to Liam's house. She would like to be the kind of person who kept in mind that there were two sides to each story, but Chris and Jett wouldn't lie to her. They had no reason to, and quite frankly, the story they told made a lot of sense.

Mrs. Hamilton opened the door for Raelyn when she knocked. Her face was still pinched and red, as though she'd been ranting non-stop since the meeting at the school.

"Can you believe this?" Mrs. Hamilton fumed as she closed the door behind Raelyn. "I've never even heard of this boy, this *Quinn Casey*. He's on the football team with Liam, did you know that?"

"Yeah," Raelyn sighed. She thought it best to keep to herself that she was actually very well acquainted with the boy who'd broken her son's nose.

"And they couldn't even get his parents to meet with us," Mrs. Hamilton continued. "Uninvolved parents. It's no wonder the boy is so troubled. Liam says this isn't the first fight he's been in either! I can't believe- they should expel him, I think."

Before Raelyn bit an actual hole through her tongue from trying to keep her comments to herself, she asked, "Is Liam upstairs?"

"Yes, sweetie. He's in his room resting." Mrs. Hamilton finally waved Raelyn in the direction of the staircase. After muttering a quick thanks, she slipped off her boots and headed up the stairs.

She didn't bother knocking on his bedroom door and entered the room to find Liam lying on his bed, staring up at his phone.

"Raelyn," he sat up, appearing surprised to see her there.

"Eventful afternoon, huh?" Raelyn said, taking another step into the room.

Liam stood up and closed the distance between them. He was wearing dark blue athletic pants and no shirt. *Lord, he did look good without a shirt.*

No. I'm angry with him right now. Ignore the pecs. Ignore the abs. Ignore the sexy V-cut pointing into his pants.

Still repeating the words in her head, she wasn't prepared when Liam wrapped his arms around her and pressed his warm body against hers. He dipped his head to kiss her but pulled back with a hiss when their lips met, "Ah, dammit." Liam put a hand to the bridge of his nose where he now had a bandage.

"Got you pretty good, huh?" Raelyn asked, her hand rising to touch the side of his face. Dropping it quickly, she inwardly cursed herself for the show of affection.

"Fucker can throw a punch, I'll give him that," Liam said.

That was unexpected. He was usually the arrogant, boastful type. Maybe getting the shit kicked out of him was a humbling experience.

"Why did he feel the need to throw a punch?" Raelyn asked, sidestepping Liam's large, half-naked form to give them some distance.

"Seriously?" Liam snorted, turning to face her. "You're taking his side?"

"I'm trying to figure out what happened," Raelyn replied, feeling her insides heat up again. "I'm trying to figure out why I had to endure guys asking if I wanted *a taste* and making blow job gestures at me after school. I'm trying to figure out why I had guys cat-calling me on my way out to my car asking if I was ready to have my cherry popped."

"Oh, give me a fucking break, Raelyn," Liam threw his hands up in the air. "Act like you that's not exactly why you were with me in the first place. You wanted some experience, I gave you that."

Raelyn narrowed her eyes, incredulous. "Just because our relationship wasn't exactly built to last doesn't mean we can't have some kind of respect for each other. Telling an entire locker room full of guys that I devour you like a gourmet meal seems like an obvious overstep."

"Well you do," Liam said, eyes glinting, "and I think we both know you enjoy it. Almost as much as that first orgasm I gave you. First one ever, right?"

Raelyn was physically shaking. This person in front of her was not the same guy she'd agreed to date. Sure, she'd known he was a bit of an ass, but this was pushing it- even for him. How had she ever trusted him? Even if it was just with her body. It was as if all the places he'd touched her were boiling now, trying to cleanse themselves from him, and she stepped away again when he reached for her.

"You just couldn't keep your damn guard dog on a leash," Liam snapped. "That motherfucker is no better than me either. Everyone knows how he gets around, but I talk about the one girl he can't have and he fucking attacks."

Fuming, Raelyn continued to glare back at him. She was still furious with how Quinn had reacted and that he'd been so quick to believe she would betray him, but hearing Liam talk about him in this pretentious tone lit a whole new kind of flame inside her.

"Some dogs weren't meant to be domesticated, *Rae*," he continued. "Should've just left him out on the street or put him down."

"What did you say to him about...about being some *charity case?*" Raelyn remembered suddenly the words that had seemed to have Quinn so incensed.

"Well isn't he?" Liam spat out. "I saw that check your dad wrote for his football team fees on the counter. I couldn't fucking believe it-talk about a fucking goldmine."

His sudden change of tone from annoyance to amusement set Raelyn's blood to boil. "That's none of your damn business. You can't imagine what he's had to do for himself. At least he's got some kind of excuse for going off! You've had everything handed to you and you're still a fucking asshole."

"And you haven't?" Liam scoffed, then rolled his eyes and lowered his voice. "Don't get me wrong, it's a cute act you've going on like you're just some normal chick and not practically royalty. Adorable, really. But even you have to know he's not one of us. He will never belong to our world, and it's just cruel to keep teasing him with it."

Raelyn let out a heavy breath and kept her fists clenched so he couldn't see her hands shaking. "You and I, Liam, are *not* the same. We are not on some level together above everyone else. Your parents' accomplishments are not your own and you're not entitled to whatever the fuck you want just because you were born to this life."

She walked around him toward the door, now wishing she'd left it open. Liam stepped in front of it, blocking her way out.

"Move, Liam. We're done here."

"I don't think so, Princess." Liam folded his thick arms over his broad chest. "See, you got what you wanted out of this relationship, but I feel like I'm coming up short."

Her pulse tripped, her stomach shrunk in on itself, and she began searching for ways out. How had she landed herself in this situation? What the hell had she been thinking coming up here? Had she expected him to be reasonable so they could part ways amicably? Whatever she'd thought of him, she truly hadn't expected this.

"I think even a caveman like you can figure out I'm not having sex with you now," she said, hoping her voice concealed her nerves.

Liam eyed her up and down a few times before landing on her face. His mouth twitched, "It's cute you think you have a say in that."

"Liam-"

He cut her off by abruptly grabbing both wrists in his hands and shoving her back against the door. Her hands were pinned over her head, and he maneuvered both wrists into one large hand, bringing the other down to unzip her coat. She kicked at him, aiming for his groin, but he simply pressed his weight against her, holding her flat against the door. When his hand aggressively shoved down the front of her jeans and into her panties, she screamed for him to get the fuck off of her. His mouth came over hers to muffle her cry for help. Teeth caught her bottom lip and she tasted blood in her mouth.

This must be that feeling Quinn had once described when she'd asked what went through his head before he got into a fist fight. White hot rage filled her, and her vision blurred red. Though she didn't know how she got out from under Liam's strong grip, and she didn't know when she made the decision to take her shot, she certainly felt the pain in her hand and wrist after making contact with something hard.

Liam staggered back, covering his already-broken nose.

"Stay the fuck away from me," Raelyn snarled, opening the door. She turned back once more and added, "And if you even think about pressing charges against him, I'll make sure you are fucking buried in a mountain of sexual assault suits. Practically royalty, right?" She slipped out of his bedroom, took the stairs two at a time, and slammed the front door behind her without a second glance back.

The final two days before winter break had passed unbearably slowly. Opting to take a break from all boys, Raelyn had invited a bunch of the girls from the swim and soccer teams to stay at her house for a stereotypical girly slumber party. They swapped gossip, caught up on each other's love lives, though Raelyn's was sort of all over the school by now, and ate pizza while watching a *One Tree Hill* marathon. It had been refreshing. Raelyn spent so much time with the guys even before her ill-advised relationship with Liam, she rarely got in any girl time.

When the girls left on Saturday, Raelyn cleaned up what was left of the mess in the living room and her dad had wandered in to help.

"It was nice having the girls over this weekend, huh?" her dad remarked as he helped Raelyn fold a large blanket.

"Yeah, I need to do this more often," Raelyn said.

Now that the house was empty and the distractions were gone, her thoughts of Quinn returned. She had tried calling him multiple times since Wednesday after leaving Liam's house, and he hadn't returned any of her texts. She hadn't given away much in the messages that she'd sent him. She was starting to think she needed to break the ice by telling him exactly what had happened at Liam's. Sure, he'd respond, but he may also take a trip to Liam's house and finish what he started. It would be a little harder trying to keep Quinn out of legal trouble if he attacked Liam at his own house.

"I get the feeling you've got a lot on your mind, kiddo," Charlie said, tilting his head as he looked at his daughter.

"Just a lot of stuff has happened this semester," Raelyn sighed.

"I can't help noticing I haven't seen Quinn recently," he commented. When Raelyn simply glanced up at him and then down to the side, he continued, "I can't imagine your injured hand and wrist have something to do with that…"

"I already told you I forgot to wear gloves at my aerobic kickboxing class," Raelyn said in what even she knew was a much rehearsed tone. Liam's strong grasp had left a very distinct hand-print-shaped mark on her left wrist, and she'd had to ice the knuckles on her right hand after punching him square in the face.

"Mhm," her dad raised a skeptical eyebrow. "No Liam all weekend, either?"

"We broke up," Raelyn stated. She grabbed an armful of blankets and left the living room, heading for the stairs.

Charlie followed her up the staircase with his arms also full of blankets and spare pillows. In the guest room, they both unloaded their arms, putting everything back into the closet.

"I'm sorry, sweetie," Charlie said, placing a comforting hand on her shoulder.

Raelyn turned away with a shrug, "I'm not."

She heard the chuckle her father let out behind her. Continuing down the long hallway and into her bedroom, she was aware that her dad was still following, not ready to drop this conversation. Raelyn flopped onto her bed with her back on her pillows, and Charlie dipped into the room shortly after, hands in his pockets and head bowed slightly.

"We don't have to talk about it," he said. "And for the record, I'm not really sorry you broke up either."

Glancing up at her father, she couldn't stop the small tug that turned up the corners of her lips. Her dad was sort of her person. The one she went to when she needed to solve life's problems. Well, actually, Quinn was her person, but as he was clearly unavailable, her dad was the next best thing. "It's sort of a long story."

Charlie lowered himself onto the edge of her bed. "I've got time."

Oh boy...where do I start? How many of the details did she really want to share with her dad? He was level-headed and understanding in almost all respects, and he was protective, but also knew that teenagers did teenager stuff and that was perfectly normal. He wouldn't freak out on her over locker room talk, and she doubted he'd flinch hearing about Quinn's new reputation. Deciding that he would let her know if she was oversharing, she began with the day Liam asked her to the homecoming dance.

"...and there was this huge fight in the locker room the other day. Chris and Jett told me Liam was sharing...*intimate* and private details of our...physical relationship," Raelyn was explaining. Her dad put a hand up and assured her he did not need to know those details. "Right, well, apparently it pissed Quinn off. And *then* Liam made some snarky comment about how I just think he's a charity case or something."

Charlie's eyebrows shot up. "What a little prick. What did Quinn have to say?"

Anxiously picking at her comforter, she continued to explain about her interaction with Quinn while he cleared out his locker. "And then!" Raelyn's pace and volume were rising as she described this scene that still had her fuming, "He walks *around* me and just shoves his tongue down Alaina Costello's throat- can you believe that? *Alaina Costello!*" Raelyn scoffed. "He knows I don't like her. And then they just walk out together like they're some couple! Just because he chose her to make out with for no apparent reason!"

"Isn't that sort of what you did to him?" Charlie questioned. "Just picked the person you knew would piss him off the most because you were upset with him at that moment?"

Staring back at her dad, she chewed her lip, reflecting on this point. "Okay, Dad, are you here to be reasonable and give me sound advice? Or are you here to back me up? Because you can't do both."

With a nearly silent laugh, Charlie put his hands up in surrender, "I'm always here to back you up, sweetie. I'm just making connections." He sighed, then furrowed his brow in concentration. "Do I know Alaina? The name sounds familiar."

"She's the girl who hates me because you and mom have money," Raelyn replied contemptuously. "I've known her since the sixth grade and she's just always been unpleasant toward me. And she constantly makes snarky comments about me being a spoiled rich girl. She's all dark and cynical and has this stupid The World Is Out To Get Me attitude. And no matter what you say or do to be nice, she just has this chip on her shoulder. It's like a vendetta against anyone who doesn't have a completely dysfunctional family."

"Sounds like maybe she and Quinn have some things in common," Charlie said thoughtfully.

Raelyn looked at her dad through narrowed eyes. "No. They don't. Quinn is nice and pleasant to be around. And funny. And fun. *Alaina* is just...moody and hates everyone."

"You do realize that's how Quinn looks to everyone except you and his closest friends, right? How many noses has he broken? How many teeth has he knocked out?" Charlie asked.

"Uh, when he was younger, yeah," Raelyn defended, "but he's not that angry, pessimistic kid anymore." Charlie raised his eyebrows and scrunched his face. "Okay, he's still a little angry, apparently," she admitted with a restrained giggle, "but he doesn't let his situation keep him down. He doesn't go around blaming everyone else because of the shitty hand he was dealt."

Nodding, Charlie waved a hand for her to continue. "So, where does your break up with Liam- and I'm assuming, your hand injury-come in?"

Raelyn told her dad about confronting Liam at his house and the things he'd said about Quinn being like a stray guard dog that should've been left outside.

"And you punched him for that?"

"Um...no." Raelyn's hands were shaking as she recalled the attack. She studied the zipper on her dad's pull-over sweater. "He...Well, we were supposed to go out that night, remember? And I guess he thought we were going to have sex. I sort of knew that...I wasn't planning on going through with it, but I knew that was his plan."

"Okay..." Charlie said with forced control.

"And...He sort of attacked me- but I got away from him, Dad. I'm fine," Raelyn said in a rush.

"He what?" Charlie's voice was clipped and threatening.

"And that's when I punched him. And then I left," Raelyn rushed the words. "Well, I told him to stay away from me and Quinn and that if he pressed charges I would ruin him. And *then* I left."

Her dad was still working to control his anger. He was staring at the wall behind Raelyn, his jaw was clenched, and nostrils flared. Charlie stood abruptly. "I will kill him."

"No, you won't."

"I absolutely will. This piece of shit...we let him into our home, shared meals with him, had conversations with him...and he *attacks* you? Because you won't have-" Charlie breathed heavily. "Does Quinn know?"

"Like I said, he won't talk to me," Raelyn said. "I'm sure he'd respond if I told him, but..."

"Do not tell him," Charlie advised. He paced back and forth in front of Raelyn's bed. "You don't want to press charges? He left marks on you."

"If I press charges on him, he'll go after Quinn. He's got a lot more to lose."

Charlie sighed and nodded reluctantly. "Fine. He'd better know what a good friend you are, even when he's mad at you for no good reason."

Raelyn slunk back into her pillows and groaned, "I don't know what to do. I hate this. I just want my friend back."

"Go over to his house," Charlie replied simply. "Just show up. He can ignore your calls and texts and turn off his phone, but he can't exactly ignore you if you're right in front of him."

"I don't know, he's pretty good at the silent treatment."

"If he still refuses to talk to you when you're making an effort to be there for him, then give me a call. I'll head on over and knock some sense into him," said Charlie. "I'm sure he's a better fighter than I am, but I don't think he'd hit me."

Two hours later, Raelyn was sitting outside Quinn's house, nervously drumming her fingers on the steering wheel of her BMW. The temperature had dropped significantly over the past week and the crisp, clean scent of snow was in the air. Parked on the street, she knew she couldn't let her engine run for long without attracting attention, and she couldn't sit in her car with the engine off without freezing. Turning the key back and pulling it out of the ignition, she made up her mind to just do it. She was going to walk into his house and find him and slap some sense into him- literally, if need be.

His mother's gold Toyota Corolla sat in the small driveway in front of a red Pontiac Grand Prix. The red car was unfamiliar, but there were always different vehicles there. Molly's various friends were always traipsing in and out of the house, likely bringing her drugs. Raelyn wasn't completely naive; she knew people who dealt with heroin were dangerous. But she couldn't bear the thought of walking around to his bedroom window and getting turned away. Quinn could pretend he didn't hear her or see her if he pulled the blinds, and wouldn't that just be embarrassing?

So, Raelyn walked straight up the walkway to the shabby front porch with its ripped screen door. She didn't knock. If Molly's drug buddies were inside, she wouldn't want to draw their attention. She tested the front door and it was unlocked, so she pushed through. The living room to the right was empty, as was the kitchen to the left. Straight ahead was the hallway that led to the two small bedrooms and the bathroom. Hoping she wouldn't run into any questionable characters in the dark hallway, Raelyn marched with purpose toward the second door on the left.

Standing outside Quinn's bedroom door, Raelyn let out a quick breath, closed her eyes for a few seconds.

It's just Quinn. He's obviously mad, but you know what you're here to say. You got this.

Raelyn opened her eyes, grabbed the doorknob and swung the door open, announcing herself with an assertive "Quinn Casey! Why-"

She was going to ask why he'd made her drag her ass all the way across town in the snow, but at the sight of Alaina in his bed she stopped short.

"-the hell is she here?" She managed to finish.

Alaina was lying on Quinn's bed, on her side, with her head propped up in her hand. Quinn sat on the floor with his back against his bed. He had a baseball in his hand, which Raelyn assumed he'd been lazily tossing into the air and catching repeatedly.

Quinn's eyes widened in surprise at the sight of Raelyn in his bedroom doorway, mouth open and frozen as if he'd been caught doing something he knew he shouldn't.

Alaina's face contorted into a sneer. "Unlike *you*, I was invited."

"Rae," Quinn placed a hand on the floor, getting ready to stand up. "What are you doing here? Did my mom let you in?"

"No, I let myself in," Raelyn replied, then with a snarky glare toward Alaina she added, "When you've been friends for nine years, there's a standing invitation. I can come and go whenever I want."

"Wow! Tell me, what's it like to feel so entitled that you think you can make up other people's boundaries as you go?" Alaina asked sardonically.

"It's phenomenal. Tell me, what's it like to be a cynical, egotistical twat?"

Alaina scoffed, and Quinn was probably lucky he wasn't facing her because his mouth made a silent "ooh..." as his eyes widened slightly and he avoided eye contact with Raelyn.

Ignoring Alaina's move to sit up and face her with a challenging stare, Raelyn looked at Quinn who had yet to stand up. "We need to talk. I don't know why you've been ignoring me or why I had to drag my ass all the way over here to witness this again," she gestured vaguely between Alaina and Quinn, "but I need some answers."

With a hand stuck out in his direction, Quinn grabbed it and let Raelyn pull him to his feet. She winced at the pain in her hand and muttered, "Son of a bitch." She shook her hand out when Quinn let go of it.

"What happened to your hand?" Quinn asked with genuine concern.

"No one ever tells you how much it hurts to punch someone," Raelyn replied.

Quinn's eyes grew wide as they flew from her hand to her face. "You punched someone?"

"Yeah, I did. You know, you, me, Chris, and Jett used to be a team. You can't expect me to not want in on the action, too."

"You hit *Liam?* Rae, he's huge."

"I'm aware. Maybe more so than most people," Raelyn said. When Quinn's face twisted to mild disgust, she laughed nervously, "That's not what I meant. I just meant, like, I've been around him a lot. Near him. I know how big he is. Compared to me. His *whole* body- *Jesus*, I cannot get out of this one."

He bit his lip, trying to hide his amusement with her word vomit. Once he'd successfully contained his expression to one of stony silence and near disinterest again, Raelyn continued with what she'd come to say. "Listen, it's been a hell of a few days and I still have no idea why you supposedly stood up for me if you were so pissed that I was sharing all your dirty secrets. I wasn't- but you seem to think I was. So...what the hell?"

Quinn's expression didn't change and she was starting to get annoyed. If he was looking for some sort of apology, he was mistaken. She hadn't done a damn thing wrong.

"Liam saw the check Dad wrote for the school for football. It was with that form they sent home and it had your name on it. I guess it got left out on the kitchen counter or something." She continued, "As far as knowing about your mom, people gossip in this town. And his dad's a family court judge. I wouldn't be surprised if your case popped up on his desk when that social worker kept coming by a few years ago."

Raelyn watched as the information sunk in and his features softened slightly.

"This would be a good time for you to apologize, by the way," Raelyn said, crossing her arms. When Quinn's brows pinched together she added, "for having so little faith in the value I put on our friendship. I wouldn't talk about you like that. I don't know what else he said, but it was either taken out of context or he was just fishing for a reaction and got lucky."

Quinn's strong chest deflated slightly as he sighed, and gave a nearly indistinguishable nod. "I'm sorry, Rae."

"That's a good start," said Raelyn, eyeing him stubbornly.

Alaina made a derisive noise from behind them, "Are you serious? She just tells you what to do and you do it?"

"Oh, I'm sorry, are you still here?" Raelyn asked with mock-friendliness.

Quinn half-sighed, half-groaned as he ran a hand down his face, "Rae..."

"What?" Raelyn snapped, exasperated. "Is this, like, a thing now?"

"We've been hanging out," Quinn said vaguely.

"Yeah, we have," Alaina got up off the bed and stood next to Quinn. "But please, feel free to barge in here with your petty, rich-girl problems. We would love to hear them. It's not like we have *real* issues going on in our lives."

"Okay, Alaina, this whole act of yours is getting stale," Raelyn sighed. "I get it. I have money. A whole bunch of it. I could raid my parents' bank vault and throw stacks of hundreds around this room and they probably wouldn't notice. Is that what you wanted to hear? I feel like you're waiting for me to just brag about my financial situation that I did absolutely nothing to help create, and I never have, so there you go."

Alaina glared at Raelyn. "Wow, I bet that felt good."

"You do realize that you hate me for something I have absolutely no control over, right? I had no more choice in the life I was given than either of you. And yeah, I know you guys can probably bond over how much life can suck sometimes, and that's great," she now turned to Quinn and grabbed both of his shoulders, forcing him to look directly at her as she spoke, "but at the end of the day, Quinn, you are my best friend. I love the shit out of you. And if you want to be mad for a while longer, then be mad. But you're better than this woe-is-me bullshit. And for someone who hates feeling pitied, you can throw one hell of a pity-party for yourself, and you're better than that."

She watched as Quinn's mood changed, the stiffness and tension in his shoulders seemed to dissipate, and the stubborn defiance of his face relaxed. Raelyn placed her hand gently on the side of his face and ran her thumb over the now green-ish bruise on his cheekbone. "When you're ready, you know where to find me." He was looking back at her, still silent, but his eyes were searching her face. He gave the vague impression of someone who'd just woken up having forgotten where he was. Ignoring the presence of this *other* girl in the room, Raelyn planted a kiss on Quinn's cheek before briskly walking back out the door.

The following morning, Raelyn was eating breakfast at the table while her dad silently read the paper and drank his coffee. She noticed his frequent curious glances in her direction out of the corner of her eye but would redirect her attention to the back of the Special K box instead of addressing him. There was actually nothing interesting on the back of the box; just different Special K products that were supposed to make you lose weight.

After several silent minutes, Charlie let out a loud and exaggerated sigh as he looked in Raelyn's direction. She looked up from the cereal box and snapped her head toward her dad.

"Is there something you'd like to share with the class, Father?"

He smirked, feeling successful that his not-so-subtle technique had gotten her attention. "You went to Quinn's last night, didn't you?"

"Yep," Raelyn stated. She shoveled another bite of cereal into her mouth.

Charlie paused, staring and waiting for her to continue. She did not. He prompted, "And...how did that go?"

Raelyn dropped her spoon into her bowl, leaning onto the back of her chair. "That bitch, Alaina, was there."

With animated enthusiasm, Charlie slapped his hand on the table, "No! Not that bitch, Alaina!"

Finally cracking a smile and laughing at her dad's level of support, Raelyn continued, "She pulled her usual crap, of course. Quinn didn't say much, but I did get him to apologize for accusing me of being a bad friend." She gave him a run-down of the scene, from barging in and wanting to projectile vomit at the sight of Alaina lying on Quinn's bed like she belonged there, to telling Quinn that she'd still be there when he was done with whatever this mood was.

"Wait," Charlie held up a hand, "you *kissed* him? In front of her?"

"It was just on the cheek, Dad," Raelyn said, "I do that all the time. Or at least I *did.*"

Charlie scratched the stubble he had yet to shave this morning, "Do you think- and I'm just throwing this out there- but do you think it's possible that you want to be with Quinn? As more than just friends?"

For some reason, Raelyn's mind went to the brief moment after the fight when Quinn had come around the corner toward their lockers and she had caught herself thinking of him differently. That image played in slow motion in her brain, and she couldn't ignore that his raw masculinity had her feeling unusually warm and flustered. A pleasant sensation spread down her belly and between her legs as she imagined Quinn grabbing her and kissing her the way he'd kissed Alaina.

Blinking the picture away, but unfortunately not the hot and bothered sensation that had no business between her thighs, she failed to make eye contact with her father as she replied, "No. Nope. He's just my good buddy, Quinn."

With a skeptical look and a chuckle, Charlie said, "Well, I don't think you could get any more convincing than that."

Raelyn glared back down at her cereal and muttered, "Shut up."

The loud gong-like sound of the front doorbell rang through the house. It was rare that anyone came to the house this early on a Monday morning. Raelyn and her dad looked at each other curiously. Moments later, one of the maids entered the dining room with their surprise guest.

Quinn stood beneath the arch that led into the large formal dining room, head lowered slightly, looking down at the floor. Without moving his head up, he flicked his gaze upward and met Raelyn's surprised stare.

"Look, Rae, it's your good buddy, Quinn!" Charlie announced loudly.

"I see that, Dad, thank you." Raelyn slid out of her chair and walked around the long dining table to stand somewhat awkwardly in front of her friend.

Quinn was wearing a black leather jacket, which couldn't possibly be warm enough for a Northern Michigan winter, and a pair of faded and ripped jeans. He'd already left his shoes at the front door. Even from this distance she could feel the cold from outside coming off him in gusts.

For what felt like several moments, she and Quinn just looked at each other. Quinn studied her, from her bare feet and sweatpants to her thin t-shirt- *his* t-shirt, actually. Their eyes met again, and she wondered when he was finally going to speak or if she should first. Before she could figure out exactly what she would say, Quinn took a step closer and pulled her into a tight hug. Raelyn's arms followed suit and encircled him, too.

His arms were wrapped low around her waist, holding her tight to him and his lips were next to her ear. "I'm sorry, Rae," he whispered. "I'm so...so sorry."

There was an unfamiliar desperation in his voice that made Raelyn question if she'd missed something. Had he found out about what Liam had done? Was there part of the story Chris and Jett had left out? His tone made her want to hold onto him tighter, so she pulled him closer and leaned into him, burying her face in his chest. She inhaled his familiar scent and closed her eyes.

Though she tried to ignore her dad's earlier interrogation about the possibility of wanting more than friendship, she couldn't help admitting that this felt right. Being held by him. Consumed by his strong arms. She didn't want to let go.

CHAPTER 22

The bright white headlights of Jett's F-250 nearly blinded Quinn in the rearview mirror of his Bronco where he sat waiting for his ride to show up. Slowly and miserably, he made his way to Jett's truck and slid into the passenger seat. He felt both sick and annoyed at the sight of Jett's disappointed dad glare as he reclined the seat back and swung his hat around to pull it over his face.

He could still feel Jett's gaze on him. "What the fuck did you do, man?"

"I got drunk and acted like an ass."

"Enough to make her leave you here?" Jett questioned.

"Apparently," Quinn sighed. He closed his eyes beneath his hat and he reflected on the past several hours. Just that morning before Rae left for the party, they'd had sex on the bathroom counter. She was getting ready to leave and had just put away all of her makeup and hair styling supplies before getting dressed. Quinn had come in, picked her up and set her sexy ass on the countertop. He'd dropped down to his knees and pulled her lacy panties down with his teeth and kissed his way up her thighs. He tongue-fucked her, using his mouth, fingers, sucking on her clit until she came. He pulled her legs around his waist and watched his cock fill her up while the first orgasm still rocked through her. Rae tangled her fingers in his hair and whispered sexy French phrases into his ear. He didn't know what they meant, but *goddamn*, they made his cock hard.

And now he was here. Asking his friend for a ride because he'd gotten drunk with a bunch of guys he'd just met and decided to run his damn mouth.

There were plenty of reasons Quinn didn't surpass the two-drink mark. In part, he was wary of substance abuse and addiction. His psych 101 course in college had taught him that he was five times more likely to become an addict because his mother- and, in all likelihood, his father- was one. He hadn't retained much from that class that he'd taken the second semester of his freshman year, but that tidbit of information had stuck with him.

Another reason he avoided drinking too much was something he'd discovered sophomore year at Arizona State when he'd ignored that psychology statistic and joined his roommates at a kegger on frat row. When he drank he became more talkative. That's normal. But when he had a little too much, he became a shit talker. He got cocky. And often his old temper would kick in. He'd find himself wanting to fight someone for trash talking back, or because they looked at him wrong, or simply because they looked like a challenge, and he wanted to impress his own ego.

While he knew this about himself, he never imagined that Rae would ever be the target of his angst or his ego.

God dammit. How did this even happen?

Quinn racked his memory for the moment he'd gone from having a good time, to whatever that egomaniacal monstrosity was that had presented itself that night.

Emerson...the moment it clicked that he'd been talking to Rae's ex, he'd flipped a switch.

"I got along with him at first," Quinn said suddenly, into the silence of the truck. "Emerson, I mean. He didn't tell me who he was."

"Ah, yeah. That'll happen," Jett replied. "He's good at first impressions. And second ones, and however many he needs to be until he gets what he wants from you."

"Well, he got what he wanted from me," Quinn sighed. "I fucked up my last shot with Rae. Only it's worse this time because I actually know what I'm missing out on now."

"You didn't break up," Jett said. "You had your first fight. Well, your first fight as a couple. You've gotten over this kind of stuff before, right?"

"I've never really been in a position to accuse her of only being with me because I make money, so...no."

Jett slammed on his brakes and snapped his head to glare at Quinn, then smacked the baseball hat off his face. "You *what?!*"

"Pretty good, huh?" Quinn said sarcastically.

"Dammit Case," Jett snapped. "Do you think she ever thought that about you growing up? When we were kids and you were poor as hell? Do you think she ever questioned your motives for being her friend?"

"I know," Quinn groaned. His first instinct told him to go back to his hotel room and wallow in self-pity. But that would probably lead to more drinking and that might lead to regrettable drunk dialing and drunk texts. He sat up in his seat and looked ahead at the road. Jett had begun driving again and was heading toward Hotel Indigo to drop Quinn off. "Go to Rae's," Quinn said urgently.

"Quinn, it's one in the morning."

"That's fine. I'm not waiting. I'll sleep on the front porch if I have to." Quinn's mind was clear enough to know he couldn't give himself time to back out. He couldn't go back to his hotel alone and beat himself up over how badly he'd messed up and would probably keep messing up. Rae had once told him he was better than self-pity, and the thing she admired most about him was that he never accepted defeat. He had to remind her that he was still that guy.

Less than ten minutes later, Quinn was walking up Rae's driveway, trying to figure out how best to get in. Maybe she would be too angry at him to sleep and would still be awake. He ran up the front porch and, after making sure that she had locked the door, began pounding and calling her name. After what felt like several minutes, he finally heard the booming bark of Harry on the other side of the door.

"Yes, Harry, help me out here," Quinn whispered, feeling his heart rate pick up.

A light flipped on inside. The inside door opened enough to see Rae in a pair of plaid cotton shorts and a thin, white camisole. Her eyes were puffy and red. There were dried tear streaks trailing down her cheeks.

She's been crying. She's been crying and it's my fault.

This hit him like a blow to the gut. He wanted to collapse to his knees and beg for her forgiveness. He *should* do that.

"Rae, please, I'm so, so sorry-"

"I'm sorry, I'm not interested in purchasing a sugar daddy today. Maybe you can try the next house over. I hear *she's* a shallow bitch." Raelyn shut the large oak door and Quinn heard the deadbolt snap into place.

"Rae, I didn't mean that. I don't know why I said it," Quinn pleaded. "Please, Rae. What do you want me to do? I'll do anything, please just let me in."

The light from inside went out and Harry was no longer barking.

Quinn hopped off the porch and went around to the garage door where the keypad was. He wasn't sure if this was technically breaking and entering, but he knew the code so he punched it in. Without waiting for the door to rise all the way, Quinn ducked underneath it and ran to the inside door, hoping he reached it before Rae realized what he was doing.

He was a little annoyed that she hadn't locked the inside door just for her own safety but was glad for the time being that his plan had worked. He was in the mudroom, and he kicked his shoes off out of habit before trekking through the kitchen and living room. Down the hall, Harry came running to greet him and Quinn gave him a few pats on the head and neck as he walked by him and pushed his way into Rae's bedroom.

"You do realize this is the definition of a home intrusion, right?" Rae fumed. She was standing just outside the door to the master bathroom, as if she was trying to get as far away from him as possible. "I know in California they're a bunch of little bitches, but according to Michigan law, I could shoot you right now."

"Rae, please just listen to me," said Quinn as he approached her. He wanted to wrap her in his arms and kiss her tears away. He wanted to make love to her any and every way she wanted. "Please, Rae. You have to know I didn't mean it."

"Then why did you say it?" she challenged, arms folded.

"Because…" Quinn hesitated, not knowing how to explain it, "Because I still don't know why the hell you would want me. Because I have these goddamn insecurities that I haven't dealt with yet. Because

I'm really good at fueling my fucking ego to try to make myself feel like I'm enough."

"You sure as hell didn't sound insecure when you were bragging to everyone about how your words turn me into some kind of sex fiend."

Quinn groaned miserably and ran a hand down his face. "I know, I know, and I have no excuse for that. Rae, I am so sorry. I acted like a fucking monster tonight, but please know that's not me."

"How can I know that? We've been together for a month. We haven't seen each other in years, and that last time we met up in college wasn't a whole lot different than tonight," Rae said.

God dammit, she's right.

"I was nervous that night," said Quinn. "We hadn't seen each other in almost four years and I wanted so badly to impress you. I'd been trying to impress you since I was thirteen, and I always fell short of the mark."

"Oh, so it's my fault for being impossible to please?" she retorted, with a hand on her chest. "Quinn, use your head. Think of the times we had the most fun as kids, the things we used to enjoy the most. It wasn't my crazy over the top birthday parties. It was playing baseball or just watching movies and talking to each other, hanging out at the park or downtown, or just walking around with no destination."

"We did that stuff all the time, yeah, but none of it ever made you think of me as more than a friend. I loved being your best friend, Rae, but I wanted more than that."

"Are you sure? Because I seem to remember sitting there, *completely* available, while you flirted and messed around with just about every other girl in school." Rae was letting out thoughts Quinn was sure she'd been holding in for years.

He found himself heating up again as she questioned his feelings for her. Fuck, he knew anger was not going to get him where he wanted, but he couldn't help it. "Completely available? Rae, you hopped from one guy to the next. You may have only had a couple of actual boyfriends, but you always had guys trailing after you, begging to be next."

"Oh, please," Rae rolled her eyes. "How is it my problem that other guys were attracted to me? I'm not the one who went around shoving my hands down the panties of everyone who looked at me."

Quinn felt his face twist into an incredulous glare before he could help it. "I did *not* shove my hands in girls' panties. And okay, you say the attention you attracted wasn't your problem? You think we didn't all know that was exactly your intent when you wore those skimpy little skorts and tight tops? Come on, you *loved* being able to make guys drool and fantasize about you. And trust me, it fucking worked. You wouldn't imagine some of the shit those guys talked about wanting to do with you behind your back!"

Rae scoffed. "Really, Quinn? Wearing certain clothes means I was asking for whatever sick fantasies you guys came up with? That's original."

She took a step closer to him and he stood up straighter and swallowed. Her sudden closeness reminded him through his fog of anger and frustration that he'd come here to apologize, to get her back, to make up for being a dick earlier. Not to criticize her and act like a dick again. *Shit*, why was he attacking her for things that had happened over ten years ago?

"Did it ever occur to you that I wore those skorts and tops because I was sick of being seen as just another one of the guys?" Rae questioned. "I wore them because I liked them, sure, but maybe part of me wanted to actually be thought of as a girl for a change."

"We knew you were a girl, Rae. We just didn't think you wanted us to act like it. You wouldn't want us to treat you differently just because you were suddenly...you know, a babe."

Rae raised her eyebrow and he could tell she was trying not to let the smirk pull at her lips. "A babe, huh?"

"We might have had conversations about it."

"Conversations? Like that locker room bullshit you pulled tonight?" Rae countered, scathingly.

Quinn put his hands over his face and groaned. "Rae, please, I'm so sorry. I know I shouldn't have talked about you like that, but...I got jealous, okay? Your ex was going on about how much you just couldn't wait for him to get home and that you were all over him all the time. I just- *we* have been having the best sex that I have ever had. Like every day. For almost a month now. I don't like thinking it was ever like this with you and some other guy. I want to know that *I'm* the only person who can make you feel like that. I've never felt this before. Being near you at all, Rae, is a fucking dream." He stepped closer and closed what was left of the gap between them. Reaching out his hand, he touched the side of her face as he peered deep into her eyes. The usual bright blue was darkened as she stared back at him, unyielding. "But being *with* you, being *inside* you…" His mouth twitched with a smirk as he watched the small intake of breath at his words. "It's all I can think about. You've got me hooked, and I don't want to do or think about anything or anyone else."

Rae let his hand rest on her face and he slid his thumb gently over the arch of her cheekbone a few times before she stepped back abruptly. Quinn dropped his hand down to his side with a sigh.

She eyed him warily. "How do I know that's not just who you are now? How do I know when you go back to L.A. that you won't just jump right back into your little 'bad boy of baseball' routine you've created over the last few years? How do *you* know you won't regret tying yourself to one woman the first time you see some hot model who wants to throw herself at you?" Rae was pacing in front him now. Three steps, turn, another three steps, turn.

"Don't you think there's a reason it didn't work with all those girls?" said Quinn, now taking his hat off so he could nervously run his hands through his mess of hair. "I didn't want to be with them. Ever since high school, all those girls I was with were a distraction from how bad I wanted you. Rae, you're the only girl who has never left my mind."

"'*All those girls*'," Rae repeated, stopping her pacing to glare at him with her arms crossed over her chest. "Speaking of *all* of those girls, don't you think it's a little ironic that you're the one who seems to get jealous all the time? You're the one who's been messing around with who knows how many women, and yet *you* get jealous of the one guy I've been with in the last few years and had a relationship with."

Quinn knew he got jealous easily. Of course he did. He used to fantasize about Rae being *his girl* for years. Ever since that day at the ballpark when she'd given him a kiss on the cheek with his hat on. He started coming up with excuses for her to wear his hats more often or offer his team shirts and sweatshirts that had his last name on them. He wanted everyone to see her with his name on her. He was possessive. He wanted to stake his claim on her but was always so sure he wasn't good enough. So he pretended.

"Yeah, I do get jealous easily, Rae," Quinn nodded. "I get jealous because- and I don't mean this in a way that's meant to treat you like an object or a prize- I get jealous of those guys because you're *mine*. You've always been mine. Everyone seems to get that except you."

Rae scoffed and rolled her eyes, looking off to the side.

"Don't believe me?" Quinn pressed, voice rising. "Nothing about those other women ever mattered. I could try to make a connection, try to feel something deeper, *try* to want more than a night or two with them. But it didn't matter. You set the bar a long time ago, and none of them ever came close." He grabbed her around the waist, forcing her to be near him, even though she resisted the embrace at first. "And no one else ever will, because I'm yours. You've made your claim, whether you know it or not. You, Raelyn DeRose, belong to me. And I belong to you. So you'd better get that through your head, because it's not changing any time soon."

Her body was tense and defiant against his. Quinn knew she was still mad, but these last words had forced her to make eye contact. There was a spark in her eyes, though he wasn't entirely sure if it was more fight flaring, or if she'd been turned on by what he'd said. Maybe both.

"Is that so?" One of her eyebrows raised as she continued to glare at him. "If I've been yours for so long, why didn't you do anything about it before now? If I belonged to you, even back then, why would you let me go out with all those guys you hated so much?"

The fire in her voice was intoxicating. Quinn was still holding her close to him, though he could feel her body pulling away. He tightened his grip on her, grabbing her hips and pressing into her. She put her hands on top of his as if to pry his hands away from her, but instead just rested them there, still fuming. Quinn watched her chest rise up and down with her exhilarated breath. He watched her nipples go hard beneath her thin camisole.

"You know why, Rae," said Quinn, his voice low and husky. "I never thought I'd make the cut. I saw all the guys you went for and I was nothing like them."

"That's a bullshit answer, and you know it." Rae lowered her voice. "I may not have known I wanted you since we were thirteen, *Case*, but at least when I realized what I wanted, I went for it. I didn't sit around for five years and wait for it to fall into my lap."

Is she talking about the night I brought her home after the bar? Or...graduation night?

Quinn searched her face for clarification. He swallowed then fought back, "You didn't want *me*, Rae. You just didn't want to still be a virgin when you got to college."

"Why do you think I chose you? By the sounds of it I could've had anyone," Rae challenged. "Why didn't I pick Jett or Chris or...anyone else if it was really just about wanting to get fucked for the first time?"

Now Quinn's breath was coming in shaky and he was struggling to keep it steady. This time it was his quick intake of breath when she'd said 'fucked' that had her grinning mischievously. She didn't usually talk like that, but damn, it did things to him. His cock was getting hard, pressing against the zipper of his jeans. He traced his eyes down her face and neck, and to where her nipples were visibly poking into the fabric of her shirt.

"Why did you choose me?" Quinn rasped, watching the steady rise and fall of her breasts.

"Because I wanted *you*, Quinn Casey. Because you're mine....and I'm yours."

Quinn's eyes flicked up from her chest to her fiery gaze. It sent an electric shock through his whole body. His hands shot up from her hips into her hair, tangling his fingers as he pulled her in hard and crushed his mouth onto hers. His tongue slid into her mouth and wrestled with hers. Quinn felt frantic. He couldn't get enough of her. He couldn't be close enough to her. He needed her- everything, all of her, all at once.

He trailed his mouth down her jaw and bit the nape of her neck. When she moaned, she arched her body into him. "You are mine," he whispered against her skin. "It's about damn time you figured it out." His hands dropped down to the bottom of her little white camisole and he slid his hands underneath it, cupping both breasts as he brushed his thumbs over those sweetly pointed nipples. The whimper that slipped out of her lips made his pants feel tight as his cock hardened for her.

Rae's hands shot to his belt and started unbuckling, unbuttoning, unzipping. She pushed his jeans and boxer briefs to the floor, then raised her hands over her head so Quinn could slip her shirt off and throw it somewhere to be forgotten. He did the same and she pulled his shirt over his head and tossed it into the room.

Picking her up, he carried her to the bed and threw her onto her back. He dropped down to his knees and yanked down her pajama shorts, pleased to find that she was naked underneath. Quinn groaned, grabbed her hips roughly and pulled her to the edge of the bed, spreading her legs. He looked at Rae, lying naked on the bed as she lifted herself onto her elbows to watch him. They locked eyes as he trailed one finger up and down the middle of her wet, pink crease before diving between her thighs, tasting her, worshipping her the best way he knew how.

She gasped and fisted his hair, lifting her hips to help him tongue-fuck her deeper. Quinn curled one arm beneath her, fingers digging into that perfectly round ass. With the other hand he found Rae's clit and rubbed it the way he knew she liked, in soft circles, while his tongue licked a slow trail up the center of her pussy, making her writhe beneath him. He got that clit between his middle and ring finger, rubbing it on both sides. He felt her back arch and she let out a long, pleasured moan.

"Yes, Quinn," she breathed. "Don't stop."

No fucking way was he stopping. Even when she finally reached that first celestial peak, it would be just the beginning.

Switching positions, Quinn pulled Rae's legs over his shoulders. He sucked her clit and slipped a finger, then two, inside her. He was not going easy on her tonight. He wouldn't be able to. He wanted to fuck her good and hard, and in every possible way. Stake his claim and ruin her for anyone else.

Rae's fingers grasped his hair tight, and he continued plunging his fingers in and out. When she cried out and thrusted her hips against his mouth, he felt her tight muscles squeeze around his fingers. She screamed his name as the orgasm ripped through her like a tidal wave, and he felt her whole body contract. As the waves of pleasure began to subside, she loosened her grip on his hair and he lifted his head up to watch with satisfaction as she caught her breath.

He allowed her a few steady breaths before roughly grabbing her hips again and easily flipping her over onto her stomach. Rae's little gasp of surprise made his fucking cock throb. Quinn pulled her hips back so her ass was sticking up and her back was arched steeply downward, giving him one of the most heavenly views he had come to know.

She pushed herself up onto her forearms, and as he bent over her body to whisper in her ear, he pressed his rock hard length up against her ass. "Feel how hard you've got me?" He pushed against her harder. "That's what this view does to me, baby. I shouldn't have said anything to anyone about it, I know. This is for my eyes only, from now on. I don't want anyone even imagining it." Quinn nibbled at her ear, then kissed his way back up to standing, gently biting her shoulder, mouth trailing the angle of her arched back. With one large hand groping her ass, he leaned over to her nightstand, grabbed out a condom and ripped it open with his teeth. He rolled it on and angled himself at that slick, pink opening. Reaching around he played with her clit some more, then grabbed both of her hips in his hands and pulled her back onto his cock.

Quinn's growl escaped from somewhere out of his chest as she moaned and he pulled her hips back onto him again. Slowly, he pulled himself out, then yanked her hips back, urging her pussy around his dick. He tore his eyes away from his cock going in and out of her and looked up to where she'd thrown her head back in pleasure, and was grasping at the comforter to hold herself together.

"Mmm, you like that, baby, don't you?" Quinn groaned. He slipped one hand from her waist down to her hair and grabbed a handful. He pulled and her back arched further. "I'm gonna make this pussy come so much, baby. I'm gonna fuck you so good tonight, you're never gonna question who you belong to again."

Rae backed her hips into him at his words and he smacked that insanely perfect ass. She let out another moan. "Oh my God, Quinn...you feel so good."

"You want it faster?" Quinn breathed. He still couldn't fucking handle hearing his name on her lips like that.

"I'm yours, Quinn," she breathed. "Take me how you want me."

Oh. Fuck. Yes.

God dammit, his chest might have fucking exploded at those words. He groaned, as words completely failed him, and gave her ass another hard smack before grabbing her hard and pounding into her until he was losing control, losing himself inside her. He fucked her hard, sweat dripped down his chest, her back arched, hips moved back to meet his movements. Their symphony of ragged breathing, moans, dirty words, and skin on skin filled the room.

Fuck, he wasn't ready to be done, but he was struggling to hold on.

"Yes, Quinn!" Rae wasn't holding back as she let herself get loud and wild. They were like animals. Nothing mattered but how goddamn good it felt. "*Oh mon Dieu!* Quinn, *S'il vous plait!*"

"Oh my God, baby," Quinn growled. "You know what that sexy French does to me."

There was always round two. Quinn pumped himself in and out, harder, faster. The way he was holding onto Rae's hips, she would be wearing bruises tomorrow. He was marking his territory.

"Fuck baby, oh my God." He knew he wasn't going to last much longer. "I'm gonna come with you, baby, tell me when-"

Rae let out another long moan, shoving her hips back into him as her pussy contracted and squeezed tight around his cock. He held her tight against him and felt her body shake and quiver around and beneath him. She reached back and fisted his hair through her fingers, and he bent his mouth to her neck.

"Oooh....fuck," Quinn drew out a low groan as he pumped in and out quickly as he came. His muscles tightened and rippled as he squeezed her hip bones harder, holding her in place. He rocked into her and let out one last shaky breath before letting his weight fall on her.

Quinn kissed the side of her neck as she panted, trying to catch her breath. Rolling off of her, he threw his hands up over his head and let his chest rise and fall until he relaxed. Rae rolled onto her back and lay next to him doing the same.

Wrapping an arm around her to pull her close, he turned her on her side so that she faced him and rested his hand on the rounded curve of her hip. "Rae, I'm so sorry about earlier. I'm not trying to blame it on the alcohol, but I know I turn into a jerk when I drink too much."

"I can agree with that assessment," Rae said as she began trailing her fingers along his chest.

Quinn swept his eyes down Rae's body, taking in every detail of this dream woman lying next to him. She was perfect and he didn't deserve her. Not one bit. She had every right to cast him out but if she'd let him, he'd spend every day trying to do better. To be better. To be the kind of man she did deserve.

She had finally talked about the biggest let down he remembered. At least she'd mentioned it. He knew Rae had a big thing about going to college while still being a virgin. He figured she'd asked him because they were friends. He was someone she trusted and that way it wasn't just anybody. But she had actually *wanted* him? Wanted to be with him? Why had she waited to realize that until just before he left the state for school?

As if reading his thought process, Rae opened her mouth to speak. He could tell she was hesitating, and she didn't meet his eyes. "About...that night. Graduation," Rae said, her voice soft and reserved. The complete opposite of what he'd heard just moments ago while he was inside her. "The reason I was so upset..."

Quinn sighed. "Because I was someone you trusted and I lied to you. Rae, you have no idea how many times I go over that night in my head, wishing-"

"That's not it," Rae cut him off. "I mean, yeah, that's part of it, but if you would've told me beforehand, I still probably would've gone through with it. But I was naked and feeling extremely vulnerable, and...I thought you were going to say something else entirely."

Quinn's hand skated up and down Rae's side, her skin like warm silk against his palm. Brow furrowed as he mentally kicked himself- *again*- for how that night had ended, he stayed quiet. He didn't want to say anything to make her change her mind about finally talking to him about that night.

"I thought…" she paused, biting her lip. "I wanted to go with you, you know. To Arizona."

This got Quinn's attention. He snapped his eyes to hers and she was looking back at him, almost nervously. "What do you mean?"

"When you said you had something to tell me, I thought you were going to ask me to come with you. I was hoping that's what you were going to say."

Quinn stared back at her for what seemed like several long seconds before he could find his words. "But…you got that scholarship to Michigan, didn't you?"

"Quinn, do you really think I needed a scholarship to afford college?" Rae countered. "I had applied to Arizona, and Louisiana, and Texas."

All the places he'd been offered scholarships to.

His mouth fell open in surprise. What was she saying?

We could've been together? If I hadn't been such a damn idiot and lied *to my best friend?*

"I got accepted to all of them, and Dad had the tuition check ready to send to Arizona," Rae said, her gaze switching from his chest to his face repeatedly. "But then…that happened. And I guess…I thought I must've had the wrong idea. I thought you were into me. Actually, I was pretty sure you had been for at least a little while. But then I guess I thought I must've been wrong. That you were only doing it as a favor or something."

Quinn put his hands over his face and released a long breath. Rae had wanted to be with him enough to leave the state for him? Enough to follow him across the country? And he'd never known it.

Goddamn, that memory plays differently now.

He laced his fingers over hers where she rested her hand on his chest. "I'd ask you why you never told me, but that's a little hollow coming from me, huh?"

If he had just told her the truth when she had first brought up that little deal they'd made, if he had just told her how he really felt, that might have changed everything.

But then again, that might've changed *everything*. They were both in good places. His dream of playing ball and getting out of poverty and doing it on his own had come true. Rae was successful, too. She was so independent, and most of the baseball wives he knew basically followed their husbands and let their ball career dictate everything. It was a show of support, of course, sort of like being a military wife. But would Rae have been happy if she'd been with him through it all? Would she have been happy following him all over the country and giving up her chance at ever having her own career? He didn't doubt she would have supported him, but would she have been unhappy just helping him live his dream and forgetting about any of her own?

Those long years spent apart suddenly felt more necessary than tragic. They'd both made a life they were happy with. And now they had each other. Now they could have it all.

"I would have loved it, Rae, if you would've come with me. I wanted you to, I wanted to be with you. Back then, I couldn't imagine four years without you. It almost made me want to say no to a scholarship and college just to stay near you, but I knew I couldn't," he said, then rolled to face her. "But there will always be what-ifs. Fuck knows I've got about a million of them when it comes to you, but we're here now."

"It's just hard not to imagine how different the last ten or eleven years might have been if I'd gone with you. I was heartbroken when you left. It's like I never actually thought you'd leave without me. You'd been a part of my life, a part of *me* for so long. I had to learn how to live without you."

Quinn reached out, cupping her chin in his hand and she leaned into it. He kissed her softly. "Well you won't have to do that again. You're coming with me this time."

Rae nearly laughed, "Quinn, you live across the country and are on the road all the time. I have a career here and my family. You want me to just pack up and leave all that behind?"

This was a conversation he'd been dreading, but the solution seemed simple now. She wanted him. He *needed* her. So they would be together. However they could make it happen.

"Yes, I do," Quinn said, resting his hand back on her hip. "The way I see it, your family and everyone has had you for the past several years. I've been generous letting them all have you."

"Oh, have you?" Rae mused, a smile playing at her full lips.

"Yes," Quinn was now speaking into her neck as he alternated between kissing, licking, and biting. "You're mine and I'm yours, and I say you're coming with me. I don't want to share what's mine anymore."

With a pleasant sigh, Rae arched into him again, and he dipped his head to lick around her nipple. He loved how her body always responded to his tongue.

"That's an awfully big decision to make for me," said Rae, her fingertips lightly tracing the hard muscles of his back.

"Do you not want to come with me?" Quinn nibbled at the soft skin of her breast.

"You might have to convince me it's a good idea."

Quinn slid his hand down her belly and between her legs, feeling where she was still wet. She bit her lip with a quiet moan, and he spoke with lips pressed to her skin, "I think you'll find I can be quite persuasive."

With a soft shove, Rae pressed his shoulder so that he rolled onto his back and she fell gracefully on top of him. "Actually, I have something in mind." Quinn looked up at her curiously. Her long hair fell over one shoulder, barely tangled, and he couldn't help running his hands through it. "I read this magazine article one time," she began, a mischievous little smirk quirking up her lips.

"Oh yeah?" Quinn returned her playful grin.

"Mhmm," she looked up as if trying to remember. "Some unbearably sexy pro baseball player claims he knows all the secrets to 'bed-breaking' sex, and," Rae's gaze swept over her bed from the headboard to the bottom posts, "I can't help noticing my bed is perfectly intact."

Eyebrow still cocked with intrigue, Quinn gave a devilish grin, "Are you challenging me?"

"I am."

"If I break your bed, you'll come back to California with me?" Quinn couldn't believe this sexy woman on top of him was real. And she was all his.

"That's my condition." Rae stared back at him, eyes both aroused and playful.

Quinn's eyes wandered to the headboard, then he gently slid Rae off of him and onto the bed. He could feel her eyes on him as he wandered to the head of the bed and rocked the sturdy wood of the headboard. This was going to take some serious work, especially after a long night of drinking. But he just knew he had to take Rae with him when he left. If this was her condition, he'd find a way.

A cocky grin pulled up the corner of his lips as he fixed his gaze back on Rae. She was peering up at him through her long eyelashes, biting her bottom lip. He gave the white oak one more shake and heard a small creak. "Oh yeah, I got this."

CHAPTER 23

Raelyn half expected Quinn to jump right on her once he'd tested the durability of her bed frame, but instead he walked around her and into her closet. She heard him rummaging through something as she waited, somewhat patiently, on top of her comforter. Her body was humming with excitement and anticipation.

Something else was humming from inside the closet. Or buzzing, rather.

Sitting up straight as she listened, she angled her head toward the open closet door.

"What are you doing?" Raelyn asked, both nervous and curious.

More rummaging. More buzzing. Different patterns of buzzing.

When Quinn emerged from the closet, he was holding various sex toys from Raelyn's pleasure box. She didn't realize he'd known where it was, or that she had it, for that matter.

"How does this thing work?" Quinn held up a curved purple vibrator that was designed for partner use. It came with a remote control and had ten different speed settings and vibration patterns. "It's not dick shaped, so I'm curious."

"Did you find the remote?" Raelyn asked, noticing that he did not seem to have a remote in his hands.

Quinn's eyes lit up mischievously as he trained his gaze from the curious object in his hand to her. "Remote?"

"Just bring me the box," Raelyn said, rolling her eyes, playfully teasing. Once she'd located the remote, she explained how it worked, "It's thin and curved so that this part can go inside and hit the g-spot, and this part sits on my clit."

Quinn grunted, "Mm, say that again."

"Which part?"

"Just the last word."

Raelyn made her best seductive pout, eyeing him through her lashes as she let the word roll smoothly out of her mouth, *"Clit."*

Quinn shuddered, "Ooh, that's almost as good as your French."

"Je suis très mouillée pour toi, Quinn," Raelyn whispered through her pouting lips.

He licked his lips as he stared at hers. "Does the pout just come with the language?"

"Oui."

"It makes your lips look like they belong around my cock," Quinn rasped, all of his focus still on her mouth, and Raelyn felt her skin go hot. "But that might have to wait, because I've got some work to do if I'm going to destroy your bed." Quinn handed the curved vibrator to her, "Can I still be inside you with this?"

"Oui." She spun it in her hand. "That's sort of what makes it a partner vibrator."

Quinn's eyes glazed over, and she felt his mood change from playful Quinn to sex God Quinn in two seconds flat. "Put it in."

Usually, with any other man she'd been with, Raelyn had been the bossy one during sex, but she just melted when Quinn got demanding. When he told her exactly what he wanted her to do. What he wanted to see. How he wanted to fuck her.

Raelyn obliged with shaky hands. As much as they'd been together and seen each other, he still made her heart flutter and her body tremble. It was all about the anticipation. Every time, Quinn presented something new. New words. New ways to touch her. New ways to make her moan.

Once the velvety smooth object was in place Quinn smirked. There was no humor in his face. It was the devilish smirk of a man who knew he was in control. That he could make her bend to his will.

"Lay back on the pillows," he ordered. Raelyn felt his eyes drinking her in and saw what the sight of her, naked in front him and taking his orders, did to his body. That magnificent cock of his was hard again. As hard as the rest of that exquisitely muscled body.

Head and shoulders now resting on her pillows, she waited for his next command.

Quinn clicked the button on the remote and watched as Raelyn's body tensed, back arching, stomach contracting, as the toy vibrated right on her most sensitive spots. He clicked it off and she relaxed with a long exhale. He pressed the button twice and the vibration pattern changed, with short buzzes that gradually increased intensity, then started over. Raelyn gripped the pillows next to her head as the sensation thrilled her.

Click-click.

It was now a steady, consistent vibration, which was always her favorite. However, she knew this wasn't the most intense setting.

Raelyn moaned and bit her lip, curving her back, pushing her hips up. Muscles tensed. Her feet slowly slid up and down on the soft down comforter, toes curling.

She reminded herself to open her eyes. When her eyes fluttered to Quinn, he was stroking himself as he watched her writhe and shudder on the bed.

Oh my God, this man thinks I'm *the sexy one here?*

He increased the intensity again. And again. And *again*, as Raelyn kept her eyes between his gaze and his cock.

Am I more turned on by these vibrations? Or the sight of Quinn getting off just watching me? How is he so sinfully sexy doing something like touching himself?

As it became increasingly difficult to keep her eyes from fluttering shut, her moans and gasps became louder, more frequent. When Quinn finally reached the last setting, she cried out. She wasn't sure if she'd spoken English or French or something else entirely. Her head pressed into her pillows, her hips pushed into the bed, and her whole body shook as she came, dizzy with her orgasm.

Before she could refocus her vision, she felt the mattress bend under new weight near her body. Quinn had climbed on top of her, leaving the vibrator at its highest setting. He pushed her knees apart and knelt between her legs. His hand was still on his cock, stroking slowly. She could see the pre-cum on the tip as she reached out to grab it and take over.

Quinn leaned over her, hands gripping the headboard behind her, and whispered, "Rae, I'm about to fuck you so hard. I'm gonna fuck you over and over until you're a gasping, moaning, quivering mess beneath me."

Yes, please.

Unable to find real words as the last few, smaller waves of her orgasm rushed through her body, she bit her lip and whimpered with a nod.

"Tell me 'yes, Quinn'," he said in a low, husky voice in her ear.

Another small whimper escaped her as her body flushed. She breathed, "Yes, Quinn."

"That's right," he nodded. He bent low and covered her mouth with his, and their tongues wrestled as their groans mingled together. Mouths separated, Quinn grabbed another condom out of her nightstand and handed it to her. "Put this on me."

Still, the sensation of her vibrator hummed along her clit and her g-spot, making everything blurry and shaky. With unsteady hands, she unwrapped the condom and slowly sheathed his long, pulsing hard cock. Quinn wasted no time squeezing his cock inside her. She was full when it was just him inside her, and as sleek as it was, this small vibrator still took up space. The pressure between her hips was nearly painful, but somehow excruciatingly pleasurable. When Quinn began to slowly move in and out of her, she adjusted to the extra girth and was almost immediately on the brink of climax.

She dug her fingernails into the backs of his arms. His triceps were hard and contracted as he held himself steady against the headboard. With Quinn inside her, the toy pressed harder into her clit and with only a few long thrusts, Raelyn was rocking her hips into his, crying out his name, feeling the full force of her fourth orgasm crash through her.

"Quinn...oh my-" Raelyn moaned and gasped for breath as her muscles tensed and quivered beneath him. Full thoughts were no longer a thing. She could only think of Quinn. His cock. Those strong, beautifully sculpted arms flexing and releasing above her.

Oh my God.

Feels so good.

Fuck yes, fuck yes, fuck yes!

He clicked the button on the remote, easing the intensity of the vibrations.

A large hand came off the headboard and caressed her breast as her body attempted to relax. The orgasm wanted to last, and her muscles seemed to have no intentions to loosen up. Quinn's thumb circled her nipple and it hardened again under his touch. With that same hand, he eased gently down the front of her stomach, over her pubic bone. The walls of her sex had contracted around him, where they now refused to let go, refused to let up. He smoothly slipped the vibrator out of her and dropped it onto the nightstand, replacing it now with his own fingers to rub her now swollen and impossibly sensitive clit.

"Fuck, Rae, I love being able to control you like that," Quinn groaned. "Just the touch of a button and I can make you come."

"I like feeling you more," Raelyn whispered. "You feel so good moving inside me, Quinn."

The groan Quinn let out was needy and imploring. He grabbed her legs and threw them onto his shoulders. Hands splayed on her thighs, he began pumping and thrusting into her. Hard. Harder. Fast, and faster. With her legs spread like this, she could take him in so deep. *So* deep. Fuck, it felt like her body only had room for him.

He leaned forward, grasping the top of the headboard again, pressing himself between her legs even farther.

Dammit, how was that even possible?

Raelyn wrapped her arms around him, grabbing that ass of his that belonged to a Greek God, and held on, pulling him deeper. Urging him to fuck her harder.

She listened to the sounds of their love making. Their fucking. His goddamn *claim* on her body. Moans and groans and grunts and growls and whimpers and breathing and gasping. The sound of his thighs against hers when he slammed into her over and over and over again. The consistent, rhythmic squeak of the mattress. The creak of the bed frame. The distinct *crack!* as the headboard clapped against the wall.

Sweat from Quinn's chest dripped onto hers and she fixed her eyes on his body. The way his broad chest and firm washboard of abs contracted with each thrust. The various beads of sweat that were now trickling down his front and onto hers as he fucked her, hard, fast, and deep.

"Quinn...Quinn, I'm-" Raelyn gasped. "Oh, fuck, Quinn, yes!" Her hips rocked against his, her body shuddered, her vision went fuzzy. She was wrapped around him so tight it felt possessive.

As she shook, a pair of rough hands grabbed her by the hips for the second time and flipped her over as if she weighed nothing. This time Quinn gripped her hands, placing them on the headboard in front of her.

"Hang on tight, baby, I don't want you to get hurt," Quinn hissed in her ear and gave it a little nibble.

With her hands where he wanted them, he rested one of his firm hands on the curve of her hip and used the other to spread her legs. "Mmm, *fuck* yes. Give me a little arch in that sexy back of yours." He placed one hand at the center of her back and pressed slightly downward. Rather than being face down, ass up, her butt was stuck out and back at an angle that reminded her of how strippers crawl on a stage. He slipped a finger into her. "You've still got that pussy so wet for me. God dammit, Rae, I hope you never get enough of me. I want you to be wet like this for me every minute of every day."

The feel of his finger inside her made her quake, even after his whole cock had just about pounded her senseless. She devoured his words and lost herself in them. "Yes, Quinn," she breathed, and couldn't help the smirk that crossed her face at the sound of his responding groan.

Quinn gripped her right hip with his right hand, and grasped the headboard with his other, next to hers. He pressed a kiss to her shoulder. "Don't worry, baby, I'll catch you when this thing comes crashing down." Then he braced himself on her hip and plunged into her from behind.

Raelyn threw her head back and found Quinn's shoulder to rest on as he buried his face in her neck. The hand on her hip wrapped itself around her front when he realized how intensely her thighs were shaking. She needed to be held up. Whether this bed broke or not, Quinn would need to catch her. Even though he knew she was coming undone, reaching her limit, he kept going hard. There was a louder creak. The pressure of three hands rocking into the wooden board was too much. Quinn's weight pounded into her from behind. Again and again.

"Je veux Jouir, Quinn!" Raelyn cried out. *"Je veux te faire jouir!"*

"Oh God, Rae," Quinn groaned. "I don't think my cock has ever been so hard."

"C'est si bon, Quinn!" She couldn't believe how good he felt. And he was right. He was so hard, *oh my God, he was hard.*

There was a crack. The bed was shaking like crazy, and then there was a definite sound of wood splintering.

Quinn's pace was wild and frantic. He was about to come. She could hear it in his ragged breath. The sweat of him rolled onto her with each hard thrust.

A sudden gasp, followed by a growl and a groan of release, "Oh...fuck...yes..." He drew out each word. Raelyn felt Quinn come, holding her against him, still pumping as he emptied himself inside her. Just when Raelyn thought he was done, he gave one more strong thrust, sending himself deep inside her, putting her so suddenly over the edge.

She gasped and sputtered and moaned as she came for the sixth time that night. Her legs were Jell-O. She would be shocked if she could walk normally the next day. She shook and shivered and shoved her hips and ass back into him as she came.

Together, they let out a sigh and leaned forward onto the headboard. The bed gave a loud creak and a snap as it tipped to one corner. Quinn grabbed her and held her as the bed frame cracked and lost balance. It may not have been in splinters, but the bed was certainly broken.

Collapsing backwards onto Quinn and the mattress, Raelyn let out a breathy laugh, "You owe me a new bed frame."

Quinn sighed heavily, wrapping an arm around her shoulders and pulling her close. He pressed his lips to hers. "I've got a really sturdy one back in L.A."

CHAPTER 24

Monday morning after Quinn's physical therapy session with Rae, where she'd given him a sling to wear as a reminder to not overuse his arm, he drove to his mom's house. This had been his routine the past few Mondays, and he was surprised to find himself looking forward to these visits.

The nurse, Sandra, was there when he arrived, and his mother was lying down on the couch looking worse than the last time he'd seen her.

"Everything okay?" Quinn asked, brow furrowed in concern as he entered the living room.

"Dialysis was rough yesterday," Sandra explained. "It takes a lot out of her anyway, but as the disease progresses, her body struggles more and more to recover."

"What can I do?" Quinn sat on the edge of the couch next to his mom who looked pale and exhausted.

Molly placed a shaky hand on his arm and forced a tight smile, "Just having you here is enough." Speaking alone seemed to wear her out. She breathed in and out in raspy, heavy breaths. "What have you and... " breath in, breath out, "...Rae been...up to?"

Quinn was focused on how labored her breathing and speaking was. Molly's eyes fluttered shut, but he could tell she was still listening, so he responded, "Well, there was some excitement over the weekend. I had the displeasure of meeting her ex-fiancé."

"Ex-fiancé?" Molly asked. "When were...you two not...together?"

"Mom, I've told you about this. We were friends growing up, nothing more." Quinn explained. His mom made a face that showed

283

she did not believe this one bit. "I wanted to be, but it never happened. Then we were apart while she went to school and started her career, and I started mine. And now we're together."

"Hmph." Molly slumped deeper into the throw pillow. "Did you… hit him?"

Quinn stifled a laugh and peered at his mom through curious, narrowed eyes. "Why would you think I'd hit him?"

She let out a harsh breath that was likely meant to be a laugh. "Oh, Quinn…Just because…I didn't go…to all those…meetings…doesn't mean…I didn't get my…messages."

"From the school?" he asked, wondering why she had never said anything to him about them. Molly nodded in response.

"I went to…one meeting. Third grade, I think," Molly wheezed.

Quinn didn't want her over-exerting herself but enjoyed hearing stories of his childhood from her perspective. It had been frustrating at first. He went back and forth between being angry that she hadn't said anything at the time and being oddly comforted knowing that she had at least paid some attention to the goings-on in his life. The more she spoke about these things, the more he remembered the rare occasions that they had actually spoken and interacted. It was still far from a normal mother-son relationship, but it made him feel like his youth was a little less tragic.

"There were two…boys involved," she continued, "and Raelyn. You two had just…become friends that summer."

"That seems to be the theme," Quinn sighed. "I swear, she hasn't been at the center of *all* my fights."

"From what I…understood, she…had thrown a…punch, too."

Quinn scrunched his brow, searching for the memory. This must have been the first fight he'd gotten in that involved Rae. *How many had there been? How many more would there be?*

"The boys had picked…on you for your…hair, I think."

"My hair?" He remembered Rae defending him on several occasions when the boys she knew from family connections and their country club had decided to make snarky comments about Quinn's appearance. His clothes, his shoes, and yes, he supposed, his hair. While they had likely thought it was dirty because it stuck up all the time, Quinn had actually been almost obsessively hygienic as a kid. His hair just had a mind of its own and liked to look messy. It was one of the reasons he'd started collecting baseball hats.

"The boys teased you...because your hair looked dirty," said Molly. "They had taken your...hat off and laughed at your...messy hair."

Now the memory was resurfacing. Quinn bit back a laugh as he remembered how that whole ordeal had played out. There had been two boys whose parents knew Rae's parents. They were in the same second grade class and had found Rae and Quinn hanging out together on the playground during recess. One boy had started teasing him and asking why she bothered hanging out with Quinn; the other had suggested that maybe she did it out of pity or some sort of charity.

Rae had immediately come to his defense and told the boys to leave them alone. At some point, one boy knocked Quinn's baseball cap off his head and into the wood chips, and the other pointed and laughed. They had started criticizing his clothes, his messy hair, his obvious lack of wealth and said he had no business hanging out with her or being her friend.

In the end, one of them had referred to him as a peasant and, while Quinn had thought it was funny- What eight-year-old called someone a *peasant?* In 1998?- it was the last straw for Rae and she took her swing. Quinn made the snap decision to join the fight, knocking the other boy to the ground, and- despite Rae's insistence- took the blame for the whole thing. The playground supervisors, teachers, and the principal were all familiar with Quinn's temper by then, and he didn't see why she should get in trouble for defending him.

Quinn looked down at his mom lying on the couch and laughed again, running a hand down his face. "Mom, the one meeting you went to was for a fight that wasn't even my fault."

"What do you...mean?" She looked up at him curiously.

"Rae threw the first punch," he said. "I just told the principal it was me because I didn't want her getting in trouble. And it wasn't really about my hair, either. That was just a cover."

Molly let out her weak, wheezy laugh. "She didn't get...in trouble?"

"No, not really," said Quinn. "She was mad and tried to tell the truth, but no one believed her. They expected that kind of thing from me, and I knew they would."

"And the boys...went along?"

"You don't think an eight-year-old boy wanted everyone knowing a girl gave him a bloody nose, do you?" Quinn smirked. "I think he was pretty grateful that I decided to take the heat for it."

"Why did she...hit them?" his mom asked, though Quinn suspected she knew.

"Because Rae's not too fond of entitled rich brats either," said Quinn. "I guess she's stood up for me as much as I have for her."

Molly hummed, then eyed him knowingly. "You didn't answer my...question...Did you hit...her ex?"

Running his hands through his hair and down his face he groaned, "No, but I wanted to."

Sandra had come back in the room from the kitchen with a glass of water. Setting it on a coaster on the end table she asked, "Did something happen? Or you just wanted to because he's her ex?"

He hesitated. "I sort of made an ass of myself when I drank too much and me and Rae had our first fight. And he was there just fueling the fire."

"How did you hurt your arm again?" Sandra nodded toward the sling on his elbow.

"Oh, that was..." he paused, feeling his face redden and a grin threatening to tug up the corner of his mouth, "that happened later."

Sandra raised her eyebrows and gave a knowing grin, "So, making up went well."

"Um...yeah," Quinn looked down to his feet, smiling shyly as flashes of that night flew through his head. He cleared his throat and looked up. "The fight was rough, but it's good now. I just...I get so jealous when it comes to her. I'm possessive. Not in a way like I don't want her to have her own life. She's really independent and I love that. I don't want to tell her what she can and can't do or anything like that. I just want people to know that she's...mine, I guess."

"Why would you get jealous?" Sandra asked, "He's an ex. You're the one she's with now. She made that choice, right? She wants to be with you, not him."

"Well, yeah," said Quinn, "but I can't help..." he worked out the best way to say it, "I didn't have much as a kid. And Rae grew up with everything. Her family was insanely wealthy. And I never got why she wanted to be friends. I didn't fit in with all the kids she knew, and they always tried pushing my buttons, telling me I had no business being friends with her and doing everything they could to let me know that Rae and I just didn't make sense."

He stuck a hand in his hair again. "I guess I heard it enough that I believed it. To an extent, anyway. I didn't want to stop being friends with her, but when we were teenagers and she started dating these guys who'd grown up like her, I felt like that kind of proved what they'd been saying. And then the other night with Emerson, her ex-fiancé," he shook his head. "This was a guy, just like the others, who just over a year ago she'd agreed to *marry*."

After he'd figured out it was Emerson he'd been talking to and sharing stories with, he'd wanted to reach across the bar and deck him. The things Emerson had said about his last ex, knowing Quinn would figure out the mystery, had him absolutely seething. He'd tried to tell himself it was made up, that there was no way Rae had been like that for this other guy. Then he remembered the story Rae had told him about how she'd caught Emerson cheating only because she went to his office wearing a long coat and lingerie to surprise him.

So, he'd spent about an hour bragging about how amazing his and Rae's connection was. About their mind-blowing sex. About how he, and *only he*, could make her feel those things.

Then out of nowhere, that comment Emerson made about him being good enough now that he had money had crept in. Fueled by jealousy and alcohol, he'd thrown that in her face, knowing full well it was bullshit.

He sat up straighter and looked at Sandra, then to his mom, who he was sure was still listening, though she looked almost like she was sleeping. "I had a moment of doubt, I guess, that she didn't want me for *me*, but for this new rich and famous person I'd become. I sort of blew up about it. In front of everyone. And she left me to find my own ride home."

"Good for her," said Molly, barely opening her eyes. Quinn peered down at his mother incredulously, and she added, "I thought we...went over all this...when she was here."

"Oh, that's right," said Sandra. "Your mom told me about your irrational insecurities." She shook her head and rolled her eyes.

"Irrational?" Quinn repeated, taken aback.

"Quinn, if you're going to be with this girl for good you have to accept that she wants you for you. That you are good enough. If you keep doubting it, she's going to feel like you're doubting her," said Sandra. Before Quinn could ask how she knew so much about the situation, she said, "Your mother has gone on and on about this. These are her words, but she needs to rest, so I'm saying them for her."

Looking to his mom for confirmation, she nodded. "What she...said."

"Once you get past all this insecure nonsense," said Sandra, "your mother would like to go with you to pick out the ring."

Quinn snapped his head from one woman to the other. "Ring?"

"That is your...endgame, isn't...it?" Molly said. "I may not be here...for the wedding...so I'd like to...at least be...part of it...somehow."

He laughed nervously and scratched the stubble that now covered his jaw. Well, okay, *yes*, he supposed that was his endgame. But they'd been together for five weeks! He couldn't be thinking about asking her to marry him yet. Granted, he'd mentally been with her for fifteen years, but his delusions he had as a teenager didn't count toward their actual relationship.

"Mom," Quinn said, putting his hands up. "Let's not get ahead of ourselves. We're not there yet. I mean, okay, maybe *I* am, because I've been in love with her since I was thirteen, but-"

"Have you told her?" his mother's voice cut him off, suddenly sounding more urgent and less weak.

"I told her when I started falling for her, yeah."

"Have you told her...you *love* her?" Molly pressed.

"Well...no, I haven't said that yet." Lord knows he wanted to. He couldn't count the number of times they'd been together and those three words had nearly slipped out before he reminded himself he needed to slow down. Saying it too soon would probably freak Rae out, and he didn't want to push her away. "I did ask her to come back to L.A. with me."

"But you can't tell her you love her?" Sandra raised a skeptical eyebrow.

"Well, that's different," said Quinn. "She had just told me that she wanted to go with me to Arizona when I left for school. That she'd applied and was about to have her dad send the tuition check, but then..." he paused. "I screwed up. I lied to her about something and it all just..." he made a motion with his hands like a plane crashing, "... blew up from there, I guess."

"She wanted to go across the country with you when you were eighteen? And you've been in love with her since you were thirteen, but you can't tell her how you feel?" Sandra's voice raised as she looked from Quinn to his mother and back in disbelief. "Quinn! You tell that girl you love her!"

The light touch of his mother's fingers brushed across his arm as she reached out to him, "If you can't imagine...your life...without her now...tell her. You could have...everything. A perfect...life. Don't...let it go because...you're worried about...telling her how you feel now."

Everything this past month had brought up- the memories, the missed opportunities, the times he'd messed up or had fallen short- all seemed to come down to him not saying the right thing. Or just not saying anything. He'd kept his feelings to himself all this time, and where had it gotten him? Chasing after women he knew he wasn't interested in just to get the only one that mattered out of his head?

Things were great now, but he wanted her to know he meant everything he'd said. He wanted her to know that he was hers. His whole self, his body, his heart, his entire being was hers to do with as she pleased. And sure, he could tell her she was his and he was hers, and he could ask her to come to California, and he could make love to her every morning and night, but did she really understand what all that meant to him? Did she understand that he wanted absolutely nothing to do with any other woman for the rest of his life? He wanted to be with her. Period. He couldn't fathom the thought of her being with someone else if, for some godforsaken reason, they couldn't make it work.

Suddenly, the idea of going ring shopping didn't seem all that crazy. It didn't mean he needed to marry her today, or next month, or even next year. He just needed her to know he was in it for the long haul.

Raelyn Casey.

It wasn't the first time he'd imagined his name attached to hers, but he still couldn't stop the smile that lit up his face.

He'd made a lot of progress in the past month, and he intended to keep pushing forward. Keeping his feelings to himself wasn't an option anymore. Next time those three words wanted to slip out, he'd let them. He would say the words, and never stop showing her how much he meant them.

After spending the rest of the afternoon at his mom's, he had one thought on his mind as he hopped up Rae's front porch steps. He let himself in, announcing his arrival on the way into the kitchen where he smelled food.

He stopped. All previous thoughts flew out of his mind at the sight in front of him.

"Um...excuse me, miss. What are you wearing?" Quinn gaped at Rae as she stood in front of her air fryer, with her back to him. Her legs were smooth and long, and her feet were bare. Draped over her and falling just below that perfectly round ass of hers was a white and blue jersey, with the number twelve on the back and his last name across her shoulders.

Rae peeked over her shoulder at him and grinned. "About time you showed up."

His heart burst in his chest. He crossed the kitchen in three long strides and wrapped his arms around her front, backing her into him. He was already hard as he pressed himself up against her ass, wanting her to know exactly what she was doing to him. He'd always loved seeing her wear his last name when she'd borrow his high school hoodies or shirts, but *this*. This was something else.

He buried his mouth into the nape of her neck and kissed and tasted her skin as his hands roamed up and down, under the white fabric. The front of the jersey- *his jersey*- was unbuttoned and she was naked underneath.

Rae's head fell back onto his chest as he cupped both of her breasts in his hands, using his thumbs to make her pink nipples go hard.

"You're leaving this on when I fuck you," said Quinn, his voice low and husky against her skin.

He kissed the corner of her mouth where her lips pulled into a coy smile. "Yes, Quinn," she breathed.

He groaned and began unbuttoning and unzipping his jeans, sliding them off right there in the kitchen while she finished making dinner. He threw his shirt off and spun her around to face him so he could kiss her deeply. Lifting her up, she wrapped her legs around him, and he carried her to the dining table. Quinn slipped a finger into her crease that was already pink and wet, wanting him. She gasped and hissed, biting his ear as he pet that sweet sensitive spot between her thighs with two fingers.

Goddamn, she's still sensitive from the other night.

Between kisses and licks and bites, he felt himself being drawn in and he stopped short of easing himself into her. "What are the chances you keep condoms in the kitchen?"

"Not good," Rae said through a moan. She tossed her head back, pushing her chest toward him and he bent his head to her tits. Her voice came out breathless as she said, "I'm on birth control, Quinn, it's fine."

Quinn stopped and stared again. As many sex partners as he'd had in the past, he *always* wore protection. He didn't care if they insisted they were on the pill or the shot or whatever. He was not going to risk tying himself to one woman, unless that woman was the one right here. Just the thought of moving inside of Rae with absolutely nothing between them made his dick throb and ache.

"Are you sure?" Quinn looked into Rae's eyes. They had a dark, seductive glaze over them as she gazed back at him.

She wrapped her legs around his hips and urged him to be closer. "Just fuck me, Quinn Casey."

Oh my fuck. Yes.

Quinn felt as his eyes darkened, blinding out anything else in the room that wasn't Rae. His heart was set to fucking explode, and he had no idea he could feel this happy and this horny and this unbelievably lucky all at once. He pressed his mouth to hers, swiping his tongue between her lips. When he pulled away, he gave her a devilish grin and spoke with his lips touching hers, "Yes, Rae."

Bracing himself, he watched as he slowly slid his rock hard length into Rae, watching her hot, wet pussy take it in. *Holy fuck*, there was nothing else like this. Nothing but her wrapped around him. He halted once he was seated deep inside, savoring this new feeling. He wasn't sure if it was a sigh or a groan that escaped him as he pressed his forehead to hers. He touched his lips to hers and began slowly moving in and out.

Shit, I am not going to last. This is going to be a fucking record.

He dropped his gaze to watch himself move into her. Nothing but him. Nothing but her. It was un-fucking-believable.

"Quinn," she moaned, her chest rising and falling with her breathing. "Quinn, oh my God, you feel so...*so* good."

"*I* feel good?" Quinn rasped. "Fuck, Rae. You have no idea what you're doing to me right now."

Another sexy grin appeared on her lips, and she tightened the grip of her legs wrapped around his waist. "I'm claiming you."

Quinn's growl of pleasure ripped through his chest and he picked up his pace. Faster and harder, he slid in and out of her. His cock was solid. How did she always make him this hard? *Goddamn*, she felt better with each stroke. Wetter and tighter as she squeezed herself around him. He watched as her grip on the table tightened, her knuckles going white as she threw her head back and cried out, raising her hips in a smooth motion to meet his thrusts as her whole body quivered. Like this, he could feel the rush against his cock as she came- and *oh...God. Fuck yes.*

He moved deeper inside her, as deep as he could go. He felt himself go from wild to insatiable, pounding hard and fast right before his release. His legs shook and he saw stars. He practically fell onto her, grasping the table top for support.

His heart was racing unlike anything he'd ever felt. This was better than any home run swing, any championship title. This right here was his fucking dream.

"God dammit, Rae. You're so fucking amazing," he groaned into her jaw before pressing a kiss to her cheek.

Rae's fingers ran through his hair and she gripped it harder, bringing his lips to hers. When at last Quinn's eyes fluttered open, he found she was gazing back at him with a completely new look in her eyes. Soft, but possessive, and a hint of nervousness. He watched as she licked her bottom lip and swallowed. She took a few breaths that appeared to steady her.

"Quinn..." Rae searched his face briefly, "I love you."

They both felt his cock respond to these words as it jolted to attention. A playful smile flashed across Rae's face. He thought his whole body would explode from sheer joy.

He let his smile light up his whole face as he felt all the pieces of his life falling into place. "I love you, too, Rae."

CHAPTER 25

The last day of summer was something of a holiday in the DeRose house. Technically, this year it *was* an actual holiday, but the pool party in the backyard was happening with or without Labor Day. On September second, Raelyn would be starting her senior year of high school. She was determined, as were most optimistic seniors, to make this the best year yet.

Junior year had been riddled with dramatic episodes; her first asshole boyfriend, fist fights, rumors, and various arguments and days spent apart from Quinn. This year was going to be a good one though. It had already started out with the excitement of Quinn getting scouted by several different colleges. There had been quite the fight over him, as each school upped their offers and sent tickets to visit their campuses free of charge. They'd paid for his hotel rooms while he checked out the schools in Louisiana, Texas, Arizona, Florida, and Mississippi. Both Grand Valley State University and the University of Michigan had sent for him to visit their programs, as well. Since Raelyn had been considering both of those schools, her parents had taken them for a visit together.

As the competition heated up between the offers, Quinn had asked Raelyn's dad to help him manage phone calls, offers, meetings, and his emails. He had been completely overwhelmed by all the attention and spent several hours in Charlie's office with him going over the pros and cons of each offer. In the end, Arizona State won out with their offer of a full ride scholarship as long as he kept his GPA above a 3.25. Quinn was a smart kid, so that was no problem for him.

So, this end of summer party was now combined with a celebration of Quinn's major accomplishment of receiving a full ride to ASU to play baseball next fall. Also, his birthday was in three days, so Raelyn's mom had ordered a huge catering spread of Quinn's favorite food, along with a large cake with the Arizona *Sun Devils* mascot on it. These extra touches had to be kept a secret, of course, because Quinn was always so reluctant to accept any sort of party or celebration in his honor.

It was early afternoon and Raelyn was waiting for the boys to show up. Quinn, Chris, and Jett would likely all be arriving together. Several of the boys from the baseball and football teams would be arriving, too. Most of Raelyn's girl friends from swimming and soccer were already at the house, getting switched over to their bathing suits as the sun was high and bright. A scorching 84 degrees, and it wasn't even the hottest part of the day.

While some people, especially from Northern Michigan, may complain that this weather was too hot, Raelyn absolutely loved it. She was a summer baby, after all. This weather reminded her of her ongoing list of reasons to apply to Arizona State for the next fall semester.

1. I love warm weather

2. ASU has a sports medicine program

3. My best friend is going and what am I going to do without him?

4. Palm trees

5. No snow!

6. The thought of not seeing Quinn for a whole year at a time makes me want to cry until I puke and then start all over

7. Ranked #2 party school in the nation- Let's make bad choices!

She had a separate, shorter, yet more weighted, list of reasons why *not* to follow her BFF across the country:

1. *Quinn is going for baseball. I don't want to distract him or hold him back*

2. *Does he even want me to go?*

3. *I'm sick of being "just friends," but what if he doesn't feel the same?*

The decision to follow Quinn to Arizona was primarily predicated on the latter. Raelyn wasn't about to move to a state based on someone else's dream if that someone was going to hook up left and right with every other girl on campus. This was college, after all. When people hooked up, that meant sex, not giving over-the-pants handies and going to third base under the gym bleachers.

Okay, so, some people were having sex in high school. Raelyn just was not one of them.

She wasn't completely inexperienced. Her first boyfriend sophomore year had helped perfect her French kissing skills and had gotten to third base. She'd even let him stick his hand down her panties. Once. Then there was Liam. *Ugh.* As much of a disaster as that relationship had turned out to be, Raelyn still couldn't say she regretted it entirely. Sure, he'd been an entitled jackass, but he'd at least been sexually experienced enough to teach her a thing or two. Taking the glass-half-full approach, having dated Liam meant she at least wasn't heading into her senior year as a complete nun.

No such thoughts were troubling Quinn, she was sure. That boy, or man, perhaps she should say- he would be eighteen in a few days- had been by her side for the past ten years. And somehow he'd managed to get with just about every available girl in their school. Maybe even T.C. Central, who knows? The rumors ranged from steamy lip-lock sessions, to oral sex, to *hook-ups.* The vague term bothered Raelyn because she had no idea if this meant sex or something else. She never had the guts, nor the desire, really, to ask him for clarification.

Back in December when they'd had their little fight and made up, Raelyn had realized for the first time that she was undeniably attracted to Quinn. Her body was physically and physiologically attracted to his.

The scent of him at times would send her thoughts swimming around in a haze and she'd find herself daydreaming about kissing him the next time they were alone in her room together so she could breathe in his intoxicating musk up close. These dreams would leave her hot and flushed with a yearning ache between her thighs.

But Quinn kept her strictly and safely in the boundaries of the friend zone. At first, she thought this was for the best. Romantic feelings could get messy- What if it screwed up their friendship? But as the daydreams began creeping into her completely unconscious nighttime dreams, and became increasingly scandalous and heated, she just became frustrated. It was hard to get a moment at school when girls weren't trailing after him, and after school he was zeroed in on getting scouted.

Raelyn had thought offering to help him with his scouting and even tutoring him on the subjects he felt less sure about was the answer to this frustration. Setting up training drills, running together, and going to the weight room was certainly one way to get more time with him and to keep him away from all those other girls who, for some reason, thought they had a more important place in his life than she did. The training drills were fine, and they could run together for miles. But sweet baby Jesus, she could not keep it together when they were in the weight room.

If she'd thought the daydreams were bad before, they were nothing compared to the actual, physical proximity to him as he benched and curled and lifted all that weight. Raelyn would zone out and focus on the way his muscles rippled, contracting and extending with each movement. To make matters worse, he didn't think he had to worry about her feeling attracted to him like that so he often went shirtless. It became a dangerous task when she would be watching her own form in the mirror as she performed deadlifts, and her eyes would wander over to where Quinn was lying back on the bench. Why did athletic pants make it so easy to see a man's penis even when it was not erect?

The image of beads of sweat dripping down Quinn's chest as he used the fly machine, and watching a stream run down his spine to the small of his back while he flexed, doing lat pull-downs clouded Raelyn's vision. Her body felt hot, and yet a shiver ripped through her suddenly.

"Girl, you okay?" Brandi Davis's smooth voice snapped her back to the present.

Raelyn blinked several times and looked at her friend. Brandi's dark skin contrasted with the white bikini she was now wearing, and she pulled her braids into a large bun on top of her head. Brandi was still looking at Raelyn curiously so she found her voice, "Oh, just thinking about...how there's too much AC in this house to comfortably try on a bathing suit."

"Yeah, about that," said Brandi, wandering over to the cubby drawer where Raelyn stored her swimsuits. "You have all, like, *athletic* suits. Like there are some bikinis, but they look like sports bras. And some tankinis, which I'm not even going to ask why. Don't you have anything a little more...feminine?"

Raelyn winced and hesitated. She had bought one bikini that was way out of her comfort zone. She had planned to wear it the last time she and Quinn hung out in the hot tub, but completely chickened out. She got nervous about what he'd say or felt like he would ask what the special occasion was or...just focus *too* much on just how much of her it revealed. She didn't want to feel like all the girls at school who threw themselves at him shamelessly. But she *did* want him to notice her as a woman, with female parts, wants, and desires.

Inside her walk-in closet, Raelyn sifted to the back where she'd hung up and left that bikini with the tags on. She grabbed it and brought it out to show Brandi, whose eyes went wide and she smiled.

"Yes, girl, that's the one," she nodded.

"Wait, Rae has girl clothes?" Heather Perch interjected, checking out the small pieces of dark and light blue fabric hanging in Raelyn's hand.

"You have all seen me in a dress and in skinny jeans and, I think there was one time I wore a jean skirt. And I always wear skorts at soccer practice. That's feminine!" Raelyn defended.

Heather shook her head and her chestnut brown hair swung gracefully behind her. "Not when you put on shin guards and knee socks."

"There are going to be so many boys here," said Raelyn as she snapped the tag off the cinched bandeau top. "This is strapless. What if it falls and I flash everyone?"

"Then Quinn will finally realize you have ta-tas," Brandi remarked. She and Heather both laughed.

"Do I, though?" Raelyn glanced down at her 32-B's. "It's a good thing I've got a nice butt."

"You've got a whole nice thing going on," Melanie Sun, one of the swim team's best divers, chimed in, gesturing to Raelyn's whole body. "I thought you were aware of that."

Raelyn bit her lip anxiously and looked to Brandi for support. Thankfully, Brandi recognized the look and said calmly, "Rae's just a bit nervous about the possibility of her friendship with Quinn going somewhere else. Which is perfectly understandable. He's, ya know, Quinn Casey. The ladies sort of love him-"

"And he doesn't seem to do relationships, and I can't just have a *fling* with my best friend!" Raelyn finished, feeling now like she might hyperventilate. "And if he hasn't noticed me by now, why would he today? I mean, we've known each other since we were seven! *Seven!* And just a few months ago, my stupid brain decides that I don't want him to look at me like that anymore. What if he still just sees the girl who, like, forced him to be her friend? Or the girl who played baseball with him like one of the boys? *Oh my God!*" Raelyn gasped, dramatically putting her hands to her face, "What if he thinks of me as a little sister?!"

Brandi put her hands on Raelyn's shoulders and backed her up, forcing her to sit down on the bed. "Rae-Rae, breathe. This is Quinn Casey we're talking about. I'm sure he sees that you are very much a woman. A hot one. But if he does see you like some kid or just his best friend who can hang with the boys," she grabbed the blue bathing suit and held it up, "I assure you, he will no longer feel that way after seeing you in this."

It was about a quarter after one when Chris pulled his Impala into the DeRoses' driveway with Quinn, Jett, and Chris's little brother Tyler in tow. Shutting the front passenger door behind him, Quinn looked around and couldn't help noticing there were more cars parked in the driveway than there had been at most of the previous end of summer parties. Camille and her friends wouldn't be there; she'd moved into her first college apartment at Northwood University three weeks prior.

Quinn gave the three boys behind him a suspicious glance, which Chris and Tyler pretended not to notice, while Jett gave an unconvincing shrug and gestured toward the door. Quinn glared but forged on and through the front door. Through the kitchen and out the back door to the patio, he shook his head as he saw the various banners hung up around the tables of food. One read "Happy Birthday, Quinn!," another "Congratulations!," and another was a picture of the Arizona State mascot.

"Okay, I see your face, but you can't complain," Rae's voice floated to his ears from behind the table topped with presents- *seriously? Presents?* "Because we combined parties and we didn't go out of our way because you know we have an end of summer bash every year anyway. So really, we did nothing extra."

"Nothing?" Quinn asked skeptically, eyes still roaming the tables of food, the ASU colors of maroon and gold on all the decorations, the banner that clearly said his name on it, and back to the gift table.

"Nope," Rae said. "So, you can stop thinking so highly of yourself. You're not that special." She gave him a playful nudge with her hip.

Finally, Quinn tore his gaze away from the decorations and looked down at Rae standing next to him. He blinked and took a step back. He blinked again and swept his eyes across her from head to toe.

Quinn had seen Rae in a swimsuit before. He'd gone to her swim meets, he'd spent countless hours in her family's pool and hot tub with her, but she'd never looked like this. He was used to her sporty swimsuits. Even the two-pieces she wore were athletic-looking.

This was most definitely a bikini. A girly one. It was strapless and the front cinched together, making the shape of her breasts more pronounced. And then the bottoms. *Holy shit.* High on the sides, and he could tell even from this angle that when she turned around there would be *a lot* of cheek showing.

He couldn't stop staring. His eyes were glued to her, and he was suddenly aware that he needed to move or sit down or adjust himself before it became very obvious what he was thinking.

"Is that…" he began, willing his eyes to look away, or at least at her face, but they wouldn't. He cleared his throat, "Is that a new…? I've never seen that on you before."

"Do you like it?" She spun in a circle and smiled up at him. "Wasn't sure if I could pull it off."

Pull it off…Well, shit. Now I'm picturing Rae taking that bikini off in front of me. This is good.

"Yeah-" Quinn choked out, then cleared his throat again. "Yeah, Rae…it looks…really good."

Rae shrugged. "It was a special occasion. Thought I'd try it out."

"I can see your ass," Jett piped in from behind Rae. Quinn glared at him, and Jett simply shrugged. "It's a nice ass. Good work, Rae." Jett clapped her on her shoulder and walked toward one of the food tables.

Jett and Rae are friends and he can act like that around her. I should be able to do the same.

Holy shit, man, stop being so awkward. And look at her face!

Rae smiled as she turned back around after watching Jett walk away. Her eyes landed somewhere beyond Quinn, and he turned to see what had caught her attention. Several guys from the baseball team and some that Quinn played football with were congregated on the pool deck behind them.

That explains the bikini.

Quinn's chest deflated with disappointment. Rae had never worn anything like that for him, but he supposed if the entire baseball team and half the football team were coming to this party, it made sense that she'd act differently. She wouldn't flaunt her insane body for him. He was just Quinn. Just her friend, who clearly had no business trying to be anything else.

He bit his lip and looked down at his feet before meeting Rae's eyes again. He gave a nod, one he was sure translated that he got the memo and went to greet the guys. He was sure Rae would be following him over to show off, but when he looked over his shoulder, she was standing next to Brandi Davis and talking, gesturing in Quinn's, or likely, the boys' direction.

"Case!" Luke Williams clapped his hand into Quinn's and they gave each other a standard bro hug-slash-back-pat. Luke had white-blonde hair that contrasted with his deep summer tanned skin, making him look like a California surfer dude. He was tall and lean-muscled and was one of the pitchers on the T.C. West baseball team. Luke's focus was trained over Quinn's shoulder. "Dang, Case, your girl's looking good over there."

The possessive monster in Quinn's chest stirred. Partially at the recognition that Luke had called Rae *his* girl. That's what he had always wanted, after all. But also because he knew that little outfit Rae was sporting was doing its job. How many of these guys would comment about how hot she was looking? How many of them knew that she was his and they would do best to keep their mitts to themselves?

"Oh yeah, she's showin' it off," Quinn grumbled.

"You guys still aren't together?" Luke asked, eyebrows raised. "What the hell, man? Go get her. Ain't nobody wanna step on your territory after what you did to Liam."

"What do you mean?" Quinn greeted a few others who'd come up and gave their general greetings, smacking him on the back or on his butt like they would before a game.

"I mean, Rae hasn't had a boyfriend since you sent Liam Hamilton to the ground in one punch," Luke explained. "I don't think that's a coincidence. I know I wouldn't go there; I don't care how fine she is."

Quinn couldn't help proudly puffing up a little and mentally giving himself a pat on the back for apparently sending out some sort of message to the other guys in school: *Mess with her? You're messin' with me.*

"Boys," Charlie DeRose's voice cut through the chatter. He put a hand on Quinn's back, "Happy end-of-summer-birthday-congratulations-surprise!"

Quinn laughed and gave Charlie a hug. "You know you didn't have to do this."

"Oh, I know. But you know my family- any chance to throw a party," said Charlie, his eyes sweeping the pool deck and patio. Quinn saw his expression change to one of alarm. "Quinn, what the hell is my daughter wearing?"

Quinn followed Charlie's gaze to where Raelyn stood next to the pool, talking to some of her girl friends. She was turned sideways and it nearly looked like she was wearing a thong with how much cheek was showing.

"That's some good work you did there, Mr. DeRose," one of the guys joked.

"Good genes," another added. "You should be proud."

Charlie glared at the boys, but his face could hardly ever look mean. Exasperation crossed his face as he shook his head and gestured toward Quinn, "I don't really need details, but I'm assuming that's some sort of birthday present for you?"

"What?" Quinn went still. *Why would he think that? Am I missing something?*

Charlie shrugged. "Better you than some of the other idiots she's brought over."

Quinn laughed awkwardly, briefly took his hat off his head to run a hand over his hair and turned to check Rae out again from across the patio. "Uh, thanks, Mr. DeRose."

Okay, so, obviously Rae was not his just because everyone seemed to think he'd claimed her by beating the shit out of her last boyfriend, but he didn't mind being able to pretend for the moment.

Another group of guys walked out of the house and greeted Quinn and the others. After the fifth comment about how great Rae looked in that bathing suit, the possessive instinct he'd been fighting kicked in. He let out a heavy sigh and grabbed one of the many pool towels off a nearby lounge chair. He unfolded it with the flick of his wrist and, sneaking up behind Rae, wrapped the towel around her shoulders.

Rae whipped around to face him, and he held the towel shut in front of her. She looked from where his hands were clasping the towel closed and back up to his face, an eyebrow quirked. "What are you doing?"

"Listen, we get it, Rae. You look hot. But you're distracting the guests and it's getting to be a problem," said Quinn. He was holding her rather close to him. That probably wasn't necessary, but he didn't want to let her back away.

"Oh, I'm sorry, *Dad*, would you like me to put some more clothes on?" Rae looked up at him, daring him to say yes. He chewed the inside of his cheek as he stared back at her, maybe stealing a peek inside the towel to where her breasts pushed the swimsuit fabric out just the slightest bit.

When his eyes met hers again, she slipped one arm out of the towel and snatched the baseball hat off his head and pulled it down onto her own. "Happy?" Rae yanked the towel out of his grip and tossed it to the side. She nodded her head toward the gift table. "I'm sure you've got a new one in there somewhere." Rae reached up on her toes and pressed a quick kiss to his cheek before turning and walking away, giving him a full view of just how much those cheeky bikini bottoms showed off.

Over at one of the many food tables, Quinn caught Jett, Chris and Tyler looking his way. Jett gave a thumbs up, with what looked like a taco in his hand, Chris was nodding approvingly, and Tyler was doing a silent slow clap. Quinn shook his head and once again couldn't help his smile before he sent a cheesy two-thumbs up back in their direction.

"I think I got his attention," Raelyn said, sitting on the edge of the pool and sticking her feet in near where Brandi was lying on a pool float.

"Oh, I think you got all their attention," Brandi replied. "Though if you wouldn't mind sticking to Quinn as your person of interest...I think I might be a little interested in Luke."

"He's a good egg," said Raelyn. "I like the idea of you two together."

"So, what's your plan?" Brandi asked. "I'm thinking if I go for Luke, by the time we get to the movie tonight- your parents are breaking out their big projector for outdoor movies, right?" Raelyn nodded in confirmation. "Well, by then, I'm thinking me and Luke should be safely in the lip-locking stage."

"You're planning on making out with him during the movie?" Raelyn asked, amused and impressed.

"Isn't that what movies are for?"

"Yeah, I guess," Raelyn said, looking over her shoulder in an attempt to locate Quinn. Would they be making out by tonight? The thought sent a ripple of pleasure through her whole body. But she also felt nervous at the idea. Quinn moved fast with every girl. She didn't want to be just like every other girl. If there was going to be something more than friendship between them, Raelyn wanted it to be big. She wanted it to mean something. That meant it was probably best to take it slow, no matter how badly her body seemed to want his.

Speaking of his body... Quinn had now stripped down and was looking particularly handsome in just his red board shorts and aviator style sunglasses. He had a beach towel tucked under his arm and spread it out on a lounge chair behind Raelyn.

An idea popped into her head as she felt the sun beating down hard on her shoulders. She smiled at Brandi and exchanged a mischievous look before turning and sauntering over to Quinn's lounge chair. He grabbed a bottle of sunscreen and began applying it to his arms, chest, and stomach. Raelyn wished she could be rubbing her hands all over those muscles instead.

She stuck a hand out to him, cupped slightly. "Can I get some of that?" Quinn didn't hesitate before squeezing way too much sunscreen in her hand and she laughed, "What am I supposed to do with all of this?"

"You've got more skin showing than usual, Rae," he replied smoothly. "I'd hate for you to burn your ass cheeks."

Enter: Flirtatious Quinn.

She'd experienced this side of him a handful of times before. It was like he could flip a switch and turn the charm on. Flip it back, and he was just her best friend who she'd known and loved since they were seven years old.

"Oh, is that what I'm supposed to do with it?" Raelyn said with a grin, rubbing her hands together. There was no way all this sunscreen was soaking into her skin. Her plan to be sexy and sensual as she rubbed lotion into her body in front of him had completely backfired. She started putting the white, creamy, and somewhat greasy liquid on her shoulders, working her way down. Everything was slippery. She got her legs to absorb the majority of the lotion and thought maybe she'd seen Quinn's Adam's apple bob a few times while she massaged it over the curve of her hips and down to what was exposed of her butt cheeks, which was quite a lot, she had to admit.

Quinn was taking a drink from a bottle of water when she stood up straight and looked down at her chest and stomach. There were still obvious white streaks and globs of sunscreen, "You're gonna have to help me out with this. It looks like I just let some guy come on my tits."

The water from Quinn's mouth flew out in a steady spray. He coughed a few times and then laughed, "Rae, you can't say shit like that!"

"Why not?" Raelyn challenged. "You think I don't know how you boys talk when you're all together? What's the difference if I say it?" She sat down on the lounge chair in front of him so they were face to face.

"On second thought," said Quinn, grinning widely, "I like it. It surprised the hell out of me, but you can definitely pull it off." He paused and, though his eyes were hidden behind his shades, she got the feeling he was sweeping his gaze down her body again. "And in case I wasn't clear before- you can *definitely* pull off that swimsuit."

The way the corner of his mouth twitched made her wonder if there was a dirty, double meaning to his words. Or was that just wishful thinking on her part?

"Thanks," Raelyn bit back a too-wide smile. "Now scoop the extra crap off my chest and rub it into my back." She held her hair back and stuck her chest out toward him.

"Um, what?" Quinn asked, his laugh disappearing from his face.

"You've got hands; put 'em to work, Case," Raelyn said, unmoving.

One corner of Quinn's mouth pulled up farther than the other and revealed his irresistible dimple. "You might wanna be more specific giving me orders like that."

Raelyn felt her body heat up as she realized what she'd said, and what he was now implying. How obvious was it that her nipples had gone hard? And how was he looking at her through those mirrored sunglasses? What did his eyes look like behind them as he said these words that sent a satisfying shudder down her front and into a sensitive area between her thighs?

Oh mon Dieu…

Her heart was racing, and she was sure he could see it. He could probably also see how her breaths were shaky, and that her nipples were poking into the polyester of her top that now suddenly felt too small to hold in her not-so-ample bosom.

"Okay," she breathed, after what felt like a long pause with Quinn staring back at her, watching her body respond to his words, though she couldn't tell exactly where his vision was focused. "How about you put the sunscreen on my back, and try not to get carried away?"

That sexy little dimple smirk appeared on his face again. "I can try."

Holy shit, dreams do come true.

That's all Quinn could think as he slowly massaged sunblock into the skin of Rae's back. Her skin was hot and soft as it had been in his dream so many years ago. Of course, that hadn't been his only dream featuring Rae since then, but this one still stuck out to him for obvious reasons. The real Rae had never interrupted any of his other fantasy dreams about her.

Her bare shoulders were smooth, her back was toned and golden from countless hours spent in the sun. He would gladly sit here with Rae nearly in his lap all afternoon and rub lotion on her. Of course he was glad that she wasn't facing him, because that would make it distinctly more difficult to hide what was going on in his board shorts.

I'm massaging my best friend's back and my dick is hard. All my friends are here. Her dad is out here somewhere. And my dick is hard.

Rae let out a relaxed sounding sigh and leaned into Quinn's hands. *Damn, that doesn't help...but can she do that again?*

Sure, it was awkward and anyone who walked by could potentially see that he was getting aroused, but this was sort of a dream come true, so he was going to enjoy it.

"Got any more lotion up there?" Quinn asked, referring to the excess sunscreen that hadn't soaked into Rae's chest and stomach. He had the urge to lean forward and brush his lips against her neck, along her shoulders...*fuck, keep it in your pants, man.*

"No, I think you got it all," she replied. "Don't forget my lower back, too. As great as this shoulder massage feels..."

Quinn felt his face redden. "Right." He'd been massaging and kneading her shoulders and upper back even though all the lotion had been rubbed in. He just loved the feel of her warm, silky skin beneath his palms.

Squeezing more sunscreen into his hand, he eyed the dimples in the small of her back and pressed his palms in the space between her bikini top and those damn bottoms. Quinn spread the lotion outward, rubbing up and down her sides, and back toward her spine. He couldn't stop himself from pressing his thumbs into those dimples in the small of her back, turning the experience into much more of a massage than a simple act of helping his friend protect herself against melanoma.

Quinn had to bite his lip to keep himself from audibly groaning when Rae arched her back at his touch. Obviously, he was getting carried away. Hey, he said he'd *try*. He hadn't promised anything. Again, he applied pressure from the small of her back and kneaded his hands outward.

"Why haven't you given me back massages before?" Rae asked, a low silvery tone to her voice.

He swallowed and cleared his throat before responding as confidently as he could, "All you have to do is ask, Princess."

Did her skin just flush? Did I just...turn her on?

This was a bad idea. But it was the best bad idea he'd ever had. He scooted forward just slightly, and the heat of her back radiated onto his chest. The shape of Rae's ass as she arched her back again was going to make him lose it. He was about to make bad choices but didn't have the restraint to stop himself. Grabbing the bottle of sunscreen with one hand, he bent his other that was still pressed to her back so his fingers were angled down, he let his fingertips slide just barely beneath the waistband of her bikini bottoms.

"Hey!" A harsh voice barked out from behind him. "Watch where you're putting those hands." Charlie's voice had come out as a growl between his teeth.

Quinn's hands flew up, having never heard Charlie sound so threatening. The hand with the lotion bottle had squeezed in reflex, sending the creamy, white substance squirting everywhere. A long stream of it landed on Quinn's chest and stomach.

Hesitantly, he looked up at Charlie who was now standing beside the lounge chair. Quinn was grateful to be wearing sunglasses. He thought it might hide some of the guilt he felt.

Charlie's furrowed glare bore into Quinn for a few seemingly long, horrible seconds. Rae turned around and grinned as she watched the uncomfortable interaction until Charlie's face transformed to a look of amusement as he raised an eyebrow and pointed at the trail of lotion on Quinn's chest. "Yeah, that'll happen sometimes."

Quinn's voice caught in his throat as he stared, jaw dropped in awkward, horrified disbelief.

"Dad!" Rae exclaimed, her face a look of equal mortification. "*Ew!* That's disgusting!" She stood up and stormed away in a huff.

Quinn watched, frozen in place, as Rae strode away. He wasn't sure what to make of Charlie's joke and didn't know that he could look him in the eye at this point in time. And to make matters worse, without Rae sitting in front of him, the evidence of his arousal was no longer hidden.

He could feel Charlie's eyes on him and nervously let his own wander up again.

"You know where the bathrooms are if you need to take care of that," said Charlie. He pulled his sunglasses off his head and over his eyes before attempting to hide a grin. "Use the old towels." And with that, Charlie slunk away to one of the food tables.

Quinn could have died of embarrassment. He threw himself back onto the lounge chair with a mortified groan and, thinking quickly, grabbed the stray beach towel next to him and pulled it over his crotch.

Despite having her sensual massage interrupted by her *dad*, of all people, the party was actually a blast. Everyone was getting along great, which is a tough feat when there are so many boys and girls in one area- who knows what kind of drama could pop up? Brandi seemed to be successfully charming Luke, and Raelyn was feeling pretty good about her odds with Quinn now, after the way he seemed to enjoy lathering her up with sunscreen.

Still wearing his white and blue baseball hat, which happened to be a favorite of hers, Raelyn stood next to the cake table, watching across the pool as Quinn emerged from the water's surface. He shook his head to let the excess water out and ran his hands through his hair.

Does he know he looks like a model from an Armani cologne commercial?

"Whatcha lookin' at?" Jett sidled up to Raelyn, following her gaze across the deck to the pool. To Quinn.

"Can you believe he's moving across the country next year?" Raelyn replied, hearing the sadness in her own voice.

"I think it'll be good for him to get away," said Jett, before shoving a large piece of cake in his mouth.

"I'm gonna miss him," Raelyn sighed. Quinn was now initiating a game of pool basketball with several of the boys and a few of the girls. She overheard one of the boys suggest that only the girls can make shots and they have to be on the guys' shoulders. *Sneaky move, Luke. I see what you did there.*

"Not as much as he's gonna miss you," Jett said, once he'd finally swallowed the dessert. He still had frosting on his lips.

Raelyn snorted sarcastically, "Yeah, because he'll have time to think about me between baseball and a whole new pool of hot babes to choose from."

Jett raised a curious eyebrow, peering at her from the side. "Does that thought bother you?"

"No," Raelyn said, probably too quickly. "Um, no. That's just Quinn, right?"

"Rae?" Jett's suspicious glance didn't let up.

Raelyn panicked at the thought of Jett knowing how she felt for Quinn. With Jett's big mouth, every person at the party would know in less than five minutes. She needed to distract him. Make him forget why he was looking at her like this. Luckily, Jett was easy to distract.

Spotting the glob of sugary, buttercream frosting on the corner of Jett's mouth, she swiped her finger across his lips to wipe it off. His eyes went wide, both alert and alarmed.

"Lick," Raelyn said, holding her now frosting-coated finger in front of Jett's mouth. This was super weird for her, too, but she hoped it wasn't showing.

Jett hesitated, "Uhm...I don't want to." Raelyn noticed as his eyes flicked over to the pool, then back to her.

Raelyn rolled her eyes. "Seriously, Jett, it's a finger. I promise not to get aroused if you don't."

With another quick glance toward the pool and back to Raelyn, he furrowed his brow and asked, "But what if you *do* get aroused?"

"Then I guess we'll have to see where this takes us," she replied with an overly exaggerated wink.

"You're weird today," Jett said. Then in what was probably the most awkward moment of their friendship, Jett wrapped his entire mouth around her finger and licked the frosting off.

Raelyn made a face, no longer hiding her discomfort at how unpleasant an experience this was for her. And for him, by the looks of it.

"You taste like sunscreen," said Jett, making a face that she imagined was similar to her own.

"Well, Jett, I think it's safe to say you and I are safely in the platonic friend zone," Raelyn said, wiping her Jett-slobbered finger on her bathing suit bottoms. "Please don't ever lick me again."

"Please don't ever *ask* me to lick you again."

Standing next to each other and looking around at anything else for fear of making eye contact, Raelyn and Jett contemplated how to get on with their lives. Raelyn's gaze drifted back to the pool where Quinn was staring, halting the game, basketball in hand. She looked at Jett whose mouth hung open as though caught doing something particularly heinous, then back to Quinn. If she didn't know better, she'd think Quinn looked...*jealous.*

Raelyn smirked, almost triumphantly at the thought. Turning back to Jett, she ruffled up his curly hair and walked off with a notable spring in her step.

The sun was going down, party food had been moved inside, and Quinn had opened his gifts, which were primarily ASU merchandise, baseball gear, and other athletic wear. An envelope from Mr. and Mrs. DeRose contained a check for *way* too much money. Mrs. DeRose assured him the card was a far better option to her husband's idea to actually purchase him a car. Charlie's argument was that if Quinn got a car, he could drive that to Arizona next fall and take Rae along for the road trip. When Quinn asked how Rae would get back if they drove his car,

Charlie waved a hand and said, "Just keep her down there with you. She'll stay out of trouble that way".

Wouldn't that be something? Bringing Rae with me to college.

She had her own plans though. Her sights were set on the amazing sports medicine program that the University of Michigan offered. If Michigan had offered him a better scholarship, he would have been on it. Him and Rae together in college? He'd be all over that option.

Rae wandered out of the house wearing a cropped racer back and a pair of blue jean shorts, and Quinn felt like a fresh breeze washed over him.

That bikini she'd been wearing earlier was a fucking treat for sure, but this was the Rae he was used to. Cool, casual, effortlessly beautiful. Her hair was down, and she was still wearing his hat. She had been right, of course; there were actually two new Arizona State University hats in his pile of presents.

As Rae approached him he smiled, maybe his first easy smile all day. "Where've you been?" he asked.

"Taking a minute to myself," she replied. She took in the new maroon colored hat that he was wearing and smiled, "That's a good color on you." Before he could respond, she wrapped her arms around him in a tight hug. She held her arms around him for a few heavy moments, and his own arms curled around her waist, pulling her in tight as he buried his face in her neck. He breathed in her hair and the familiar summery scent of coconuts and vanilla consumed him.

When she let up, she only half pulled away and Quinn forced her to look him in the eyes. "What was that all about?"

There was a hint of sadness in her smile as she replied, "I'm just really going to miss you next year."

Quinn's chest swelled, feeling both elated that she'd expressed this feeling to him, and also sharing her sadness that they would be separated for the first time since they'd met. "You don't know the half of it, Rae."

She backed up a little more, her arms dropping from his shoulders to rest her hands on his biceps. Her smile brightened. "Can you believe we've been friends for ten years?"

"*Best* friends," Quinn corrected.

"You're not allowed to replace me," said Rae. "If I hear you have a new best friend, I'm not going to be happy. You can call him your college best friend, but not your *real* best friend."

"What if my new best friend is another girl?" Quinn questioned. He wanted her to get defensive, even possessive. Give him some clue that she felt like she had a claim on him the way he did with her.

"Bitch better step aside. That's not happening," said Rae, completely straight-faced.

Quinn laughed, feeling satisfied with her response, "Deal. No girl best friends. No new best friends. Just college friends. And probably teammates."

"And I promise not to have any new guy best friends. I don't think college works that way anyway. I'm pretty sure if a guy expresses interest in you in college, it's strictly because he wants sex."

The thought of Rae spending her days on campus and in the dorms with some other guy, laughing and talking, close like Quinn was with her, made his stomach tie in knots. Even more so was the thought of that new friend actually having the guts to say and do what he never has. It made him sick.

"I'd fly back up here just to knock his teeth in," said Quinn.

Rae grinned brightly. "You do realize we will probably both be having sex in college. It's a whole different ball game. I don't think people just hook up for hand stuff."

"Is that what you've been doing with everyone?" Quinn teased.

She laughed and sighed, "It's funny that you think I do anything with anyone."

Quinn looked at her curiously. He'd endured enough locker room talk about this girl to fill his head with all sorts of jealousy and envy toward the guys who bragged about going out with her. Though now that he thought about it, he realized Rae had never mentioned anything about them. Would she have told him what goes on when she's out with guys? Quinn sure as hell didn't tell her about anything he'd done. The rumors were exaggerated, but he'd always been adamant about avoiding any discussion of the things he did with other girls while wishing he could be doing them with her.

Truthfully, he hadn't even been out with a girl in a long time. Several months, in fact. After the new semester began the previous year, he'd been completely zeroed in on baseball and deciding on a college. Between training, which he'd been thrilled Rae had offered to help with, and school, and actually playing the game, he really hadn't had time for anything or anyone else. And over the summer, well, that's when he got Rae to himself. No other guys gawking at her, no shoving his anger down when someone made crude comments about her in front of him.

"Nate O'Reilly said you guys sixty-nined in his Escalade. I didn't think that sounded like something you'd do," Quinn said, remembering how he'd wanted to knock the guy out, and then go puke after hearing this random brag.

"Ew," Rae scrunched up her face. "False."

"Bryan Wilmot? He said you gave him a hand job when you met up to tutor him for French."

"If you're going to lie about a hookup, why not make it a little better than a hand job?" Rae asked. "Also false. What else?"

"Drake Vaughn-"

"Absolutely not."

Quinn laughed. "Yeah, I didn't really believe that one either. Um...Greg Mink?"

"The guy wears eyeliner, Quinn- What do you think?"

Laughing again, he shrugged. "I don't know, some girls like that *Jack Sparrow* look."

"Not this girl," Rae said. "Okay, how about you? Kimberly *and* Olivia Brooks? You were making out with Kim in their hot tub and Olivia joined?"

"Nice- but no. I did go out with Olivia, but nothing particularly exciting happened."

"Did you hook up with Hallie Thomas?"

"Nope."

"Rachel Price?"

"Also no."

"Nina Parks said her dad caught you guys fooling around."

Quinn winced. "True."

Rae gasped. "Quinn Casey...Did she really have your dick in her hand?"

"Why do girls share these things?" Quinn groaned.

Rae laughed. "Isn't her dad a pastor?"

"Mhmm."

She let out another high laugh. "That's brilliant."

"Most of the rumors are false though," Quinn sighed. "I just sort of...fuel the fire. I think it's funny, so I go along with it. Encourage it, even. It seemed a lot easier than fighting the rumors."

"Interesting strategy," Rae said. "Maybe I should do that."

"That might attract the wrong kind of attention," Quinn replied, shaking his head. No way did he want the guys at school thinking those stories were true.

Rae was looking at Quinn curiously now, her eyes searching his own. It was rare that he didn't know what to make of her expression. Today had been a bit of an anomaly, between Rae coming out like some kind of *Sports Illustrated* swimsuit model, and the horrible moment of watching Jett- *fucking Jett!*- lick her finger. Quinn didn't think he'd ever let him live that down.

"Are you staying at your house tonight?" Rae asked.

"Probably should since tomorrow's the first day of school," said Quinn. He nodded toward the pile of opened boxes on the patio. "Although, I think your parents got me a whole new wardrobe, so maybe it doesn't matter where I stay."

"I see Mom talked Dad out of buying that car for you," said Rae, looking over her shoulder toward the gifts, too.

"I don't know what I would've done. You guys do too much for me as it is."

Rae shrugged. "You deserve it." Her gaze floated down to where her hands were still resting on Quinn's arms. He had almost forgotten he was still holding her like this, with his arms hanging loosely around her hips. He wanted to pull her closer and inhale her again. "Why don't you just stay?" she suggested.

"Stay?" Quinn questioned, his mind wandering from their conversation and floating off to a dream land where holding Rae like this meant they were more than friends.

"Here, I mean," Rae said. "Tonight."

"If you want me to."

Her responding smile was contagious. He grinned down at her, wondering for what was likely the millionth time in his life why this girl wanted to be close to him, why she was letting him hold her like this.

"You know I love you, right?" she asked after a few silent beats. She was looking up at him from beneath her long lashes and he felt his heart flutter, and his stomach must've done some sort of backflip.

"You might've mentioned it before," said Quinn, his voice low. Of course she just meant it as her friend. Rae told all of her friends she loved them. He always struggled to say the words back to her because she had no idea what weight they held for him.

For the second time that day, Rae reached up on her tip-toes and planted a kiss to his cheek, though with this one she lingered a moment or two before stepping back out of his arms. One of these days he was going to see those cheek kisses coming and turn his head to "accidentally" catch her lips on his.

All right, probably not. But it was a nice thought.

Everyone had comfortably posted up in the lawn on chairs, blankets, towels, and pillows for the movie viewing on the large projector screen. It hadn't been much of a race between *Harry Potter and the Order of the Phoenix* and *Superbad*, and in the end, *Superbad* won out. Rae was particularly displeased, having been the only one to vote for the *Harry Potter* movie, but made Quinn promise to watch a marathon with her the next weekend they both had available.

In a mass of pillows and blankets, Quinn and Rae had essentially made themselves a nest from which to watch the movie. Several others were coupled up, but *actually* coupled, and it was hard to ignore the fact that many of them were making out rather than watching the film. Rae and Quinn were loudly commenting and laughing at the movie and whispering to each other about the unlikely pairings that had come together, making bets on how long some of them would last.

After the show, Quinn said his goodbyes and thank-yous to everyone. He let Chris know he didn't need a ride home because he'd be staying with Rae. He'd given Jett a back-slapping hug and whispered threateningly into his ear, "Fucking put your mouth on her again, man," before pulling away and laughing at the wide-eyed expression on his friend's face. Jett's look of worry cracked into a grin, and he shoved Quinn's shoulder, insisting he'd told Rae that he didn't want to do it.

Quinn started cleaning up but Charlie waved him off, assuring him they'd get the rest later. He and Rae grabbed all the gift bags and hauled them up to the guest room across the hall from Rae's bedroom before taking turns in the shower, cleansing themselves of chlorine and sunscreen and the remnants of summer.

There was a vanity dresser in the guest room that had socks, underwear, t-shirts, and even a pair of blue jeans he'd left behind. Some nights he had very little notice that he'd be staying at the DeRoses' and after the third or fourth surprise stay, Margaux had reserved the drawers for him. She'd also made sure there were always new toothbrushes and tubes of toothpaste, even razors, shave cream, and any other toiletries he may need in the guest bathroom for these occasions.

Fresh out of the shower, wearing only a pair of gray sweatpants, Quinn folded his new clothes, trying to figure out what to wear the next day. He looked up at the sound of a knock on the frame of the open bedroom door.

Rae was leaning in the doorway, hair still wet, in a pair of pajama shorts and a spaghetti-strap top. His pulse tripped and his chest inflated. This wasn't the first time he'd seen her like this, but it never seemed to be an image he could get used to.

It took him a moment to see that she was holding a gift bag in her hand. He narrowed his eyes and asked hesitantly, "What's that?"

Rae pushed herself away from the door frame and entered the room. "Well, the stripper-gram I ordered didn't show, so I suppose this will have to do."

Quinn snorted a laugh and shook his head, reaching his hand out to take the bag. He laughed again when he realized the bag read 'Merry Christmas, Ya Filthy Animal!' on both sides. He held it up. "Is this literally something you found laying around because you forgot to get me a real present?"

She shrugged, holding her hands up. "I just know you don't like people going all out for you, so I didn't want you feeling guilty that I spent five dollars on the bag alone."

Setting the bag on the bed and beginning to pull out the tissue paper that also looked like it had been pre-used, Quinn remarked, "That's actually oddly thoughtful, if you think about it."

Rae plopped herself down on the bed. "Well, what can I say? Work smarter, not harder, am I right?"

Quinn pulled the wrinkled tissue paper out of the bag and reached to the bottom where there was a white jersey folded, with maroon and gold lettering. He pulled it out, shaking it to unfold it and held it up. It was a customized Arizona State baseball jersey, with *Devils* on the front in maroon letters, outlined in gold. The back read 'CASEY' with the number twenty-one underneath.

He looked at her and quirked up an eyebrow. "My jersey number is seven."

"Right," said Rae, "which is a lucky number because we were seven when we met. But I think your new lucky number should be twenty-one. Because it was on the twenty-first."

Quinn looked at the jersey and back to her, smiling. "It's also your birth date."

"Happy coincidence. Now you'll never *not* be able to think of me when you wear that," she replied, rather smugly.

"What if twenty-one isn't available?" Quinn asked teasingly. He was absolutely elated that she'd thought to put something personal for *her* on his jersey. It was better than her adverse reaction to him having a new girl best friend.

She looked thoughtful for a moment and hummed. "Then I guess twelve would be okay. It's the same two numbers. I think you'd still think of me."

Quinn nodded, "I'll see what I can do." Looking back at Rae, sitting cross-legged on the bed, he bit back the extra-wide smile that threatened to show itself.

She stretched out on the queen-sized guest bed, leaning back on the pillows and was giving him the same look as earlier when he couldn't quite figure out what she was thinking.

"Did you know Arizona is, like, the second highest ranked party school in the country?" Rae turned on her side and combed her fingers through her long hair.

"I don't really plan on partying much," Quinn said, grabbing one of his older t-shirts from the vanity drawer and pulling it on.

"That's what you say now, but when you realize that's where all the hot babes are, I'm sure you'll cave," Rae said playfully.

Well, there's only one hot babe I want, and right now she's on my bed.

"I feel like I'm going to be the only virgin on campus next year," she commented, seemingly out of nowhere.

Every muscle in his body froze as a frequent fantasy of his flashed through his mind. Only this one now featured that new blue bikini. Quinn couldn't look at her, unsure what his face would do, but he had a feeling he might get a little carried away like he did with the sunscreen earlier.

"I guess there's a whole year between now and then, though." Rae continued playing with her hair, twisting it, tousling it, sliding her fingers through it.

"Is that some goal of yours?" Quinn asked finally. "To lose your virginity before college?"

"Uh, yeah," Rae said, flinging her hand out as though it were obvious. "Quinn, all people do in college is have sex. Between classes you study, and then you have sex. And then you get a study partner so you can act like you're being a good student, but really, you guys just hook up in bed on top of all your books."

Quinn let out a bark of laughter, "Rae, I think you watch *The O.C.* too much."

"Those are high school students! So I feel like that really drives my point home."

"So, what, you want to lose it now so you're prepared for all the sex you plan on having in the library and on top of books?" Quinn could hardly take this conversation seriously.

"I mean, it would be nice," said Rae. "Think about it. The first one is a big deal, right? So once that's out of the way...well, I guess I don't know. Does it get more casual?"

"Why are you asking me?" Quinn asked, stretching out on the bed next to her.

"Wouldn't you know?" Rae looked at him with narrowed eyes. "Wait, would you have told me? We are best friends, and that seems like something friends would share."

"Would you have told *me?*"

"Well, yeah. You would've been the first person I told," she replied. Quinn furrowed his brow and made a face. "I probably would've come right over to share that we were finally on the same level. Although, by the sounds of it, I would've just been bragging."

"I have never been more glad that I punched Liam in the face the day you two were supposed to have sex," Quinn said, imagining the revulsion he would have felt if Rae had come over just to tell him she'd just lost her virginity to her piece of shit ex-boyfriend.

Rae looked at him thoughtfully for a moment, and Quinn didn't know what to think of the look on her face. She bit her lip for a beat, then spoke. "I have a proposition."

"You're propositioning me?" Quinn teased.

"That's one way to put it."

"Rae, you know what that means, right?" Quinn chuckled. She always managed to say sexual things that she'd never intended to come out that way.

"Yes, I do," Rae stated. "Would you want to have sex with me?"

Blink.

I, uh...what? I must be hallucinating.

"*What?*" Quinn stared, eyebrows shooting up into his hairline. His whole body froze, and he no longer had any knowledge of what was going on. Where he was, why he was lying in bed with his best friend, what in the world had led to this conversation? What the hell was Rae saying?

"Not right now," Rae said, holding a hand up. "I mean, it is awfully convenient that we're in bed together, but I mean...you're obviously, ya know, aesthetically pleasing, and I trust you probably more than anyone. What if we make a sort of...pact?"

Quinn's heart was pounding in his chest, his blood rushing in his ears as he listened to the one girl he'd wanted for four years tell him the reasons she wanted to lose her virginity to him. The image of Rae's sun-kissed skin as he gave her an overly sensual sunscreen massage clouded his mind, along with all the thoughts he'd had during it. The memory of his first full look at her in that bikini had the beast in his chest stirring with excitement once again.

He cleared his throat, which had suddenly gone insanely dry. His voice still cracked when he asked, "Um...what kind of pact?"

"What if we agree that if neither of us has had sex by the end of the school year. Or prom? The school year? I don't know," Rae shook her head and waved her hand. "Whatever. If we haven't lost our virginity by the end of the year, the date is yet to be determined, then we do it with each other. You'll be my first, and I'll be yours."

Holy shit. Yes. One-hundred percent yes.

Quinn forced himself to stay calm, to not just blurt out his response. Of course he would agree to this. How much of an idiot would he have to be to turn it down?

He considered for a moment before realizing this wasn't exactly what he'd had in mind. He didn't want to just have sex with Rae because she didn't want to be the only virgin on her college campus, but this was at least a good sign, right? She was attracted to him enough to consider getting naked with him and engaging in intimate acts she had yet to do with anyone else. Of course, she was asking them to *both* lose their virginity...

"Are you sure?" Quinn asked. "I mean, you don't want it to be more...special? With someone you're actually dating?"

"A lot can happen in one school year," Rae said, grinning shyly. "You don't have to say yes, it was just an idea. I feel like I'm completely freaking you out."

"No, no," Quinn said quickly, perhaps too eagerly. "Um, I mean, I'm good with it."

"You're good with it?" Rae said, eyeing him skeptically.

"Yeah, I'm in. It's a deal...or a pact, or whatever."

"Shake on it." Rae stuck her hand out, her winning grin pulling up her lips.

He slid his hand into hers with a triumphant grin and shook it once.

CHAPTER 26

"Quinn Casey, you clean up damn good." Raelyn smoothed her hands up his arms and over his shoulders. His black suit jacket fit his muscled arms and shoulders perfectly. He was also wearing a tie, which she hadn't seen since prom night. Quinn always opted for the more casual, open-collar look, but seeing him dressed to the nines like this sent all sorts of warm and needy feelings thrumming through her whole body.

Grabbing the lapels of his suit jacket, Raelyn pulled Quinn to her and pressed her lips to his. When she swept her tongue between his lips, he groaned and brought her in closer to him.

"Can I ask you something?" Raelyn said, reluctantly separating her mouth from his. "Why are you paying for the most expensive hotel suite in the city when you stay here every night?"

Quinn sighed and hummed as though contemplating a very tough question. "Well, the closet has all my stuff in it now."

"Stuff can be moved."

"Rae, are you asking what I think you're asking?" Quinn's mouth was curved into a grin. "Because that's a pretty big step."

"I know we've only known each other twenty-two years," she said, sliding her hands down his chest beneath his jacket. "But I have this complex, I think. Back in high school I forgot to tell my best friend how I felt and he got away. So now when I see something I want, I just go for it."

"And you think you want me?"

"Oh, I know I do."

Quinn flashed his sexy one-dimpled grin before another heart-racing, breathtakingly fervent kiss. When he pulled away, Raelyn's chest was rising and falling with the exhilaration of the kiss, eyes still fluttered shut. "Good, because I *need* you," Quinn said before nipping playfully at her ear.

Raelyn peeked at the alarm clock on her nightstand and groaned. "This is going to hurt me more than it hurts you, but we need to get going if we're going to make it on time."

Quinn threw his head back with exasperation. "I know this is your *other* best friend's wedding, but I'm not looking forward to it as much as I should be."

Laughing at the emphasis that Amira was the *other* best friend, Raelyn narrowed her eyes. "You're not going to get all jealous, are you? Because you have absolutely nothing to worry about. The past is in the past, and it can stay there."

"I'm not *worried*," Quinn insisted. "I just don't like that he's put these images in my head of the two of you. It's like, every time he looks at you I feel like he's just picturing things, or replaying those memories in his head. And I don't want anyone but me seeing that."

With a grin, Raelyn wandered over to her closet and picked a little black bag off her dresser. Bringing it back to Quinn she said, "I thought this might come up. So, I got you something. Well, I got *us* something."

Quinn looked at the bag, and then curiously up at Rae. He reached his hand in and pulled out the couple pieces of tissue paper on top, and the object hidden beneath. He held a small black and silver, oval-shaped remote in his palm and there was a mischievous glint in his eye when he peered back up at her.

"This one's different than that other one we used," said Quinn, turning it over.

"It's new," Raelyn replied. "And it goes to...these." She pulled back and lifted up the side slit of her dress's long skirt and snapped the band of her lacy black thong.

"Vibrating panties?" Quinn's eyes widened, his devilish smirk looking hungry.

"Just bought them for this occasion," said Raelyn, dropping the skirt back down. She wrapped her hand around his so that he was holding the remote, thumb hovering over the little plus sign button. Making her voice a silky, low whisper, she explained, "So, this puts you in control. I'm all yours, Quinn. But if you feel like you're getting a little angry or annoyed with anyone trying to make you jealous, or you just want to remind me who I belong to throughout the night, you can just use this. And I'll instantly be thinking about you."

Quinn's shuddering breath as he stared back into her eyes told her all she needed to know about how this made him feel. She liked when he took control and knew that he felt like it slipped away at times. Raelyn had racked her brain for a way to let him know, beyond a shadow of a doubt, that she *wanted* him. Wanted to be with him, and only him. His reaction to her little gift was exactly what she had hoped it would be.

The dark, seductive gleam in his eyes threatened to make Raelyn come undone. "Is it pretty intense?" he asked.

"Haven't tried it yet," Raelyn shrugged.

Almost immediately, Quinn pressed the button. Raelyn was grateful that the vibration was almost completely silent but was not prepared for the intensity of the sensation. She gave a surprised "Oh!" and placed a hand on Quinn's shoulder. He turned it off, smirking. "Oh yeah, I can feel that."

"This is gonna be fun."

Raelyn held up a finger, pointing, "With great power comes great responsibility. Do not abuse it."

On anyone else, the mischievous grin Quinn displayed would have made her nervous, but on him she had to stifle a whimper, biting her lip. He leaned in and hovered his lips over the space between her ear and neck for a beat before whispering, "I wouldn't dare."

The thirty-five minute drive to Chateau Delacroix, also known as Raelyn's family's winery, was spent with sparkling banter and teasing about the night ahead. Quinn seemed ecstatic that Raelyn had given him, quite literally, the key to her pleasure, and had joked that he was going to put it on high and watch her orgasm at the head table from where he sat in the dining area. However, when Raelyn pointed out that he would then be allowing everyone to know exactly how she looks and sounds in the midst of climax, he quickly changed his mind. Those sights and sounds were for him alone, she knew.

The chateau had a long, twisting drive, and overlooked a large garden, with the vineyard beyond. Finding a parking spot, Quinn gaped at the massive structure before them. It was built to resemble a fifteenth-century French chateau, with a large stone frame, tall, decorative chimneys, enormous arches, steeply pitched roofs with elaborate dormers, and several angled towers. It looked somewhere between a medieval fortress and Sleeping Beauty's castle.

"Okay, Rae," said Quinn, still staring. "Your family owns an *actual* castle. I might have to call you Princess just one more time."

"It's a chateau, not a *castle*," Raelyn said. "Queens and kings and princes and princesses live in castles. Chateaus are for high-born Lords and Ladies."

"In that case, shall we go, *My Lady?*" Quinn replied with a sideways glance to Raelyn.

Knowing she could drive him wild with this one, she leaned across, lightly placing a hand on his upper thigh as she put her lips to his jaw, "Yes, *My Lord.*"

His answering growl melted into a groan, "Save that one for later."

The wedding rehearsal was being held in the back garden, and the dinner would be served on the patio beneath the tall, domed stone covering. There was hardly any need for decorations with the flowers in full bloom and the large fountain with its intricately carved architecture. At this time of day, the sun was still bright, but beginning to sink in the sky, and the air was warm.

After mingling and casual introductions between family members, Amira rounded up the bridesmaids and began giving instructions, talking over her wedding planner, about where the girls were to line up, how slow they were to walk, where they would link up with their groomsman, and precisely where to stand. When Brody and the guys finally found their way over, most with drinks in hand, Amira and the wedding planner repeated the instructions.

It was less seeing than sensing Emerson's presence when he stood behind her when they lined up in order. Raelyn could practically feel his steely gaze on her back. And probably her ass. She craned her neck to look around for Quinn who had been intercepted earlier by one of

Brody's family members who was eager to ask hundreds of baseball questions. She had barely peered over her shoulder when she felt the gentle pulse of the vibrator against her clit. It was a burst of pleasure, gone as quickly as it came. Her muscles tensed as she gasped, then bit her bottom lip, trying to hide her amusement at this little secret that only she and Quinn were sharing.

In the white garden chairs set up in front of the fountain, she spotted Quinn surrounded by a cluster of mostly red-haired and black-haired guests. There was a boy with red hair as flaming bright as Brody's who looked to be about eighteen, and another Indian boy near the same age, who seemed absolutely awe-struck to be sitting next to the Major League All-Star. She made eye contact with Quinn and couldn't help reflecting his own wicked grin back to him.

Emerson's deep voice felt too close to her ear as he said, "Lookin' good, Rae."

She didn't bother to turn around, keeping her eyes on Quinn when she gave a confident, "I know" in response.

Another shot of quick pleasure shivered through her.

She smiled and shook her head at him. *I know, I know, I'm yours.*

The wedding planner called out over the lined-up bridal party, "Okay, we're getting ready to head down the aisle!"

Raelyn looped her arm through Brody's older brother, James's arm. He looked very similar to Brody, except while Brody was lanky, clean-shaven, and a little bit nerdy, James was more broad and had a short red beard. He gave off a vibe that he knew how to do more with his hands than type, sign, and fill out legal documents. James pulled Raelyn's arm toward him slightly, anchoring and stabilizing their connection more than anything else.

Two short buzzes.

She involuntarily squeezed James's arm with her elbow as the vibrations rippled into her and let out the smallest whimper.

James glanced down at her curiously. "You okay?"

Keeping her mouth pressed shut, she gave a nod. "Mhmm." She was certain that if she opened her mouth she would laugh. This feeling was increased when she chanced a glance up at Quinn who was now attempting to hide his own laugh. He was having too much fun already and the evening had barely even started.

Music began to play, and the first pair started their way down the aisle, through the chairs and separated at the end near the fountain. The rest followed suit, and once Raelyn and James were passing the row where Quinn was seated, she braced herself for it, and...*there it is*.

A longer, steady vibration sent a thrilling shudder down her spine as the familiar warm, needy feeling pulsed between her legs. She chewed the inside of her cheek, trying to hide anything that would give her away. James seemed to notice when her grip tightened on his arm again, this time actually grasping his forearm. He was getting suspicious, she could tell. He'd probably have it figured out by the end of the night.

It didn't take too long to walk through the ceremony and the exit, but of course, Amira wanted to go again. It took four more runs before she was completely satisfied and felt that even if the men had something to drink before the ceremony, they'd be able to figure it out.

They were dismissed for dinner, and Raelyn was thankful to discover the head table had yet to be set up, which meant she could sit with Quinn. When she went to tell him the good news, a few of the guests seemed disappointed that she was taking away their shiny new toy. He wrapped his arm around her, and they headed off to find a table when they were quickly flagged down by Amira.

"Come sit with us!" Amira squealed. "I can't believe it's actually happening!" She grabbed Raelyn's arm and pulled her into the seat next to her.

The dining tables were round, with eight chairs per table. Brody sat on the other side of Amira, Raelyn and Quinn sat to Amira's left, James and his girlfriend, Bethany, sat on the other side of Quinn, and Ethan sat between James and the empty chair next to Brody. Letting out a long sigh, knowing exactly who would be sitting in that empty seat, her eyes swept from it to Quinn, who seemed to be on the same page.

It wasn't long before Emerson strolled over, a rocks glass in one hand and a shot in the other. He slid the shot glass across the table to

Quinn. With the table set up as it was, Quinn and Emerson were seated directly across from each other. This was certainly going to be entertaining.

Quinn eyed the shot glass and looked back up at Emerson without saying a word. His face was calm and unfazed- for the most part. Raelyn figured she was the only one who saw his jaw twitch just the slightest bit.

"Got that for you, All-Star," said Emerson, taking the final seat at the table. "Thought maybe we could get dinner and a show." He let out a satisfied sigh, "I just love to watch couples fight."

Clearly, Quinn had no intention of taking the shot of what was most likely Jameson. He put his arm around the back of Raelyn's chair and continued to stare Emerson down. Silent and stoic. At least that's how he appeared on the outside. Raelyn was sure his insides were beginning to boil.

An awkward silence fell over the table as the two men waited for the other to cave. Raelyn's eyes must have flitted back and forth between them a dozen times before she decided to make a clean cut through the tension. Her arm reached out and snatched up the shot glass. She tossed the shot back- *yep, that was Jameson, all right*- with a severe wince.

"Ugh, I do *not* miss drinking that," Raelyn said with a shudder, setting the glass back down and sliding it back across toward Emerson.

Buzz buzz.

Another, completely different kind of shudder ripped through her, and she put a hand to her mouth as a giggle threatened to slip out.

"No?" Emerson questioned. "It seemed like you enjoyed it that night there was a power outage. You remember that, right?"

Of course Raelyn remembered it. It had been one of the first times Emerson had let his guard down with her. About his family, about his dad. So, naturally, they had fucked like rabbits for hours.

"We sat on your couch and played drinking games." His malevolent gaze drifted from Raelyn to Quinn. "She always used to keep Jameson on hand for me; you should check her cupboards and see if it's still there."

It wasn't. She had dumped it out less than a week after she'd caught him cheating.

"Emerson, dude," Brody said cautiously, shaking his head.

"What?" Emerson lifted his hands, playing innocent. "It's all in the past, right? Besides, I doubt anyone who's gotten as much tail as All-Star over here is going to care that his girlfriend used to get drunk and have wild animal sex with her former *fiancé*."

Raelyn opened her mouth to say something but was interrupted by an intense, drawn out vibration on her clit. She gasped and grabbed Quinn's thigh. He didn't let up. She tried hard not to squirm too much in her seat as she looked up to read his face. His jaw was clenched, and his eyes were set across the table on the yammering jack-wagon trying to get a rise out of him.

Finally, after digging her nails into his leg through his dress pants, he clicked the remote and gave her relief. Well, sort of. She was now wet and wanted to drag Quinn off to a quiet corner and ride him until she truly felt relieved.

"Can't you at least switch to beer?" Amira suggested to Emerson, sounding annoyed after taking a sip from her wine glass. "You're at least kinda-sorta-somewhat tolerable when you're not drinking liquor."

"Me?" Emerson retorted. "Shit, I don't remember ever getting so drunk that I accused Rae of being with me for my money." The gleam in his eyes proved what satisfaction he was getting from all this. His stormy blue eyes met Raelyn's again. "I might've accused her of being with me for my *cock*."

There were uncomfortable groans and winces, Ethan even let out a quiet *'whoa'*, but Quinn's hollow laugh was all Raelyn paid attention to. She'd never heard him *laugh* when he got mad. Not even a completely humorless one like that. And she had seen him angry on plenty of occasions. She was often witness to his fist fights and knew exactly which steps his anger came in before throwing a punch. This was new- and that made her nervous.

Quinn shook his head and an amused- angry, for sure, but still amused- smirk slanted up the corner of his mouth.

Mmm, that dimple. Please don't push that button now, or I will come undone just looking at you.

"Listen, Emerson," Quinn began, his voice low and shockingly casual. "I don't know what the fuck your problem is. Maybe you just hate to lose. Maybe you feel like you made the biggest mistake of your life letting her go- I know I would."

He chose this moment to click on the vibrator. Raelyn again tried not to wiggle around too much. She shifted in her seat and the little vibrating device rested itself on just the right spot. *Oh yes, that feels...so good...*

"I've been in love with her since I was fourteen. Thirteen? Maybe even before that. I know how much it sucks when you feel like you've blown your last shot with her."

The intensity of the vibrations was gradually increasing. Raelyn angled her head down, eyes shut tight, and did her best to hold in any pleasured, porn-star sounds that threatened to escape her lips. One hand was gripping her seat and the other had a tight hold on Quinn's thigh. His legs were sprawled in a wide man-spread, inviting her to take hold of him. The hard length pressing against the inside of his dress pants made Raelyn slick with need between her legs.

"And you know what else? When I first met you, I thought you were all right. I didn't know who you were, of course, but we talked. We had a good time. And I guess, yeah, Rae must've seen something in you to want to marry you at one point in time. So, instead of doing my usual shit and punching your ass to the ground, I'm going to say thank you."

Oh. My. God. How is it going faster?

She was grateful for the chatter and the clinking of glasses in the space, because she was sure the buzzing sound would otherwise be audible at this level. She peeked through eyes that wanted to flutter closed or roll back, and saw where Quinn's hand was in his pocket, holding the remote. His corded, contracted forearm told Raelyn that he was squeezing it. Maxing it out as he spoke. She struggled to control her breathing. His hand wrapped tight around that little black remote might as well have been finger fucking her beneath the table.

She couldn't sit still. The sensation against her clit along with Quinn's voice and words had her on the edge.

"Because if you hadn't fucked up so bad, I wouldn't be here right now, with the woman I've been in love with for the last fifteen years. And I really want you to know that you're responsible for this right here."

"Mhmm, *fuck* yes!" Raelyn threw her head back, her breasts heaving as she found her breath.

"Yeah girl!" Amira exclaimed.

Raelyn was aware of the curious glances in her direction. Quinn wouldn't make eye contact with her, but she could see him grinning and he still wouldn't release his grip on the remote.

"That was a little more than enthusiastic," Emerson's voice was cautious and searching. He glanced back and forth between Quinn and Raelyn, Quinn's strong stare never faltering. Emerson threatened to let out an actual grin. "Okay, now I'm not saying this to be a dick, but I know that 'fuck yes'."

Raelyn's body was humming as she nearly vibrated out of her seat, gripping Quinn's leg, then grabbing at his suit jacket.

"Think so?" Quinn asked. He and Emerson exchanged challenging glares across the table, staring each other down.

"Quinn, we need to go. *Right* now," Raelyn panted, swiveling to get out of her seat and tugging at his arm. At this point, she really didn't care who found out. She just needed Quinn. Now. With his pants off.

With one last triumphant glance across the table, Quinn stood and followed her out of the dining hall.

CHAPTER 27

The morning of the wedding arrived with a rush. Raelyn had a to-do list about a mile long to help get Amira ready for the big day, and yet all she wanted to do was lie around in bed with Quinn, as per usual. However, she had things to do and places to be, so after a quick yet satisfying round of love making in bed, Raelyn set off for Amira's, leaving Quinn looking both fulfilled and sleepy. It was a good look on him.

As crazy as the entire morning had been, the ceremony was absolutely beautiful. Raelyn was so happy for both Amira and Brody and was actually impressed at how well Brody's sword had tied into their castle-like surroundings. After the ceremony, the wedding party spent a little over half an hour doing group photos around the Chateau, both inside and out. There were so many natural backdrops for wedding photos at this place. The fountain, the gardens, the balconies, the winding staircases. When Raelyn was little and had seen her first wedding hosted by the Chateau, she had wanted so badly to have her own wedding here. As much as she despised being called a princess, she was at least willing to accept that her wedding day would be the one time that it wouldn't just be okay to be treated like a princess, but it would be expected.

With the formal pictures out of the way, the wedding party moved into the first ballroom where the tasting room was now cleared out except for the bartenders. The larger ballroom was being filled with guests for the reception. On the bar, there were twelve glasses of champagne in crystal flutes waiting for them. Amala passed the drinks out to everyone, and they all toasted to the new Mr. and Mrs. Kalahan.

"So, when they have kids, do you think they'll get Amira's skin tone with Brody's hair?" Emerson was leaning back against the bar next to Raelyn as the two watched their best friends link arms to drink the rest of their champagne. "Is that even possible? What would that look like?"

Caught off guard by this casual, breezy, tolerable version of her ex-fiancé, she glanced sideways at him, mouth open, ready to make a comment. She thought better of it, though, and shook her head. It was probably best not to draw attention to it; she wouldn't want him thinking she was enjoying his company or giving him a compliment. "Let's just hope they look more like Amira, but with Brody's height."

Emerson chuckled, which was a rare occurrence, "Yeah, well, at least they'll be smart."

Raelyn couldn't help the furrowed brow and somewhat stupefied expression as she looked at him.

"What?" Annoyance seeped into his voice now.

That's more like it.

"You're just being oddly...pleasant. It's freaking me out a little," she admitted.

"I can be pleasant," Emerson said defensively. "You liked me once. You know I can be nice. I don't always have to be..." he seemed to search for a word, "combative."

Both Raelyn and Emerson were laughing before he'd finished the word.

"You can't even say that with a straight face. Yes, you *always* have to be combative. And competitive and manipulative." Raelyn took another sip of her champagne.

There was a silent pause between them as they simply observed the members of the bridal party around them, drinking, laughing, making good conversation, taking selfies.

"Do you ever think about...what our wedding would have been like?" Emerson attempted to make eye contact as he asked this. "Is this what you wanted? Your family's place?"

Is this what happens when he drinks wine instead of whiskey? He's not going to try getting sentimental with me, right?

Feeling more than a little uncomfortable, she felt the best thing to do was to simply respond, not giving him a reason to think he'd thrown her off guard in any way. "Honestly, we weren't even engaged long enough for me to work out the details," Raelyn replied, determined to avoid his piercing blue gaze. She was pretty sure it was focused on her face, but for all she knew he could have been staring at her chest or the small bit of flat stomach showing between her top and skirt.

"Doesn't every girl have an idea of what she wants from the time she's like seven years old or something?" Emerson pressed, still not taking his eyes off of her.

Seven years old? Quinn...I think I've wanted Quinn since I was seven years old.

Raelyn smiled at the thought. The image of him skipping rocks by himself on the beach, and her unexplainable need to have him join her party, and then her life.

"Maybe we do," she said, unable to conceal her smile at the fond memory. She met his gaze and he looked back at her curiously. "I'm not *every girl* though, so no, I didn't have a wedding all planned out already."

Emerson snorted a laugh, "You're not wrong about that." He tossed back what was left of his champagne and set the glass on the bar behind him. "I can't wait to get into that reception and get a real drink."

Raelyn was also ready to get into the reception, but for a whole different reason. She wanted to zoom through dinner and toasts and get straight to the dancing. She had always loved the dancing portion of wedding receptions, but after Quinn's make-shift prom and homecoming, she couldn't wait to get him back on the dance floor. And here, there were nearly five-hundred people to watch as she showed him off in front of everyone.

Sorry, ladies, Quinn Casey is off the market.

It wasn't long before the wedding party made their entrance, and the bride and groom were introduced to the ballroom full of guests. At the head table, Raelyn scanned the tables for Quinn and found him at one close to the front. He was sitting with Chris, Jett, and Victoria, and there were a few other guests sharing their table.

On Quinn's right was a woman with a natural bronze tan, long shiny hair that was nearly black, and she was wearing a tight-fitting red dress. Raelyn couldn't tell from where she sat, but she suspected the dress was short. It seemed odd that Quinn was sitting between this woman and Jett. Assuming she was single, it would make sense for Jett to trade places with Quinn so he could chat her up since he'd come without a date.

Raelyn watched intently as this admittedly gorgeous woman talked to Quinn, leaning in and making her rather large bust more pronounced. Seriously, those things were about to pop out of her dress. Raelyn's eyes narrowed as she continued to watch their interaction.

The woman laughed at something Quinn said, tossing her head back gracefully and placing a well-manicured hand on his upper arm. Her laugh sounded whimsical and feminine. Quinn was grinning, too, as he leaned toward Jett and motioned to the woman who still had her hand on his arm.

Hands off what's mine, bitch.

Raelyn angled her head toward Amala and asked, "Hey, who's that girl next to Quinn? Skimpy red dress, XL ta-tas."

Amala skimmed the crowd until she saw where Raelyn was looking. "Oh, dang. She needs to put those babies away," Amala said, eyes widening. "I'm not sure, actually. Might be a friend of Brody's or something."

Unsatisfied with that explanation, Raelyn huffed and tried Tessa on her other side. Again, Tessa didn't know, but admitted she had been silently envying the woman's perfect cleavage that looked photoshopped.

Raelyn stared, intensifying her gaze as she focused on Quinn. She hoped he would feel her glaring at them and look up. His hand was on his water glass in front of him and Raelyn couldn't help noting his body was angled ever so slightly toward the voluptuous creature next to him.

Look up here.

See my face.

Switch spots with Jett.

Quinn Casey, stop talking to that woman and look at me.

Oh! It worked!

Quinn smiled wide when he found Raelyn staring intently at him, but his smile faltered for a second when he saw the narrow-eyed glare. She cocked one eyebrow and nodded toward the mystery woman and mouthed, "What the fuck?"

His smile returned. Glancing at the woman and back to Raelyn he mouthed, "Are you jealous?"

Um, yeah!

Attempting to make her glare look more threatening, she tried mouthing to him again that she needed to keep her hands to herself. He failed to lip read this message, so Raelyn rolled her eyes and grabbed her phone off the table to text him.

Raelyn: Tell her to keep her hands off.

She watched as Quinn read his phone, then looked up at her with an amused, near laughing expression. Raelyn was not laughing. She was giving her best Don't Mess With Me stare with a little bit of attitude. Quinn bent his head over his phone as he wrote her back.

Quinn: I've never seen you jealous. It's kinda cute.

Cute?!

Raelyn scoffed and lifted her gaze back up from her phone to see Quinn still smirking in her direction.

Raelyn: Switch places with Jett. She can hit on him instead.

Quinn laughed again at her message when he read it and looked up at her, mouthing, "Seriously?"

Raelyn nodded vigorously and made a criss-crossing motion with her hands, gesturing to Quinn and Jett, and said, "Switch." Quinn chuckled, running a hand through his hair and shaking his head. He leaned toward Jett and got his attention again. Raelyn watched as he spoke and made various hand motions between the two of them and pointed to his seat. Jett leaned forward and took a look at the woman on the other side of Quinn, shrugged, then got up so they could swap places.

Once in his new seat he looked back up at Raelyn, "Happy?"

She smiled in response, and he laughed again, shaking his head. Her smile brightened when she saw the woman's confused and disappointed expression. It was brief, however, as she looked Jett over and realized that he wasn't too bad either. He wasn't Quinn, of course, but he did look good tonight.

Dinner was served, toasts were made, and dancing began. Amira and Brody had their first dance, the bridal party had the dance floor after the parents' dances, and then it was open for everyone. Raelyn felt like she could have run into Quinn's arms once she no longer needed to be in any particular place.

At his table, Quinn was turning to get out of his seat and greet her when she grabbed his hands and pulled him up to drag him to the dance floor with her. He brushed a piece of hair behind her ear before tilting her head up to him. When he covered her mouth with his it was demanding and hungry. It still amazed Raelyn how exhilarating their kisses were. She could forget all of her surroundings and feel like it was just her and Quinn in the room, and all she could feel were the sensations of his lips, his tongue, his breath, the stubble scratching her as he kissed deeper, his hands behind her head, forcing her to give in to him. Not that she was offering any resistance.

Breathless and a little dizzy when Quinn pulled away, Raelyn smiled up at him, "I missed you."

Quinn smirked. "I've been fifteen feet away."

"I missed touching you," Raelyn replied, sliding her hands up his stomach to his chest.

"Well, by all means, touch me all you want."

"You're wearing far too many clothes," Raelyn observed, running her hands back up and down his torso. "You look great, but I prefer you in a little…less."

"Oh yeah?" Quinn cocked an eyebrow. "Usually when I get jealous about someone checking you out I want to cover you up. Make sure no one sees enough to get too creative with their imagination."

Raelyn looked around Quinn, searching for that woman who'd been feeling up his arm through his suit jacket. "She can look all she wants as long as she quits fondling your biceps." Finally catching a glimpse of that tight red dress, she saw that the woman was at the bar, no Jett in sight. "Did she ditch Jett already?"

With a chuckle, Quinn replied, "They didn't really hit it off. I hope he can find someone here tonight. I mean, even just to take home."

"Yeah, he'll be thirty this year; it's about time he loses his virginity," Raelyn said, still not taking her eyes off the red dress which, she had guessed right, was very short.

"Poor kid…" Quinn shook his head. "Hey, what about Amira's sister? Is she single? She's pretty cute."

"She's also twenty-one," said Raelyn. "Although maybe that's a good thing. She might be just inexperienced enough to handle a thirty-year-old virgin."

"Were you innocent at twenty-one?" Quinn eyed Raelyn knowingly.

She cringed as a reel of her college sexpeditions flashed through her mind. "Okay, maybe that's a bad idea."

As they danced, they pointed out any potential girl for Jett to take home when they saw one, but mostly they enjoyed each other's company, the feel of being close and in each other's arms. After several songs, Raelyn expressed her need to give her feet a break and Quinn offered to head up to the bar and get them each something to drink. Almost as soon as Raelyn sat in Quinn's seat, she saw the blur of red moving toward the bar.

You've got to be kidding me.

Raelyn watched Miss Skimpy Pants casually act as though she just happened to be in line at the bar at the same time as Quinn. Eyes narrowed, she witnessed yet another graceful touch on his arm. This time Quinn glanced at the hand on his bicep then lifted his gaze slowly back up to the woman talking to him.

What the hell did she have to say to him anyway? She doesn't even know him. How can she just go on and on like they're old friends?

"That's quite the look." Jett had taken his seat in the chair next to her and was loosening his tie.

"Who the hell is that chick anyway?" Raelyn snapped, still glaring toward the bar.

"Her name is Regina," Jett replied. "She's Brody's dad's...best friend's...daughter? Or something like that?"

"Well, I hate her," Raelyn stated. "Don't you think you could try a little harder with her? I mean, she's super hot, so it's not like I'm asking you to take one for the team. It's a win-win."

"I tried talking to her already," Jett replied. "We really have nothing in common."

"I disagree. You both want to get laid tonight. That's plenty," said Raelyn. "Seriously, she will not stop touching him."

Jett laughed. "You sound like Quinn talking about you and any guy who's ever looked at you since you were sixteen."

"Come on, Jett," Raelyn groaned. "Don't you want to lose your V-card to a hottie like that?"

"I'm not...I've had sex, Rae," Jett snapped, frustration tinging his voice. "I went to college and got crazy just like you and Quinn." Raelyn gave him a skeptical glance. "Okay, maybe not *just* like you guys, but I had sex. I had a few girlfriends. But I'm not going to have sex with Regina just so she stays away from Quinn. That's ridiculous."

Scrunching her face up in disappointment, she let her gaze drift around the room for a better solution than Jett Miller. In any other circumstance, Raelyn wouldn't say that Jett was exactly out of this Regina chick's league, but she needed someone with the charisma and charm to get her away from Quinn Casey. Surely part of the appeal was that he was famous. Not only was he a professional athlete, but he also had that whole 'sex icon' reputation going for him.

Raelyn was about to give up the task and resort to handling it how she knew Quinn would- a punch to that pretty face of hers, perhaps?- when the tall, broad, blonde, and bearded solution she didn't know she was looking for strutted right by her and Jett. Gasping, she reached out and grabbed Emerson's arm and pulled him around as she stood up to face him.

"Hey!" Raelyn beamed brightly.

Emerson glanced at Jett, who was laughing with a hand to his brow as though embarrassed for her, then back to Raelyn. "Hi?"

"So, I was just thinking," Raelyn began, now realizing she had no idea how to ask him for a favor. Surely if she posed it as a favor, he would refuse. Especially if it meant helping her and Quinn. She took a deep breath and continued, "You like hot girls, right? Big boobs, small waist, that kind of thing?"

"Okay?" Emerson looked, if possible, even more confused now.

"See the girl in the short red dress, legs for days, and cleavage that should only be on an airbrushed Cosmo magazine cover model?" Raelyn turned Emerson to face the bar where it would be impossible not to see her.

Oh no, she did not just brush her hand down his chest like that!

"You mean the one putting moves on your man over there?" Emerson asked.

"Yes," she said, exasperated. "She won't leave him alone. And I don't want to cause a scene by punching her, so I thought that maybe… possibly…you'd take her off my hands."

"Why would I do that?" Emerson got that competitive gleam in his eye that was so familiar. "She's hitting on him pretty hard. If he gives in-"

"He's *not* going to give in," Raelyn stated firmly. "Besides, you owe me."

"Do I?"

"*Yes*, because you cheated on me *twice!*" Raelyn glared. She turned her focus back to the bar and added offhand, "Actually, I *caught* you twice. For all I know, you could've cheated on me way more than that."

Emerson smirked. "Look at you, beauty *and* brains."

Raelyn snapped her head back and glared at Emerson for a few silent moments, comprehending this admission. She heard Jett's *"seriously, man?"* from where he was still seated. She was overcome with the urge to smack him, but finally blinked and focused on the issue at hand.

"Whatever…" She shook her head. "The point is, Quinn isn't going to cheat on me, unlike some people, but that bitch won't leave him alone and you might be the right person to distract her so we can enjoy our night. And so can you. Because you'll have her. And you can find out how the hell she gets her boobs to look like that."

"I don't know," Emerson sighed. "She *does* have a nice rack, but I don't know how I feel about helping my ex have a good time with her new guy. Especially after he tried to fight me."

"Consider it a competition," Raelyn suggested. "If you can get her away from Quinn, who is extremely hot *and* rich *and* famous, then that's a big win for you."

Emerson's expression told Raelyn she'd hit the right note with that one. That competitive gleam shined a little brighter as he smirked. "Fine. But I'm not helping you. I'm helping myself. To a *delicious* slice of cake, by the looks of it."

Raelyn made a face, then shook off any weirdness she felt at having just set up her cheating ex-fiancé with a complete ten. "Just go! And send Quinn back."

She sat back down and watched as Emerson made his way to the bar. Quinn and Regina were at the front of the line and ordering drinks when Emerson slid past the line and leaned against the bar next to Regina. He placed a hand on the small of her back and she turned to face him. For a split second, the woman looked annoyed that her attention was being brought away from Quinn, but when she registered the undeniably handsome second option that was being presented, her demeanor changed quickly. Her eyes swept Emerson from head to toe and back up to his charming grin, or at least it would have been charming if Raelyn didn't know the truth behind that look. If Regina hadn't just had her hands all over Quinn, Raelyn may have felt bad for inflicting Emerson on her.

Guess you should keep your hands to yourself, bitch.

Emerson leaned in and whispered something in Regina's ear, and Raelyn noticed the placement of his hand on her hip already. The way Regina grinned and bit her lip, it was probably safe to assume she was also blushing beneath her bronze tan. On the other side of them, Quinn was watching curiously for a moment, until the bartender handed him a glass of wine and a rocks glass, and he slipped away unnoticed.

Sitting in the chair next to Raelyn, he handed her the glass of red wine. "I hope this doesn't mean I have to thank him twice."

"No, you can thank me," said Raelyn, taking a sip of wine. "I sent him up there."

"Wow, a year later and he'll still take orders from you, huh?" Quinn teased.

"I can be persuasive when I need to be," Raelyn shrugged, then paused abruptly, seeing Quinn's eyebrows shoot up in alarm. Behind her, Jett laughed. "That's not what I meant. I didn't mean, like, sexually. I mean, I guess I *can* if I need to. I don't know why I said that. I wouldn't with him. Or anyone else. I don't- I didn't-" Raelyn covered her face with her hands, "Oh my God, just make me stop talking."

Still laughing behind her, Jett leaned back to look at Quinn. "I assure you, there was no sexual persuasion. I witnessed the whole thing."

Quinn smiled at her. "I love when you do that. Say the wrong thing and then completely word-vomit to try to excuse it."

"I'm glad you're amused, because it's stressful," Raelyn replied, taking a larger sip of her drink this time.

The three of them sat, talking and drinking for a while before returning to the dance floor. Raelyn pointed out a cousin of Amira's who was clearly checking Jett out. She was petite, and very pretty, with long dark brown hair, matching dark eyes, and perfectly manicured eyebrows, wearing a gold two-piece dress. Jett looked at Quinn and Raelyn as if asking for instructions, and Quinn simply nudged him in her direction. After some time, Amira slid in and stole Raelyn away from Quinn for a few dances together, plus the bouquet toss. She dragged Quinn up for the garter toss and Raelyn was pretty certain she'd asked Brody to aim the garter at Quinn, because it hit him square in the chest.

Their night was full of dancing, selfies, making out in the photo booth, and indulging themselves in the open bar. By the end of the night it was clear neither of them was fit to drive, so they called a cab to take them all the way back to Quinn's hotel. Maybe it was the alcohol, maybe it was the first real flash of gnawing jealousy, or maybe it was just the fact that Raelyn found it almost impossible to keep her hands off of him, but as soon as they were in the back seat of the cab, she was on him.

Ignoring the fact that they were obviously not the only ones in the vehicle, and that it was likely a distraction to their poor driver, she sat in Quinn's lap, straddling him, and crashed her mouth into his. Their tongues wrestled, his hands held her steady by the hips, keeping her in his lap, her hands loosening his tie, and unbuttoning his vest. She couldn't wait to get back to his hotel room and rip his clothes off the moment they walked through the door, but they managed to keep it PG-13 in the taxi on the ride there.

The rain from earlier in the week had returned, and it was a complete downpour by the time they got back into the city. At the entrance to the hotel, Quinn kept a hand firmly on Raelyn's lower back as he tossed a wad of cash to the driver. He then rushed her inside, trying to shield her from the rain with his suit jacket.

The excitement and need buzzing between them was palpable as they waited for the elevator doors to close, hoping that no one else would be needing a ride up with them. Alone, Quinn pressed Raelyn's back against the wall and kissed her deeply, letting his hands roam from her neck, down over her breasts, to her hips, and around the curve of her ass. Leaving his hands there, he pulled her into him and she could feel the hard length of him through his dress pants. Raelyn moved her hands up his chest and neck and into his hair, grasping it tight as she refused to let her mouth part from his.

The elevator dinged and the doors opened. They stumbled out, still holding onto each other, pulling and grasping at clothes as they made their way down the hall to his door. There were two women in pajamas entering the room next to his with a bucket of ice and a few drinks who stopped to stare at Quinn and Raelyn's tornado of passion breezing toward his door. Again, he pressed her back up to his hotel room door and kissed her hard, with a deep, throaty groan as he pinned her with his hips. He took a moment to fumble around for his room key in his inside jacket pocket. He swiped the key and the door swung open so they could fall into the room, a flurry of fervent heat and desire that would fuel the night ahead.

CHAPTER 28

Quinn woke up to the sound of his phone going off. The text tone was dinging over and over, and without much thought, he reached to his nightstand, searching blindly for the source and flipped it to silent. Eyes still closed, he rolled himself to face Rae, wrapping his arm around her waist and pulling her so that she was up against his body. Her back was to him, and he buried his face in her neck, pressing light kisses into her skin.

Images from the previous night took up space in his mind; Stripping clothes off themselves and each other as soon as the door shut, pinning Rae against the wall, her legs wrapped around his waist as he entered her roughly, the rattling picture frame next to them as he worked to give her that first climactic release. Taking her on the couch, the floor, the bedroom wall, turning her around on the mirrored closet doors so he could watch everything. *Oh God*, Rae dropping to her knees and taking him into her mouth.

He was hard again, his cock pressing against Rae's backside now. His hands slid up to her breasts, caressing and sliding gentle fingers over her nipples. He seemed to have roused her and her hips were now rolling back into him slowly. Matching the motion of her hips, he slid a hand down and between her legs, stroking gently. Her responding groan was groggy and heavy with sleep, but her body was responding how he needed it to.

"Rae, baby, I need you right now," Quinn whispered into her neck, kissing and sucking at her skin, as he pressed his hard length against her.

She let out another sleepy groan, arching her back when he circled her clit with his finger. She parted her legs, making room for him.

Quinn angled himself at her opening and slowly thrusted, first just allowing the head of his cock inside, then further with the second and third thrusts until he was buried deep.

Rae continued rocking into him and he gripped her hips firmly. She reached back, fisting his hair as he made his movements more aggressive, demanding more and more from her half-sleeping body.

The doorbell to the suite sounded through the room. Quinn's eyes shot open, wondering who the hell would be at his door this early. And why now?

Closing his eyes again, he chose to ignore it, resetting his focus on Rae and pleasure and satisfying their needs.

The doorbell rang again, accompanied by knocking.

Quinn groaned, aggravated, and leaned over Rae to kiss her on the cheek before reluctantly parting himself from her and getting out of bed. Hastily pulling on a pair of boxers, he made his way through the living room to the door. His raging erection was perfectly visible inside his shorts, but he didn't care. Hell, the person who'd taken him away from his bed should know what they were interrupting.

"This had better be an emergency," Quinn sighed as he pulled the door open. A short brunette with a ponytail stood next to a tall, thin man with black hair and a natural tan. They both wore professional clothes; the woman in a blazer and a blouse with a pencil skirt and the man wearing a suit. Quinn registered their name tags and realized they must work at the concierge desk. He didn't miss how both sets of eyes widened and swept him from head to toe, taking in his near-naked and fully erect presence.

"Um, yes, Mr. Casey..." The woman was staring either at his torso or his barely-concealed cock, he couldn't quite tell. Her eyes snapped up to his face, redness blossoming under her fair cheeks. "We thought we should tell you that there are quite a few cameras out front. It's a bit of a scene down there."

"After those articles popped up this morning, it seems like someone must've let slip where you're staying-"

Quinn cut the man off, "What articles?"

"With all the pictures of you and your...girlfriend?" He said hesitantly.

Furrowing his brow, Quinn turned and looked into the room where Rae was now walking out of the bedroom wearing his button-down shirt from the previous night. Her hair was tousled, falling over one shoulder as she looked at him curiously.

"Is everything okay?" Rae asked, glancing from Quinn to the hotel workers at the door. "It's not your mom, is it?"

"No," Quinn said quickly, "no, nothing like that. Um, Rae, just stay away from the windows. And maybe get some clothes on."

"All I have is my bridesmaid's dress," she replied. "I totally didn't think to grab my bag out of the changing room last night."

"Oh right," Quinn turned back to the man and woman outside his door. "Could you guys go get some, like, pants or sweatpants or leggings. Women's...small." He found his dress pants on the floor behind the door where they'd been dropped and dug out his wallet. He handed the woman a hundred-dollar bill. "Keep the change. How many cameras are we talkin' down there?"

"About a dozen, I'd say," she replied, folding up the cash and tucking it away.

Quinn cursed under his breath and stole another glance at Rae, whose attention was now glued to her phone. Folding her legs under herself, she sat on the couch and started scrolling.

"We'll be here until you get back, and then we'll go from there," Quinn said. The two concierges both gave short nods, and he closed the door. Sitting down next to Rae on the couch, he smoothed down his hair, looking at her anxiously. He'd completely forgotten about this part of them being together. The media, the paparazzi, the ruthless reporters who would no doubt dig into Rae's past and try finding something that would make a good story- of course good stories were never the happy ones.

"Well, *mon amour*, I hope you're ready to hang up that playboy reputation of yours," Rae said, still staring down at her phone. "Amira, Camille, and Alexis were all sending me links. I literally had over twenty texts this morning. I even have a text from Dad congratulating us on making it official."

Quinn groaned and rested his forehead on Rae's shoulder. "I'm sorry. I completely forgot about the whole...being famous thing. I just feel like I've been on vacation to a completely different life." He lifted his head so that his chin was now resting on her shoulder, "The hotel people were letting me know there are cameras out front, wanting to know more about us."

"You're okay with people knowing, right?" Rae asked, eyeing him curiously.

"Yes, yes, of course," Quinn said, placing his hand behind her neck and pulling her in, pressing his lips to hers. "I want people to know. I do. I just didn't think about all this. I don't like the idea of all these strangers trying to follow you around and dig up dirt. Happy stories don't sell. They like me because I've got the whole 'bad boy' rep. That's why I get so much media attention, and now I'm putting that on you. I'm sorry."

"It'll be an adjustment, but I kinda like you," she kissed him and pulled away just slightly, "so we'll make it work."

"You're already moving across the country for me, and now you have to put up with this," Quinn said. "I feel like I'm not worth all that."

"Stop it," Rae scolded, tracing his jaw with the tips of her fingers. "We've been over this. You always underestimate yourself. I love you. I want to be with you. And you want to be with me, right?"

"Only for over half my life," said Quinn.

"Good. Then we'll make it work." The corner of Rae's lips tugged upward as she said this, and he stared back into her bright blue eyes. The same eyes that had always made him feel so at home, so calm and grounded when he thought he might lose it.

Does she have any idea how bad I want to see those eyes every morning for the rest of my life?

"Have you seen the pictures yet?" Rae asked, excited. "We look damn good together."

"Oh yeah?" Quinn stood up and slipped into the bedroom to grab his phone off his nightstand. Though he'd been woken up by multiple text message tones, he hadn't actually checked it. His eyes went wide at the number of text notifications he had, and he suddenly wished he had Zoey here to manage and smooth everything over.

The first text, or thread of texts, he opened was from Zoey.

Zoey: First of all- I am SO happy for you and proud of you right now. Second, this is going to be huge. I hope your girl is prepared for this craziness!

Zoey: You two might be the most gorgeous couple ever! Did you plan this?

There was a link attached to her message with pictures of him and Rae at the wedding. Quinn wondered who was taking pictures of them to sell, but also felt like an idiot for not seeing this coming. Of course someone would have a camera at a wedding and notice him. Hell, it could've been the photographer.

The first picture was of him and Rae wrapped in that first fiery kiss on the dance floor when she'd dragged him up out of his chair. There were several of them laughing and dancing, a few more of them kissing. There was a picture of them sitting at the table with Jett, smiling and talking while Quinn massaged her feet in his lap. There was a photo of him holding the garter he'd caught on one finger as he stood in front of Rae with a suggestive smirk on his face. The final photos were of them getting into the taxi at the end of the night.

Thank God they didn't take pictures inside that cab.

There were several other links to pictures and even some articles with various headlines: *"He's Stealing Bases, She's Stealing His Heart,"* *"Quinn Casey Can't Dodge Cupid,"* *"Casey Hits Hard- Love Hits Harder,"* *"Who's Quinn Casey's New Catch?,"* *"Can She Take Him All the Way to Home?,"* *"Casey Gets a Curveball."*

Quinn couldn't help smiling as he read the headlines, making his way back into the living room and plopping himself back down next to Rae. She had swapped her phone out for his iPad and was reading the article titled *"Who's Quinn Casey's New Catch?"*. The featured photograph was of the two of them, head to head, embraced closely for a slow dance.

"We do look good together," said Quinn, leaning over and peering at the screen. "Of course I've known that for years. You're a little behind on the uptake."

"How do they know so much about me?" Rae asked, her eyes moving back and forth across the page. "'*Raelyn DeRose, of Traverse City, Michigan, is no stranger to a life of luxury. The daughter of Charlie and Margaux DeRose'*- They know my parents, too?- '*Raelyn was cloaked in wealth from day one. Chateau Delecroix, the scene of these hard-hitting photos, is one of four upscale wineries owned by the DeRose and Delecroix family. A bottle from Chateau Delecroix can range from $32, for a newer selection, all the way up to $800 for the aged fine wines-*'"

"You guys sell eight-hundred dollar bottles of wine?" Quinn's eyebrows shot up as he looked at her. *No wonder they were so damn rich.*

"Most of those are at the wineries in France. We've got one in Paris and one in Bordeaux," Rae didn't take her eyes off the screen as she spoke to him. Her face was intent and concentrated on the article.

"Well, your family isn't exactly low-profile," said Quinn. "I'm really not surprised they already filled up a whole article about you."

Rae was silent for a moment as she read, then she gasped, "Oh look! It says here that we've known each other since childhood! I wonder how they figured that out."

"Hmm...maybe there was a reporter at the wedding. I mean, there were hundreds of guests. It's not unlikely that out of that many people, one of them was a journalist. Did you tell anyone you didn't recognize about us?" Thinking back, he realized he had mentioned it to a few people. "Maybe that was me, actually. I told that Regina chick that I was with you and that we'd been friends since we were kids."

"And she was *still* putting her hands all over you?" Rae snapped her head up to him.

"Now that I think of it...she was asking *a lot* of questions." Quinn recalled how chatty the woman was, and how curious she seemed about what he'd been up to since his surgery. She'd asked how he knew the bride and groom, and once he'd pointed out Rae as his date, she had bombarded him with questions about how they had met, if their relationship was serious, and other details. At the time, Quinn had thought she was just sizing up her opponent. Guys do that sort of thing when they find out a girl they're interested in is taken. Ask questions about him to figure out what kind of competition they're up against.

"Oh my God, *Quinn!*" Rae put her hands over her face, dropping the iPad into her lap, "That bitch was a reporter and I delivered her my *ex-fiancé!*"

Oh. Shit.

Well, at least they knew where any bad press she'd receive would come from.

"How likely do you think he is to really talk shit about you though?" Quinn tried imagining what kinds of things Emerson would say about her. Would he talk about what kind of sex life they'd had? Would he tell her about their big fight at the bachelorette party? What kinds of things would he say that even Quinn didn't know yet? And maybe didn't *want* to know? "I mean, you were together once. He obviously had some kind of feelings for you. He wanted to marry you, right?"

He didn't blame her for the exasperated look she gave him. How much could he have wanted to marry her if he snuck around so soon after popping the question?

"These are just assumptions," Quinn said, trying to sound calm and soothing. He hoped he could make her feel the way she always made him. "We don't really know that she was a reporter. And we don't know that Emerson actually spent the night with her. It *does* explain why she was so quick to turn her focus from me to him, though."

A burst of laughter bubbled out of her lips before she clamped her mouth shut.

"What? Why is that funny?" Quinn narrowed his eyes. "Do you think he's more attractive than me? A better smooth-talker? More seductive? Come on, Rae, what is it?"

"No, I just think it's funny how competitive you both are over women you don't even want," Rae said, grinning. "He doesn't want me any more than you wanted that Regina chick, and yet you guys would get in a fight just to try to prove who's better."

He shrugged sheepishly. "It's not even a question. It's me. I'm better."

Rae leaned toward him and gave him a peck on the lips. "Yeah, I agree."

About an hour later, the concierge arrived with a selection of leggings for Rae. After slipping on a pair of black leggings, Rae grabbed one of

Quinn's t-shirts and pulled it on, and finished off the look with one of his baseball caps. Quinn threw on a pair of blue jeans, a t-shirt, and his Chuck Taylors. His hair was especially messy since he hadn't taken the time to shower yet, but Rae assured him it looked sexy.

Rae had called her dad and had him send one of their drivers to the hotel to pick them up since both of their vehicles were elsewhere. As they waited for the call that their driver had arrived, Quinn and Rae worked on responding to some of their text messages, reading some of their friends' reactions to the news.

Quinn's teammates were more than a little surprised that he was now a one-woman man; most of them offered their congratulations, and others expressed their disbelief that it was for real. Some were convinced it was being hyped up by the media. He assured them that it was very real, but they said they'd believe it when they saw it.

He couldn't exactly blame them for being so reluctant to believe it. All they'd known of him was the version that lived and breathed baseball and had women all over him when they went out, and a new one in his bed nearly every night during the off season. He cringed at the thought that he'd been sleeping with different women only days before coming back to Michigan. It seemed like a lifetime ago. When he thought of that version of himself, it felt like a completely different life. A different person. The person he was when he was with Rae? *That* was the real him. This was the guy he wanted to be.

Finally, the call came that their ride had arrived.

Quinn took Rae's hands in his and studied her. "Are you ready? These people can be crazy, but I'll get you through them."

She bit her lip nervously and looked down at her feet. "I wish I had shoes that went a little better with my outfit." Her gold sandals from the previous night did seem a bit out of place with the casual leggings and oversized t-shirt she had on. She quickly tied a knot in the front of the shirt, making it more fitted to her. "There, now it looks a little less like I just had to throw on clothes to avoid the walk of shame. I could have planned this."

"I think you look great," Quinn assured her, handing her a pair of sunglasses.

"No, *you* look great," said Rae. "I look like a sorority girl who partied too hard and is on her way to get a Frappuccino from Starbucks so she doesn't fall asleep in her nine o'clock class."

Quinn laughed. "That's oddly specific." He brought her hands to his lips and kissed them. "Come on, baby doll, let's get this over with."

He kept his arm around her the whole way down the hall and held her close in the elevator. It wouldn't surprise him if she were nervous, but she didn't seem to be showing any signs of anxiety until they got to the lobby and looked outside at the crowd that had likely grown in the past hour and a half. Rae stopped walking at the sight of everyone waiting for them. Quinn spotted the all-black Mercedes Benz waiting for them just beyond the crowd and put his arm around her shoulders again. He wished he could wrap himself all the way around her and protect her from the crowd, but he held her as close as he could and forged ahead.

Through the glass doors, they were submerged into the crowd of cameras and flashes, getting bombarded with questions, reporters and photographers shouting their names to get their attention. Quinn told Rae to keep walking and not to answer questions. If anyone grabbed her, he would be sure to take care of it.

Having successfully made it to the car where the driver was holding the door open for them, Quinn dropped his arm from her shoulders to wrap it around her waist. His voice was low so that only Rae could hear, "Up to you if we give them a little something."

She looked from the crowd and back to him, giving a shy, lip-bitten smile and a nod. Relieved, he drew her in close with one arm, and cupped the side of her face with one hand and his smile brightened right before pressing his lips to hers. His heart raced. He was letting everyone know that he was hers now. And more importantly, that she was his. Any other guys who thought they were interested would have to go through him. He felt himself give further into the kiss.

Keep it tasteful, man. PG. We can drive each other crazy in the back seat.

Their lips parted and Quinn let out a shuddering breath. *Every time.* She did this to him every time.

He let himself half turn toward the crowd and held up a hand in a brief wave before ducking into the car behind Rae. When the door closed behind him, he pulled Rae to him again and gave her a deeper, more passion-fueled kiss, sliding his tongue between her lips and letting his hands slip beneath her shirt where he knew she wasn't wearing a bra. His mouth trailed down to her neck and he breathed her in. "It's about time we get to finish what I started this morning."

Arching her back at the feel of his hand palming her breast and brushing his thumb back and forth over her perky nipple, Rae moaned, "Not yet, we can't."

Quinn pulled back. "Why not?"

"Because that divider is *not* soundproof and I actually know this driver," Rae said. "I'm not doing this within earshot of him."

With a loud and exasperated groan, Quinn dramatically fell onto Rae, burying his head in her chest. "Nooo! Why me?" He cried out, "Why must I be tortured like this?"

He felt Rae giggle as her chest and stomach moved up and down. "Your life is so hard, I know. Between the money and the paparazzi and everyone being obsessed with you. I don't know how you do it."

"It's not my *life* that's hard right now," he mumbled into her chest. Grabbing her wrist, he lowered her hand and wrapped it around the hard bulge pressing against his zipper. "I'm suffering, Rae. Only you can fix it."

"Patience, *mon amour*," Rae sighed, brushing her fingers through Quinn's hair as he rested his head on her chest.

He let out a long, heavy sigh and settled into the shape of her, the feel of her body against his. This vacation he felt like he'd been on was about to be over, he could tell. They were about to be in the spotlight every time they walked out of their homes or went grocery shopping. They'd have photographers popping up when they were out on dates or taking her dog for walks on the beach. Patience didn't seem likely. He wanted her to himself *now* before he had to start sharing her- sharing *them*- with everyone else.

CHAPTER 29

Charlie met them at the door to his home, welcoming and ushering them inside enthusiastically.

"Good morning, good morning!" Charlie beamed, "Well, I suppose it's afternoon now."

"You seem rather chipper, Dad," Rae observed, making her way past him and into the kitchen.

"And you look like you were at a toga party last night," Charlie commented. "Jeez, Rae, did you swing by Starbucks on the way here? Where's your Frappuccino?"

She shot a glance at Quinn that said *I told you so!* He couldn't help laughing. Charlie and Rae always thought and acted so much alike; it directly paralleled the way Margaux and Camille were so similar.

"Well, I'm sorry I don't look more presentable. That's apparently what happens when you get woken up by the concierge informing you that there's a mob of people waiting to take your picture in the lobby," said Rae, rifling through cupboards and finding the supplies to make her own iced coffee.

"Oh, well forgive me, Princess Rae. Us common folk don't know what that's like," Charlie mocked. He faced Quinn. "Great, she has one paparazzi experience and is already a diva. It's like she's a teenager all over again. The drama never stopped with this one."

"Oh, believe me, I remember," Quinn replied, smirking when Rae made a face at him.

"I still can't believe it took you two this long to get together," Charlie said, "but I suppose, better late than never."

"You're tellin' me," Quinn muttered under his breath, but it didn't go unnoticed.

Charlie smiled in his direction before saying to the both of them, "Well kids, I have some work I need to get done, so I'll be in my office if you need me." And with that, he ducked out of the kitchen toward his study.

When Rae's coffee finished, she poured it into two cups, giving one to Quinn before gesturing out of the kitchen and toward the stairs. He followed and eventually found himself feeling as though he'd gone through a time warp as he stood in the doorway to Rae's bedroom. The walls were still the same silvery gray, with the lavender accents throughout the room. The vanity dresser, the desk, and the bedframe were all the same. New curtains had been put up, and on the collage wall over her desk, there were now pictures from her college years mixed in with high school, middle school, and earlier.

Quinn gravitated toward the collection of photographs, wanting to see the familiar ones he hoped would still be up there. And there they were: Quinn and Rae at the pool when they were eight years old, the two of them playing volleyball in her backyard when they were ten, and another sitting in one of their many blanket forts, watching a movie with a giant bowl of popcorn between them. In middle school when Chris and Jett had joined their duo, there were pictures of the four of them at the baseball field or at the park. Quinn laughed at one in which they must've been playing soccer beforehand. They looked to be about thirteen, and Jett was on his knees, ripping his shirt open, looking like he was screaming, Chris was posing like a bodybuilder with his arms flexed in front of his body, and Quinn was standing between them, the soccer ball under his arm at his hip and Rae on his back, arms wrapped around his shoulders.

In so many of these group pictures, Quinn and Rae were a pair. They were coupled, but not a couple. They had arms wrapped around each other, leaning back-to-back, Quinn giving her a piggy-back ride or picking her up in his arms. There was one from their senior year that he was shocked to see displayed. He wasn't sure who had gotten the shot, but was glad the single best moment of his high school career had been documented.

It had been his last baseball game of high school- the state championship game. The game was close the whole way through, but they didn't have to run any extra innings because of his final home run hit. As amazing as that hit had felt, nothing could have prepared him for what met him at the end of that run on home base.

"You were so mad all this time, but you kept all these pictures up," he said, his gaze swiping over all the memories. Pointing to that championship photo, he grinned. "That was quite possibly...the best moment of my life."

"It's funny looking at these again with how different everything is now," Rae said, searching the photos. "I guess I kind of get why everyone just assumed we'd date back then. We were all over each other without even trying to be."

"It's like on some level," said Quinn, still zeroing in on his favorite picture, "we knew when we met. Maybe we fell in love when we were seven and just didn't know what to call it."

"I had that thought yesterday," said Rae, smiling. Quinn glanced at her now and saw that her eyes had fallen on the same photo he'd picked out. Her smile turned a little mischievous and she peered at him from the side. "Tell me something, some thought or fantasy you had when you were seventeen or eighteen."

One eyebrow raised as a grin tugged the corner of his mouth up.

"We spent so much time in here," Rae looked around the room, "lying next to each other in bed, sleeping across the hall from each other. Even spending time in the pool or hot tub...you had to have fantasized about *doing* something at one point or another."

He could feel himself blushing as he bit his lip. His high school fantasies were far more innocent than anything he thought of now. Hell, they were more innocent than a lot of things he and Rae had actually done together. Why was it so weird to express the thoughts he'd had about her when he was a teenager? He almost felt like he was sharing someone else's secrets. Like the ghost of his seventeen-year-old self was sitting there in the room, waving his arms and saying *"Oh my God, do* NOT *tell her that!"* Little did seventeen-year-old Quinn know, keeping his thoughts to himself was a stupid idea that kept Rae from him for way too long.

"Okay, but they're probably going to seem pretty mild," Quinn said. "I mean, I was still innocent back then."

"Not *that* innocent," Rae reminded him.

Quinn nodded his head from side to side, trying to remember specific fantasies and daydreams he'd had about the two of them. He remembered zoning out at times when they were together, especially in her bedroom, with images of himself grabbing and kissing Rae finally, taking her off guard. He'd always imagined the kisses escalating into so much more, but that wasn't really a fantasy. That was just something he'd wished he had the guts to do. He sat on the bed and thought back.

"Well, I remember that first time Jett walked in on you changing, actually," he admitted. "I obviously wished it was me. And would imagine you just letting me see you, and I'd slowly walk over and kiss you...you'd let me finish undressing you and I'd just...explore your body, I guess."

"I do undress myself a lot," said Rae, sitting next to him on the bed. "I suppose I could let you do that more. What else?"

"I remember when we were in the hot tub once- just the two of us. And I got hard," Quinn chuckled shyly. "We were sitting next to each other and you were wearing that strapless bikini top. The one you wore at my eighteenth birthday party...so it looked like you were naked. And I just kept imagining that you were. And I think I was half hoping you'd figure out I was hard for you, like if you knew you'd just...go with it. I pictured you grabbing onto me by accident and being shocked but then turning naughty with it."

"I probably would've," Rae laughed. "If it was our senior year, I was definitely into you by then. We'd go to the weight room together after school and I'd wait for you to get all sweaty and I'd just stare. Just waiting for the sweat to drip down your muscles. It was dangerous. I almost dropped weights on myself a few times."

"How did I not notice that?"

"You are very focused when you lift. That might be another reason it was so sexy," she said. "Did you ever think about sneaking into my room when you slept over?"

"I thought about you sneaking into mine," Quinn replied. "You'd come in while I was in bed and slip under the covers and already be naked." This was a regular fantasy that he'd had, especially after the pact they'd made. He kept hoping she'd forget about waiting until the end of the year and just join him in bed and they'd take it from there.

"Would you be mad if I told you I totally considered doing that? I just didn't want to be like all the other girls who threw themselves at you. I wanted you to come to me, I guess."

"Why would I be mad? We were clearly on the same page at some point." If Rae had done that, he didn't know how he would've reacted. The fantasy version of himself was a lot cooler and more collected. In those dreams, he obviously knew what to do, but if it had actually happened, he likely would have been a fumbling, awe-struck mess.

Thinking back again to his eighteenth birthday party, he remembered Rae asking him to rub sunscreen into her back. He'd been caught off guard at first, but quickly gained composure and was able to play it cool. Until, of course, Charlie had interrupted. Shit, Quinn had never been more afraid of Rae's dad in his life. He wasn't exactly intimidating, but *damn*, that was a whole different situation. He wondered if Rae's intention was to turn him on.

"At my birthday party that you guys combined with the end of summer party," Quinn began, "you had me turned on when I was rubbing that sun lotion into you. I wanted to pull you right into my lap and show you how hard it made me just to touch you."

"That might've been my goal," Rae grinned. "I was trying to figure out if you thought of me in any other way than just your friend. I guess neither of us were particularly good at communicating our feelings."

"Oh!" Quinn remembered another frequent fantasy dream he'd had when he stayed at Rae's. "The shower. Any time I took a shower here I'd fantasize about you getting in with me. Sometimes if we'd just been swimming or in the hot tub I'd picture you getting in the shower in your bathing suit and letting me take it off of you. I always wanted to un-tie those tops." Quinn's eyes gleamed mischievously. "Then I'd drop to my knees and slip off the bottoms and...well, do what I could to drive you crazy. Not that I knew anything about that back then, but I would've been willing to try." Seeing Rae's blush, he added, "Other times, I'd fantasize about you being the one on your knees."

"Naughty boy," Rae chided. "You had these fantasies in the shower, huh? Where no one could walk in on you doing anything to satisfy these dirty thoughts?"

Quinn's lips slanted to one side. "Perhaps."

"Quinn Casey Casey," Rae gasped. "You're telling me you *pleasured* yourself in our shower? Thinking about me on my knees in front of you?"

"Maybe a few times."

"Wow, I thought you were just really hygienic, but now I know you were just itchin' to touch yourself," she teased.

"I didn't shower here just to do that!" Quinn laughed. "It was just, ya know...I'd been holding back urges all day around you. I needed a release. And a shower. Because we usually got dirty."

"*You* got dirty."

"You've got like five showers in this place anyway," he said defensively. "I'm the only one who ever used that bathroom to shower in."

"Um, wrong, *I* used that shower!" Rae replied, giving him a playful shove. "Usually after you!"

"Oh yeah," Quinn held up a finger. "I definitely remember thinking about you taking your showers. Being in there after I'd let myself go, thinking about you."

Leaning over him, she brushed her lips against his. "I guess that means I'm taking the first shower this time."

Rae grabbed clothes out of her dresser which still held a few outfits in the event that she needed to stay at her parents' place, then headed to the shower. Quinn waited downstairs, trying to remind himself that Charlie was home, so he couldn't exactly slip into the shower with her like he wanted to. He was beginning to wonder when he and Rae would finally get some alone time so they could finish what they'd started in bed that morning and cursed himself for not just finishing before answering the door. It wouldn't have changed anything, except he would have gotten relief and would be able to think a little straighter. God, could he possibly be more addicted to one person? The way he always craved Rae was like an addict itching for a hit, putting that high before anything and everything else.

Sitting at the kitchen island, having downed his second cup of coffee, Quinn answered more texts and checked more links and updates. The pictures from only an hour ago would likely show up soon, and he couldn't help the nervous excitement about seeing those photos. He was actually finding himself loving this attention. Not being in the media, necessarily, but loving that he was getting recognized for being with Rae. That she was being referred to as "Quinn's girl" all over the internet.

He wasn't exaggerating about feeling like his L.A. life was completely different from the one he'd been living in Traverse City over the past several weeks. Seeing this dream life come together with his other was confirmation that he wasn't just experiencing some sort of long-term hallucination. He wasn't going to wake up in the hospital, just coming out of surgery to discover he'd dreamt it all. This life with Rae was real, the love was real, and she was going to be part of his life even once this *vacation* was over and reality set back in.

A pair of arms wrapped around him from behind and lips pressed behind his ear. Quinn let out a groan at her touch and she nibbled his ear. "Anything new?" she asked, resting her chin on his shoulder and peering at his phone.

"Same stories and pictures so far," he replied. "I was just reading some of the comments. People really don't want to believe I can be in a serious relationship."

"Well, we were photographed together for one night," said Rae. "I'm actually a little surprised people assume it's a relationship based off of that. They're really just going off of whatever you and anyone else told that one reporter."

"Does it bother you?" Quinn was reading the comment section of one article, where one reader had expressed his opinion that this was just Quinn's way of getting media attention while he was benched for the season.

"Not really, no," she sighed. "I know it's real. The opinions of thousands of strangers is their business, not mine."

"Good," said Quinn. "Just try to remember that when they start attacking you."

Rae took the phone out of his hand and set it face down on the counter. "Don't worry about it. I'm sure this will all sink in for me at some point, but can we just pretend for the moment that my life isn't about to get flipped upside down?"

He spun on his stool to face Rae and smiled. She kept her arms around his shoulders, and he wrapped his arms around her waist, pulling her between his legs. His voice was low as he splayed his hands on her phenomenal ass, "I think that's a great idea." She lowered her lips to his, sweeping her tongue into his mouth. Quinn pulled her closer as he moved to the edge of his seat, wanting to press his now semi-erect cock against her.

Damn, her kiss woke me up quick.

A deep groan emitted from his throat as he rubbed against her thigh. Rae leaned into it and his heart rate picked up speed. Slipping a hand beneath her shirt, his palm felt the warmth of her skin and he nearly forgot they were in the middle of Rae's parents' kitchen.

"Hey, hey-" Charlie's voice cut through the quiet of the room. "Tongue out of my daughter's throat! I'm happy for you guys, but I don't need to see that."

Quinn put his hands up, but Rae didn't remove her arms from his shoulders or step back from him. "Technically, Dad, it was my tongue in his throat."

"Gross," Charlie stated flatly. He opened the pantry and began rummaging through the shelves.

Rae giggled and planted a kiss on Quinn's cheek. "Why don't you take a break from the tabloids and go take a shower."

"Better make it a cold one!" Charlie shouted from inside the pantry.

Color filled his face as Quinn glanced down at his pants where his cock was pressing hard against the denim along his thigh. Telling himself Charlie had seen nothing and was simply guessing, Quinn nodded, smirking at Rae before he stood. Her eyes swept down to the bulge in his jeans and back up to his face, grinning mischievously.

God dammit, how much longer do I have to wait?

Upstairs in the guest bathroom, Quinn stripped down and stepped into the hot shower. The bathroom had been updated since he last used it, and rather than the bathtub alcove with a curtain, the shower was now fully tiled with frosted glass doors. There's no way he would've taken the risk of relieving himself back when he was a teenager with how exposed he was in this shower. There had been times when Rae would come into the bathroom while he was still showering because she needed her hair dryer or she'd come in to brush her teeth. He would have absolutely died of embarrassment if Rae had actually caught him in the act.

Eyes closed as he rinsed the shampoo out of his hair, he contemplated turning the water to cold, as his erection would absolutely not go away. It was either that or risk being caught jerking himself off. Would that be better or worse now that Rae knew he'd done it before? Would she be offended he wasn't saving it for her?

Images from last night crept into his mind again. Rae's mouth wrapped around his cock as he held her hair back in his fist. Looking up at her as she rode him hard, her body leaning over him, bracing herself on the headboard as he thrusted into her from beneath her. The way her back arched when she threw her head back as she climaxed. The way her muscles squeezed and contracted around him as the waves of her orgasm crashed through her.

Before he could make a conscious decision about it, he was grasping his cock, slowly stroking himself to the memory of their love making. Watching himself enter her over and over, harder, and faster. Leaning his forearm against the shower wall, bracing himself as he worked toward finally getting some kind of release, his old fantasy of Rae joining him in the shower came back to him.

He imagined being eighteen again after making that pact with Rae. He would tell her no to the pact. That if she'd let him have her, they could do it now. He didn't want to wait anymore.

How the hell did I ever wait to take her?

Too far into his fantasy, he didn't hear the bathroom door open, and he didn't hear the shower door swing open or closed. His eyes were shut, still bracing himself with his arm against the wall, his head bent down, getting closer and closer to his release.

"Need some help with that?"

Quinn's eyes snapped open, and he grinned at the sight in front of him. With his fist wrapped around his cock, he eyed Rae hungrily. She still had that sexy blue bathing suit from his eighteenth birthday party and it still fit. Actually, it might fit even better now.

"I'll take it if you're offering."

Rae stepped closer to him, taking his cock in her soft, gentle hand. The water was coming down hard on Quinn's back as he watched her stroke him, top to bottom, giving his balls a light squeeze. He groaned, drinking in her appearance. How many times had he imagined this? And she was making it come to life for him.

"What do I need to do?" Rae asked, looking up at him from beneath her long eyelashes. "I want to make this as close to your fantasy as possible."

Quinn's breath hitched as his pulse kicked up a notch.

Fuck, this girl is amazing.

He swallowed hard, wondering where to start. He was good at giving commands during sex. Why did this feel so different? He felt like he was actually a love-struck teen again, and the girl in front of him was completely out of his league. Out of reach. But here she was. And she wanted to do everything she could to make this just right for him.

Goddamn, how did I get so lucky?

With one last shuddering breath, he pushed through the giddiness he felt and focused on making this perfect for both of them. "On your knees," he said, his voice managing to sound confident. "I want to see your lips wrapped around my cock."

Rae's eyes darkened with lust before she lowered herself to her knees, still holding his cock in her hand. She licked the length of him up to the tip, circling her tongue around it before taking him deep into her mouth. He loved how deep she could take him, even though he could tell she had to stretch her mouth to fit around him. Quinn held her hair back in a messy bun in his fist and watched as she devoured him. She moaned and he felt the vibration of it on his dick. His eyes threatened to roll back as he thrust slowly into her, bracing himself again with a hand on the shower wall.

He grunted as he thrusted into her mouth again, a little rougher this time. He'd never fucked her mouth like this, always letting her take control when she went down on him, but goddamn, he was having a hard time not getting carried away.

Another moan vibrated up his cock, telling him she was enjoying his roughness. Her hand and mouth now worked up and down his length. *Fuck*, he was hard. But his fantasy didn't end here. He still wanted to undress her. He wanted to explore her body. Though he'd done it several times, he wanted to pretend it was his first. He wanted to make sure he licked and kissed and tasted every inch of her, like he'd dreamed about doing when she was his untouchable, unreachable obsession.

God, that mouth felt so good on him, but he had to bring her to her feet. He watched as she took him in and out a few more times, then tightened his grip in her hair, pulling upward slightly. He groaned and whispered hoarsely, "Get up here, baby."

Slowly, Rae got to her feet, his hand still tangled in her hair. He tugged, angling her head back so that her neck was arched and exposed. Quinn dipped his mouth, kissing and sucking at the skin below her jaw. Trailing his tongue down her neck and back up to her mouth. "*God, Rae, that mouth of yours,*" he growled into her lips. His mouth came over hers hard and possessive, his tongue wrestling with hers, tasting her, claiming her. "Do you have any idea how much power you have over me when you use your mouth like that?" He met her lips with another dominating kiss, his fist still wrapped in her dripping wet hair.

Letting his hand drop, he took hold of her hips and spun her around. Quinn pressed his chest to her back, his rock hard length against her ass. From her shoulders, he smoothed both hands down her arms as he bowed his head to her ear, biting it before whispering, "Tell me, Rae...did you wear this sexy bikini just for me that day?"

As he traced his fingers back up her arms, she nodded, "Yes."

Quinn groaned, pressing himself against her further, "Correct answer." His lips brushed the nape of her neck. "You had everyone staring, wishing they could have you. But they all knew you belonged to me." His hands trailed down her arms one more time before wrapping one arm around Rae's front, teasing her, slipping his fingers beneath her bikini bottoms, then back out. He watched the rise and fall of her breasts as she let out a needy whimper. Lips pressed to her wet skin, he whispered, "I'll give you what you want, baby, but you'll have to keep quiet. Think you can do that for me?"

Rae's voice came out in a breathless moan, "Yes, Quinn."

He slipped his fingers back into her bikini bottoms, dipping lower this time to find her clit. She leaned into him, biting her bottom lip as he rubbed and circled her most sensitive spot softly. He slipped his hand lower, sliding a finger inside her slick crease, and fuck was she wet. It took every bit of restraint he had to not bend her over and dive into her. He needed to feel her pussy wrapped around him, but he wanted to drag this teenage dream out as much as possible. His middle finger found her clit again, working and rubbing it on all sides, making sure to give Rae every bit of pleasure she deserved. A strangled moan escaped her as she struggled to bite it back, and she bucked her hips into him. He continued brushing his fingertips along her sensitive clit, and when finally a shiver rippled over her skin, he knew she was close. He thrusted one finger, then two inside her, pumping in and out steadily while the pad of his thumb circled and rubbed her clit.

She was wrapped around his fingers so tight, and he could tell she was losing the ability to hold back as her hands found his neck and slipped into his water-soaked hair, grasping frantically. It was like she was trying to physically hold onto the last bit of control in her body. She gasped and stuttered, "F-fuck, Quinn...oh my...feels s-so good."

His hand holding her hips against him slid up and clamped over her mouth, "Shh, baby, you're gonna get us caught." Quinn's lips grazed her ear as he whispered. Rae's head lulled back into his chest and her moan came out muffled by his palm. Despite his warning, he didn't let up or slow down. He could tell she was on the edge of ecstasy. "Come on, baby, come for me."

Another moan was muffled by his hand on her mouth. Rae rocked her hips into him, grinding against his hand, craving friction. Fingers pumping, massaging, circling her in all the right places, he watched as another shiver came over her. Goosebumps sprinkled over her skin, even beneath the heat of the steaming hot water. Rae's eyes shut tight, throwing her head back, strained with the sounds she wasn't allowed to make. Quinn felt her warm, wet flesh contract hard around his fingers as she gave herself over to wave upon wave of pleasure.

He waited for her orgasm to subside before slipping his fingers out of her. He caught the waistband of her bikini bottoms with his fingertips and slid them down her legs, kissing and nibbling her body on the way down and back up. With one hand rubbing up and down her side, the other found the tie of her bikini top, undoing it with a quick snap. Dropping the top to the shower floor, he slid his hands around her and palmed her breasts, massaging and squeezing them, brushing his thumbs and fingertips over her pink nipples.

Taking his time still, he enjoyed the feel of her skin, her breasts soft and smooth in his hands. Again, he tried to imagine what his younger self would have done in this moment- apart from coming instantly at the chance to touch Rae like this. He wanted to be inside her. Feel his cock fill her up and then release into her.

Quinn walked her forward a couple steps, grabbed her hands and placed them on the tile in front of her. Slowly, he smoothed his hands back up her arms, over her shoulders, and down her back to rest on her hips. Rae spread her legs, widening her stance slightly without having to be prompted now. He didn't think he'd ever get enough of this view. That ass was something else, and the way she arched her back for him when he entered her had him in pieces every time.

Watching water drip down her back, Quinn grabbed his cock and stroked it up and down to the erotic sight before him. He could get off to this image alone and come all over her ass. He groaned at the thought, but he wanted to feel her wrapped around him. To make her come again. Make her legs quake so bad that she'd drop back to her knees if he didn't hold her up.

"Remember, baby, don't make a sound," Quinn breathed, settling his hand at the base of his cock before gently and deliberately squeezing himself into her tight, wet heat. He sunk himself deep and let out a shuddering groan. Leaning over her, he bit her shoulder to try to muffle his own sounds. Rae's head bowed forward, the arch in her back steepening closer to her hips, and her ass popped out toward him further. He wanted to smack it and hear the sound of his hand against her skin ring out but refrained.

They'd never been in a situation that required them to hold back. While letting it all go and being as wild as possible was a fantastic way to fuck, there was something about having to keep himself in check that was driving Quinn to his breaking point. Having to hold back, knowing they could get caught. This built up so much more tension than he was used to. The build alone was dizzying.

His thrusts started slow and deliberate as a way to keep control. But he quickly learned that going slow like this, he could feel everything. He felt every inch of him slide against her wet skin. Every contraction as she squeezed around him, wanting each and every bit of him to fill her up. This pace was torturous. Satisfying. Tormenting. Indulgent. He felt greedy with every thrust in and out, wanting to draw out each separate sensation and make it last.

The sound of Rae's hollow, gasping breath told him that he wasn't the only one finding pleasure in this new pace. Quinn kissed the nape of her neck, and bit and licked and sucked her skin, groaning as he slid all the way in and mostly out of her. Everything but the head of his dick pulled out, then he pushed himself in until he couldn't press forward anymore. He watched as Rae's hips rocked back and forth with the motion of his own hips. She was threatening to make him pick up tempo, rolling her hips a little faster, letting another needy whimper escape.

"Quinn…" Rae whispered through gasping breaths. "Quinn, you're so hard, oh God."

His head buried in her neck, he picked up his pace just slightly, and sent his thrusts with more force. Rae threw her head back, feeling the extra strength of his movements deep inside her. His hands found her tits again and he played with her nipples, rubbing them beneath his thumbs, massaging her breasts, then holding on tight as he pulled himself hard into her. The sleek muscles of her back tightened and she gasped. He pounded himself into her with a series of hard, deliberate strokes, and she came undone. She was wrapped tight around his cock, tighter than she'd been around his fingers, and she braced herself on the wall for support as her orgasm ripped through her, biting down on her forearm to keep from crying out.

When her legs shook, she refused Quinn's help to stand her up, letting herself drop back onto her knees. Rae spun around to face him, level with his throbbing cock and brought it to her mouth, devouring him once more. Quinn groaned and wrapped a hand in her hair, fist tight, as he thrust himself into that amazing mouth. Her tongue licked his whole length, from balls to tip, and he shuddered as she sucked him in. His hips rolled toward her as he leaned his back against the shower wall. Rae licked and sucked and tasted every inch like she was hungry for it. Quinn's eyes were focused on how her lips looked, stretching around the width of him. He pumped into her again, trying to reach the back of her throat, and felt the release coming.

Keeping one hand in her hair, the other dropped to the base of his cock, holding it steady while she sucked him in and out. "Rae..." Quinn rasped. "Fuck, I'm gonna come, baby." He pumped quick strokes down part of his length and pulled himself back and out of her mouth as he came hard. Stroking himself through his release, his hot, white cum squirted on her lips, her neck, her collar bone, her tits. His lips pressed together hard as he tried to keep the animalistic sounds inside as he finished. He rested his head back on the shower wall, his breaths escaping long and shuddering. Now he was the one with shaky legs.

His chest heaved with a heavy sigh and he glanced back down at Rae. Still on her knees, she peered up at him from under long lashes. She swiped her finger across her bottom lip where he'd come and, without breaking eye contact, licked it off.

Fuck, that was hot.

"Teenage me never came on you," Quinn confessed through heaving breaths, as he watched her clean herself off under the spray of the hot water, "but if you're not mad, I don't regret it."

Rae didn't say anything, but she raised an eyebrow, then dropped her gaze from his face to where he was still erect and pulsing. Before he could see it coming, she wrapped her mouth back around it and sucked him in one more time. Quinn groaned and dropped to his knees

369

in front of her. Rae slid her hands behind his head and pushed her fingers through his hair, pulling his lips to hers.

"I'm not mad," Rae said, between kisses. "I liked it. I felt like you were staking your claim."

"I thought I'd already done that," said Quinn, touching his forehead to hers, eyes trained on her pink lips.

"Never stop," Rae breathed. Quinn met her bright blue eyes and smiled. Pressing his lips to hers again as the hot spray from the showerhead came over both of them, he knew he never would.

Chapter 30

The days following the breaking news of Quinn and Raelyn's relationship had been a crazy whirlwind of phone calls, new privacy arrangements and dodging the press. Raelyn had taken a few days off work so that she could adjust to the new media attention and find a way to do her job without disrupting the practice or the patients. Alexis called her several times over the weekend to warn her about the sudden increase in appointment requests. There were other physical therapists at her office, but all of these new patients seemed to be requesting Dr. DeRose. Alexis had expressed her concern that these were reporters or photographers hoping to get a chance to speak with Quinn's new girl directly. Grateful that her secretary had seen the ruse these people were trying to pull, she told Alexis to simply let anyone who called know that she would not be seeing any new patients at this time.

They were still staying with her parents. Raelyn was itching to get back into her own house, but Quinn insisted they wait until the excitement over their relationship faded, not wanting too many reporters and paparazzi to be able to bother her at home. He assured her they would find someone new and more scandalous to follow around soon enough, and then they would be able to live more normally again. There would probably still be a few cameras to dodge here and there, but the crowds would eventually diffuse. They would be safe to drive their own vehicles rather than take her parents' chauffeurs everywhere, and she would be able to go get groceries or go to the gym without a hat and sunglasses.

New articles and photos of them continued to pop up daily. Most recently was a story with several photos from the wedding- photos of Raelyn and *Emerson- ugh!* They had been photographed in the moments before the bridal party had entered the reception, in that rare occurrence of Emerson being relatively bearable. There was a photograph of them laughing together, another of him with his eyes focused on her while she looked into her champagne glass, and one in which he appeared to have his arm around her, but Raelyn knew he was just setting his own champagne glass on the bar behind her.

Predictably, Quinn was displeased. He knew the photos just looked bad, and the implication that she was using or playing him was complete crap, but Raelyn had caught him studying the photos on more than one occasion. She had taken the iPad away from him and managed to distract him in the best way she knew how- They'd had quiet sex in her walk-in closet- or they'd tried their best to be quiet at least- and he hadn't mentioned or looked at the photos since.

While she was feeling a little cabin fever-ish, she knew Harry was certainly not complaining about the recent changes. With both Quinn and Raelyn being home all the time, he'd gotten two long runs each day, in the morning and evening. During the day, Harry could be found poolside, beneath an umbrella or shading himself in the many grape vines beyond the backyard.

It was Thursday evening and Raelyn had just gotten out of the shower after a long run with Quinn and Harry. Having to shower scparatcly and keep their clothes on more frequently was an adjustment, and another reason she couldn't wait to get back into her own home. They had gotten better at having quiet sex, but she was ready to get home and have Quinn throw her on her back and go crazy with it.

Wrapped in a towel, she slipped across the hall and into her bedroom where Quinn was on the phone, head leaning back on the headboard. It appeared he had taken advantage of the fact that there were multiple bathrooms with showers in the large house and was already clean and back in a pair of vintage-wash blue jeans.

"...okay, room four-oh-two?" His eyes flew up to Raelyn as she entered and lowered his voice into the phone, "Okay, yeah I'll be there.

I gotta go." He quickly pulled the phone from his ear, pressed the red button to end the call and tossed the phone on the bed, face down.

Leaning back against the door as she closed it all the way, she flipped the lock then swept over to the bed. Raelyn climbed onto the mattress and straddled his lap, letting the towel fall. She kissed him deeply. His hands like magnets found her hips and slid their way up to hold her breasts. The groan rumbled through his mouth and into hers, sending a warm and needy sensation between her thighs.

"Who was that on the phone?" Raelyn asked, slipping her hands beneath his light cotton t-shirt, splaying them on his unbelievably hard, broad chest.

Quinn spoke around their kisses, never fully parting his lips from hers, "Jett is picking me up later." His lips traced her jaw. "People are snooping around my mom's house." His tongue slid down her neck and across her collar bone. "Want to make sure everything's okay there." Raelyn pressed into his mouth as he sucked at her skin. "Then checking out a new hotel room...We booked a few so they don't know where to find us...But now we can have somewhere...we don't have to hold back." At this, he dipped his head and sucked a nipple into his mouth.

Raelyn's neck arched back as she muffled her own cry of pleasure and wrapped her hands around the back of his neck, pulling him closer. "But I still can't go home yet?"

"I know, babe, I know." Quinn maneuvered her onto her back, holding himself above her now. "I was looking forward to moving in, too." He started back in, licking and sucking at her nipple while toying with the other between his fingers. "We were going to break that place in. Leave no surface untouched."

"I think we have a pretty good head start on that." The last words came out as a small moan, curving her spine away from the mattress when Quinn scraped his teeth gently across her nipple. "Ugh, Quinn, why did you put clothes back on?"

"So I can watch you take them off." Quinn's smile pressed into her soft skin and she lifted his shirt up and over his head.

The ding and vibration of a phone sounded from beneath her, and Quinn slipped his hand under her back to retrieve it. Lifting his head up, he glanced at the phone. His brows pulled together and he sat up with an aggravated groan. "Shit…" Quinn sighed. "I have to call my agent."

"Right now?" Raelyn asked, propping herself up on her elbows.

"I'm sorry, *ma chouette*," said Quinn, leaning forward for a quick kiss.

Raelyn's eyebrows scrunched, confused. "*Chouette?* Are you sure that's what you meant?"

"That's 'my darling', right?" Quinn asked, sitting on the edge of the bed, glancing away from his phone.

"Uh, no," Raelyn giggled. "You're looking for *ma chérie*."

"What did I say?" Quinn's eyebrows pulled together again.

"My owl," she replied, "but it's super cute, I like it."

Quinn's lips pulled up into an adorably embarrassed grin. "I'll never be able to speak French."

"I love that you're trying," said Raelyn, rolling up to make her way to the dresser.

By the time she turned back around to ask more about their trip to Paris in December, his phone was pressed to his ear again. With a quick apologetic look, he took the phone call out to her balcony, closing the door behind him.

Raelyn got dressed and watched him for a few moments. He was never particularly animated on the phone, and he kept his voice low. She wasn't a huge fan of how much he had been on the phone lately, but she figured that was part of the package. With the knowledge that she would have to save her sexual appetite for later, she decided to head downstairs while he finished up his phone call and start making dinner for the two of them.

Quinn had just enough time to eat something and pack an overnight bag before Jett arrived to pick him up. With a short peck on the lips, Raelyn sent him out the door and then wandered back into the living room where her dad was watching TV. Since staying with her parents, Quinn and Charlie would spend their evenings watching MLB network, but tonight her dad put on *The Big Bang Theory* instead and they watched a few episodes together.

Around nine o'clock, Raelyn made her way back up to her bedroom to pack her own overnight bag- she was *not* getting caught leaving the hotel again in leggings and Quinn's t-shirt. And no bra. Of course, in that particular instance she had been grateful for her lack of endowment in the chest region. Under Quinn's large shirt, it was hard to tell she'd been braless in those photos.

Earlier in the week, Camille had been kind enough to go to her house and grab a large section of her wardrobe to bring over to their parent's house. Searching through one of the bags she had yet to fully unpack, Raelyn was about to mentally kick herself for not making sure her sister had grabbed some lingerie when she came across a pile of lacy, strappy, mesh, and silky fabrics at the bottom of the bag.

"Oh, bless you, Camille," Raelyn said under her breath.

Sorting through the various sets of bras and bustiers, thongs, and even a pair of crotchless panties, Raelyn settled on a black strappy bustier with lace so thin it looked almost silver. There was a pair of matching panties she knew she had yet to wear for Quinn, but the mere thought of keeping them on and watching him slide down her body, putting his face between her legs was enough to make her blush and feel that familiar warmth spread from her stomach, into her breasts and between her thighs.

It took a few tries to get all the straps in just the right places, but once she managed, she checked herself out in the full-length mirror. She couldn't help nodding an approving *dayum, girl* to herself. Tempted to snap a picture and send it to Quinn, she refrained. Partially because she wanted him to be surprised when he saw it in the flesh, but mostly because she didn't need photos like that leaking all over the internet.

Raelyn rifled through her closet and found a blue sundress with a large white floral print, trying to look as innocent as possible. The cameras could catch her in this All-American girl sundress, and behind closed doors, Quinn could tear it off and they could set each other free. She could absolutely not wait for a full evening of raw, fiery, passion-fueled love making. She wanted to be able to take her time, do it hard and rough, then slow it down and be soft with each other. Her body was humming with anticipation, needing this night with Quinn as much as she needed to breathe.

It caught her off-guard to realize how intensely she had fallen for him in such a short period of time. But this didn't feel like the typical new-relationship buzz. It was more than that. Looking at the pictures scattered on the wall over her desk, she took time to appreciate each one with her and Quinn together. These feelings had been building for almost a lifetime. She'd found the person who she could be her truest self with, and they were finally learning other ways to express the raw nature of who they were, both separately and as one.

It was past ten o'clock now, and Quinn had yet to text her that he was back at the hotel. Antsy and unable to stay put any longer, she made the decision to get out of the house. She'd been cooped up for days and was sick of feeling like she couldn't go anywhere. She needed a drink. She was pacing back and forth with her overnight bag sitting at the front door, just waiting for the go-ahead from Quinn.

"Dad, I'm taking your car," Raelyn said, grabbing the keys to his new Beamer.

Charlie had been pouring himself a glass of white wine in the kitchen and looked up at his daughter curiously. "Everything okay, Peaches?"

"I haven't driven a car in days. I've barely left this house, and waiting for Quinn's text is slowly killing me," Raelyn explained, twirling the key ring around her finger. "I just need to get out."

"Sure thing, kiddo," Charlie said, then took a sip of his wine. "Drive safe. Call me if you need me."

Raelyn gave her father a quick hug and headed to the far end of the house to the garage. When the garage door raised and the light turned on, Charlie's new black BMW 840i was so shiny, it looked chrome, reflecting everything in its surface. Raelyn had given him crap about buying his mid-life crisis vehicle -he usually opted for the SUVs- but sitting in the soft leather of the front seat and feeling the way it cushioned and wrapped her body so perfectly, she took back every mocking comment, every jab that she'd given. This car was perfection. The engine purred, and she thought she might simply drive this baby around until Quinn messaged her.

Aimlessly driving for about half an hour, she inevitably found herself parking across the street from Trojan Horse. She could easily have one glass of wine and still drive back to the hotel without issue.

Taking her time to once again admire the gleam of the car's brilliant surface beneath the streetlights, she eventually broke away and set off for the bar.

Holy Moses.

There was a line out the door. Sure, it was a Thursday night and there were games on, but Trojan Horse didn't typically get quite this busy. Traverse City had more hipster vibes than jock aesthetic, and while any bar serving locally brewed craft beers could pull their weight, Trojan Horse had a more finely tuned demographic of customers.

Raelyn weighed her options. She could probably slip past the line, being a friend of the owners, but that might draw attention to herself. It hit her that the bar was likely getting more traffic since the articles about Chris and Jett being friends of Quinn's had been printed, as well as the casual mentions of Quinn having spent much of his time at the bar in the past several weeks. Would Raelyn walking in make things completely blow up?

A glance down at her phone told her that Quinn had still not arrived at the hotel. She knew his room number but didn't have the key yet. It was possible that he'd told the concierge to give her a key upon arrival, but he hadn't told her that she needed to stop at the desk. She contemplated again before deciding to get into the bar through Jett's apartment rather than use the main entrance.

Raelyn ducked her head low, hoping that no one would recognize her as she passed by the long line. The dark of the night was working in her favor in that regard, but she was silently wishing there was a little more light in the alleyway behind the bar.

Quickly slipping through the door, she ran up the stairs and into Jett's apartment. The thunder of the music and crowd of people below was muffled, but the bass still vibrated through the floorboards. Her plan was to find something in Jett's apartment that might disguise her so that she could sit at the bar. It was probably a ridiculous idea, but then again, no one seemed to recognize Clark Kent was Superman when he combed his hair and put on thick-rimmed glasses, right?

Just over a year ago, this apartment had been much like her second home, but Jett had made some updates and decor changes since then.

The red-brick walls of the living room were both manly and trendy. The glass-top coffee table was sleek, and surprisingly had coasters on it. She didn't realize Jett was a tidy, coaster-using kind of guy. The kitchen wasn't huge but was certainly big enough for one person. There was a bar with black bar stools separating the living room and kitchen, but no kitchen table. She figured Jett either sat at the bar or, more likely, ate his meals on the couch in front of the TV.

All the appliances were black stainless steel, and Raelyn found herself feeling rather impressed with Jett's interior decorating skills. The place was definitely a man cave, but it was a classy man cave. Classy, but fun and cool. It gave off the vibe that the person who lived here was someone you could easily chill and have a beer or two with over good conversation.

She noted the cherry red and black Gibson Les Paul mounted on the wall in the living room, along with an all-black Fender Stratocaster next to it. On a guitar stand next to the couch was an acoustic Gibson.

Jett was the only one of their group who had any real musical talent, apart from Chris who would occasionally grace them with a sample of his singing voice, which was completely untrained. But he liked to brag that he used to sing in his church choir...when he was eight. Jett was possibly the only person who had ever actually played the multi-thousand dollar grand piano in Raelyn's parents' living room. Her eyes swept to the piano pushed against the wall next to the window near the fire escape and she smiled fondly at the memory from over a year ago when Jett had offered her a place to stay when she didn't feel like being alone.

It was a week after she and Emerson had broken up. She had come into the bar, *alone*...for shots. Exclusively for shots. And she got tanked. She had no reason to worry, of course, with big brothers Chris and Jett hanging out at the bar, shooing away any guys giving off rapey vibes. When Chris had asked if she needed a ride home, Raelyn had insisted on staying in Jett's apartment. She'd been terrified that Emerson would show up at her door trying to explain away his infidelity like he had before. Or worse, admit it, start a huge fight around it, and they would inevitably crash together in what could only be deemed break-up sex. She'd felt horrible enough, she didn't need the shame of giving into him one last time.

So she'd stayed here in Jett's apartment. He had come up after closing the bar down and locking up, and she was still wide awake on the couch. Jett had gone to the piano and played and sung various pop songs before she fell asleep on the couch to something more classical sounding. The next morning, she'd woken up having been moved into his room, and Jett had taken the couch for the night.

He might be the easiest to tease and give shit, but he was probably one of the most sincere and fiercely loyal friends any of them ever had.

Raelyn spun around, looking for the hallway. Hopefully she'd be able to find something in Jett's room, like a baseball cap or a beanie. Maybe some non-prescription glasses. Who knew?

When she lifted her head to face the hall entrance, she gasped and jumped back.

Jett did the same- well, it was more of a shriek- but *he* was only wearing a towel. A towel that he hadn't seemed to tuck in just yet, and when he jumped, his hand slipped and the bath towel was whipped away from his body, falling into a pool at his feet.

"Oh my God!" Raelyn shouted, hands flying up to her face.

"WHY ARE YOU HERE?!" Jett screamed, scrambling to cover himself up with his hands.

"Why are you *naked*?" Raelyn yelled back, turning to the side and shielding her eyes.

"Because I'm in my own apartment, Rae!" He kept dipping to grab the towel off the floor but missed each time.

Raelyn cast a squinted side glance at him before blinking in shock. "Holy shit, Jett! Good for you," she said sincerely. "Seriously, have you ever considered doing porn? That thing's a fucking beast."

"Would you stop LOOKING AT MY DICK?" Jett's shouts came out panicked, the last words more of a shrill screech than anything else.

"I'm sorry, but *damn*," Raelyn turned away, but her eyes darted back a few more times, confirming that she had in fact seen correctly that Jett's penis was enormous. "Why aren't you working? You realize you have a line wrapped around the building down there?"

"I was supposed to be off tonight," said Jett, finally getting the towel wrapped around his waist and tucked in. "I went with Quinn to his mom's, then we had an incident that resulted in getting covered in mud, so I showered and now I'm going to have to go help out downstairs anyway. The joys of being a business owner."

She processed this information as she peered at him again from the side. "Do you pass out when that thing gets hard? From all the blood in your body rushing to it?"

Jett let out a heavy sigh, "That's a bit of an exaggeration, I think. But thank you. Make sure you tell Quinn that. He can be famous and rich, Chris can be happily married, but of the three of us guys, *I* have the biggest dick. That's all I need to know in life." He puffed out his chest and smiled with pride.

"Is Quinn downstairs? I thought you were with him," said Raelyn, facing Jett again, but not putting her hands down all the way just yet.

"I dropped him off at the hotel already," Jett replied. He glanced at the clock on the stove top. "Like an hour and a half ago. At least."

Instinctively, Raelyn pulled her phone out of her purse and checked it. No new messages. Not from Quinn or anyone. She frowned at the screen. "Maybe my phone's not receiving texts. It might need an update."

Without being asked, Jett padded over to the kitchen counter where he'd left his phone. He shot off a text and seconds later, Raelyn's phone buzzed. More confused, and now starting to get a little worried, Raelyn could barely laugh at Jett's message- *On second thought, don't tell your bf you saw me naked. He scares me.*

"I hope he's okay…" Raelyn stared down at her phone for a few seconds, pondering. If they'd had an incident, whatever that meant, and got covered in mud, he likely had to shower again. But he didn't take that long in the shower. "Maybe his phone's dead."

"Shouldn't be," said Jett. "He was charging it in my truck. Pretty sure it was over fifty percent when he unplugged it. That guy gets a lot of phone calls."

"Hmm…" Raelyn chewed the inside of her lip, brow furrowed. "Well, I guess I'll just go to the hotel. He told me what room it was. I'm sure there's some sort of explanation."

"Yeah, I'm sure he's fine. Maybe he got held up by reporters and had to make a run for it," Jett suggested. "*Maybe…*" Raelyn could hear the conspiratorial tone in his voice, "they ran out of Quinn Casey bobbleheads, and Bobble Corp had to have him flown out for a new replica."

Raelyn giggled, appreciating the lightening of the mood.

"*Maybe* he was trying to set up a sex swing in your hotel room and decided to try it without supervision and got stuck!"

Laughing again, Raelyn shook her head.

"*Maybe*...and just hear me out on this one- *maybe*... he's Batman."

Raelyn nodded, smiling. "Yeah, that could be. Money, abs, anger issues...that vigilante urge to carry out justice on his own terms."

"See? The bat signal apparently comes before whatever weird sex plans you had tonight," Jett said with a shrug, attempting to conceal his own amusement with himself.

"There's nothing weird about buying nylon rope in bulk and-"

"Oh *God*, no! What?" Jett's look of horror made Raelyn laugh even harder.

"Aw, poor little virgin ears can't handle that," she pouted mockingly.

"I'm *not* a virgin!" Jett insisted through gritted teeth.

"Sure you're not, Flower," Raelyn reached up and ruffled his curly hair and he ducked away from her. "Better hold onto that towel." Raelyn smirked and made her way to the door to head back down to the alley.

"Wait, Rae," Jett grabbed her by the bicep and turned her around. "You can't go down to the alley by yourself. It's almost eleven o'clock. I'll get dressed and walk you out."

"It's fine, that's how I came up."

"Well, that was dumb. Just give me a minute." With that, he turned down the hallway to his bedroom. It did only take one minute for him to get on a pair of shorts and a t-shirt. He slid on some shoes at the door and walked Raelyn out to the car.

"Let me know when you find him, okay?" Jett said, holding the door open as Raelyn slid into the front seat.

"Will do, Flower," Raelyn teased and gave a wink. Jett shook his head, exasperated, and shut the driver's side door.

It wasn't a long drive back to the hotel. Quinn was still staying at Hotel Indigo because they had the best safety measures around for guests. Some false leaks had been made that he was staying in other hotels, which at least kept the cameras from all congregating outside one building. Raelyn managed to duck into the lobby unnoticed and get the elevator to herself. She pushed the button for the fourth floor and waited.

Room four-oh-two, right? Four-twenty-two? Two-twenty-four? Shit.

She specifically remembered hearing the number four-oh-two, but she could've sworn that the room number Quinn had given her had a twenty in it somewhere. Oh well. Quinn hadn't texted her yet asking her to show up, so she wasn't in too big of a hurry. She could check those different rooms with the hope that the occupants weren't complete weirdos.

Stepping out of the elevator on the fourth floor, she spotted the sign that directed which way to go for rooms 400-412, and the other way for rooms 413-424. It looked like the floor did a full circle, or rectangle, rather, so she supposed it didn't matter which way she went first. Since rooms were equally close, she opted to start with room 402.

She knocked. Waited. Nothing. Knocked again. Still nothing.

Raelyn whispered a brief, "Sorry if you're sleeping in there…" and continued down the hall to find room 422. As she passed the little nook to get ice and other beverages, she heard a door open and looked up at the sound of Quinn's familiar voice. The excitement she felt was stopped short at the sound of a female voice, and the sight of a woman exiting his room in front of him.

Panicking, Raelyn slipped inside the nook and peered around the corner.

No. Fucking. Way.

No.

This is not fucking happening.

Quinn was standing just outside the doorway in a t-shirt and boxer briefs. He was wearing his fucking underwear and a t-shirt. In front of some woman. A woman in his hotel room. She was beautiful, of course. She was petite with dark brown hair that fell in waves down her back, and was wearing black pump heels, a pencil skirt, and an emerald green sleeveless blouse, with her blazer tucked under one arm.

Raelyn's stomach was an empty pit. It felt like her stomach was falling and falling into endless blackness. Her heart clenched. It physically hurt. The lump in her throat grew in seconds, and the harder she tried to swallow it down, the larger it seemed to get. Her eyes burned with tears begging to pour out.

No, no, no, this was not happening again.

Not with him. Not Quinn.

He loves me. I know he does.

So what the fuck...is he doing here? With someone else?

She strained to hear past the rushing in her ears and listened for the words being exchanged that had to, *absolutely had to*, provide some explanation other than what it clearly looked like.

"...*so* good," the woman's voice came to Raelyn's ears. Her voice was velvety and warm, smooth and sexy. *Of course it was.*

"Good to see you again, Mamacita," Quinn said, his voice full of playfulness and charm at the same time. Raelyn peeked ever so slightly around the corner of her nook in time to see the two step out of an embrace. The woman's hands lingered on Quinn's biceps. It made her want to sob and scream and fall apart all at once.

"Tomorrow, then? Eleven o'clock? We can do lunch and then go from there," the woman said. Raelyn leaned against the wall, standing still as she heard footsteps advancing. Eyes closed, trying to just breathe and keep the inevitable flood at bay, she waited to hear Quinn's door close.

The click of the door and the electronic beep of it locking behind him sounded through the empty hall. Raelyn stood still, unsure of her next move. Should she confront him? Should she walk away and let him figure it out? Should she confront *her?* This woman that Raelyn had never seen, but apparently Quinn had and was going to see again? She swallowed around the lump in her throat, considering how to move forward. How to handle this. How...how she was supposed to just carry on once this had officially come to an end.

The thought of their final goodbye brought the first sob out. She put a hand over her mouth and tried to keep control. She thought of how little sense this made. How she knew, she *knew* Quinn loved her. *Loves* her. Was this really just some act between them? Was this something fun to do while he was benched? The questions seemed absolutely ridiculous, but what else could she think?

Closing her eyes again, she was taken back to the doorway of Emerson's office at the law firm. The woman lying on his desk with her legs wrapped around his waist. His pants slung just low enough on his hips that he could fuck her. She remembered that entire scene, and how humiliated she had felt. She hadn't wanted to face him, talk to him, be anywhere near him. She hadn't wanted to give him a chance to explain or try to excuse it like he had the first time.

Raelyn considered going to Quinn's door and knocking. Then she imagined him opening the door for her to see the scene of whatever had just happened in that room. Jett said he'd dropped him off close two hours ago now, and she was just leaving. What kind of mess had they made in that hotel room? Had they shaken picture frames off their spots on the walls like she and Quinn had only days ago? Knocked over lamps? How tangled were the sheets?

No. She did not want to see that. She wanted to get as far away from that as possible.

Having found the motivation finally to push herself off the wall and head back to the elevator and out to the car, Raelyn concentrated on her breathing until she was comfortably behind the wheel again. Then she let it out. The tears, the sobs, the struggle to catch her breath. Her chest was tight and her heart felt like it was shattered into a thousand broken in pieces. Her stomach was still dropping out of itself into nothingness, and she had no idea where to go from here.

The chime of her phone in the passenger's seat made her gasp and pause. She slowly reached her hand over to look at the screen.

Quinn: Hey, baby. I'm so sorry that took so long. I promise to make it up to you when you get here. You want it soft, we can do it soft and slow. You want it rough and wild, you know I can do that, too. I love you. See you soon.

Closing her eyes with silent tears streaming down her cheeks, Raelyn felt the last piece of her heart break.

CHAPTER 31

2009

Quinn's eyes fell on the scoreboard. They were tied 6-6 in the bottom of the ninth. Traverse City was up to bat, and if they struck out before they could make a run, they'd be running extra innings. The guys on his team were good, but Bay City had one hell of a pitcher. The announcer had mentioned the pitcher's scholarship to play for Texas A & M in the fall, which meant Quinn wasn't the only player here who'd been scouted, recruited, and fought over by multiple universities. He felt it leveled the playing field, so to speak, knowing that he was up against guys who were just as good as, or maybe even better than he was. The cocky punk in him didn't want to admit they could be better, but he pretended to believe as much.

He stood up from the bench and leaned, crossing his arms to rest over the top of the fence in front of the dugout. His eyes scanned the crowd and gravitated toward the long blond hair beneath a worn navy blue ball cap. Her white t-shirt read 'Traverse City West Baseball', and was short enough to show just the smallest fraction of skin between its hem and the waistband of her blue jean cutoffs. Though he couldn't see it from where he stood, he knew she was wearing her low-rise black Chuck Taylors, and that she had a number seven- his jersey number- painted on one cheek just behind her crescent-shaped dimple.

God, could that girl be more perfect?

Rae caught him looking at her and smiled brightly, then stuck her tongue out at him before smiling again. Quinn's lips slowly curved upward in response, his chest inflating with warmth as he thought about how great the past couple weeks had been.

Their relationship had changed notably. Not in a huge way, but there were subtle differences Quinn couldn't help noticing. Rae had always been very hands-on, never afraid to wrap him into a hug or plant a soft kiss on his cheek or steal his hat off his head and ruffle his already messy hair. She'd loop her arm through his as they walked or take him up on a piggy-back ride simply walking down the hall at school or in the parking lot to and from her car. But ever since his mom's car accident on Prom night, these actions had become more frequent, and more...well, just *more*.

Watching movies in the theater room at her house, she'd sit closer, or sit leaning her back on the arm of the couch with her legs draped over his lap. She'd suggested more hang-outs in the hot tub, and had worn that tiny blue bikini from the end of summer party on more than one occasion. It had caused problems on his end a few times, but he wasn't about to ask her to change. And she almost always wore something of his. A hat, a hoodie, his team t-shirts with his last name and jersey number on the back.

He wasn't complaining, of course. Actually, he loved it. He just didn't know how to interpret it. Any other guy would probably take it as a sign that she liked him, but Quinn was skeptical. He'd wondered if she was doing it because she felt bad about the car accident. His mom had been in rough shape, and he'd been taking care of her more than usual. Quinn wasn't sure if this was just Rae's way of trying to relax him. Make him feel better and ease his anxiety over everything.

Another explanation could be the pact they'd made at the beginning of the year. She made sure to ask him every now and then if they were still on for it, if he'd met anyone or had been with anyone since shaking on their agreement. Obviously he hadn't. Holding out to be with Rae was absolutely not a problem for Quinn. However, there were a few things regarding the arrangement that had been gnawing at him.

When he thought about the pact they'd made, it made him excited, exhilarated, and a little bit like he'd dreamt the whole discussion and that it was all in his head. That it was never going to actually happen, and he and Rae would simply remain friends who didn't touch or kiss each other or get naked together. There was also the issue that he didn't want it to just be about sex. He wanted so much more than that with her. He wanted everything. He wanted to call her his and let everyone around know that she was off limits.

But for Rae, he was pretty certain it was just sex. She didn't want to arrive on campus at the University of Michigan in the fall and feel like the only inexperienced freshman around. If it was more than that for her, Quinn was sure she would have told him. She would have made a move, right? Because what reason did she have not to? There wasn't a single guy in their school who'd turn her down if she expressed interest, and she had to know that.

Just sex or not, Quinn was determined to make it as special as he could for her. Maybe she'd understand how much she meant to him. He wasn't much of a talker and had no idea how to put into words what he felt for her. He'd practiced it on several occasions, but the words seemed inadequate. Maybe if he said them as he was being intimate with her, being gentle and caring and showing her how much she could trust him with her body, with everything...maybe then the words would feel like they meant something.

There was also the small matter of the pact being a *virginity* pact. And...well, Quinn wasn't exactly a virgin. It was only one other person, but Rae was still operating under the impression that they were both sharing their first time together. He doubted she'd find out. The girl he'd had sex with the previous year, almost a year before the virginity pact was in place, wasn't someone Rae ever talked to if she could help it. But...if the important part of this pact was that Rae wasn't going to college with zero sexual experience, he didn't think that point mattered much. Quinn didn't care about his first time. It wasn't a big deal. He cared about Rae's, and he knew he was the best guy for the job.

"Case, you're on deck to bat!" Coach Garcia called to him with a grin. He gave Quinn a pat on the back as he grabbed his batting helmet and walked out of the dugout. Gloves on, helmet secured, Quinn grabbed his bat and moved to the circle, readying himself to bat.

Tim Hoyt, a tall, dark-haired senior player was at the plate. The pitcher had been doing a good job striking out their players, and the bases were empty. Tim needed to make it to a base or they'd be going into a tenth inning.

Quinn gave a few practice swings as he stood in the on-deck circle, not taking his eyes off the pitcher. He breathed in and out, long, slow breaths. Stretched his arms and shoulders. Gave another practice swing and another round of steadying breaths. If Tim struck out, Quinn was set to pitch the next inning. He told himself confidently he'd make it a no-hitter and then he'd be first to bat. He'd get a run, and the game would be done. One way or another, he'd win this game for his team.

The pitcher wound up and sent the ball in. Tim didn't swing. Good call.

"Ball!" The umpire called as the catcher threw the ball back to the tall pitcher.

Brows furrowed in concentration as he studied the pitcher. His wavy blond hair flipped out beneath his ball cap. He was sun-tanned and baby faced. His young features were a stark contrast to the ferocity with which he threw a baseball.

A wind-up and a pitch.

Crack!

Quinn's back straightened and he watched as the ball flew into the outfield- *Yes!*

Tim ran to first base, then chanced it to second.

"Safe!"

Quinn let out the breath he'd been holding and grinned. The section of the crowd sporting green, gold, and white roared, cheering and clapping, getting to their feet.

The announcer's voice boomed through the stadium, "With Hoyt on second base, we have Casey up to bat! Quinn Casey, a senior player for the Trojans, will be playing at Arizona State University in the fall. This just might be the guy the Trojans need to get their third consecutive state championship victory."

"Damn right, I am," Quinn muttered to himself with a smirk as he took his spot at the plate.

"Quite the ego there, huh?" The catcher remarked, having heard Quinn's own confidence booster.

Without looking back at the catcher, Quinn kept his cocky smirk and replied, "It's only ego talking if it's not true."

Quinn kicked the sand and clay mix at his feet and took one last look around to find Rae. Ever since that day with the clowns in the dunk tank, he felt like knowing she was there and seeing her cheer him on, giving him encouragement, was the ultimate good luck charm. He found her easily in the crowd and they locked eyes. She smiled and gave him two thumbs up, scrunching up her face goofily. He smiled back, brought his bat up to point it at her and winked with his sly, one-dimpled grin.

Turning back to the pitcher, he focused himself back into the game. Deep breath in, slow breath out. He smelled the grass, the red clay, silt, and sand. The chalk. The leather of the catcher's glove. He tuned out the sounds, focusing on his breathing, then focusing on the pitcher. That was his world right now. The player on the mound, the ball, the bat. Quinn rocked his weight back and forth, shifting from one foot to the other. He gripped the bat, angling it up and behind him as he stared the pitcher down.

"Yeah, you're in my world now, buddy," Quinn whispered roughly.

As if in slow motion, the pitcher wound up and threw in a fastball. Quinn's weight shifted back. His front foot lifted off the sand as he felt the force that he was about to unleash gather in his core. Time came back to normal speed, and he swung, full-force, hitting straight through the ball with a loud *crack!* His lips curved back up into that familiar confident one-sided grin as he watched the ball fade, flying...flying...flying over the fence.

This was his victory lap. He saw Tim thrust both fists into the air as he continued to third base, then home. Quinn started toward first base, jogging without urgency and tossing his bat into the air on the way. The ball was out of here, he could take his time making his last lap of his high school career.

Again, the crowd in green and gold stood up, cheering and pumping their fists as they shared the victory with their team. By the time Quinn was at second base, the team was spilling out onto the field, jumping and shouting, clapping each other on the back, grabbing fellow teammates in tight, squeezing hugs. At home base, they all waited for him to finish his run before jumping on him in celebration.

The giant huddle of boys jostled him back and forth, messing up his hair even more as he dropped his batting helmet to the ground. Chris and Jett found him in the mass of bodies and both grabbed him up into a tight group hug.

"We fucking did it!" Jett shouted, followed by a loud howl as he tossed his ball cap in the air.

"We knew you had it in the bag for us, Case," said Chris, slapping him on the back. Then he grabbed Quinn's arm to bring him to a halt.

Their huddle had gradually moved, jumping and skipping, to the middle of the field. Chris turned Quinn around to face the fence near the dugout, bringing his attention to the absolutely stunning picture of Rae squeezing her way into the field. Quinn gave Chris and Jett each a pat on the back before jogging over to meet his favorite person on home base.

Rae jumped into Quinn's arms, wrapping her arms around the back of his neck, and he held tight around her waist as he spun her around, making her feet leave the ground. When Quinn stopped spinning, she set her feet back down and giggled as she steadied herself. He waited for the 'Congratulations, All-Star' or 'You did it, Case!' but it didn't come. Instead, she looked him in the eyes, her bright blue ones twinkling back at him as she smiled, then for a brief moment he saw her gaze flit down to his lips. His heart jolted into action a split-second before he could register what was about to happen. Her arms tightened around the back of his neck as she pulled him down to her and kissed him.

Her lips were pressed against his, and his eyes went wide with stunned disbelief. When she didn't release him or take her lips away, he closed his eyes and sunk into the kiss. Wrapping his arms tighter around her small waist, he pulled her body against his. Her lips were soft. They felt full and just completely perfect against his. She tasted like cinnamon and smelled like her familiar scent of coconut and vanilla. He wanted more. More of her. More of her mouth, her scent, her taste. He wanted to freeze this moment and stay in it forever. His heart was beating out of his chest and he was breathing her in, leaning over her, making her back arch slightly as he greedily demanded more of her lips.

At that cursed moment when they finally parted, she looked up at him and he was pleased to see she was just as breathless as he was. Quinn brought one gloved hand up and cupped the side of her face gently before pulling her toward him, joining their lips again. He had a hard time closing his eyes, because he wanted to watch this moment as long as it lasted to make sure it wasn't a dream. He allowed his eyelids to flutter shut to give himself the courage to take the kiss one step further. Slowly, he slipped his tongue out and licked her lips. Quinn delighted at her small gasp of surprise, and smiled into her lips as she parted them enough to let him in.

Holy Mother of sweet baby Jesus. I'm kissing Rae. On the mouth. I'm French *kissing Rae. And she tastes like a cinnamon roll. That's my new favorite food. Fuck, I don't want this to end.*

He felt as she began to let her arms loosen and her mouth started to pull back. Quinn shook his head in protest and pulled her closer to him. He loved her body pressed to his. He could devour her with his body and wrap her up in it. He could feel where her hips and the small mounds of her breasts pushed against him. It was only when he realized *other* parts liked pressing into Rae, too, that he finally let up.

Quinn's forehead rested against hers where his hat was flipped backwards on her head. He let out a slow shuddering breath as he held her close and smiled. He tried to be cool, he really did. But *dammit, this was Rae!* He couldn't help the stupid, big grin that wouldn't leave his face.

"Good game, Case," Rae said through her own grin.

Oh shit, that's right. I just won the state championship game. Again.

"Yeah, thanks," Quinn said breathlessly.

"I'm sure you guys will have a party somewhere, but feel free to come over when you get back," she offered.

God, how did she sound so cool about this? Like she hadn't just made out with her best friend?

"Oh, right," Quinn glanced at the team still celebrating. "You could come. I mean, the guys like you. You know how to fit right in."

Rae smiled up at him. "Go celebrate with your team, Quinn. I'm not going anywhere."

"Ho-ly *shit!*" Jett exclaimed, plopping into the seat across from Quinn and Chris's bus seat.

The bus ride home was going to be loud and rowdy, buzzing with the excitement of this final win. Everyone was on cloud nine, high on the feeling of winning a major game, and Quinn was high on the lingering taste of cinnamon and frosting Rae had left on his tongue.

"You finally did it!" Jett threw his hands in the air. "You finally fucking did it! How was it? Everything you hoped for? Is it weird to say you guys look good together? I thought it would be weird, and, well, it kind of was, because you're two of my best friends, but...holy shit! Good for you!"

Quinn hadn't been able to wipe the dopey, love-struck grin off his face. "It was...*fuck*, it was amazing! Guys...that happened. I can't believe it happened. She told me to come over after we get done partying and I feel like I'm going to get there and kiss her and she'll be like 'what are ya doin there, Case?' like it never happened. But it did! I was there and it happened."

"You being there is sort of an essential part of the equation," Chris chortled. "Does this mean you guys are gonna be...a thing? You gonna do the long distance thing from Michigan to Arizona in the fall, or what?"

"Whoa, whoa!" Jett put his hands up. "Don't be a downer, Chris. Come on, let him enjoy this. They still have the whole summer to be together. Dude, her parents are never home. It's gonna be so easy to fool around and not get caught. You guys can make out and have sex all summer." He paused and made a near-horrified face. "Oh, God, this is Rae! Why are we talking about having sex with her?"

"*We* will not be having sex with her, first of all," Quinn said pointedly, "and on that note...I wonder if this changes things."

"Of course it changes things, Case," said Chris, as though explaining to someone particularly idiotic that fire is hot. "You guys have been best friends for eleven years and now you're going to start developing deep love feelings and getting physical and touching. That's how relationships work, dude."

"No, not that," Quinn waved a hand dismissively. "No, I mean the pact that we made at the beginning of the year."

"We made a pact?" Jett asked curiously. "About Rae?"

Rolling his eyes, Quinn replied, "No, me and Rae made one. About...having sex."

Chris and Jett both went wide-eyed and their eyebrows shot upward. Chris leaned his head in closer, "I'm sorry, you guys made a sex pact? What the- Why didn't you tell us?"

Quinn shrugged. "It was just supposed to be between us, I think. I don't think she told anyone. But it might not even matter now. We can just have sex on our own terms, when it feels like a good time in the relationship."

"Explain, please," Jett said, looking thoroughly confused, as well as a little concerned. "What were the terms of this sex pact?"

"Well," Quinn nodded his head from side to side, feeling awkward at discussing this private arrangement, "Rae has this thing about not wanting to be a virgin her first day of college, I guess. I told her it was dumb and that no one would care or know, but she has it in her head that college is just like sex and parties and more sex and study partners that you have sex with. So she wants to be prepared."

Jett chuckled, "That sounds like Rae."

Chris nodded his agreement, "Always thinkin' ahead, that girl. Even if her view is a little distorted by that TV drama shit she watches."

"Well, basically, that's it. She just said if she hadn't had sex by the end of the year, that I would be her first." Quinn gave another lame and awkward shrug.

"And...you agreed to that?" Chris quirked an eyebrow skeptically.

"Yeah, so?"

"Quinn, you're crazy about this girl. You don't just want sex with her, you want to *be* with her," said Chris, again using his Explaining Obvious Shit to a Simpleton voice. "You're telling me you agreed to have no-strings-attached sex with her? You were gonna just blow your load, pat her on the ass and say 'Go get 'em, Tiger' and send her off to a sea of horny college dudes?"

Quinn narrowed his eyes into a glare. "That was unnecessarily crass, and *no*, that's not what I was going to do."

"Wait, wait," Jett held a hand up to pause the conversation. "Rae was completely fine with you hooking up with whoever you wanted all year...and as long as *she* hadn't had sex, it didn't matter how many chicks you'd been with, she still wanted to do it?"

Ahh, shit. I was hoping they wouldn't get to this part.

"Um...well, not...not exactly, no," said Quinn, feeling the heat rise from his neck up into his face. He knew they'd have a problem with this part. He'd struggled with it himself but had tried his best to glaze over it and not give it too much thought. "Okay, um...the thing is...this is supposed to be more like a *virginity* pact."

"But you're not a virgin," Chris stated, eyes darkening even in the limited light. Even Jett's always-friendly face looked incredulous and mildly threatening.

"No...No, I'm not," Quinn cringed as the reality of the lie set in.

"Case...no," Jett shook his head. "You cannot do that to Rae."

"What am I really doing though? I mean, she gets what she wants. She loses her v-card and it's not with some asshole like Liam-"

"Who lied to her about the conditions and intentions of the relationship?" Chris cut in. "Liam pretended to like her and dated her for two months because he wanted to have sex. You have been lying to Rae for the *entire school year* so you can have sex with her. Quinn, no."

"I didn't *lie*, technically," Quinn said, and even he heard how weak that sounded. "I mean, I never *said* that I'd never had sex. She just made the assumption based off a conversation we had...and I didn't correct her."

"Lying by omission is still lying," said Chris. "How many times has she asked you if you still haven't had sex?'

"A few..." Quinn mumbled, no longer able to make eye contact with either of them. "Well shit, what am I gonna do? We're supposed to do it next weekend after graduation."

Chris and Jett looked at each other, pondering and mulling over the limited options.

"You *have* to tell her," Jett said, "but maybe you can start by telling her how you feel about her. And that because you want to start something real, that it's best that you just forget the pact."

"Okay, but what if she's just happy with that? Then do I have to tell her? Because...no pact, no problem, right?"

"But your relationship is going to get there eventually and she's still going to think that she's your first, and that might bite you in the ass later," Jett replied, looking to Chris to add on.

"The problem is that the girl you *did* have sex with is basically Rae's arch-enemy. You don't have to tell Rae who it was, and she probably won't ask. But just imagine, if you will...Rae runs into Alaina at the gas station. And you're with Rae, of course, because you're a happy couple now, having regular intercourse. Alaina sees you two together and makes a snide comment about Rae getting her sloppy seconds or some shit like that, because those two girls cannot resist making jibes at each other. Rae says 'what did she mean by that, Quinn? I thought I was your one and only?' and Alaina hears this-"

"Okay, I get it! That would be very bad," Quinn brushed his hand through his hair and then sighed, landing his face in his palms. *"Fuck!* So how do I get out of this without Rae being pissed?"

"My vote is that you tell her the bad part first, and then soften it up with the crap about how you've been in love with her for years and want to marry her and have her babies," said Jett. "Bad news first, then soften the blow. And hope like hell she's so delighted by the good news that she completely forgets that you've been lying to her for nine months."

Quinn slumped in his seat, leaning his head back as he pulled his hat over his face. How could he go from feeling so blissfully elated to *this* in such a short period of time? His stomach churned and his head was suddenly throbbing.

A few hours ago, this felt like a non-issue. But sharing it out loud to his friends, he realized how terrible it was. They were right. He was lying to his best friend to have sex with her. That's not even what he wanted. It's not *all* he wanted, anyway. He'd have to go over to her house tonight and come clean. About everything.

"You taste like strawberries today," Quinn groaned into Raelyn's mouth, his tongue sweeping in and tasting hers. "Cinnamon rolls...and strawberries...are my new favorite foods." He was lying on top of her, pressing her into the bed, her head resting on the pillows. Raelyn's hands were roaming over him, up the flat plane of his stomach and chest, around the back of his neck and pulling him, urging him to kiss her deeper.

Kissing Quinn was like no other experience she'd had before. She couldn't get enough. Their lips fit so perfectly, and when he slid his tongue into her mouth, *dear God*, her heart pounded, she had butterflies in her stomach and chest, and her skin tingled everywhere. His hands were gentle but firm as they explored her. He had been tentative at first. Hesitant about where and how he should touch her. But over the last week they'd spent every possible moment like this, tangled together in a mess of limbs and eager hands and hot breath and kisses, learning each other in a completely new way.

When Quinn had come over after the championship game, she had practically grabbed him by his shirt and covered his mouth with hers before he could get out even half a greeting. His arms had slowly wrapped back around her, and she had dragged him upstairs to her bedroom before her parents or Camille could catch them making out in the foyer. If they found out she and Quinn were getting physical, she doubted her parents would be as lenient about him staying the night as they always had been.

Quinn's hand felt warm and steady as he slipped it beneath her shirt and held her just above her hip bones. He pulled her upward, forcing her back to arch just slightly off the mattress and pressed his body into hers. If her eyes hadn't been closed, they would have rolled back in her head at the incredible, sensational pressure between them. The daydreams and weight room fantasies had absolutely nothing on the actual feel of him against her. His scent fogged up her brain when they were this close and all she could be aware of was him and his hard body, soft hands, tender lips, his wet tongue on hers. She loved the sounds that seemed to escape him from some deeply buried primal part of him. His groans and his steady touches. Every action felt territorial and she *craved* it.

There was a flash of hesitation as Quinn lifted his hand from her skin, and she instantly wished for the return of his warmth. He placed his hand back, lighter this time and Raelyn groaned needily against his lips. His hand slid up her stomach slowly...slowly...until it was covering her breast through her bra. Raelyn's small gasp of surprise made him pull away just slightly, interpreting his touch as unwelcome or too much.

Raelyn rocked her hips up into him and whimpered, begging for him to return his touch. His hand came over her breast again and massaged it expertly. His thumb trailed along her soft skin, threatening to dip into her bra and find that sensitive pink peak.

Oh my God, yes, please...just a little closer... His teasing thumb was making the ache between her thighs pulse.

"Quinn," Raelyn breathed as he trailed his mouth down her jaw to her neck. "Quinn, it hooks in the front."

He buried his face in her neck with a deep groan and let his hand find the bra clasp between her breasts. His hips rocked against her and she could feel how hard he was beneath his jeans, rutting against the ache between her legs, giving her the intense pressure she craved.

The sudden opening of her bedroom door cut straight through all the need and desire and intensity between them as Jett's voice boomed into the room, "Who's ready to get their taco on? Aye-aye-aye!" Then realizing what he'd walked in on, "Oh my *God!* Put a damn sock on the door!"

"Whoa, sorry guys," came Chris's low, much quieter voice.

"*Shh! Jett!*" Raelyn whisper-yelled. "You think my parents would be okay with my door being shut if they knew about us?" She gestured between herself and Quinn as he rolled off of her with a heavy sigh.

"Jett, you really need to learn to knock, dude," said Quinn, reaching a hand down to adjust himself. He was visibly hard through the denim of his jeans and Raelyn's skin heated at the sight of it pressing against his zipper.

"And *you* really need to do something about your one-eyed trouser snake, bud," Jett replied casually, taking a seat in Raelyn's desk chair.

"Could you just...not?" said Quinn, sitting himself up to lean against the many pillows at the head of the bed.

"Don't like that one?" Jett questioned. "How about hardwood?"

"Tent pole," Chris added, sitting in the cushioned chaise lounge in the corner.

"Stiffy,' Jett continued.

"Boner- always a classic," said Chris.

"Love stick."

"Hard-on."

"Ramrod."

"Pocket rocket," Raelyn contributed, earning her an amused sideways glance from Quinn.

"Chubby," Chris said.

"Lieutenant Dangle!" Jett called out in his best Forrest Gump impression.

"Louisville Slugger!"

"The ol' custard slinger," Raelyn winked and shot finger guns.

"Aghh, Rae, too far! *Too* far!" Jett shouted as he and Chris cringed.

Raelyn bowed and waved her hands with a flourish. "Thank you, thank you, I'll be here all week."

"Thanks for finishing that, Rae," said Quinn. "I feel like that could've gone on all night."

Raelyn stood up off the bed and straightened her t-shirt and blue jean shorts. Shooting Quinn a mischievous grin over her shoulder she remarked, "Hm, I wonder if you'll be saying that again later."

Quinn's face went red as he grinned, eyes glinting back at her. Chris and Jett erupted in groans and shouts of disgust, causing both Raelyn and Quinn to laugh.

"Too far again, Rae," Jett shook his head, "Damn, girl."

"I think he means *daaayum, girl*," Quinn said with a wink.

Raelyn leaned over the edge of the bed and planted a kiss on his lips. In a high, dainty, southern belle accent, she announced to the room, "Now if you boys will excuse me, I have to go powder my nose," and ambled to the door and across to the bathroom.

Graduation was the following morning, and Raelyn's dad had been generous enough to reserve three rooms at Grand Traverse Resort for Raelyn and her friends to celebrate the end of their high school careers. She may have told him there would be more people joining than there really were so that he would reserve a third room. There were only four boys and four girls, which put the rooms at capacity, but the third room was for her and Quinn. Where they would stay together. And sleep together. And make good on their pact.

At this point, the pact seemed somewhat inconsequential. She still wanted to do it, but not just because they'd made the agreement months ago. The chemistry between her and Quinn was intense. Fiery. Explosive. She wanted all of him in the worst way. And she was more and more certain that with each hot and heavy make-out session, he wanted it too. Not just the sex, but she felt like he really wanted *her.* In the same way she wanted him. The possessive way he always had to have a hand on her, the way his mouth felt like a territorial claim, she felt...coveted by him.

It was more than just physical, she *knew* it was. So, after they'd had their intimate, romantic night together, she would tell him about Arizona. She would tell him that if he wanted her to, which she was sure he did now, she would go with him. And she would be his and he would be hers and they would be there for each other just as they had for the past eleven years.

Back across the hall, the sounds of low, intentionally hushed but vehement male voices came from the other side of her bedroom door that was cracked just slightly. She pushed her door open, and all three boys looked in her direction, silently, having immediately ended whatever discussion or argument they'd been having.

Raelyn looked from Quinn to Jett to Chris, and back to Quinn, one eyebrow arched curiously. She took a breath and opened her mouth and paused before speaking. She was tempted to ask what they had been arguing about that had to do with her. They got in surprisingly heated arguments about sports or movies or superheroes every now and then, but they wouldn't end an argument over whether Wonder Woman or Poison Ivy would win a wet t-shirt contest just because Raelyn walked in the room. Quinn gave a tight-lipped smile and looked away, smoothing his hair down anxiously.

The fact that Quinn was avoiding eye contact and Jett had yet to break the awkward silence made her feel like she'd better wait and ask

Quinn about it in private. Storing this astonishingly uncomfortable moment in her brain for later, she then asked, "Jett, didn't you say something about tacos?"

Saturday evening arrived: They walked the stage, collected their diplomas, sat through the corny, life-inspiring speeches, and took pictures in the school's courtyard in front of the T.C. West High School sign. Raelyn's parents had followed Chris's and Jett's parents to take pictures of the boys on the baseball and football fields and had taken them all out to lunch.

Raelyn and Quinn had been having fun sneaking kisses all day while her parents weren't looking, though Camille had definitely caught them at least once. Raelyn made a zipper motion over her lips and Camille had repeated it, miming locking and throwing away the key. Her sister was a huge gossip, and had absolutely no trouble spilling people's deepest secrets, but she was a good big sister and knew better than to share this admittedly huge secret before Raelyn was ready for it to be out.

Having checked in to the resort and dropped their bags in their respective rooms, they all gathered in one room to go over everything the resort had to offer. There was a full spa, a pool and hot tub, a golf course, tennis courts, and of course, the beach. The girls all opted to try spa packages, with massages and the sauna while the guys went to the pool.

After her relaxing spa experience, Raelyn went back up to the room that held only her and Quinn's bags. She showered and got dressed before meeting the girls back in their room, which was a fog of hairspray and perfume by the time Raelyn got there. The girls all got cute for dinner and dancing. The resort's restaurant was in a large hall with floor to ceiling windows that overlooked Lake Michigan. That night, the reception hall that was frequently used for weddings was open for dancing with a DJ. It would be like a mini-prom, which Raelyn was looking forward to since they had missed theirs.

Once the girls and guys met up again, Raelyn and Quinn couldn't keep their hands off each other. Quinn's arm constantly draped over her shoulders, or his hands found hers. Raelyn let her hands scratch up and down his back lazily as they sat down for dinner, and his hand rested on her leg at the hem of her skirt, letting his fingertips trail just under it. Raelyn glanced down at his hand and back up at his face. He grinned, one side of his mouth pulling up farther than the other, displaying that dimple of his. Her heartbeat picked up and she blushed, feeling goosebumps cover her skin.

They ate. They kissed. They danced. They kissed some more. They had quiet, head-to-head conversations about the upcoming summer, their plans to be together every day until Quinn had to leave for school. Their lips came together, over and over, becoming more heated, their breaths coming in heavy and gasping and greedy at the very thought of having to live so far away from each other for so long.

Her arms wrapped around the back of Quinn's neck as he held her close, and she rested her forehead against his as he bowed his head. She could feel the heat of his breath on her lips. Her words came out breathless as she looked into his golden, honey-brown eyes, "Should we...?"

Quinn's Adam's apple bobbed as he swallowed. He licked his lips, and his breath came out shuddering as he nodded, "Sure." His breath hitched when Raelyn smiled up at him and pressed her lips to his again. His arm curled possessively around her waist as he guided her out of the hall and to the elevator.

On the way up to their room, Quinn kept his arm around her, skating his hand up and down her side, dipping just below her hip bone and back up. Raelyn let her finger slip into the belt loop of his jeans, keeping him closer still. Her heart was pounding, her pulse fluttering with nerves and excitement and anticipation. She felt the butterflies return to her stomach and chest that were always there when he swept his tongue into her mouth and found hers. Attempting to ease her nerves, she let out a long sigh and rested her head against his chest, closing her eyes and breathing in his familiar scent.

This feels right. It's Quinn. And me. We're best friends and he wouldn't do anything to hurt me. He's the right person to do this with.

Quinn bent down to press a kiss to the top of her head, resting there for a few moments until the elevator dinged and the doors slid open.

He took her hand in his and brought it to his lips to kiss before leading her to their hotel room. Raelyn didn't miss the tremor in his hands as he dug out and swiped the key card. He pushed the door open and held it for her to walk through.

Looking around, she took in the beautiful, romantic space before them. The room had one wall of floor-to-ceiling windows, and the adjacent wall boasted a king-sized bed with a fluffy white down comforter covered in red rose petals. There was a small iPod speaker on the nightstand next to a shallow, silvery glass bowl.

Raelyn chuckled when she saw that the dish was filled with a variety of condoms. She wandered over to the nightstand and picked a few of the packets out of the dish. "Looks like we're supposed to find out what sensations we like the most." She smiled back at Quinn who was standing near the foot of the bed. "When did you set this all up?"

"I had help," he replied. "Brandi, Melanie, and Heather decorated the room. But I," Quinn walked over to the nightstand next to Raelyn and pushed the button on the iPod that was docked into the speaker, "made the playlist."

The slow, smooth, familiar tunes played out of the speaker and Raelyn's face lit up. "Hey, I always said this would be a great song to have sex to."

"I know," Quinn nodded, biting his lip shyly. "You mentioned a few, actually. I thought maybe you were hinting at me to take notes. So I did. Literally, I wrote them in a pocket notebook."

Raclyn's grin grew wider. "That might be the cutest thing I've ever heard." She took both his hands and pulled him close and their lips gravitated toward one another.

They parted for a moment while Quinn glanced toward the large open windows. "Hang on," he said, and crossed the room to find the remote that controlled the black-out curtains that rolled down from the top of the windows. After a few tries, he found the right buttons to roll the large curtains down, and it suddenly felt as if they were the only two people in the world.

Impatient and needy, she met him at the end of the bed where their bodies crashed together and he kissed her again, slipping his tongue between her lips with a groan. She let her hands roam over his shoulders, down his chest and stomach, and back up. Within a minute, their desperate gasps and heavy breaths had returned as they got lost in each other's touch and scent and tastes and sounds. Still standing, they were grinding against each other, into one another, needy, craving, and possessive.

Raelyn slid her hands beneath the hem of Quinn's shirt, grasping desperately as she pulled it over his head. She gazed at his bare chest and stomach, eyes hungry as she slowly ran her hands down his body, feeling each warm, rippled muscle beneath her touch.

When Quinn reached behind her for the zipper of her dress, he suddenly slowed. Their lips parted and the tension and heat still buzzed between them, but he made sure to pull the zipper all the way down her back in a measured, deliberate motion. He pushed the sleeves off her shoulders and down her arms, and Raelyn was mesmerized at the sight of him watching her. Undressing her. His eyes were glazed over with desire as he drank her in. Quinn finished pushing the dress down over her hips, letting it pool on the floor at her feet.

Raelyn stood in front of him in her lavender lace bra with her matching boyshort panties. His chest rose and fell steadily as he stared at her, taking in her body before him. She watched as his eyes swept over her from head to toe and back up. His gaze hovered at her chest for a few beats before sliding back up to her face.

The look on Quinn's face was so much more than lust. Raelyn could see the same longing in his eyes that she felt throughout her entire body. He took a breath in and let it out, long and steady and slow. "Rae…" his voice was barely a whisper, and there was a low, husky quality that she'd never heard from him in the eleven years they'd known each other.

She wanted him to always speak to her like that, like she was the only girl in the world, his everything, his center. And she felt possessive and covetous and greedy with the knowledge that she was the only one who had heard him like this. The only one he'd ever looked at the way he was right now.

Wanting more of this from him, Raelyn reached behind her back and, with surprisingly steady hands, unclasped her bra. She watched as it fell to the floor, then slowly lifted her gaze back up to Quinn's face from beneath her lashes. His eyes darkened with desire and he bit his lip, as if he could contain the deep, needy growl that escaped him.

He reached his hand out for her, brushing her forearm with his fingertips, "Come here." Raelyn let him pull her in and close the gap between them. He wrapped his arm around her and held her close, as one hand slid from her hip to her breast. Gently caressing her soft, light skin, he dipped his head low and she met his lips with a slow, deep kiss.

Raelyn's hands found Quinn's belt and worked to unbuckle, unbutton, and unzip his jeans, and pushed them to the floor. He fumbled just slightly as he stepped out of his shoes, his socks, his pants, then regained himself as he backed her up to the bed. She lay back and grasped at his hands, urging him to fall over her.

With him on top of her, they fell into the new rhythm that they'd learned over the past week. Sliding up further on the bed so her head was resting against the pillows, she felt Quinn's body press into hers, the weight of him familiar and reassuring. Comforting. It was the first time they'd had so little between them as his hips rocked into her, feeling his hardness rub against the sensitive ache between her thighs.

Dear God, it felt so good. The thin lace of her panties and the cotton of his boxers was all that separated them now. Nearly self-conscious of the moisture accumulating between her legs, she reminded herself that it was a good thing.

It's the same as him being hard as a rock right now...I'm turned on, this feels good, fuck *does it feel good, and it'll make it better for both of us.*

Quinn was propped up by his forearms on either side of her, kissing and sucking the skin of her neck, trailing his mouth to her breasts. He teased and traced one nipple with his tongue before covering it with his hot, wet mouth. Raelyn arched her back and moaned at the sensation.

More, she wanted more. Needed more. More touch, more heat, more wet. More of him and his scent and his sounds. *Dear god,* she wanted him inside her. She had never had such an intense craving. She wanted him to become a part of her.

She felt as his hand slipped down her body, between her breasts, down her stomach, over her navel, and beneath the lace of her panties. There was a moment's hesitation before he continued lower, before slowly and gently sliding his finger down her center, feeling her wet crease.

"Oh my God, Rae," Quinn groaned into the smooth skin of her breast. "You're so perfect, oh my God…"

At his praise, she rolled her hips up to him, begging him to enter, begging to feel him inside her. To relieve the ache and this hot-blooded need for him. She whimpered, "Quinn, please…"

Quinn lifted his head, meeting her gaze, and she saw again the same fierce need reflected in his eyes that she was feeling everywhere. Every limb, every nerve, every cell of her body needed him.

Finally, mercifully, Quinn slid a long, firm finger into her. She let her head fall back with a moan, closing her eyes. His lips covered hers and she was moaning and gasping into his mouth as he pumped his finger into her, slow and sure, getting her used to the sensation. Raelyn grasped at his shoulders, digging her fingernails into his skin as she moaned, biting her lip as Quinn's mouth pressed kisses along the line of her jaw.

Extra pressure came between her hips as he added another long finger. Raelyn's eyes closed, her mouth opened with a silent cry of pleasure. She could feel how tightly she was wrapped around him, and *god*, if this is how his fingers felt…

She was suddenly acutely aware of his hard cock pressing against her thigh as he worked to get her ready for him to fill her completely. He was *not* small by any means. But Quinn wouldn't let it hurt. He'd be gentle and make sure she enjoyed it just as much as he did.

The most amazing pleasure sent a shock through her body as he lightly swiped the pad of his thumb over her clit and she couldn't help thrusting her hips, making his fingers go deeper, letting each and every touch take over.

She couldn't imagine a more perfect first time. A more perfect person to be with. It just made sense. How had they not realized it before? They could've been together like this all through high school. Kissing and touching, making love. Is that what this was? This was more than just sex, right? It sure as hell felt like it. At least they could be like this all next year. In Arizona. She was definitely going to Arizona now.

She couldn't possibly stay away from him after this. And she was sure he was feeling this connection, too.

Quinn's lips met hers again as he continued his soft, slow strokes of his fingers, the circling of his thumb around her clit. She was ready. She needed him now.

"Quinn," Raelyn breathed when their lips parted for a beat, "Quinn, I'm ready...please, I want you now."

His growl vibrated into her as he slipped his fingers beneath the waistband of her panties, and he pushed them down. He sat up, chest heaving, and worked his boxers off, and *dear God*, he was ready, too.

"Should we get under the covers?" Quinn's low, gravelly voice made her even more impatient.

Raelyn nodded and they quickly got beneath the sheets and comforter, and Quinn lay on top of her again. Fully naked. They were both completely naked. Not a thing between them. And she swore nothing ever felt more natural than the two of them in this moment. The corner of her lips pulled up in a small smile as she looked up at him. She wanted to say something, to tell him how perfect this was, to let him know she couldn't have asked for a better person to be with, or a better best friend. Instead, she kissed him and wrapped her arms around the back of his neck, pushed her fingers into his hair and held him tight.

"Did you grab the...?" Raelyn asked, gesturing generally toward the nightstand with the dish of condoms.

Quinn brought a hand up, smirking as he held the condom between his index and middle finger. Raelyn bit her lip as she smiled back and, for the first time, reached down to feel his hard cock that was pressing into her thigh. He let out a low groan at her touch, burying his face in her neck as she softly stroked up and down his length. His skin was soft, but he was hard and long, thick and warm.

She felt the soft, wet kisses he was pressing into her neck, and she rolled her hips into his again. "Quinn, please," she breathed into his hair, "I want you, Quinn, *oh God*..." He brushed his fingertips across her clit again and slid a finger back into her.

After a few more strokes in and out, Quinn pushed away, up onto his knees as he fumbled with the condom packet. His fingers trembled slightly, and Raelyn found it actually sweet that he was a little nervous. He looked down at her, sweeping his gaze down her bare body and there was no doubt he was craving her.

His eyes met hers again. His brow furrowed. He swallowed hard. Then bit his lip. He let out a heavy sigh and his expression changed, "Rae…" Quinn lay back on top of her and pressed his forehead to hers, "Rae, baby, I have to tell you something…"

She couldn't help smiling at him calling her *baby*.

Is it that this evening has been perfect?

Is he going to point out that he's on top of me completely naked and we've been friends for eleven years and this should be weird but totally isn't? The only weird thing about it is how it's not weird at all?

Is he going to tell me he doesn't want to go to Arizona without me? Because I have a big surprise if that's the case…

There was a long pause as Quinn simply breathed, eyes closed, resting his head on hers. "Rae, I haven't…I haven't been completely…honest," his voice shook as he spoke, but he continued, "about the…pact."

"The pact?" Raelyn repeated, blinking. *Did the pact still matter?*

"Yeah, I…" he lifted his head and sat up a little. "I lied. I'm not a…I…I've had sex before. This, um…this isn't my first time."

Raelyn blinked and she swore time around her stopped. Or maybe it was more like it started back up again. They'd been in their own world and suddenly with these words, this confession, the rest of the living world was intruding on their moment. They'd crashed into some weird alternate reality where her best friend…had *lied* to have sex with her?

She processed what he said. The individual words and what they meant. That for the past nine months, every time Raelyn had asked him if he'd been with anyone or if they were still on for the pact, he had an opportunity to come clean and chose not to. She stared up at him, with one eyebrow cocked in confusion as though he were speaking a different language. As she contemplated what to say, how to respond, Quinn continued speaking.

"I'm sorry, Rae, I just…I know this was more for you…you wanted it to be special and, I mean, I've wanted this for *so* long. Us, I mean.

God, I've dreamt about this so many times, Rae. I couldn't believe you wanted...with *me*...but...and we still can. I can still," he lifted his hand with the condom in it. "I just thought I should tell you first. I didn't want...I thought you should know."

Again, Raelyn processed this new information, peering up at him through narrowed eyes as though he were a complete stranger. *We can still have sex if I want? If it will make me feel better, he'll still fuck me so I can at least say I lost my virginity? What a fucking gentleman...*

Opening her mouth to speak, she closed her eyes and let the first thought pop out from the tornado of dizzying questions and angry comments that were now buzzing around inside her head, "Why...did you lie in the first place? Because you just wanted to have sex with me?"

"What? No," Quinn's eyes widened with panic. "No, that's not what I meant. I mean, I have wanted you for a long time, but-"

"So you just thought, 'hey, if I pretend to be a virgin I can screw my best friend and we'll both be happy?'"

"Technically, I never actually *said* that I was a virgin...you asked if sex gets casual after your first time and I said I didn't know, because I only had sex once, so..." Quinn trailed off.

"So, because you lied by omission you thought it was okay?" Raelyn challenged.

Quinn ran both hands through his hair anxiously. "That's exactly what Chris said..."

"Chris?" Raelyn snapped. "Chris knows about this?"

"Well, I kind of...yeah, I told them about our...the pact...on the bus ride home from the state championship game." He looked like he was talking more to himself than Raelyn at this point, "They told me I needed to tell you the truth, and then every time we hung out just the two of us, you'd start kissing me before I could say anything. And then I couldn't say anything because...I just wanted to keep kissing you."

Suddenly feeling completely bare and vulnerable, Raelyn attempted to cover her breasts by laying one arm across her chest. "So...let me get this straight, Quinn," her eyes were piercing as she looked up at him where he still knelt between her legs. Only moments ago her body was warm and wet and eager, and now was cold and rigid. "You let me believe you'd never had sex so that we could have our first time together, only not really. And you continued to lie all year. We see each other *every* day. You could have told me any time and chose to keep it from me. And *now* you tell me the only reason you're coming clean at all is because Chris and Jett told you it was shitty to lie to your best friend of eleven years? Just to get in her panties?"

"Rae, no, that's…"

"Is that all this was for you?" Raelyn's voice was getting higher and louder. "The stupid pact?"

"The pact was *your* idea, Rae," said Quinn. "I just wanted to be with you-"

"So tell me you want to be with me!" She was shouting now. "Don't lie to me!"

"Fine, I want to be with you," he said the words so fast, it nearly sounded like one word.

Gesturing to their naked bodies in bed together, she scoffed, "Yeah, I see that." Still holding an arm over her chest, she slid out from under Quinn and flung her feet over the side of the bed. She felt the burn of tears behind her eyes and had to avoid his gaze. Forgetting about her undergarments, she found her skater dress and stepped into it, pulling it back on.

"Rae, no, come on," he climbed off the bed and grabbed her arm to pull her toward him. "Baby, come on, this week has been so amazing. I'm sorry, I'm so, so sorry. None of this came out how I meant. I just couldn't do it knowing I hadn't been totally honest with you. But now I've told you and we can go from there."

"Go from there?" she repeated, incredulous. "Gee, Quinn, I'm flattered that you're still willing to make all my dreams come true by *fucking* me tonight-" she caught the way he winced as she said this, "-but I don't need you to do me any favors." She yanked her arm out of his grip and turned away from him. The burning behind her eyes was winning out and the tears were welling up in her eyes

"Please, Rae, don't…I didn't mean it like that, *fuck*," Quinn fisted his hair as he watched Raelyn grab her things.

"I know how you are with girls, Quinn, but I thought at least I might be different," Raelyn said around the lump in her throat. She needed to leave. She needed to be gone, away from here, away from the scene where she discovered the truth about her so-called best friend. The one person she just knew she could trust above anyone else.

"You *are*, Rae," Quinn said, his voice pleading. Raelyn ignored the desperation in his tone as she slipped her sandals back on by the door. "Rae, you're *all* I've wanted since-"

"All you've wanted?" Raelyn shot back, glaring at him from over her shoulder. She shook her head as the first tears spilled down her face. Quinn reached for her again and she pulled out of reach. "Quinn, don't." She couldn't look at him. Didn't want to be near him.

Pushing her fingers back through her hair, she tried to think of something to say, but there was nothing. Absolutely nothing that could fix this. Nothing that could make her feel better about his lie. Nothing that could change how foolish she felt for thinking this was more for both of them. She let out a shaky sigh and shook her head again. Without looking back, she pulled the door open and stormed out.

CHAPTER 32

Sleep had not come easy, and it wasn't until around four or five in the morning that Raelyn had finally managed to get some rest. Still, her sleep was interrupted, tossing and turning in the unfamiliar bed.

After leaving the hotel, she'd contemplated places to go where she knew she would be left alone. She wanted to go straight back to her own house but knew that was likely the first place Quinn would have looked for her. If he'd gone looking, that is. She needed to be completely alone until she could fully grasp what she had witnessed outside Quinn's hotel room. Knowing that Amira and Brody were still on their honeymoon in Maui, she had taken advantage of the spare key Amira had made for her and slept in one of their upstairs guest bedrooms.

The queen-sized guest bed was soft and plush and in any other circumstance would likely have provided an amazing night's sleep. But Raelyn had been lost in thought after tormenting thought about Quinn and the woman leaving his hotel room. Trying to come up with alternate theories and other possible explanations than the obvious, she couldn't help coming back to the fact that Jett had dropped him off nearly two hours before Raelyn had shown up, and Quinn had been in his underwear.

It had barely registered that she'd gotten any sleep at all until the bright morning sun was shining in through the sheer curtains, making her squint awake. She yanked the covers over her head and groaned, burying her face into the pillow. The fresh pain in her chest hit her with renewed intensity as she pictured the scene from last night and ran through the fragments of conversation she had overheard.

If only she'd mentioned where they were going to get lunch, I could show up and cause a scene. Throw his drink at him, maybe even his plate. There'd probably even be a photographer around to catch it.

No, she wouldn't have done that even if she had known. She didn't want to be anywhere near that woman or Quinn right now. Especially together. Her eyes burned and her eyelids felt swollen from the lake of tears she cried throughout the night. They stung and felt dry, but she knew if she thought too much about the fact that Quinn was cheating on her...*Quinn*...cheating on *her*...the flood of tears would easily return.

If not for the fact that she had to pee at the same time every morning, she likely would have stayed in that bed all day. But her internal clock was stubborn. Slipping her feet out of the bed and sitting up slowly, she caught sight of her phone on the nightstand. She had turned it off after Quinn's first text, not wanting to be tempted to respond or call. She was sure he would continue texting, and likely call her when she didn't respond or show up. Raelyn picked up the phone and tapped her fingers on the case nervously. Pushing her hair back out of her face, she powered it on, set it back on the nightstand, and got up, making her way across the hall to the bathroom.

After washing her hands, she found a hairbrush and ran it through her tangle of hair. She wet her face with cold water and stared at herself in the mirror, trying to compose herself. Steady her breathing. Get a grip. Definitely do *not* start crying again. She swallowed hard and let out a long breath before making her way back to the bedroom to check her phone.

Quinn: Rae? You didn't fall asleep on me, did you?

Quinn: I'm so sorry I took so long, baby. I didn't mean to make you wait around on me all night.

Quinn: I just tried calling but your phone must be dead. Please call me when you get it back on. Let me know you're ok.

Quinn: Ok, baby, I called your dad and he said you took his car and haven't come home yet. Call me when you get my messages. Please.

Quinn: I've been up all night worried about you...I hope you're ok, baby. I love you.

There were also messages from her dad, and several missed calls from both her dad and Quinn. She checked a few of the voicemails: five from Quinn and two from her dad. Of course they both sounded panicked, and hearing Quinn's voice filled with worry made the tears pool at the corners of her eyes again. She blinked them back and deleted the messages. As a courtesy to her dad, she sent him a quick text: *Dad- sorry I freaked you out last night. I'm ok. I'll explain later. Love you.*

She wondered if Charlie would immediately call and bombard her with questions, or if he would text Quinn and let him know he'd finally heard from her. At that last thought, she was tempted to turn her phone back off, but simply flipped it to silent. Grabbing her overnight bag from the end of the bed, she pulled out a pair of blue jean shorts and a t-shirt, along with her change of underwear and got dressed.

She thought of the espresso machine in Amira's kitchen and the magnificent iced coffee it brewed and thought maybe she just needed a fix to get her brain working again. Raelyn shoved her phone in her back pocket and padded quietly, barefoot down the stairs, stretching and ruffling her hair. She rounded the corner into the kitchen where she stopped short with a gasp.

"What the hell are you doing here?" Raelyn snapped, a hand to her chest, startled.

"*Jesus!*" Broad and bare-chested, her ex-fiancé jumped as he turned around, spilling coffee down his front. "*Fuckin' hell!*" Emerson winced at the hot coffee now running down his stomach.

"Why are you here?" Raelyn asked, completely unremorseful about the scalding coffee burning his skin.

"What the fuck? When did you come in?" Emerson grabbed a couple squares of paper towel and mopped up the dripping coffee from his chest and abs.

"Last night," Raelyn replied. "I slept here."

"You slept here?" Emerson quirked an eyebrow as he looked up at her. "I slept here. How did I not notice?"

"Your car wasn't here," said Raelyn, confused.

"It's in the garage," he replied. "I've been staying here while the newlyweds are on their honeymoon. My apartment's having work done."

"Are you staying downstairs?" Raelyn asked, continuing into the kitchen and taking a seat at a bar stool around the island. The basement layout was essentially a full-sized apartment. Brody had joked about renting it to his younger brother while he saved up for a house. While Amira enjoyed Ethan's company, she hadn't been particularly enthusiastic at the idea of a house guest for an indefinite period of time.

Emerson nodded and took a sip of what was left of his coffee. She set her phone face down on the counter. "I got here around midnight. You sleep like a rock, so I'm not surprised you didn't hear me come in."

Emerson was peering at her curiously, brow furrowed, and she hadn't even thought about how she was giving away information. Now he was bound to ask...

"Why would you stay here?" He leaned cockily back against the counter. He wore only black sweatpants, slung dangerously low on his hips. There was a tattoo that looked like a knight's armor extending from his right pec, over his shoulder and down to his elbow. His shoulders were large and stacked, his chest broad and imposing, his stomach rippled and hard, all with a matching confident air that stated he knew exactly how he looked. "Not hiding from All-Star, are we?"

Raelyn nearly laughed at the irony that the first person she had the opportunity to tell about the previous night was only someone who could empathize with Quinn in this situation. She hedged, sweeping a brief look down his body, her eyes catching on the blackletter script of his tattoo before looking back at her hands. "Will you please put some clothes on? Or at least pull your pants up?"

Even his laugh was smug. "Why? Am I too distracting?" She ignored this, still not looking at him. He grinned. "It's okay, Rae. I don't mind you sexualizing me."

Turning back to him, she fumed, "I'm *not-*" He cut her off with a pointed stare and she blinked away, attention back to her fingers drumming on the quartz countertop, "I'm not talking about any of this with you."

Emerson shrugged. "Okay." He turned back around and refilled the espresso machine.

Shit, that's what I came down here for.

"You know, I might be able to help," Emerson offered. "I mean, I know what it's like to date you. I might be able to give some insight. Maybe give you an idea of what you're doing wrong."

Raelyn scoffed, "What *I'm* doing wrong?"

"Yes," Emerson replied, straight-faced, leaning against the counter again. "Believe it or not, Princess, you're not perfect. Close. But not entirely."

"Yeah, I'm aware, thank you." She rolled her eyes. "If my boobs were a cup size bigger, I'm sure that would be a good start."

"Just one cup size?" Emerson said, the corner of his lips twitching in a near smirk.

"You are such a dick." Raelyn shook her head, exasperated.

"At least I'm honest."

"Says the man who cheated on his fiancé a dozen or so times."

"A dozen?" Emerson sipped his coffee casually. "Nah, just three."

"Wow, you really suck at sneaking around then," she said, now wishing she'd made it to the espresso machine before he could make himself a refill.

Emerson nodded. "Probably the only thing I suck at." Raelyn felt him studying her for a few silent beats. Pushing himself off from the counter, he walked around and set his coffee mug down on the island, then took the bar stool next to her. "I take it All-Star sucks at it, too?"

Raelyn was staring at a swirled pattern on the countertop as she chewed the inside of her lip, trying not to let the tears fall. It felt like her heart fell into her stomach. Her eyes burned, her throat was sore with the lump that filled the center of it, and she absolutely did not want to cry in front of Emerson.

"I gotta say I'm surprised," Emerson sighed. "After hearing how crazy he's always been about you, I thought he meant it."

"Me too," Raelyn's voice came out a squeak, barely more than a whisper.

More silence passed between them. The espresso machine beeped and Emerson stood up, grabbed a glass out of the cupboard and filled it with ice. Raelyn heard him getting something out of the fridge, still focusing her gaze on that spot on the countertop. Emerson set a glass of iced coffee with just the right amount of sweet cream right on the spot where she was staring. She blinked and looked at the glass, then furrowed her eyebrows before looking at Emerson.

"I'd give you something stronger, but then we might end up sleeping together again," he said, sitting back on the seat next to her.

"You really think you're that irresistible." She took a long drink of the iced coffee. *Perfection. At least he got this part right.* "Thank you."

"So," Emerson began, looking as if he were contemplating how or if he should continue, "Why didn't you guys get together forever ago? You were best friends as kids and then...what?"

"You're seriously asking for our story?" Raelyn looked at him skeptically.

"I'm curious. I remember that time I went to your parents' house and you showed me your old room...there were pictures of you guys everywhere. And you just shrugged it off like he was some kid you knew once and now he was famous."

Raelyn remembered Emerson asking her about the boy in all her childhood pictures. She'd just said "Oh, that's Quinn." He'd spotted a picture of them at a high school baseball game and asked "Quinn *Casey?*" After confirming that she had indeed been friends with the professional athlete, he'd asked several questions.

Then he'd found the picture of them kissing at the state championship game their senior year tucked away, hiding behind a few other photos. Emerson had pulled it out and held it out to her, with a "Just friends, huh?" to which she had responded that they'd kind of dated for a week, and then he went to college and she hadn't really seen him since. Emerson had been the one to leave that picture out front where it was actually visible.

Raelyn remained silent, waiting for the iced coffee to sink in, and contemplating whether she should really say anything. She took another long, silent sip of her beverage.

"Did you catch him cheating?" Emerson pressed on, and she wondered why he was so insistent. Why did he care? What was he getting out of this?

Maybe it was the familiarity of waking up in their best friends' home and sitting down to have coffee together as they had done so many times before, or maybe it was just that she really needed to talk about it out loud, but she decided to take the bait. She sighed, "Not in the way I caught you. But I think I saw enough."

"What's enough?"

Raelyn glanced sideways at him, and after another swallow of her coffee, she explained the previous night's events. Getting too antsy to stay at home, going to the bar, then sneaking up to Jett's apartment. Finding out that Quinn had been dropped off already, and finally the scene in the hallway outside his room.

"What did he say when you confronted him?" Emerson asked, and she felt he knew exactly what he was getting at. When Raelyn didn't respond, he let out a dry laugh. "He *might* have another explanation. Maybe it just looked bad. If Amira and Brody got home early and walked in here to see us having coffee together like this, they'd probably think we hooked up last night." This was a good point, but she wasn't going to admit that to him. "Or maybe he did cheat and he'd fess up, but at least you'd know. I know your life has been next to perfect, but you can't just hide because it could hurt you."

"I don't *hide-*"

"When was the first time you spoke to me after that night?" Emerson cut in. "I get that it was a little more cut-and-dry, but still. I had to leave town for work the next day and you'd turned off your phone so we couldn't talk about it. And then when I got back you just hid in Jett's apartment for like a week."

"I didn't feel like there was anything to say," Raelyn said quietly. "I couldn't even think of what I wanted to say. And honestly, I was kind of just scared that it would escalate the way all our fighting used to. And I sure as hell didn't need that."

Emerson laughed, but it was more of a hum. "Fair point." He scratched his jaw where his beard was getting longer than he usually let it. "I still think it's a big assumption. Unless you have a reason to believe he'd do that to you…"

"I don't," she admitted, and she felt her heart squeeze tight in her chest. She thought more on what he'd said about it simply looking bad and hoped beyond all hope that's all it was.

"Has he ever hurt you before?" Emerson questioned. "Apart from acting like a dickhead when he drinks?"

Raelyn shot another sideways glance at him. "Why?"

"Why what?"

"Why are you asking? Why are you so concerned?"

"I'm not, I'm just nosey," he replied, though there was a smirk that suggested he simply wasn't willing to admit that he actually might care. Just a little. "You never told me why you guys quit talking after high school…"

She looked at him for some sign that this was a joke, but he just looked back at her, ready to listen. "I already know I'm going to regret telling you this," she said, head falling into her hands as she thought of where to begin. From the beginning? That seemed like a lot to share, and way too personal. Emerson didn't need to know all the intimate details of Quinn's life, his mother, and their friendship.

She'd give him the cliff notes version: They met when they were seven, became best friends, this continued through high school until junior year when she realized she felt more than that, but was worried about his ability to have an actual relationship. Then the pact. At this, Emerson laughed, saying it was the dumbest thing he'd ever heard.

"Come on, I had no other way to appeal to him without pouring all my feelings out, and I was terrified that it would backfire. It seemed like a good idea at the time," she said defensively, her face turning slightly pink. "You wouldn't have taken me up on it?"

"I lost my virginity at fourteen, so definitely not. I don't do virgins. Too dramatic." Emerson shook his head in absolution.

Raelyn laughed. "Well, he did. Only, he wasn't actually a virgin. So he lied to me about it until the last possible second. I mean, he was opening the condom wrapper and decided to tell me then."

Emerson let out a low whistle. "Bad move. He should've kept his mouth shut."

"He should've told me from the beginning," Raelyn insisted.

"Would you still have wanted to do it?"

"More than likely," she replied. "Well, actually, yes. I'm sure I would have. I didn't really care about the pact at that point. We'd practically been dating for a week by then and I was crazy about him. Like, ready to move across the country with him."

"So, why didn't you tell him it was more than sex to you?" Emerson asked with genuine intrigue. "Isn't it just as deceitful to have sex with him under the guise of it being 'just sex' as it was for him to do it under the guise of it being his first time? I mean, that sort of put him in a bad spot. Imagine telling him afterwards that it was more than that, and he *didn't* feel the same way. That would've been a shitty position with him being your best friend, and you would've felt like shit. It was risky to just assume he felt the same thing."

"That is not the same," Raelyn said. "And if he hadn't felt more than that...well, I would've probably been even more humiliated."

"But...you told him that's all it was."

"But he lied."

Emerson snorted. "But you didn't even care about *what* he was lying about."

Glaring intently at him, trying to ignore the point he was trying to make, she repeated, "He lied. We were best friends for eleven years and he lied." She gave him a pat on his shoulder, "I wouldn't expect you to understand how upsetting it is to be deceitful towards women when they actually think you care."

"So, how did you end up not seeing each other for so long then? You both did something stupid, but were both into each other...what happened after you talked it out?"

Raelyn looked away and bit her lip. Wow, somehow his entire point had come full circle and she was less than amused. She winced as he shook his head again before saying, "Oh my God, Rae. You fucking hid and never talked it out, didn't you? You knew you could get hurt, so you avoided it."

"I was humiliated, okay? And I just...I don't know. I was terrified at how hurt I was. I didn't want to feel like that again. If I'd talked to him and I had to hear him actually say that he didn't feel more…" she trailed off.

"Rae, just go talk to the guy," said Emerson, finishing his last gulp of coffee. "You can't just leave loose ends with someone you love that much."

Raelyn studied him for a moment, not taking her eyes off him as she tipped her glass to her lips. She set it down and looked more curiously at him, one eyebrow raised and the other furrowed just slightly. "You're weird today."

Emerson smirked. "Yeah, well, if it doesn't go well, you'll be at the bar getting drunk tonight and I'll make sure I'm there when you're ready for rebound sex."

Laughing dryly, Raelyn nodded. "*There's* the motive. I knew there was one somewhere."

"Where the hell is she?" Quinn paced back and forth in the living room of Jett's apartment. Jett and Zoey sat on the leather couch watching Quinn's panic heighten each minute that passed without hearing from Rae. "What time did she leave here last night?"

"I walked her out to her car at 11:15," Jett said, for what seemed like the hundredth time. "I walked her out, shut her car door, and watched her drive away. It shouldn't have taken her more than ten minutes to get to the hotel. Even if she had to stop and fuel up the car or…buy condoms."

Quinn fisted his hair with both hands as he groaned, "Ugh, this is my fault. I am the reason crazy people are following her. What if she stopped at the gas station and someone recognized her and…I mean, people can get obsessive. Especially over a beautiful girl like her. You wouldn't imagine the kind of creeps…" he trailed off, not wanting to think too hard about it.

When Rae hadn't responded to his text, he figured she was just going to show up. And when she didn't show up within a half hour of his first text, he thought maybe she'd fallen asleep. It was a lot later than he'd meant, after all. He had known it was going to be a late night getting back anyway, but Rae wanted to have a night alone, outside of her parents' house and he was all for it.

He and Jett tried to make their trip quick but driving on unfamiliar roads and with the recent rain over the past week, they'd managed to get stuck in the mud and had to push the massive truck out while Quinn's mom sat in the driver's seat, heavy on the gas pedal, flinging mud everywhere. Once back at the hotel, he'd swung by Zoey's hotel room, told her he needed to shower, but that they could talk and go over everything when he was out. Zoey's visit had gone long, and next thing he knew, it was nearly midnight and he hadn't had a chance to even send Rae a text.

Quinn had called Charlie first, then Amira, forgetting that she was on her honeymoon. Then he called Jett who had told him that Rae had left his place only a couple of hours earlier. When Jett said that she'd left with the plan to go straight to the hotel, the panic started. Quinn woke Zoey up, who was staying just a few rooms down from him, and told her what was going on. Once she'd dressed they'd set off for Trojan Horse, waiting in the upstairs apartment while Jett and Chris closed the bar down. Chris had hung out for a few hours but had to get home before Victoria left for work in the morning.

"Where haven't we checked? Is there anyone else we could call?" Quinn asked, impatiently tapping his phone into his hand. "Alexis at the PT office said she'd already planned to have today off, she's obviously not at her parents' house, we already checked her house. Amira's not even home, so I can't imagine why she'd be there. Camille doesn't know where she is..." He let out another frustrated groan. "Who else? Who haven't we thought to contact yet?"

He felt like it was silly to ask who might know where she was. If she was with someone she knew or somewhere safe, he was sure she would have contacted him, responded to the texts he'd sent, or called. It was eleven o'clock in the morning, about twelve hours since the last person had seen her.

"I can make some calls and get it out there that she hasn't been seen in twelve hours," Zoey offered. Quinn's publicist had all the connections to make this news available everywhere. "I know it might be a mess and will completely backfire my attempt to tamp down the publicity, but if it gets us some tips as to where she is, I think it's worth it."

Quinn nodded. "Yeah, make whatever calls you can. If she is in danger for some reason, it's best to get the news out faster."

Zoey took her phone out of her bag and stood up. Placing a comforting hand on Quinn's arm, she consoled him, "I'm sure she's okay, Quinn. We'll find her. I'm sure there's some kind of explanation."

He ran his hand through his hair and scrubbed his hands down his face. "I have to do something. I have to be out there looking or asking around, *something*. I can't just sit here and wait for her to show up."

"So let's check her friend's place," Zoey said. "I know you said they're not home, but maybe something happened and they got home early? Maybe there was an emergency or...I don't know. But it's better than sitting around here, right? And maybe while we're out we'll think of new places to look."

Jett was staring at a spot on his coffee table, bouncing his leg up and down anxiously. Having been the last one to see her, he felt bad about not doing more to make sure she got to the hotel safely. Not that there was anything he could have done or that he could have predicted that something would've gone wrong. He looked up at Quinn, seemingly interested at the prospect of having something to do. Jett got up and grabbed his keys off the kitchen counter.

"Jett, there's nothing else you could've done," Quinn reassured him when his usually boisterous and talkative friend still didn't speak. "At least you had the sense to walk her down to her car."

On the way down the stairs to Jett's truck, Quinn's phone buzzed. He paused halfway out the door into the alley to pull it out of his pocket. He gasped and swiped hastily to answer, holding a hand up to pause Jett and Zoey. "Hey, Charlie, is she home?"

"No, not yet, but I got a text from her saying that she's okay." Charlie's voice was only slightly less worried than the last time they spoke. "I called her right away and her phone is ringing now, but she still didn't answer."

Quinn sighed, frustrated. "Well that's something at least. I'll try calling again. I wonder why she didn't text me..." He pulled the phone from his ear to check that he hadn't missed anything. Both Jett and Zoey looked hopefully at him. "Did she say anything else?"

"Just that she was sorry for making us freak out, she's okay, and she would explain later," Charlie replied. "A little cryptic, but I'll take it. I'm going to stay here and hope she turns up."

"We were just about to go check Brody and Amira's place," said Quinn. "Do you think it would be best to just stay put? I'm going crazy just sitting around."

"She does have a spare key to their house," Charlie said thoughtfully. "I still don't know why she'd hide out there. You didn't do something to piss her off, did you?"

"Not that I'm aware of," Quinn said, brushing a hand through his hair again as he tried to recall anything he could've done. She wouldn't get that upset because he'd taken too long to text her. Jett said she'd seemed concerned that he hadn't contacted her yet when she'd shown up at his place, but was otherwise in a good mood when she left for the hotel.

"I didn't figure," Charlie sighed, "but it was worth checking. Last year when she found out about, ya know, that scumbag sneaking around on her, she disappeared, turned her phone off, and basically refused to talk to or see anyone for a while."

Furrowing his brow, he thought hard about if there was anything he might have done or said that would have upset her. Had an article come out about him like the one about her and Emerson? She would have known better than to believe it, though. Had she simply decided that being with him wasn't worth all the trouble after all? Maybe one of *his* crazed fans had seen the article and attacked her. Seriously, there were some nut jobs out there.

Though he couldn't think of anything he'd done recently, he suddenly felt like it was the best explanation. Or at least one he could deal with. It was better than the alternatives. Quinn remembered how impossible it was to talk to her after graduation. He'd shown up at her house the next day and she had simply refused to see him. She wouldn't come down to talk, wouldn't answer his texts or phone calls.

He had sent Chris and Jett over to try to talk for him, and they had also been unsuccessful, and explained that she wouldn't even respond to anything that had to do with him. If they talked about sports, she'd respond as if nothing was wrong. If they asked about getting ready for college, she was fine. But the second they'd mentioned Quinn, she was practically ready to kick them out. And then she'd gone to visit her dad's family in Canada for two weeks, then to France. By the time she finally agreed to see him, he was a week away from moving to Arizona.

"I'll think on it," Quinn said into the phone. "Thanks, Charlie. I'll let you know if I hear anything."

"I'll do the same," Charlie said before ending the call.

Shoving his phone back into his pocket, he continued out the door and gave Jett and Zoey a quick run-down of his conversation with Charlie. Once in the truck, Jett driving, Zoey in the middle, and Quinn in the passenger seat, he asked, "You're sure Rae wasn't pissed about me not messaging her?"

"No, she was worried," Jett replied. "Plus, there's a big difference between catching your cheating dickbag of a fiancé and forgetting to send a text."

"Yeah, that's sort of what I thought," said Quinn, staring out the passenger window. "I can't imagine Rae getting mad at me now and not coming to talk to me about it. She might talk to Amira first, but…I can't think of anything that I've done. She wasn't mad before I left."

They continued their drive and Quinn went over every detail he could possibly remember from the previous evening. Everything he and Rae had said or done. He found himself regretting how much time he'd spent on the phone with Mitch and Zoey and the coach and every other person who had called yesterday. Maybe there was something going on that he hadn't noticed because he'd been too busy.

Turning into the large suburban neighborhood where the Kalahans lived, Quinn sat up eagerly in the front seat, eyes open for the sight of Rae or Charlie's new Beamer. Brody and Amira's house was toward the end of the winding street, before turning off into a new subdivision.

Quinn breathed a sigh of relief when he saw the black Beamer parked in the driveway in front of the two-story craftsman. Already unbuckling his seatbelt, he was ready to hop out of the truck before Jett had come to a complete stop. He raced up to the front porch just as the door was opening and Rae stepped outside. His breath was even more relieved as he took in the sight of her- completely unharmed. Her hair was damp and tousled, as if she'd just taken a shower and briefly towel-dried it, and he wanted to pull her in and inhale her fresh scent and never let go.

But when she stopped to look at him, she looked surprised, and then...*hurt.*

"Hi," she said softly. "I was just coming to see you."

"Rae, thank God." Quinn tried to embrace her, but she stepped back and averted her gaze. "Baby...what's wrong? Is everything okay?"

He hated the way she was looking at him. Guarded, tentative, wounded.

"That depends." She stood up straight and her eyes were filled with challenge.

It was then that he noticed that her eyes were puffy and red. *She's been crying? Why couldn't she call me? What the hell is going on?*

"Okay? Depends on what?" Quinn studied her and knew he was about to hear the explanation. The reason she'd disappeared and had him worried sick to his stomach for the past twelve hours.

"I came to the hotel last night," she said. "Jett said he'd dropped you off hours ago, so I decided to just show up."

"You did? Are you sure you went to the right room?"

"Quinn, you weren't alone," she stated, her eyes traveling back and forth between his. She was searching for something, but he didn't understand what. "Imagine my surprise when I saw you standing in the hallway in your boxers with some other woman giving you a hug and telling you what a great time she had."

Comprehension dawned. All morning, they'd been operating under the assumption that Rae had never even made it to the hotel, but of course if she'd left Jett's when he said she had, she would've gotten there just in time to see Zoey leaving his room.

He threw his head back, grateful there was such a simple explanation. It was a misunderstanding, nothing more. "Oh my God, Rae, I'm sorry. I should've told you my publicist was coming. She was going to help manage some of the press. She stopped by my room and we lost track of time catching up. I'm sure what you saw looked bad, but I swear Zoey's not even remotely interested in me that way."

"Your publicist?" Rae questioned. "You hang out with your publicist...in your underwear?"

"Well, no, not usually. My pants were in the dryer because of all the mud."

"What the hell did you and Jett get into?"

He grinned and looked down at his feet, knowing he couldn't tell her where they'd been. "It's a long story. But Zoey is actually in the truck with Jett. You can meet her. You'll find out she doesn't really even like me that much."

Rae studied his face again and he could tell she was assessing, deciding whether or not she should believe him. Finally, her features softened and he saw the tension leave her shoulders as she sighed. "Thank God. I knew there had to be some other explanation. I just...I've heard a dozen different excuses in the past."

Quinn reached for her, slipping his arm around her waist. "Rae, I would never do that to you-"

Just then, the front door pulled open and Emerson- *Emerson?!*- stood in the doorway. In nothing but a fucking bath towel wrapped low on his hips.

"Hey Princess, I think these are yours." Emerson handed Rae a pair of black and white plaid pajama shorts that Quinn recognized as hers. "They were under the bed upstairs." Emerson then glanced at Quinn and a slow grin dragged across his face. "Mornin' All-Star."

There was a heavy silent moment in which Quinn swore time stood still. He glanced from the pair of shorts to Rae's wet hair to the towel around Emerson's hips, and that fucking smug punch-me-now face.

Rae's mouth hung open for a beat before laughing uncomfortably. "This is another example of something that just *looks* really bad."

Quinn looked at Rae, eyes narrowed as he tried to piece everything together. What the hell was *he* doing here? Had they spent the night here together? Had she been so upset when she assumed he'd cheated that she'd jumped back in bed with *that* asshole? The guy who'd already proven to her that he wasn't worthy of her trust?

"Did you guys make up?" Emerson asked. "What did I tell you, Rae? He just might have another explanation. Or at least a believable excuse."

"What the fuck are you doing here?" Quinn snapped, glaring at the man who could never seem to keep his damn mouth shut. He glanced back at Rae. "What is he doing here?"

"Apparently he's been staying here all week," she replied.

"And you stayed here last night? With him?"

"Aw, come on, All-Star. Cut her some slack. You had a lady friend in your hotel room last night."

"Nothing happened," Rae insisted. "He was already asleep when I got here and I slept upstairs."

Emerson gasped mockingly and put a hand to the large tattoo on his chest. "Rae! *Nothing? Nothing* happened? I made you iced coffee! That used to mean something to you."

Quinn's jaw clenched and he removed his arm from Rae's waist and took a step back. His hands balled into fists as he held back from finally giving that asshole the broken nose he deserved. "You talked to him about us? You told him you thought I cheated on you? That's none of his fucking business. Why are you talking to him anyway? *He's* the one who cheated, Rae. Not me. I wouldn't fucking dream of it."

He exhaled, and it felt like the wind had been knocked out of him. He shook his head and finally broke eye contact, turning around without another word.

"Quinn, wait," Rae called after him. "Quinn!" Rae's hand caught him around the elbow and she forced him to face her, but he wouldn't look at her. Instead he kept his gaze over her shoulder, on the porch where Emerson was now standing on the top step.

"Quinn, please, talk to me. You don't actually believe something happened between us, do you?" Rae said, her voice panic-stricken and already near tears.

"I don't know, Rae. I really don't. What I'm finding hard to comprehend right now is that you *confided* in him rather than confronting me." He was trying to hold onto his anger, working around the lump in his throat.

"I know, I know." Rae still held onto his arm with one hand as she pushed the other into her hair, "I panicked. I'm sorry. I know it's not how I should've reacted, but-"

Quinn scoffed. "In hindsight, you don't think it was a good idea to spend the night with your cheating ex-fiancé?"

"I didn't- no, Quinn, I didn't *spend the night with him*," said Rae defensively. "These are both misunderstandings. Neither one of us cheated, so can we just move past this?"

"Maybe you didn't cheat, but you talked to him before coming to me," Quinn stated. "You *lumped* me in with him, after everything we've been through, after all I've done to show you how much you mean to me- how much you have *always* meant to me, Rae. And you assume I'm just like him. And then you talk to him about shit that's none of his business." Taking a step back, he pulled his arm out of her grasp and shook his head in disbelief again. "I was going to take you back to L.A. with me Monday, just so you could see my- *our* home- but...I think I'll just leave by myself."

"Quinn, no, don't go," Rae pleaded. "Come on, let's talk this out. Please, I know-"

"*No*, Rae, I don't think you do," Quinn cut her off. "I don't think you have any idea how much this hurts." He dropped his gaze as her face fell, tears streaming down her cheeks. Quinn turned around and got into the back seat of the truck.

Quinn avoided Jett and Zoey's looks of concern as he slumped in his seat and scrubbed his hands down his face. He thought about how he'd spent the entire previous day working to fit Rae into his life in L.A., and their plans to spend their futures together. He took a shaky breath in before grumbling to Zoey, "Find the next flight home. We're leaving today."

428

CHAPTER 33

By Monday evening, Raelyn was feeling good about her plans that she'd worked out over the weekend. She was back in her own house with Harry, and though it felt completely empty without Quinn, she was grateful for the solitude while she figured out how she was going to make this right. She hadn't wallowed or hid away from what happened Friday morning. She was simply determined to get to work on each and every detail to make sure she was successful when she went to Los Angeles to get Quinn back.

It had been a long weekend, having to explain everything to her dad, and even explain in further detail to both Jett and Chris exactly what had led to her being alone with her ex-fiancé that morning. Jett had stormed into her house, shouting in his stern disappointed-dad voice that he'd completely mastered, and she wasn't too ashamed to admit that she cried her whole way through the story. Jett didn't typically get uncomfortable with tears- he was the guy who comforted his younger sisters through all their breakups- but seeing Raelyn cry was a whole different story. He'd toned down his intensity almost immediately.

While they understood why she had jumped to that conclusion upon seeing Quinn and Zoey in the hallway, especially given her previous experience with similar situations, they agreed she should have been able to knock on his door and confront him. And that's exactly why she was no longer running from her problems. She was prepared to face this head-on.

Every morning and every night at the same time, Raelyn tried calling Quinn. She wanted to explain, she wanted him to know that she knew she was in the wrong. She wanted him to know that she had also been making plans for their future together, and *dammit*, she just wanted to hear his voice again. But each call would ring until it went to voicemail. Each *good morning* text went unanswered, and each *goodnight, I love you* was also met with stony silence. This didn't deter her, though. If anything, it made her more determined to fix the giant mess she'd made.

All of Raelyn's appointments for the next few days had been rescheduled, her bags were packed, and her plane ticket was ready. On Tuesday morning, Charlie, Raelyn, and Harry were in her Jeep, heading to Detroit Metro where she would board her nearly five-hour flight to LAX. It wasn't Harry's first time on a plane, and being a certified therapy dog, he got to sit in first class with Raelyn, but he did still require doggie Xanax to get through the flight.

"Got everything you need?" Charlie asked, as Raelyn grabbed her bags and Harry's leash in the drop-off lane.

"Yep." Raelyn nodded.

"Plane ticket? License? Wallet? Phone? Resume?" Charlie listed.

"All of the above."

"Okay, good," he said as Raelyn leaned over the passenger seat to give him a quick kiss on the cheek. He then turned to her, his expression sincere. "Now, no matter what happens, Rae, I love you. But don't come back until you've got my future son-in-law in tow. I don't care if you have to put Harry's leash on him and drag him back as a carry-on."

Raelyn's eyebrow twitched upward. "That could be fun."

Charlie scowled. "Raelyn Elise, that's...just gross. But whatever works."

"Love you, Dad," she said, smiling as she closed the door.

It was just after noon, Pacific Time, when Raelyn landed at LAX. The three-hour time difference had allowed her to take a slightly later flight and still get to her interview with time to check in to her hotel, get dressed, and get something to eat. Her hotel had a gorgeous view of the ocean, and as much as she would have loved to sit on the balcony with Harry and stare out at the water, she had places to be, so the view would have to wait. She was hopeful she'd only be staying one or two nights in the room, but there was a lot riding on both her interview and Quinn's reaction to her showing up unannounced.

At 4:30, she met with the Director of Player Health as well as the head and assistant athletic trainers. The meeting was set up to be intimidating, with Raelyn at one end of a long table, while the director and trainers sat at the other end grilling her about her professional experience, offering different hypothetical situations, and asking about her intentions to stay with the team. Their team's physical therapist had taken up a position with the Rays in Florida because of the proximity to his family, and with Raelyn being from Michigan, it was a concern that they felt necessary to address.

Then, of course, there was the matter of Quinn Casey, their star hard-hitter and alternate pitcher. They had all been impressed with his recovery thus far and were confident he'd be able to re-join during the next year, even if it was in the middle of the season. They had asked several questions regarding his specific condition, and what she recommended for his next steps. The Director of Player Health was strongly adamant that he continue therapy with her, as she clearly knew what his condition was from the beginning.

Near the end of the interview, the head coach of the team entered the room, beaming as he set his eyes on Raelyn sitting at the far end of the table.

"Dr. DeRose, isn't it?" He grinned as he walked over to shake her hand. "I've been looking forward to meeting you in person." He turned to address the men sitting at the other end of the table, "This is the woman who's going to keep our star player up and running *and* out of trouble, if I heard correctly."

"Well, I've known him since we were seven and he still managed to get himself in trouble a handful of times back in the day," Raelyn replied with a grin. "Though I have noticed tremendous progress on that punching reflex of his."

The coach chuckled, "Yeah, he's a bit of a hot head, our guy. I bet he's excited you're here."

"Actually, he doesn't know," said Raelyn quickly.

The coach and former outfielder nodded, "Well, I'll hold off on making him sign certain forms given the unique circumstances here then."

Raelyn tried not to smile too wide at the implication that they'd already made up their minds. *Well, Quinn had better forgive me then. Otherwise this is going to get weird.*

After a few more questions and friendly conversational exchanges, she shook hands with everyone again, telling them she looked forward to hearing from them soon. Leaving the stadium and clubhouse, she felt both more confident and more anxious than when she'd arrived.

Back in the hotel, she changed into a set of exercise clothes and running shoes, hooked Harry to his leash and took off for a run on the beach. There wasn't a whole lot more she could do until she received a call from the director. And who knew how long it would take for them to deliberate? Running would clear her head, and it would also keep her from making the rash decision to go straight to Quinn's place. She was sure the urge to do so would only intensify once she got back to her hotel room, alone, and began running through various scenes of her showing up on his doorstep, and Quinn pulling her inside for hours of wild make-up sex.

He was genuinely upset and had every right to be. This wasn't something she could fix with sex.

I mean…it couldn't hurt…

No, no, I have a plan I need to stick to.

Raelyn ordered room service and ate dinner on her balcony, also ordering an extra grilled chicken breast for Harry to devour. At 7:00, she was hesitant about whether or not she should try calling Quinn like she had every other evening since Friday, but opted against it. Knowing she was in the same city, she'd be too tempted to head straight over when he didn't answer. And what if he *did* answer? What would she say to him? She sucked at keeping secrets and would be sure to tell him she was in L.A., which she just wasn't ready for him to know yet.

At 10:30 when she slipped under the covers and Harry hopped onto the foot of the bed, she sent him the usual text: *Goodnight, I love you.* Plugging her phone into the charger, she set it down on the nightstand and clicked the lamp off. Not ten seconds passed before her phone lit up and dinged. She propped herself up on one elbow and checked her new message.

Quinn: Late night? You didn't call.

Raelyn thought for a moment before she remembered the three-hour time difference. She always texted him at 10:30 from Michigan, which was 7:30 in California. *Shit.* Well, it was a hell of a lot easier to keep her poker face through text. Re-reading his text, she couldn't help the swell in her chest that he not only received her texts and calls, but he maybe even looked forward to them. Even if he didn't respond, he waited for them. Raelyn smiled and sent back: *Long day. Were you planning on answering this time?*

Nearly a full minute passed before his response came through: *Probably not.*

Shaking her head, she sent back: *So stubborn. Now quit screwing with my routine. Goodnight, Quinn. I love you.*

It wasn't until morning that she read Quinn's responding text that he'd sent several minutes after her last: *I loved you first.*

"You're meeting with the trainer at the stadium at ten, and then there's a meeting inside the clubhouse with the whole team," Zoey rattled off as she scrolled through her phone.

"A trainer, but no physical therapist?" Quinn questioned. He was back at his house- his very large, very empty house- in his living room, working on some of the exercises Rae had gone over with him at their last PT session. He was officially out of the six-week phase, which meant he no longer needed a brace and could start strengthening his rotator cuff and scapula muscles.

Without looking up from her phone she replied, "You left your PT in Michigan, remember?"

"There are therapists here," said Quinn, stubbornly.

He was partially regretting his moment of weakness the previous night when he'd responded to Rae's text. It was late, he was in bed by himself, thinking about how much he missed pressing up against her shape at night, and curling his body around hers. He'd been annoyed when his phone hadn't rung at 4:00, and again when he hadn't received the usual goodnight text at 7:30. He was worried she was done trying to contact him after his silent treatment. When she'd refused to talk to him all summer after their senior year, he still called, texted, and showed up at her house regularly. He hadn't given up on her, and he panicked a little, both hurt and a bit angry, when he thought she'd already given up on him after a few days. The thought that maybe she had decided to go back to Emerson after all had him grinding his teeth, brooding, and being unnecessarily short with Zoey before she'd left for the night.

"But only one who knows where you're at with your progress," Zoey said, still looking at her phone.

"Yeah well, some things just don't work out how we want them to," Quinn sighed.

"You're being stupid," Zoey said bluntly.

"Oh, am I?"

"Yes. You finally get the woman you've wanted your entire life and you come back here *without* her?" Zoey replied. "You ignore her calls and walk around brooding all day. Just answer your damn phone and make it right."

Quinn let out a groan of frustration. "You were there, Zoey. So was she- *and* her half-naked ex-fiancé."

"You know just as well as I do that nothing happened between them," Zoey said, with an exasperated eye roll. "She got upset when she saw us in what appeared to be a compromising position- and quite frankly, *Quinn Casey*, with your reputation, I really don't blame her."

"You don't?" He glared.

"Speaking as the person who rushes in with fake emergencies so your one-night stands don't stay the night? No, no I don't."

Quinn looked at her through narrowed eyes as he contemplated his response. He watched as her phone screen lit up, she read something, then giggled and bit her lip at whatever message she'd just received. "Who are you texting?"

Zoey looked up at him for a beat, quickly wiping her smile off her face. "Just making more appointments," she responded quickly. Too quickly.

"You giggled," Quinn held his arm at a forty-five degree angle, dumbbell in hand. Slowly lowering it, he took a couple steps toward her and craned his neck to try seeing her phone screen.

"I did *not*," Zoey replied defensively. "I don't giggle."

Quinn eyed her suspiciously. "Not usually, but you just did. *And* you bit your lip. You're flirting with someone."

Zoey stared back at him, mouth open. "I have had a lot of time to myself over the last month, not having to follow you around and clean up your messes. I'm a young woman, and I am single, so I don't see why you're so surprised that I could flirt with someone."

"What's his name?" Quinn asked, a grin curling up his lips. "We spent all that time talking about me and my now-failed relationship. Why didn't you say you were seeing anyone?"

She broke eye contact with him briefly before saying, "You didn't ask."

"Wow, you're right. We only ever talk about me." Quinn sat down in the chair next to the sofa where she was curled up. "I'm sorry, I feel so selfish now. Tell me about him...what's he like? Where'd you meet? Was he upset that I stole you away to a different state?"

"It's...really new. There's not much to tell. It's...It may not even be anything. We *just* met. I just...It's probably nothing anyway," Zoey stuttered and stumbled over her words.

"You just met? But you said you had a whole month while you weren't..." Quinn trailed off, peering curiously at her. His eyes widened and he grinned. "No...wait...Let me see your phone."

"No!" Zoey pulled her phone close to her chest. "It's private."

"Are you sexting?"

"*No!* Oh my gosh, Quinn," Zoey squealed. "I'm allowed to keep things private from you."

"You know everything about me," Quinn reasoned.

"Yeah, because it's literally my job."

Quinn lunged forward and began wrestling her phone out of her hand. She tried prying his fingers off and shoved him back. Quinn cried out in pain and Zoey gasped, loosening her grip as she turned her attention to his injured elbow. "Oh, no! I'm sorry! Are you okay?"

Quinn snatched the phone with its gold, sparkly case out of her hand with a smirk. "Wrong arm, Mamacita."

She stared back at him, incredulous. "Ugh, *that's* just...oh, you play dirty, Quinn Casey!"

He grinned, turning around and looking down at her phone screen as it lit up with another message. Zoey tried grabbing it out of his hand again and he held it way above her head. He looked at it from that angle, holding it high in the air. "Oh, would you look at that? New message from *Jett Miller!*"

Zoey blushed slightly as she looked away. "Okay, but don't tell him I said it was anything. Because it's not. We've just been texting since we got back...and he's...funny. I enjoy talking to him, okay? But that's all it is."

"Your secret's safe with me," Quinn said, and made the zip-the-lips motion across his mouth and handed her phone back to her. "Are you a virgin?"

"I'm sorry, *what?* No, Quinn, I'm twenty-four years old, I'm not a virgin!" Zoey snapped.

"You're only twenty-four? Shit, I thought you just looked young."

Looking at him with a look of mild offense, she asked, "You thought I was older, but still a virgin?"

"No?" Quinn replied, uncertainly. "I just never hear you talk about having a love life or anything."

"Yeah, well, as I've already stated, my job keeps me pretty busy," Zoey said, sitting back on the sofa. "And I know you guys are just teasing when you call Jett a virgin. Just because we don't hook up with a new person every night..."

Quinn chuckled at the mention of Jett the Virgin, "Well, I approve, if it matters. He's a good guy. Probably the nicest guy I know."

"Good to know," Zoey nodded. "Not that it's going to turn into anything."

"If it helps," Quinn began, trying to conceal a grin, "he's practically a horse from the waist down."

"What?" Zoey arched an eyebrow, appearing somewhat confused, and fully exasperated.

Quinn shrugged. "I always felt bad; he's got all the equipment but absolutely no game."

Shaking her head, she rolled her eyes. "Thanks for the warning? Like I said, though, we're just talking. And he lives across the country, so…"

"Right, of course," said Quinn.

A new silence settled over them and her phone buzzed again. Another grin, another giggle, and Zoey looked back up at Quinn who was watching intently. "Would you stop staring at me? Go get ready!"

Walking out onto the field for the first time in over a month was like a breath of fresh air. Quinn took his time taking in the familiar scene, breathing in the grass, the clay and sand.

His trainer was waiting for him on the field. It was rare that he was the only one out there, but his teammates were resting and gearing up for their evening game that night, which Quinn was looking forward to, even if he had to watch from the bench.

After giving his trainer a run-down of where he was at in his physical therapy, and that he'd been working on strengthening his rotator cuff and the muscles surrounding his scapula, they got to work. They ran through cardio exercises, and with the Southern California heat, he was drenched in sweat from head to toe by the end of his workout session.

Walking back to the clubhouse locker rooms, he realized just how much he'd missed these kinds of training sessions. His head felt clear, and his body felt awake. Though he'd soon be feeling a lot more awake once he got in the showers. Not that he was complaining, but it was a little frustrating that ever since Rae had made his teenage shower fantasy come true, he couldn't take a shower without getting hard as fuck. Being in the clubhouse showers made this a hell of a lot more difficult to manage.

Cold shower it is.

Back in the meeting room of the clubhouse, Quinn greeted his teammates as they filed in, giving them back slapping hugs, fist bumps, and awkward left-handed handshakes. Nearly all of them had asked about his arm, and just as many asked about his girlfriend.

"Did you bring your girl back with you?"

"When are we meeting the girlfriend?"

Dean Bennett, the third baseman and Quinn's closest friend on the team said, "I still can't believe you're settling down, man. I give it another month."

"Ouch! You know I expected more support from you," Quinn replied, a hand to his chest as though wounded. He was good at pretending. Had he been excited at the prospect of no longer having to pretend around these guys? Sure. But if he had to pretend that he and Rae were still fine for a while longer, he would.

"How about that article with all those pictures of your girl with other guys? Was that whole thing photo-shopped? Or did you have to show half the guest list your fightin' skills?" Rob DiMarco asked, nudging Quinn as he took a seat on the bench next to him.

"Nah, they weren't photo-shopped," Quinn replied. "Just guys at the wedding. Rae used to be a total tom-boy, believe it or not. She may not look like it, but she could probably run bases around you assholes all day."

"With long legs like hers, I definitely believe it," said Dean, wiggling his eyebrows.

Quinn glared at his friend and made his voice low and threatening, "Watch it."

Dean chuckled, then asked, "So you really have been friends since you were kids?"

Quinn nodded. "Met when we were seven."

Dean grinned. "Oh, I can't fucking wait to hear stories about what you were like as a kid. I hope she's got some embarrassing ones. Lord knows that ego could use some humbling."

"All jokes aside," said Rob, "we really are happy for you. Glad you finally got your girl, Quinn."

Quinn was only able to give a half-hearted smile and ran his hands through his damp hair anxiously. *What were these guys gonna say when they realized he'd only lasted a little over a month in a real relationship?*

He caught up with the guys for a while longer until they all turned their attention to the door where the coach was now entering, followed by the athletic training staff and the health director.

The manager addressed the room of men, some sitting, some standing. Quinn was leaning back against a table near the front. "This meeting was called so that we could introduce you all to the newest member of our health staff. As you all know, our former physical therapist got a job with another team, and though we wish him the best, that's left us without our own traveling PT for the rest of the season. But after interviewing several qualified candidates, we have finally landed on a decision."

The door below the large, blue clubhouse sign swung open, and the man Quinn recognized as the Head Athletic Trainer walked in, followed by-

"Everyone, meet our new team physical therapist, Raelyn DeRose," the athletic trainer next to Rae announced, gesturing toward her with a *Vanna White* flourish.

Quinn's heart jolted at the sight of her. She was here. In Los Angeles. Showing him she was every bit as invested in their future together as he was.

Her hair was down, her long, blonde locks falling over one shoulder. While the rest of the health staff wore the signature navy blue polo with the team logo and a pair of khakis, Rae boasted a royal blue shirt with the logo, and a black athletic skort.

Well, motherfuck. If that's not cheating, I don't know what is.

Quinn straightened and pushed away from the table, having to hold himself back from completely consuming her. He slowly took in her presence from head to toe. His eyes took their time drinking in her long, tanned legs, stopping at the low-rise Converse All-Stars and sliding their way back up to her face. She was looking at him knowingly. Yeah, there was no hiding how hard he'd just eye-fucked her in that skort.

Trying to bite back the grin that had involuntarily plastered itself to his face, Quinn sucked in his bottom lip and shook his head in disbelief as he looked back at Rae. He wondered how long she'd been planning this. When had she contacted the manager and all the health staff? When had she set up her interview? That had all taken a lot of planning. Far more than she could've done in just the past few days. He knew now she'd have every intention to come to California with him. To be with him. This argument, this conflict between them was temporary. They'd had fights before. And they would probably have more. But she had absolutely no plans to give him up.

He was dying to wrap her in his arms and feel her against his body. It had only been a few days, but he fucking missed her. How could he have thought things might actually be over between them? He wanted to be alone with her and be able to kiss her and hold her, and *fuck, can she leave that damn skort on during our make-up sex?* Instead he kept his hands safely in the pockets of his athletic pants and tried to remain calm and collected.

"Dr. DeRose already has experience working with one member of our team," the health director's voice yanked Quinn out of his fantasy, "and she has an impressive history with athlete recovery. We feel she's the best fit to our team and will keep you all in good shape so we can keep winning those championships."

Rae stepped forward to address the team, "As I'm sure you all know, I've been working with Quinn on his recovery over the past seven weeks, and we've been making some serious progress-"

One of the guys in the back interjected, "*Yeah* you have. You've tamed a damn wild animal!"

Blushing slightly, Rae laughed. "Yeah, well, I promise to do my best with all of you, but don't expect the same level of special treatment."

Her eyes met his and her smile hit him right in the chest. He couldn't take it. Without a word, he briskly closed the gap between them and slid one arm around her waist, pulling her flush against him, and his other hand cupped her cheek.

"Quinn!" she gasped, surprised by his sudden move.

"I'm sorry, Rae, I know this is unprofessional, but I am just so fucking glad you're here," he whispered. He dipped his head and brushed his lips over hers, reveling in their softness and the small little sigh that escaped her as she relaxed against him.

The locker room erupted in shouts and exclamations and whistles of excitement. Quinn couldn't help smiling at his team's response and felt when Rae began to laugh against his kiss.

"Why do I feel like that was really for their benefit?" she asked, nodding her head toward the team.

A slow grin dragged across his face, and he puffed up his chest. "Gotta let them know you're *my* girl." He turned toward his team. "And no one messes with *my* girl! Got it?"

There was a chorus of hearty laughter and more shouts and caveman-like noises from the guys. Facing Rae again, he wiped the pad of his thumb over the perfect arch of her cheekbone. "And you'll always be my girl."

A small part of him wanted to remember why he'd been so mad for the past few days so that the planned speech in his head didn't go forgotten. But with Rae *here*, in Los Angeles, in his arms inside the clubhouse, having made the huge, life-altering decision to bring her life on the road with him and spend her days working where she could see him and be with him….it was nearly impossible to remember why he'd been so upset in the first place. After the meeting concluded, Rae had to go back with the health staff, and Quinn gave her another quick kiss before sneaking back out to the ball field by himself to let everything sink in.

The game wasn't until later that evening, but the concessions in the stadium were bustling with people cleaning and prepping, setting up their food stands, and various merchandise carts. Quinn stood on home base, listening to the faint sounds of everyone getting ready for a big game, while going over and trying to process everything that had happened in the past half hour. He pulled his blue L.A. hat low as he closed his eyes and remembered what he'd planned to say to Rae when he went back to Michigan. He knew he'd go back. He knew he'd see her again. He knew, on some level, that his departure wasn't permanent. He'd just needed time and space to think and process. To be mad and sad and whatever else he needed to be until he could figure out his next move.

"I know you didn't come out and say it," Rae's voice made a warmth spread through his body like nothing else could, "but is it safe to assume you forgive me?"

Quinn turned around to see Rae entering the field, with her trusty, fuzzy companion, Harry, at her side. Harry took off at a run when he saw Quinn and nearly knocked him over with his enthusiastic greeting. Crouching down to pet Harry as the giant dog licked his face, Quinn couldn't help laughing. He looked up at Rae who was still walking toward him, a smile on her face.

"He's been moping around the house looking for his running buddy," Rae said, squatting down next to them, scratching behind Harry's ears.

"This really isn't fair, you know," said Quinn, peering at Rae. "Using your dog to guilt trip me *on top* of wearing a skort...you're playing dirty."

"But I thought you already forgave me. Or, was that really just some macho move to let all your teammates know I'm off limits?"

Quinn shrugged. "I thought I'd be able to keep it together, but I might've lost control."

"Am I preventing you from acting mad so that I have to beg for your forgiveness?" she asked, grinning slyly.

"Yes," Quinn replied, concealing his own smile. "I was looking forward to it. I had it all planned out in my head."

"Well, we've acted out your fantasies before," Rae shrugged. "Let's hear it."

His eyebrow arched mischievously as he looked around. Attention back on her, he finally said, "Not here."

The familiar gleam in Rae's bright blue eyes lit up her face and made the possessive monster in Quinn's chest want to break free and go wild, but he kept his calm demeanor. He'd let it loose soon enough. But first he wanted to address what was bothering him the most.

"Rae," he began, and the tightening in his chest that he'd felt the previous night after she hadn't called or texted on time returned, "why did you stay there with him? Why wouldn't you have left right away?"

"I didn't know he was there until morning," she replied. "I had gone straight upstairs to one of the guest rooms, and I guess he was already sleeping in the basement. I didn't see him until maybe forty-five minutes before you showed up. He was in the kitchen, and I needed caffeine. So I endured his interrogation for some kick-ass iced coffee."

"Interrogation?" Quinn snorted, unable to help himself.

"I know he's a bank lawyer, but he should really consider criminal law. That guy could make a mime talk."

The corner of Quinn's mouth pulled up slightly. She wasn't wrong. Quinn had always been known for being somewhat mysterious when it came to his past but remembered how easily he had given away some of his deepest secrets within an hour of meeting Emerson. He'd thought it was strange at the time, and still couldn't quite put his finger on what had made him so easy to talk to.

He nodded, understanding. "And when he saw you there without me, he obviously wanted to know everything. I wouldn't expect him to let up."

"Still, I shouldn't have jumped to conclusions," Rae said, looking at Quinn, the big dog still between them. "My brain just immediately went to what I walked in on a little over a year ago, and I didn't think I could handle it if..." she trailed off and let her gaze drop to where she was still petting Harry.

Studying her, he found himself caught between wanting to be completely understanding, and being offended that she'd even think for a second that he could hurt her like that. He tried not to think too hard about how she must have felt that whole night, imagining he'd been with someone else, and feeling like she had reasonable suspicion to back it up. Then he remembered the other part of that night that had upset him.

"Promise me, Rae," Quinn said, placing his hand on top of hers, "you won't ever take off without letting at least *someone* know where you are or that you're okay. You have no idea the kinds of scenarios I was running through my head. Seriously, baby, even if you tell me that you're mad and don't want anyone bugging you, just let me know you're safe. *Promise* me."

"I promise."

"I was terrified something had happened...someone who'd seen you in the tabloids could've developed an obsession or something, and..." Quinn shook his head. "I know it seems far-fetched, but there are some whack-jobs out there. You can't do that to me again."

"I'm sorry, Quinn," Rae said, letting her fingertips brush against the scruff on his jaw that had grown over the past few days.

Taking her hands, Quinn stood up and brought Rae to her feet with him, gazing deep into her eyes that twinkled turquoise in the California sun. He pulled her so that her body was pressed against his, and brushed her hair back, curling his fingers in the sun-gold strands and holding firmly as he tilted her face up to his. He quirked an eyebrow and let a smirk cross his lips. "You can make it up to me later."

CHAPTER 34

Watching a Major League game from the view of the dugout with the entire team and the rest of the trainers that evening was an experience unlike anything she had ever had. Raelyn had interned during her undergrad with the University of Michigan baseball team as an athletic trainer but being at this level with world class athletes was something else entirely. The energy of the ballpark, the tension when the score got close, and the comradery among the players was something Raelyn couldn't believe she would actually be part of in a month's time.

She hadn't been sure the health director would even consider her with the position she was in with Quinn, but he obviously had his reasons for wanting her as a member of the player health staff. The important thing was that she'd gotten the job on her own. She had been itching to tell Quinn all about it when she'd made her first contact with the director only days after their initial conversation about moving to Los Angeles together, but she really wanted to get the job independently, rather than feeling like she'd pulled strings to get there.

As much as she'd wanted to chase after Quinn the day he left for Los Angeles, her interview was already set up and she wanted to get things in order and prepare herself for the massively intimidating interview.

The team won their game that night, continuing their winning streak. They'd only lost two games so far this season, and they'd both been early in April and May. Even though Quinn had watched from the bench, he was celebrating with his team as though he'd also been out there making runs. Raelyn hadn't forgotten how much she enjoyed watching Quinn play or get engrossed in a baseball game, but it had been a long time since she'd been able to share it with him. It was almost more exciting to watch him watching the game. He was so intense and passionate about it, it almost hurt to imagine how much he must miss playing.

Since it was a late game and they'd be playing again the next afternoon, most of the players only celebrated on the field and in the clubhouse for a short period of time before turning in to rest up. Quinn wrapped his arm around Raelyn's shoulders and they walked out of the clubhouse together to his Jeep Rubicon. She eyed the vehicle curiously, finding it funny that with all the money he was making now he'd still gone for a Jeep, rather than a Range Rover or something higher end.

When they pulled into the driveway of Quinn's ultra-modern L.A. mansion, however, she took back her thoughts of how thrifty he still seemed to be despite his massive salary. The house was all sleek, straight lines and floor-to-ceiling windows. The white walls contrasted with all the black trim and accents. Behind the house she could see the million-dollar ocean view and the silhouette of palm trees.

"Look at you, Mr. Fancy Pants," Raelyn said as they pulled into the garage. To the right of the Jeep's parking spot were two sports cars- a black Audi R8 and a cherry red classic Mustang GT, both of which looked like he could've been bought at a Barrett-Jackson car auction.

"Is it weird?" Quinn asked, glancing sideways at her. "Seeing me live like this instead of...what you were used to? When we were kids?"

"No, it's not weird. You've earned it, and I'm happy for you."

Quinn led her inside and they walked past the mud room into an open, spacious kitchen with high, vaulted ceilings and beams. Each appliance was stainless steel, the countertops were white and spotless. The window over the sink displayed a view of the infinity pool and ocean. Raelyn's smile brightened as she looked around. "I feel like I just stepped into the Cohens's house."

"Yeah, I'm pretty sure I felt like Ryan Atwood the first morning I walked out and realized I was actually living here," Quinn replied.

"I didn't think you actually paid attention to that show," said Raelyn, amused, remembering how many times she'd made the boys watch *The OC* when they hung out at her house.

"Oh, we were all pretty invested. We just didn't want to admit it." Quinn put a hand possessively on the small of her back and led her forward and into the next room. He took his time giving her a tour through the house, Harry wagging happily beside them into each different room which looked perfectly designed, every piece of furniture and decor precisely placed by a decorator. Raelyn wondered how much time he actually spent in each room, figuring he likely used only the main living space, the kitchen, and his own bedroom often. There were five bedrooms in his house- *five!* Was he planning on having a big family one day? Or had he just let his buddies use the extra rooms to sleep off their partying? Raelyn assumed the latter was far more likely.

Finally Quinn stopped in front of the open door that he'd pushed past earlier in the tour, clearly wanting to save this room for last.

"Is this the Red Room?" Raelyn asked, arching an eyebrow mysteriously.

"Red Room?" Quinn repeated, brow furrowed.

"You know, Christian Grey, Fifty Shades...secret sex dungeon?"

The furrow in Quinn's brow deepened as he stared back with utmost confusion. "If I had a secret sex dungeon, wouldn't it be in the basement?"

Raelyn shook her head. *The OC* he understood, but this reference was clearly lost on him. "Never mind. Dungeon or not, I assume this is the place you plan on giving me back-to-back orgasms until I pass out."

Pulling her into the room which was obviously his bedroom, his eyebrow twitched up and a mischievous grin crossed his lips. "Is that what you think?" Quinn released her hands, slipped behind her, and she heard the quiet latch of the door closing.

"Been thinking about it a lot, actually," Raelyn admitted, eyes sweeping the room. His California King bed ran parallel to a wall that was entirely made up of a large window. The beach and ocean view beyond were stunning, and she found herself mesmerized by the flashes of moonlight reflected in the restless waves.

There had barely been any time for intimacy or affection throughout the day, but Raelyn had begun to wonder at the game if it was intentional. If he was holding back on purpose. Perhaps he was still hurt. Or perhaps he was working on keeping himself composed in front of everyone- his coach, his team, and now *her* new employers.

Hands, warm and large and familiar, found her waist as Quinn pressed himself against her from behind. Sliding them down to her hips, he tightened his grip and pulled her toward him, her ass to his crotch, and she could feel him again through the fabric of their clothes just as she had on the baseball field that morning. He'd kissed her then, but it hadn't been the full, deep kiss she'd been anticipating that would leave her breathless. Her heart rate had picked up at the feel of his lips on hers, but...then he stopped. And that was it. Quinn had never left her *wanting* like that. Feeling like she didn't get everything she'd asked for and then some.

His lips trailed along her neck as he held her hips in place so that she felt the full length of him. *God, he was fucking solid.* Her heart was racing with anticipation and her head lulled back, leaning into him. She had no idea what to expect from him tonight, but the tension and energy between them was suddenly a physical presence in the room.

"Know what I've been thinking about a lot?" Quinn murmured into her skin. Her nipples went taut at the low, gravelly tone of his voice, and he continued before giving her a chance to respond, "I've been thinking...about how hard and ready I was for you Thursday night. How much we needed to get a little loud...a little wild..." he bit just behind her ear, his teeth stinging just enough to make Raelyn gasp, "maybe a little rough."

Quinn slid his hands back up her body, pushing her arms up so that he could peel her shirt off in one quick motion. He felt his way back down slowly, grasping and massaging her breasts through her bra before continuing downward. Fingers catching on the waistband of her skort, he stripped it off her legs and came around to stand in front of her. She was on display, and he was still fully clothed. She would have felt exposed, but she yearned for the hungry look on his face as he swept his gaze across her body.

His eyes were afire with something far deeper than lust, but when Raelyn tried to pull his shirt up and over him, he grabbed her hands and held them back at her sides. She looked up into his face, searching.

"You left me needing you so bad the other night, baby," he said, brushing a hand back through her hair and holding it, "and then I find out it's because you doubted me."

The swell of Raelyn's chest rising and falling was noticeable as she realized how hard she was breathing already. Anticipation and need coursed through her entire body. She was hanging on his every word, wanting his thoughts, and needing to make his lingering hurt vanish. When he looked like this, *sounded* like this, *damn*, he was intoxicating.

"I told you I love you, Rae. And I meant it," said Quinn. "I thought you knew that."

"I do," her voice was barely a whisper. She licked her lips.

He paused, his gaze sliding from her mouth to her eyes. "Do you?"

"Yes," Raelyn breathed. Quinn tightened his grip in her hair and dipped his head so that his lips were nearly touching hers. She just wanted to feel his mouth on hers, taste him, get lost in him. The warmth of his breath covered her lips, but he wouldn't close the gap. He was teasing. Withholding what he knew she wanted. She swallowed, eyes fixed on his mouth. "Yes, Quinn."

The satisfied smirk tugged up the corner of his lips again as he rasped, "That's my girl." His mouth came over hers, hard and demanding as he kept his possessive hold of her head through her hair.

Raelyn tangled her fingers in his shirt, pulling him close, but it still wasn't close enough. She wanted his body on hers, his skin against her skin, and *God*, she wanted to feel him moving inside her. His tongue swept into her mouth, and she let out a needy groan, moving her hips into his. The feel of her thin cotton panties against the fabric of his athletic pants made her crave more. She craved the feel of him, his skin, his cock, hard and ready to plunge into her.

Without thought, her hands moved to the waistband of his pants to move them down, but again, he stopped her. Quinn held her hands in his and Raelyn let out a whimper. "Quinn, please... I need you."

"Not yet," he replied in a thick whisper. "Do you trust me?"

Raelyn blinked up to Quinn's eyes. "Yes. More than anything." It occurred to her then when he grinned in response that this was the fantasy he'd been referring to earlier. The one he wouldn't go into detail about at the stadium. And she wondered if his careful, calculated distance all day was part of it.

"Lie back on the bed," Quinn said, nodding behind him toward the large, perfectly made platform bed.

Raelyn obeyed, lying back into the pillows at the head of the bed, and waited for more instructions. Every nerve in her body was hovering on the edge, waiting for what was coming. She found that she was still in awe of how easily Quinn could go from calm, easy-going lover to Alpha-dog Sex God and never skip a beat. She watched as he stepped closer toward the bed, his eyes surveying her nearly-naked body, making goosebumps appear all over her skin. He pulled out the drawer of his nightstand and retrieved a silky black rope.

Her heart jumped into action at the sight of the rope, and she let out a gasp before her eyes narrowed at him.

Holding up a hand as he read her expression, he explained, "I've actually never done this before. It always sounded like a good idea, but...I wouldn't ask someone to trust me with it if I knew I couldn't do the same." Quinn then climbed onto the bed, straddling Raelyn. He unhooked her bra and tossed it aside. "Arms up, baby."

Heart pounding in her chest, she let her arms float up over her head so that she could grasp the spindles of the headboard. Quinn proceeded to wrap the rope around her wrists, through the spindles, and back around several times before securing it with an intricate knot.

"That okay?" he asked. "Does it...does it feel okay?"

Raelyn couldn't help the warmth that spread through her chest at his look of genuine concern but prepared herself for the drastic transformation back into alpha-dog once she assured him the rope wasn't too tight. And then the warmth was spreading elsewhere. The yearning, pleasant ache between her thighs was like a reflex when Quinn looked at her with his cocky one-dimpled grin, as was the involuntary thrust of her hips.

He settled himself between her legs and his palms slid from her tied wrists down her arms, over her breasts. He dipped his head and took a nipple into his mouth as he caressed the other, brushing the pad of his thumb over the pink tip in smooth circles. Raelyn reflexively tried to move her hands down, wanting to wrap her fingers in his hair and pull him toward her, but was met with the strong resistance of the rope against the headboard. She could feel the rope, smooth as it was, bite into her skin. She gasped and whimpered. Hips thrusted, lifting off the bed to meet Quinn's.

Oh…oh, yeah, okay. The forced restraint was…satisfying. To say the least. Gratifying? Titillating? Thrilling? *Fucking* awakening. Raelyn found herself pulling harder against her restraint, enjoying the pleasure mixed with a little pain as the rope rubbed and dug into her wrists.

"You like that?" Quinn grumbled into the soft curve of her breast. He nipped and bit harder than his usual soft nibbles on her skin, and she arched her back, pressing into his mouth as she moaned with pleasure. "Oh fuck, baby. Yeah, that's right, I knew you liked to play rough."

One hand slid over her stomach and down into her panties. He traced a finger along her sex and groaned, feeling what he was doing to her. He teased her, trailing his finger up and down, and pulling away when she rocked her hips into him. His palm pressed against her thigh as his fingers returned their light touches, soft, playful taunts that he knew would only be enough to make her crave him more.

"Oh my God, Quinn, *please*," Raelyn moaned, once again rolling her hips to demand more.

"*Fuck*, I love when you say my name," Quinn groaned. He lifted his head and pressed his mouth to her ear, biting before demanding, "I wanna hear you beg."

Raelyn pulled against the rope again and moaned, "Please Quinn, I need you so bad." He was sucking at the indentation where her jaw met her neck, teeth scraping, likely to leave his mark. Fingers still teased and danced around the spot between her thighs where she needed him to be.

"More," he growled.

She didn't hesitate to give him what he wanted, "Please Quinn, *fuck*, I want to feel you inside me." His fingers trailed up and down. "Please, baby, I'm here. I'm yours." Fingertips circled around her clit lightly and he grinded into her, making her feel the length of him pressed into her thigh. "Take me however you want, Quinn, I just need to feel you."

He groaned and cursed under his ragged breath. Sitting up, he hastily peeled off his shirt and pushed down his pants and boxers, kicking them off the bed. Raelyn looked down at Quinn's magnificent naked body over hers. His cock was thick and hard and standing at attention for her. The rope kept her from reaching for it, but she still pulled roughly as though she could break free.

Quinn saw Raelyn's gaze as she zeroed in on his cock, imagining it filling her up as he pounded into her over and over, making her scream and gasp and shake. He knelt between her legs and closed a hand around the shaft, sliding his hand up and down, watching her. She let out a whimper again, wishing she could touch it. *Oh baby*, he was good at this teasing game. She bit her lip as she watched him, eyes flitting from his full cock in his hand to his face. His eyes were heavy-lidded and glazed with need, and he bit back a groan.

"You want this?"

Raelyn nodded, still biting her lip as she pulled against the rope.

"What was that, babydoll? I didn't catch that," he cocked his head as if to hear better.

With an impatient groan, she answered, "Fuck, Quinn, *yes*."

His eyebrow twitched and he looped his fingers around the waistband of her panties to pull them down. He smoothed a palm over her spread thighs as he sunk between them, holding his cock just at her opening. Just as he'd done with his fingers, he traced her with the head of his cock, up and down, slowly and torturously, pulling just out of reach when she rocked her hips toward him.

"You're so wet for me, baby," Quinn whispered as he watched himself tease her. "So fucking perfect." The hand on her thigh slid up and he brushed his fingers gently over her clit. Two fingers rubbed either side of that perfectly sensitive spot and she moaned. The headboard creaked with the tug of the rope.

Quinn leaned in and hovered over her, his mouth to her neck just below her ear. "Tell me, Rae...am I the only one who can make you feel like this? The only one who's *ever* made you feel like this?"

"Yes, *oh God*, yes," Raelyn moaned as he dipped the head of his cock in ever so slightly.

"And if you ever have a problem, if you're upset or if you think I've done something to hurt you, do you promise to come to *me?* No one else, baby, you come to me. And we'll sort it out."

"Yes, I promise." She thrusted her hips up to force him inside, but he shoved her back down, pressing her thighs into the mattress.

"One more thing," Quinn said, eyes glazed over as he looked down at her, inching his way back into her again slowly.

"Okay?" She was practically panting.

"Make sure you scream my name when I finally let you come," he said darkly, taking his time to watch how her body responded to his words. "I want you hoarse and gasping and begging for more."

She sighed with relief, smiling blissfully as he rubbed her thighs. She braced herself for the sweet relief of him finally giving in to her. His hands grasped her hips and he plunged into her all at once. She gasped and threw her head back, giving over to him, reveling in his control.

If he wanted her hoarse, he knew how to get it. He was hard and full and long as he sunk into her again and again and *again*. Deep strokes making her feel so full, the roughness making her go wild with him. Her hips raised to meet him as he pushed in, she cried out and called his name over and over, pulling hard against the restraints around her wrists.

She wanted to touch him, but she was relishing that she couldn't. She was still being teased and was sure the rope would leave a mark. The thought left her feeling greedy and coveted. She wanted Quinn to leave a mark on her. She wanted everyone to know she belonged to him. And fuck if that's not exactly what he was doing to her now.

His hips pinned her hard into the mattress as he moved deep inside her, thrusting, pounding, and taking every bit of her. She wasn't even doing any of the work and she was panting, gasping, sweating, *pleading*. "Oh yes...*harder...faster...fuck* me... Oh God, *fuck yes, fuck yes!...Please* Quinn, *please*, oh *God!*"

His skin slid over hers, slippery with their sweat as he fucked deeper, giving in to her pleas, getting lost in his own greedy desires, his needs.

Raelyn gasped as she felt her skin flush. She was close. *So* close. Quinn knew her body well enough to recognize how close she was and he slowed down. Way down. Leaving her hanging just on the edge of her climax. She moaned as her head fell back, exposing the arch of her neck. Quinn's mouth sucked at her skin just below her jaw, scraping his teeth down to her collarbone.

"Don't come yet, baby," he growled into her neck.

She moaned, a pained and tortured sound, "*Please*, Quinn...oh my *God*, please." Her pulse was thrumming, she was dizzy with being so close, hanging just out of reach of that perfect release. When she finally came, she was going to implode.

"No, baby, not yet." His right hand toyed with her nipples while his left kept him propped just slightly over her. Mouth tracing the line of her jaw and coming over her lips, he trapped her bottom lip between his teeth and sucked gently. He pressed a soft kiss to her lips again before demanding, "Look at me."

Raelyn peered into his eyes, like liquid gold. He could hypnotize her with his gaze. She would do anything he asked. *Anything* he wanted.

"Rae, I love you," Quinn breathed. "I'm so *fucking* in love with you, you know that?"

"Yes," Raelyn whimpered. And oh God, his intense sincerity mixed with his fevered, unhinged fucking was enough to make her ache and yearn for him even more. He was right here, inside her, and she still craved more of him. *All* of him. "Yes, Quinn, I love you, too."

"I belong to you, Rae. I always have."

Yes, that's all she wanted. He looked down at their bodies, watching himself enter her slowly, watching her hips raise to meet his. She bit her lip, wanting him to look at her face again. She wanted to see his eyes, the look he gave her that let her know she was it. She was his whole world and everything around them melted away when he looked at her. He'd always looked at her like that. How had she taken so long to return it?

"I'm yours, Quinn," Raelyn said, and he lifted his eyes back up to her, still moving, pushing into her at his deliberate, unhurried pace. All of him in...all of him out...all of him in...Feeling every inch of his hardness against her softness. "You know that. I'm undeniably, helplessly, irrevocably yours."

Quinn exhaled through his smile- a relieved, genuinely happy smile- and brushed her lips with his. Pressing his forehead to hers, he asked, "You wanna come now?"

"Oh *God*, yes," Raelyn moaned. His hips settled back onto hers, the pressure familiar and welcome. He ran his palms down her sides, over the curve of her hips, to her thighs where they gripped, strong and solid. The flick of an eyebrow and flash of dimple were all the warning she was given before he thrust into her, hard and determined. Each snap of his hips brought a new gasp or cry or moan. His husky, gravel-coated voice met her hoarse pleas for more...more...*fuck me, yes!*

"Oh fuck, Rae," Quinn groaned into her neck. "Fuck yes, *oh goddamn*. It's so good, baby. You feel *so fucking good*."

Within a minute, she was there. Back on the edge, about to free fall, and *oh my God...*

Raelyn screamed, Quinn's name echoing through the room as she erupted. She was a shaking, gasping, convulsing puddle of pure satisfaction beneath him. Stars flooded her vision and she thought she truly might pass out as she pulled hard against the rope, having wrapped her hand around the small length between her wrists and the headboard.

Quinn's breath caught in his throat as he watched the tidal wave of pure bliss and pleasure wash over her. "Oh fuck, baby...fuck that was so good," Quinn growled.

He brought her legs onto his shoulders and leaned over her, thrusting and pounding deep, the sound of skin smacking against skin as his hips snapped into her. "*Fuck, oh fuck!* I'm com-" the rest of the word was lost to a masculine, guttural sound that emerged from his chest. He pumped into her, emptying himself as he covered her mouth with his.

Their groans melted together, tongues wrestled, and chests heaved against each other until he was still. They were both gasping, breathing hot breath into each other's necks, their hair. Pressing soft kisses onto salty, sweat-soaked skin.

As Raelyn's body relaxed and her legs dropped back down onto the bed with Quinn still between them, he pushed himself up, staying inside her, and reached above her to untie the knot that bound her hands. Once released, she slowly brought her arms back down, and like magnets, her fingers curled around his hair, pulling his mouth to hers.

Her arms were sore and the skin of her wrists burned from the friction she'd created against the rope, but she still grinned when she saw the marks it left. Quinn smoothed his palms over her shoulders, down her biceps, her forearms, and to her hands. Holding each delicate hand in his, he inspected the red marks where the rope had bitten into her skin. He pressed his lips to her pulse and made a trail of kisses around each wrist, taking one hand at a time.

"Did you like it?" He spoke into her palm and his breath tickled her skin.

"Yeah, I did," Raelyn said, voice just louder than a whisper.

"I like dominating you," Quinn smirked, the familiar, cocky tone teasing. His eyes changed now, his eyebrows pulled ever so slightly together as if the thought pained him in some way, tortured or scared him. "It's the only time I feel like I have control with you. With...how I feel for you. I let myself finally take the leap, and...sometimes I feel like I'm in free-fall. It's exciting and it's thrilling and I love it, but if I mess it up...that's it."

Raelyn considered this, watching as he studied the marks he'd left behind. "I don't want you to feel like that. I want you to feel grounded. I want to be the one you know will be there. Your constant." His golden brown eyes flickered back up to hers and she suddenly remembered the first time she realized how much she loved the color of his eyes. Her heart swelled at the memory of their seven-year-old selves.

When their friendship was new, she had spent a lot of time studying him. Maybe it was weird, but Quinn Casey was just so different than anyone else she knew. And his eyes were just as unique. She'd never seen anyone whose eyes turned golden in the sun, and when she realized this, her face had slowly turned up into a beaming smile. He'd looked back at her curiously, maybe like she was a little crazy.

"I've still never seen anyone with gold eyes like yours," Raelyn said, smiling up at him.

"They're not gold," Quinn let out a short breath of laughter. "They're just light brown."

"They're like liquid amber. And I love them."

"You've mentioned that before," he said. "No one else has seemed to notice though, so I think maybe it's just you."

"Good," Raelyn grinned. "I like being the only one who can see it. It's like a special part of you that belongs only to me."

"All of me belongs to you, Rae."

With a smirk and a playful yet forceful shove, she rolled Quinn onto his back and landed on top of him. Her hair spilled over her shoulder onto the pillow next to his head. He smiled up at her and she knew all he saw was her. She only wished he realized he did the same to her.

"I love you, Quinn." She got lost in his golden gaze again as she spoke, "I know we've made our mistakes. We've pretended to be just friends, we've said and done things we regret. I never should've shut you out years ago, after graduation. Something so small, so…trivial, had hurt me so badly, and I was absolutely terrified that you had that kind of power over me. The ability to hurt me like that, even if you never meant to.

"And the way I reacted Thursday night…it was childish. I knew better, but I just…the 'what if' was so petrifying I couldn't face it." She looked down where her fingertips were trailing along his chest, then back up again with a swallow. "I can't believe we got another chance, and I just don't want to hold anything back this time. I'm so in love with you, and I don't know if it just happened this summer or if it's been there since we were seventeen or thirteen or seven. But I do know that I want you…for as long as you'll want me."

Quinn's serious stare broke into a playful grin. "That's a long time, my little *chouette*."

Giggling, Raelyn replied, "Probably still not long enough to teach you decent French."

"Probably not," Quinn laughed as he cupped the side of her face with a large hand. Their lips met, soft and slow, melting into each other.

Within minutes, their kiss turned to frenzied grasping and moaning as their bodies moved with one another. Quinn flipped off the light and they kissed and felt and made love in nothing but the moonlight shining through the window. Laying on his chest afterward, listening to the sound of the steady rhythmic thumping of his heart, Raelyn knew without a doubt that *this* was what she wanted above all else. She'd known she wanted him, and she wanted to finally get her chance to see what this could be. Less than two months had gone by, and never would she have imagined that it would come to her this hard, this fast.

She could fall asleep just like this every night, here or at her house or a random hotel in a strange city after a ball game. His strong, muscled arms holding her, lightly tracing his fingers along her bare skin. This was it. *He* was it. She was completely, entirely where she wanted to be.

CHAPTER 35

"Run! Run to third- go, go!" Quinn shouted over his familiar hometown baseball diamond. They were back in Michigan for two more days, then Rae was making her big move with him to Los Angeles. Quinn had been helping coach one of the local teams after Rae had mentioned her patient asking if he'd be able to stop by and see the team. It was the last game of the summer season before school started and his team, The Pirates, were officially undefeated.

Quinn watched as Avery Aimes slid into third base.

"Safe!" the referee called out, and Quinn pumped his fist.

The kid was good. Rae had told Quinn about his injury last spring when he'd taken a fastball to the wrist. It had healed up really well and he was back in the game as if he'd never left. In any case, the injury hadn't stopped the kid from running bases like the Flash.

"I'm seriously considering adopting that kid," Quinn said to the coach who also happened to be Avery's father.

Mike Aimes let out a bark of laughter, "Yeah, I might have to fight you on that one."

"He's gotta be getting scouted already, right?" Quinn asked, watching Avery stand up and brush his pants off a little before turning his attention to where the next batter was stepping up to the plate.

"Oh yeah," Mike nodded, "he's got some options. Mississippi, Louisiana...*Arizona*."

Quinn smirked. "I am partial to Arizona."

"Ball!" The umpire's voice rang out and Quinn refocused his gaze on the player up to bat.

He'd only been working with these kids for a little over two weeks and he'd already found himself getting attached. He wanted to come back and watch them play during their school seasons and was trying to figure out how to get some sort of VIP experience set up in LA or with the team here. They held baseball camps for kids, but they weren't cheap. Quinn supposed he wouldn't mind footing the bill to give some of these kids an experience like that.

He knew some of the boys on the team just played to keep busy, stay active, and be social. But there were also some like Avery who reminded him of himself in ways; their focus and dedication, their readiness to take any instruction or constructive criticism when he offered it. For some of these boys, the sport was part of them, embedded in their identity.

The Pirates beat the Wildcats 8-5 after a strong last hit with loaded bases had earned them three runs. Quinn stood back and watched in delight as the mob of black and red uniforms jumped up and down on the field together, celebrating their undefeated season. He couldn't help thinking of his final championship game in high school, celebrating with his team and then getting his first mind-blowing kiss from Rae.

Looking around the park, he noticed the familiar faces in the stands who had come to watch after Quinn had pestered constantly, telling them they needed to come see his amazing team. It was true he was proud of his team and was grateful for having taken part in their season, but there may have been a different motivating factor to having everyone here at the park where he, Chris, Jett, and Rae had played so many games.

He scanned the crowd, seeing Rae's parents standing up, and Chris, Victoria, and their little girl, Sophia. Brody and Amira had come to show their support, too. Even his mom had come out to watch the game and was sitting next to Sandra. He may not have been playing, but he still felt his chest swell at the thought that his mom had finally made it to one of his games. He grinned when he saw Jett sitting on the bleachers next to Zoey. Jett was smiling as he spoke and Zoey had her head thrown back in laughter.

"Hey Coach," Rae said as she slid her arms around Quinn from behind and bit playfully at his shoulder.

Quinn spun around, wrapping his arm around her as she kept hers circled around his torso. She wore a plain white t-shirt and a dark blue athletic skort with her usual Converse on her feet. A timeless look on this woman, honestly. Her hair was down and resting over her shoulders. "Look," he nodded toward Jett and Zoey with a smirk, "what do you think of that?"

Rae followed his gaze and found the smiling couple. "I think if she's into centaurs, she'll be thrilled," Rae replied, one corner of her mouth tugging up in a playful grin.

"Centaurs?" Quinn questioned, brows scrunched as he looked down at Rae. "Those are the half-man half-horse...wait," he stared, incredulous. "How the hell did you find that out?"

"Accident," Rae giggled. "I tried to look away, but I had to keep doing double and triple takes to confirm that was in fact what I was seeing. I was in shock."

"You *had* to?" Quinn pressed, skeptically. When Rae simply shrugged, he sighed, "Great, now I'm competing with Jett *fucking* Miller. Who would've thought?"

Rae swiped the hat off his head and pulled it onto her own, then pressed her lips to his cheek. "Oh, there's no contest."

Quinn cupped her jaw and rubbed his thumb across her cheekbone before meeting her mouth with a deep kiss. His heart was racing as he breathed her in and he wondered if she would ever stop having this effect on him. It seemed unlikely.

"Great team there, kid," Charlie said, his friendly and sonorous voice cutting through the commotion around them. Quinn broke away from Rae to face him and smiled. "You know, you could just stay here and coach. I'm sure your old school would hire you in a heartbeat."

"You want me to retire from the majors to coach high school baseball?" Quinn replied, his crooked grin showing his skepticism.

"Sure, why not?" Charlie shrugged. "You've got enough money to put away to be more than comfortable. Why do you think we went through all the trouble to get you on travel teams and make sure you could play ball any chance you got? You think we wanted you to be in the majors?" He shook his head. "No, no, we wanted you to stay right here in your own hometown. LA is overrated anyway."

"Oh my gosh, Dad," Rae said, rolling her eyes, and Quinn couldn't help smiling at how much she sounded like her teenage self. "Why don't you just adopt him and get it over with? Trade me for Quinn like you've always wanted to do."

Charlie gasped theatrically. "Raelyn Elise, how could you think such a thing? I just don't want him taking *you* away from me."

"Uh-huh…"

"We'll come back during the off season," Quinn assured Charlie as Margaux now sidled up to her husband. "We can even stay at your house again and make you get sick of us. You'll be ready for the season to start up again."

Charlie replied "Perfect!" just as Margaux and Rae shook their heads and gave an "I don't think so" in unison.

"Well, I'm still out for the rest of this season, and probably part of the next. While Rae's traveling with the team, you can come stay in LA. We'll have a men's weekend. Jett and Chris can come, too. Although, I suspect Jett might ditch us while he's there," Quinn said, eyes wandering back over to his friend and his publicist still sitting together, smiling and laughing amiably.

"Wait, wait!" Rae put a hand on Quinn's arm. "I took a job so I could be with you, so that we didn't have to be away from each other again, and you're going to ditch me as soon as we get back to spend time with my *dad?*"

Quinn shrugged. "I'll have the guys keeping a close eye on you on the road. They'll make sure you stay out of trouble." He did his best to hide his grin at her responding scoff and eye roll.

The baseball field and stands were clearing out and people from both teams were scattered, parents of players talking to one another, teammates making plans and talking about the upcoming school year and next baseball season. The field was empty now and Quinn took in a slow steadying breath, reimagining for the ten-thousandth time that day when he'd given Rae batting lessons.

Chris and Victoria, along with their young daughter, came down from the bleachers and greeted Rae's parents. Margaux doted on Sophia while Chris and Charlie exchanged comments about the game.

Chris turned to Quinn finally and said, "Celebratory dinner at Trojan? We'll open it up to the kids for the evening. It's a special occasion so they can stay past nine." After the bar had gotten so much recognition for being a place Quinn frequented while everyone was buzzing about his new relationship, they'd put in place a rule that those under twenty-one weren't allowed inside past nine o'clock.

Nodding, Quinn said, "Yeah, I'll tell the coach. Just give me a minute. I wanna do something first." He then grabbed hold of Rae's hand and lifted his chin toward the empty ball diamond, "C'mere, I have to show you something." He tried, and failed, to not meet Charlie's gaze before pulling Rae toward the field. Charlie's eyes went wide, then crinkled in a knowing grin, and it made the task of keeping his own smile and emotions under control that much more challenging.

"You're not going to make me run bases again, are you?" Rae asked as they stepped out onto the field.

"No," Quinn laughed. Holy shit, his heart was thumping so hard in his chest, he could feel it reverberating through his entire body. He was nervous and excited and anxious, but also somehow completely content that he was exactly where he wanted to be.

He stopped at home base and brushed his foot across the plate a few times before shifting his gaze to look at Rae. This woman was his entire life. She was his center, his constant, his best friend, his soul mate. He'd known it for so long, and how could he not? The proof was everywhere. In the way she looked at him, how he looked at her. The way he'd always felt so calm and grounded in her presence. He'd never wanted or needed anything more than he needed her. He tried to work out what to say, even though he'd rehearsed it several times, the words suddenly felt as though they weren't enough. There were absolutely no words, no script he could go off of that would accurately depict how deeply and desperately he loved her.

Finally he grinned playfully. "I have one more fantasy I want to make a reality."

Rae was grinning, but her eyebrow ticked up and she glanced sideways at the small crowd of their friends and family gathered just outside the dugouts. "Okay, but you do realize my parents are here.

And your mom. And I think Jett would absolutely implode if he saw me naked."

His laugh let loose the tension and anxiety that had knotted in his chest, though his heart was still pounding like an eight-oh-eight drum. Catching her gaze he asked, "Do you trust me?"

She grinned. "Of course."

He placed his hands on her shoulders and directed her to a specific spot just off the plate, concentrating hard on where her feet were placed. He then walked behind her and grabbed her hips, pretending to care where they were placed, though it was really just for show and being reminiscent of his favorite memory here with her.

Walking back around to face her, he tried to poke her lower hip at her ticklish spot, but she was prepared and swatted his hand away. He smiled down at her, meeting her gaze from beneath *his* ball cap. "Rae…" he began, and was suddenly caught up in emotion. A million memories of them together swarming in his mind. He swallowed hard, reached into his pocket and knelt in front of her and produced a small square box.

Quinn watched her face as her expression changed from wide-eyed surprise to absolute delight, her bright beaming smile lighting up her face.

"Yes!" She exclaimed before he could say or do anything else.

Laughing, he looked at the box that was still closed in his hand, "Rae, I haven't even asked you anything yet."

"*Yes!*" Rae repeated, hands on either side of her face.

"You don't even know what's in here," Quinn replied, though his heart was already bursting with joy and excitement and complete fucking bliss that Rae had already said yes. "It could be a cock ring or a butt plug."

"Okay, we're going to completely gloss over those words when we retell this story," said Rae, though the smile had not disappeared from her face.

Quinn shook his head, then finally flipped open the box to reveal a shining, bright white diamond ring. Tears rolled down Rae's cheeks as she beamed down at him, and he felt the same emotional intensity building up inside himself but swallowed around it.

"Raelyn DeRose," he began again, "You are my best friend, my favorite person, my soul mate. I've loved you my entire life, and I will spend every single day for the rest of it trying to prove that I deserve you. I know this might seem fast to you, but I feel like I'm running about ten years late. We don't have to get married this month or this year or even next...all I'm asking is to spend forever with you." Quinn paused, taking in this moment as she swiped another happy tear off her cheek. "Rae, will you marry me?"

Rae nodded vigorously and extended her hand out. "Quinn Casey, you know I will."

His smile split across his whole face as he slid the diamond ring on her finger and stood up to pull her around him, covering her mouth with his, claiming her, kissing her deeply as he felt her tears wet his cheeks. He was smiling and laughing into their kiss because finally, fucking *finally* he knew she was his.

And he was hers.

And it was all he ever wanted.

EPILOGUE

Raelyn flopped back on their brand new bed panting and glistening with sweat as she brushed her hair back out of her face. Quinn's weight fell into the spot next to her, also catching his breath with a hand on his chest.

They had just gotten Raelyn moved into Quinn's house in LA and were having a house warming celebration of their own. There might have been a bit of an argument earlier about how Raelyn was absolutely not sleeping on the same bed Quinn had had so many meaningless one-nighters in. Nope. Not happening.

Quinn pointed out that she'd already slept on it before, but she was adamant. Hot head that he is, and a bit of a drama king, he decided to throw the old mattress off the balcony and into the pool before storming out to buy a new bed. Of course when he'd come back, he was more than happy to break in the new mattress and maybe challenge the durability of the new frame and headboard. It was still intact. So far.

"Fuck. We're. Awesome," Quinn declared between heavy, gasping breaths. He grabbed Raelyn's hand and pressed her palm to his chest, "Feel that. Fuck, I hope this is how I go. You're gonna make my heart explode. I'll be coming and going at the same time."

A burst of laughter escaped Raelyn's lips, "That's horrifying!" She rolled and slung one leg over his, kissing the line of his jaw down to his neck where his pulse was visible. Her diamond ring glimmered in the low light of her bedroom, her hand slid across his chest, feeling his strong muscles, slippery with the sweat they'd just worked up.

"It would traumatize you and you would never be with another man again," Quinn said, and she could hear the curve of a grin on his lips as he spoke.

"You're a little twisted, Quinn Casey Casey," Raelyn purred into his skin. Her fingers traced down his long torso, feeling those familiar solid, hard, defined muscles. She felt the dips and lines of his abdomen, the sharp V-cut next to his hips, then down his dark happy trail. Already, she knew his body well, but her heart fluttered and a heat melted into her at the thought of having forever to completely learn him. With her hands, her mouth, her tongue.

"Should we pick a date?" Quinn asked after a few silent moments of letting their breath slow as they touched and felt each other skin-to-skin.

"Right now? Sure," she laughed into him. "Just call Zoey up and ask her to relay your entire schedule for the next year and a half."

"Spring? Summer?" His fingers massaged into her lower back where he held her with one arm around her, while the other brushed lightly up and down her arm.

"That's baseball season. Aren't we going to be a little busy?"

"I think summer," Quinn said, ignoring her concerns, "on the beach. And it should be small and intimate."

Raelyn bit her lip, smiling as she propped her head up to look at him. "You've given this some thought."

The corner of his mouth tugged up enough to give the smallest flash of dimple and he looked up to the chandelier hanging from the ceiling as he spoke. "The first time I imagined our wedding, it was on a nude beach in Jamaica or somewhere tropical." Raelyn laughed again but urged him to continue. "I was fifteen, I think. Maybe sixteen. I had just gotten over the guilt I felt at picturing and fantasizing about you naked. It was a big deal. But once I gave in, I just went all out."

Since Quinn's confession a few months ago about how he'd been in love with her for so long, she'd done a lot of reflecting, revisiting past memories, trying to remember if there were signs. There were. Lots of them, in fact. And she wondered how she had been so oblivious. Especially junior and senior year when she'd started having similar feelings toward him.

"I didn't feel guilty the first time I pictured you naked," Raelyn confessed. "We were seventeen. Well, I was sixteen, *you* were seventeen. It was glorious."

She felt Quinn's chest compress and decompress quickly with his silent laugh.

"The second time I pictured our wedding," he said, "I added bathing suits. It was a sexy white bikini from a *Sports Illustrated* magazine. I figured if we were getting married your parents would want to be there, so we'd better wear something. But it was still on the beach."

"And the time after that?"

"The time after that I pictured you in a white dress. I remembered how much it took my breath away seeing you in your fancy homecoming dresses. I wanted you to dress up like that just for me." Quinn pressed a kiss to the top of her head then added, "Although, I don't know that a *white* dress is the right choice here."

Raelyn swatted his chest with a *"Hey!"* and he laughed playfully.

"Either way," he continued, "I always picture it on the beach. Maybe it's because that's where we met. Whenever I think of you I think summer and sunshine and waves. California is going to look great on you, baby."

"Yeah, I think I'll adjust." She turned her head toward the window where the ocean was turning pink against the glow of the sunset. "Just look at that view...I want to go jump in."

Quinn laughed under his breath, "You do that, I'll stand on shore and watch."

"What?" Raelyn exclaimed, "Are you afraid of the ocean?"

"I'm not saying I won't pee on you if you get stung by a jellyfish, but I don't know that I'd fight a shark if I see a fin pop up out of the water," he replied, and his body gave an exaggerated shudder.

"You would let me get eaten?" Raelyn asked, incredulous. "I seriously doubt that."

"Even Superman has kryptonite, babydoll."

"Noted," Raelyn giggled quietly into his chest and placed a kiss there.

A few more quiet beats passed and Quinn inhaled before asking, "So...how many?"

"How many what? Wedding guests? You want small and in-"

"No, not that," he interrupted, then paused. Another inhale before, "How many...kids...do you want?"

"Oh," Raelyn paused. She realized they had never talked about having a family. Creating a family. Quinn never talked about kids or wanting them, wanting more than just her. It wasn't something she had given much thought to either, to be perfectly honest. She wasn't filled with any sort of need to reproduce and spend her days raising miniature humans who would talk back and make messes for her to clean up.

Now, however, she was hit with the idea that their kids would be half her and half him. Obviously, that's how that whole thing worked. It was just the realization of how fun it would be to raise a version of herself that had Quinn's edge, or a little boy with both their athletic abilities and wit and charm. She thought about her dad as a grandfather, like he was to Camille's children, and how he would absolutely love the shit out of anyone who looked or acted remotely like a miniature Quinn.

"I have four other bedrooms in my house," Quinn said, "but we could always upgrade if we needed. It's not like-"

"Four?" Raelyn repeated the number. "You want four kids? Or more?"

Quinn shrugged. "I wouldn't mind filling you up more than a few times."

"You can *fill me up* without the babies, you know," she replied, nearly laughing, but not sure how serious he was.

"Yeah, but seeing you like that, knowing *I* did that. Knowing part of me is actually a part of you...I don't know that I could get enough of that."

"You do realize that eventually the baby belly goes away and there's an actual living breathing human with a self-destruct button on the top of its head and it's our responsibility to keep it living and breathing and to absolutely *not* mess with the self-destruct button, right?" This of course came out far more panicky than she had meant.

His laugh rumbled through his belly and into his chest, "Oh my God, Rae...*you're* afraid of babies!"

"I'm not *afraid* of babies," Raelyn scoffed defensively.

"Sure, give me shit for not wanting to be eaten by a shark, but here you are terrified of an infant."

"They're so tiny and fragile!" Raelyn argued through a laugh. "I'm not afraid of them, but the concept is a bit daunting."

"So...no babies?" Quinn asked, and she could hear the disappointment in his voice that he was trying to mask.

"I didn't say no babies," she corrected. "I said the idea of taking care of them is a bit scary, but I have to admit we would make some adorable children. And they'd be sassy and a little edgy, and way cooler than anyone else's kids. So maybe let's start with one and see how that goes."

"Half me, half you," Quinn sighed. "The world won't know what hit it."

Raelyn's hand slid back down his abs until she grasped him, massaging gently and feeling him grow again in her hand. "You know, I'm still on the pill, but we can always practice making babies, if that's something you think you're interested in."

The satisfied growl inside his chest started a fire between her legs and she pressed her hips into his thigh.

"Practice makes perfect," Quinn said, his voice low and gravelly, "and that's not something you want to get wrong, so I think we're going to need *a lot* of practice." He dipped his head to catch his mouth on hers, groaning into her lips, sliding his tongue inside to meet her own.

"Well then, how do you want me?" Raelyn bit playfully at his lip, sucking it into her mouth.

Quinn flipped her onto her back and rolled on top of her in one swift and well-practiced movement. "Let's start with the basics: You on your back. Me, moving inside you. I'll hold you down, and I'll know how good it feels when you scream my name. Got it?"

"Got it, Coach."

"I love you, Raelyn DeRose," Quinn said, voice and eyes softening briefly.

"I love you, too, Quinn Casey." She smiled back up at him before his grin turned wicked and he got ready to claim her once again.

She thought of all their history, their connection, their friendship, the miracle of finding each other again, and all that lost time in between. Already they shared so much; love, hope, countless memories, maybe some regret. But he was hers forever now, and she knew this was just the beginning.

information can be obtained
'CGtesting.com
the USA
'50080822
'0011B/264

9 781639 373000